COTSWOLDS HOLIDAY

ALSO BY KASEY STOCKTON

Contemporary Romance

Snowflake Wishes: A Holly Springs Romance

His Stand-In Holiday Girlfriend

Snowed In on Main Street

Melodies and Mistletoe

Regency Romance

The Jewels of Halstead Manor

The Lady of Larkspur Vale

Properly Kissed

Sensibly Wed

Love in the Bargain

A Duke for Lady Eve

A Forgiving Heart

All is Mary and Bright

Scottish Historical Romance

Journey to Bongary Spring

Through the Fairy Tree

The Enemy Across the Loch

COTSWOLDS HOLIDAY

A CHRISTMAS ESCAPE NOVEL

KASEY STOCKTON

GOLDEN OWL PRESS

Copyright © 2022 by Kasey Stockton
Cover design © 2022 by Melody Jeffries Design

First edition: November 2022
Golden Owl Press

ISBN 978-1-952429-30-9

For Maisie Peters & Olivia Rodrigo,
whose music was the soundtrack to this book

Christmas Escape Bingo

Read all seven books in the series to get a Christmas romance blackout!

Broken elevator	Sleigh ride through the mountains	Allergic reaction	Snowstorm Power outage	A walk down main street
Candlelit house tour	Define the boundaries chat (multiple answers)	Ice Skating on a frozen pond	Mint hot Chocolate	"Highway to Hell" ringtone
Boat ride	"Fresh" chocolate milk	FREE SPACE	Reindeer Attack	Miniature Christmas Tree
Hot chocolate at a Christmas market	Trip to Ikea	Burning hot chocolate	Home Alone movie night (multiple answers)	Listening to Bing Crosby
An angry dachshund	Blanket fort	Snowy Beach	Mandalorian pajamas	Snowmobile ride through the mountains

ONE

I NEVER KNEW I WOULD FEEL SO STRONGLY ABOUT AN embossed square of luxury cardstock, but apparently paper had the ability to produce a visceral reaction. Like the kind that required keeping a bucket close, or one of those bags on the airplane for motion sickness. I ran my thumbs over the velvety smooth envelope, still holding half the invitation in its grip, and my stomach rolled over. I legitimately wondered if I would throw up.

I hadn't removed the invitation entirely from the envelope yet. My fingers had frozen the moment my eyes hit those familiar names inked in gold, scrolling font. *Together with their families, Aubrey Schenk and Jake Hunt invite you . . .*

Now my breathing was coming in quick, heaving gasps. I'd never been so grateful to find myself alone in my parents' kitchen so I could freak out in private. It wasn't just the expensive wedding announcement that threw me into a tizzy; it was the actual wedding itself. I had learned about the engagement when my best friend—I mean *ex*-best friend—posted a picture of herself beside her then-new fiancé at the beach a few months ago, her hand close to the camera to show off her giant rock. The wedding wasn't news, but the invitation in my hands was physical proof it was happening.

A quiet sob escaped my chest, and I sank down to the floor, leaning against the cabinets while I stared at the gold letters. It was like Medusa's snaky hair. I *couldn't* make myself look away. Meanwhile, a slow, boiling hatred built in my chest. I didn't just hate this expensive piece of stationary, I *loathed* it. I wanted to crumple it into a ball, set it on fire, spread the ashes over the compost bucket, and feed them to Dad's pig.

The mere fact that I'd been invited to this wedding sent me into a full-on rage. But my anger was justified.

I wasn't an awful person, I promise. This was not like one of those chick flicks where the girl was *so* sad because everyone around her was moving on in the world, and now her best friend was getting married and leaving her behind too, and *oh, woe is me*. To be fair, all of that was true, but not the reason I was hyperventilating on my mom's cold linoleum floor.

No, the minor hysteria was because my best friend got engaged to my ex-boyfriend four months after he had ended our *five-year* relationship.

Yeah, I thought it was kind of messed up, too. But hey, they decided they were soulmates, and who was I to stand in the way of true love? I'm no ogre. I preferred to bury my hurt and anguish deep inside and avoid both my feelings and my exes entirely. Yes, plural. My ex-boyfriend and my ex-best friend. Aubrey and I stopped speaking when they got together. It was much easier to drop her from my life than face her happiness while I wallowed in mountains of Twinkies and old Pinterest wedding boards.

Heavy boots thumped on the porch outside, and I grimaced. Mascara was likely running down my wet cheeks in heavy rivulets, making me look like a KISS costume gone wrong, and my dad was about as good at facing emotions as I was—so, not at all.

The kitchen door leading to the back porch swung open, and Dad paused mid-step into the house, his eyes widening while they ran from my KISS face down to the invitation still half-cocooned in its envelope and clutched tightly in my claws. He turned his head, keeping his eyes on me, and shouted. "Maeve! We have a problem!"

Dad's shout was as slow and deep as the rest of his movements. He was a California cowboy down to his roots, and he had that deep, molasses voice of John Wayne mixed with the steady wisdom of Dumbledore. He'd always been a patient teacher with my sister and me, showing us how to ride horses, bottle feed baby calves, and hold a chicken. But he left anything emotion-related to Mom.

It was a good thing she was never very far away from him. The quick-paced click of her boot tread crossed the back deck, and she slipped under Dad's arm while he held the door open, her radar-like gaze focusing on me.

"Talk to me, Luna." Those four words were a mood—weighted blankets or candlelit baths. I'd heard them often growing up. Mom didn't believe there was a problem she couldn't fix if she hit it head on. The annoying thing was she was usually right.

I lifted the invite, and she snatched it from my hand, slipping the cardstock from the envelope easily. She didn't even look like she might gag. Unfair.

She scanned the paper quickly, then lowered it, gazing at my face with fiercely calculating eyes. Her open button-down shirt swayed a little over her ribbed tank, and she tucked a strand of faded brown hair back into her clip. She was probably stressed about the idea of watching me spiral again like I had the last time I'd run into Aubrey in town. Jake, fortunately, had not been with her then. But seeing Aubrey in person instead of on social media had been a hit to my gut that led to a few late nights of

3

sappy 90's chick flicks and inordinate amounts of mint chip ice cream.

That was the blessing about being my own boss for a completely virtual job: I could take three days off to wallow and no one could tell me not to.

The downside: when those three days turned into weeks and I started to lose followers because of it.

It's all about balance.

"Come on," Mom said, reaching for my hand and taking it in a vise grip. "Outside."

I allowed her to pull me to the swinging bench seat on the front porch and sat beside her. She pushed tissues into my hand, and I wiped the mascara streaks from my cheeks. The sun was setting over rolling hills of naked grapevines that lined the field opposite our property like rows of obedient soldiers, glowing orange and yellow. The beautiful scene was at odds with how ugly my mood felt.

My breath came out in a shudder. "I just can't believe . . . I mean, *married*? Seriously? The last time I brought up marriage to Jake—"

"Nope. Not a good idea." Mom slid an arm around my back. "Why compare their relationship to the one you had with him? What good would that do?"

"It's not going to help anything at all. But telling me not to compare them is pointless. I've already been doing it on a loop in my head."

Mom sighed. "He wouldn't have made you happy, Luna."

Wrong. He already had made me happy. That was why I stayed with him for five years. Then Aubrey had to return from her master's program, they finally got to know one another, and it was practically love at first sight.

At least they did me the *courtesy* of breaking things off slowly, after months of agonized longing for one another despite the fact that I stood in the way.

I mean, I was essentially the villain in every chick flick. I was the woman who was wrong for him. And there was so much great tension in our story, because the *right woman* was my flipping best friend.

It was really obvious I hadn't moved on in the last eight months of being single again, right? Jake had stolen five years from my life. I'd put off traveling for him, focused my career on what he thought it should be, and I was still sitting at my parents' house wallowing like a frumpy banana slug.

Gravel crunched around the side of the house, and I heard Dad's truck door open and slam again.

"Dad's going to pick up dinner at El Azteca. Why don't you go with him? It might be good to get away for a minute."

It would feel great to get away from Geyserville. Or even completely away from California. Anywhere I didn't have to see the places and things that reminded me of my failed relationship or the lifelong friendship now missing from my boring, lonely life. But leaving the house just to pick up tacos? No thanks.

I slumped back against the swinging bench and sighed.

Mom squeezed my shoulder. "I know this is hard, but it won't be hard forever."

"Easy to say when you're not the one going through it," I mumbled.

"Come on," Mom said, her voice raising in its no-nonsense way. "Up. You're going with Dad, and you're getting your mind off it. I'll burn the invitation while you're gone."

Gravel groaned beneath the truck tires, indicating he was already leaving. "Too late."

Mom raised one dark eyebrow at me and pulled out her phone. "Start walking. I'll tell him to wait."

There was no getting out of this. When Maeve Winter believed something was good for me, she didn't give me a choice. It didn't matter that I was twenty-four years old; I still had to listen to my mom.

I ran my fingers through my mid-length hair and shook out the loose, brown waves. November in northern California was cold, and I would have layered up in more than yoga pants and a chunky sweater if I had known I was going into town.

I started down the long, gravel driveway. The brake lights lit up on Dad's red pickup truck, and I hurried to get into the toasty cab.

He looked at me warily. "Tacos for dinner."

"Sounds great."

This was likely why Mom sent me on this errand. Dad wouldn't ask questions, and I wouldn't expound on the finer points of why I had a right to grieve. We could each keep our thoughts and emotions tightly and securely bottled for the next thirty minutes.

We rode into town to the sound of country twang, and I averted my eyes from the little shop on the corner where Jake's law office was situated.

"I got a call from your sister this morning. She just heard back about her English paper. She aced it."

"The one about training horses?" I checked my runny makeup in the visor mirror and wiped away the remnants I hadn't gotten earlier.

"That's the one."

Sometimes I think it would be nice to be back in college, where the only things I had to worry about were getting to work on time and completing all my homework. My sister, Callie, didn't have to work, though. Her uber-smart brain had gotten her enough scholarships to ride her way through four years without assembling pizzas or wiping tables.

We pulled in front of the best taqueria in Geyserville, and I hopped out of the truck. Cold hit me in a gust of icy wind, and I tugged my sweater sleeves down over my hands and ran into the taco shop. Okay, so it was low sixties, and I realize that's not *cold* to everyone, but cold is relative. To this California girl, it was practically frigid.

The bell rang above the door, and I stepped aside for a young family to slip past me on their way out. When I raised my eyes, my heart stopped. I actually felt the blood drain from my cheeks. Because there, standing at the counter, holding hands and looking right at me, were Jake and Aubrey.

If there was ever a time I wished for the power to rewind my life and make a different decision, it would have been when Jake asked me out the first time. I would have said no and stopped this trainwreck before it had a chance to leave the station. But the *second* thing I'd choose would be the moment I was living right now. I would rewind thirty seconds to when we pulled into the parking lot, and I would stay in the truck.

As it stood, I had no choice now but to face the perfect newly engaged couple ahead of me. Yes, *newly* engaged. They had the fastest dating-to-engaged-to-married timeline of anyone I knew. I'd search for the fire lighting their tails to explain how outrageously quickly Aubrey had managed to get Jake to the altar, except that I couldn't tear my gaze from their faces.

The door swung open again to the sound of the bell, and Dad stepped up beside me. "What's the holdup?" He looked at the two holdups at the counter. "Oh."

This was likely his worst nightmare. I sucked in a deep, yoga-trained breath and pasted a wide smile on my face. We'd made eye contact, so there was no avoiding them now. But I did approach the counter at my dad's side, like he could maybe shield me a little from their radiating fumes of joy and happiness.

No luck. He left me the moment we reached the cashier so he could place our order.

"Luna! Oh my gosh, I can't believe we ran into you. We were just talking about you!" Aubrey closed the gap between us and crushed me in a hug. Her voice was high, doing that thing where she infused it with false positivity to cover her intense anxiety.

I was glad not to be the only one struggling.

"Good things, I hope," I joked, like a sandals-and-socks-wearing dad.

Jake nodded. "Of course." He looked like he was about to go in for a hug, too, but I crossed my arms over my chest and brightened my smile until my cheeks felt stiff. His sleek blue Oxford shirt fit him well, and his golden hair was freshly cut. He looked good, as always. Jerk.

Aubrey laughed awkwardly. "I don't know if it arrived yet or not, but we sent you an invitation to . . . well, the wedding."

"Yeah, I got it today. It's beautiful," I bit out. Could they tell how difficult it was for me to speak right now? I felt like I had Mom's Christmas caramels in my mouth and hoped I was hiding it.

"Oh, nice. I'm so glad." Jake affected massive relief, and I knew at once the invitation was not his idea. He didn't want me at the wedding, and who would blame him? I was his ex-girlfriend. The one he left while she was dreaming about engagement rings and sending him little houses on Zillow every day.

Which meant this was on Aubrey. What I didn't understand, though, was why? Despite stealing Jake, Aubrey was a saint. She wouldn't invite me to the wedding just to rub my nose in her happiness. That wasn't like her. Even if it was a wedding that we'd spent years developing together with magazine cutouts and artfully scrapbooked color schemes. I didn't know any other woman as obsessed with their wedding as Aubrey had been for most of our lives, and up until she took my boyfriend, I had been by her side as the scrapbooks transitioned from the Barbie-influenced dreams of a seven-year-old to the vision she had today.

Dad eyed me from the register warily, and I shot him a reassuring smile.

"Listen," Aubrey said, stepping forward and lowering her

voice from the fake falsetto back down to normal. "I know this is unusual, but I . . . well, I've really missed you, Lu. I've spent my entire life imagining you standing by my side on the day I got married. You holding my bouquet, planning my bachelorette party, helping me pick out a dress. It's just not the same without you."

Did she want me to apologize? I'm sorry, but when you steal your friend's boyfriend, you lose that friend as an option for maid of honor. Besides, we both knew she didn't need help picking out a dress. She'd had the perfect classic gown earmarked since college.

I swallowed my snide remark. "I'm sure Natalie will do a great job. Or whoever you've chosen."

"No, I didn't ask my cousin." She pulled a face, and I fought an understanding laugh. I felt too raw to connect with her right now. "I actually asked Michelle."

"Michelle Riedman?" I couldn't keep the shock from my voice. We'd grown up with her, and she was awful to me in high school—mostly because she wanted my best friend.

"We've gotten close recently, and I think she'll do a good job," Aubrey said defensively.

Of course Michelle swooped in once I vacated the picture. How could Aubrey be so blind?

I pushed away my irritation. Not that I was even considering attending before, but now there was nothing that would entice me to go to that wedding. I couldn't sit there and watch that usurper stand in my place as Aubrey's new best friend. It hurt too much.

Aubrey smiled widely. "So anyway, I know things have been weird between us—"

Understatement of the year.

"—but I was really hoping you would agree to be one of my bridesmaids." She grinned hopefully, pushing her long, blonde hair over her shoulder. "You wouldn't have to do much, but I really miss you. It just wouldn't be the same without you there."

She. Had. To. Be. Joking.

I wasn't sure if my mouth actually dropped open and hit the sticky tiled floor, or if it just felt that way. I closed my lips and looked at Jake. He watched me with trepidation. Was he worried I would say yes?

Good heavens. Did the man not know me *at all*?

"I'm sorry. I can't."

Aubrey ducked her chin. I saw her hand reach for Jake's and immediately lifted my gaze. "You can't, or you won't?" she asked.

What kind of question was that? It was my choice, and the distinction didn't matter. But her stung expression and Jake's hopefulness that I wouldn't agree to this ridiculous scheme set off a boiling rage in my gut. I could not let them win. "I *can't*. I'll be out of town."

"Really?" Aubrey's eyebrows shot up.

It wasn't that difficult to believe. I went on trips. I vacationed. I had driven down to Anaheim with my sister just a few months ago to hit up the happiest place on earth during her summer break.

The trip had definitely been an effort on Callie's part to pull me out of my depressive funk—I was sure my mom put her up to it, since she's convinced I'm going to turn into a hermit—but that wasn't relevant to the current conversation.

"Where are you going?" Jake asked, his brows pulled together.

He didn't believe me.

Well, I'd show him. This wasn't just a trip; it was the trip of a lifetime. The trip I'd dreamed of going on since I was fifteen and had to do a report on my ancestry, leading me into vast rabbit holes of the United Kingdom. It was also the first thing that popped into my head because my mom had watched *Pride and Prejudice* on the TV last night.

"I'm going to England."

"England?" he questioned, his golden eyebrow lifted.

"Yes," I said, more firmly this time. "I can't make it to the wedding because of a trip I have planned to *England*."

Thank you, Mr. Darcy, for putting the idea freshly in my mind. Those rolling green hills were calling my name. Maybe I really would book the trip. I'd always wanted to go, and then when Jake or Aubrey ran into my parents in town and asked how I was holding up—like I *know* they had been doing—Mom could respond with how much I was adoring the old manor houses, Cadbury chocolate, and hot British guys.

"You're going to England for Christmas?" Jake repeated, his eyebrows inching further up.

Christmas? That was unexpected. I should have read the entire invitation.

Dad came to my side with a bag full of heavenly roasted carnitas. I'm guessing he either didn't hear my lies or intended to leave it to Mom to handle. "Ready?"

Was I ready for this? The question hit me in the chest with the weight of Jake's disbelieving stare and Aubrey's slightly suspicious one. Neither of them believed I was really going. So I had no choice.

Get me a neck pillow and a supply of wasabi almonds, because this girl was gonna book herself a flight to London.

TWO

"EXPLAIN SOMETHING TO ME," MOM SAID, PAUSING *WHITE Christmas* and turning to face me on the couch. My computer sat on my lap with more tabs open to different Airbnb apartments and flights than there were animals in the yard outside. And we ran a fairly decent-sized farm here.

I leaned my head back against the sofa and expelled a breath. We'd gone over this at least sixty times since I'd run into Jake and Aubrey a few nights before, and I wasn't changing my mind about the trip to the UK.

"Why do you have to go so early? It's not even December for two more days. You have weeks until the wedd—until Christmas."

Because if I stayed here, I would be roped into being Aubrey's bridesmaid. Luck was not on my side, and I was bound to run into Aubrey and Jake again repeatedly at town functions, the grocery store, or the post office between now and Christmas Eve. It was inevitable. Even if it wasn't, my own inner voice would hound me until I reached out to Aubrey. Weddings weren't as big of a deal to anyone else in the world as they were to her, and I knew that intimately. You weren't a woman's best friend for more than twenty years without that kind of knowledge.

I mean, we'd spent a week of our summer vacation before sixth grade practicing various walks down a makeshift aisle in her bedroom so we could narrow down the type of slow stepping we would do on her actual wedding day, complete with a stuffed animal audience.

But then there was also that other reason. "If I go now, I don't have to think about the wedding. My trip will be a distraction, and it will keep me safe from succumbing to guilt. Win-win."

Mom readjusted her position on the cushion. I could see her working out my reasons and choosing not to argue against them. "How do you plan to get from Heathrow to the Cotswolds?"

"I'll rent a car."

"But then you'll have to drive—"

"On the left side of the road, yep."

"You know it snows in England, right?"

"I've seen *The Holiday*."

She looked at me shrewdly. "Just so long as you aren't trying to find a boyfriend over there—"

"I've *seen* the movie, Mom. I don't want to try to live it." Not that I would reject Jude Law if he just happened to knock on my cottage door and needed a place to stay. "Anyway, the movie sets an unrealistic standard. No one would actually trade houses with a stranger for a vacation and then just happen to fall in love with that stranger's brother."

She didn't seem convinced by my indifference. "But you'll be gone for so long."

Which was kind of the point. I'd wanted to visit England for so many years but had never made the time to go. In college I really couldn't afford it, and during my years dating Jake we vacationed in Tahoe during the summer or his aunt's beach house in Santa Cruz. He never had the desire to go to England, and I wasn't about to leave the country alone.

Except now that was precisely what I was doing. Kind of annoyingly poetic, right?

I shoved aside all Jake-related thoughts. "As long as I work while I'm there, I can write off the whole thing in my taxes. I might even be able to get enough yoga segments filmed to fill the next few months."

"In the snow," Mom said.

Snow couldn't be as bad as she made it sound. It wasn't like I planned to kneel in it and film a downward dog routine. My yoga channel on YouTube had a wide enough following that I couldn't get away with ridiculous segments, anyway. I posted quality content only. "Maybe I'll just stay there until spring, so I can shoot some videos in famous scenic places *without* the snow. Like the cliff Elizabeth stands on in *Pride and Prejudice*."

She wrinkled her nose. "Too windy."

"Or the park they meet up at in *Notting Hill*."

"The gated private park?"

"Or in front of a cozy fire with snow falling outside the window behind me."

Mom opened her mouth to argue, then tilted her head to the side and conceded the point. "That sounds restful."

"Or the top of Mount Doom, with Frodo—"

"Isn't that one filmed in New Zealand?"

So it was. "I guess I'll have to extend my trip." I chuckled. "My followers would probably love that, actually. I can start a new segment and call it *Yoga Around the World*."

"Alone, though? That sounds far too dangerous."

"Yet also a little dreamy," I said quietly, scrolling through my choices for apartments in various small towns. I'd chosen the Cotswolds since that's where my people had come from before they'd hitched a ride on the Mayflower, and it seemed as good a place as any. "Oh, look at this one. It's in Snowshill, for heaven's sake. How does that sound for the holidays?"

"Lonely."

"Mom," I scolded. "We can video chat on Christmas Day, and I'll even make sure I've got the whole dinner set up so I'm not missing out on the important things."

"Granny's mashed potatoes are more important than spending time with your family?"

"No," I said, squirming a little on my seat. "Getting away from here is more important than being Aubrey's bridesmaid." I scoffed. "I mean, who gets married on Christmas Eve anyway? It's just selfish."

I didn't know if Mom could sense the hurt radiating from me in palpable waves, but she pressed her lips together and scooted closer to me on the couch. "All right. Let's find you a nice, safe, clean place to stay."

I clicked on a charming little apartment. "This one in Snowshill is near Linscombe. I could still travel over there and see the church where your great-whatever grandparents got married." I enlarged the pictures of a small apartment on the first floor. There were a few basic photos of the compact interior and a description explaining the apartment had its own entrance.

Mom waved her finger around the screen. "Zoom in on the door. I want to see how well it locks."

I rolled my eyes but complied. "Look, a key goes in there, and there's another bolt at the top." I looked at her. "I am an adult, you know." Though the argument fell flat, since I currently lived at home. I couldn't be alone after the break up, though, and Mom had swooped in to the rescue like a stalwart golden retriever.

"You'll always be my daughter."

"I'm going to request the apartment." A thrill ran through me, and I filled out the form and submitted it.

Mom reached for the remote and unpaused *White Christmas.*

It was only November twenty-ninth, but we started Christmas prep as soon as the Thanksgiving turkey was cleared from the table in this house.

"I wish I could go with you," she said absently. "We could make a family trip out of it."

But who would watch the farm? Feed the animals? Water the fields? It wasn't a possibility, and we both knew it.

I tried to sound light. "I'm fortunate in my line of work that I don't have to answer to anyone else."

Mom said nothing. She supported my YouTube channel completely. She was the one who had taught me my first downward-facing dog pose when I was little and helped me perfect my bird of paradise pose when I got older. She had even designed the small studio space Dad built for me in the guest room upstairs.

My channel had grown exponentially in the last few years, and my followers with it. I wouldn't call myself a celebrity at all, but someone recognized me in the line for It's a Small World and the resulting dopamine boost from the woman's praise had made the ride bearable.

A buzz vibrated my phone, and an email popped up from the owner of the charming Cotswolds apartment. I did the math. It had to be like five in the morning there.

rhysnorland@eemail.co.uk: I just approved your booking, but I need to know something. Do you have allergies to animals?

I took a quick peek at Mom, but her eyes were glued to the TV. I didn't want a hairy apartment, but my heart was kind of set on this idyllic little place. That, and the price tag made it a hundred times more attractive than any of the other rooms I'd looked at so far. Were the Cotswolds a Christmas vacation spot or something? It was slim pickings.

yoga4lyfe@eemail.com: No allergies, but I have an aversion to being covered in dog hair.

rhysnorland@eemail.co.uk: I can assure you there will not be a blanket of dog hair in the room.

Then why had he felt the need to ask me about it? Something was off.

yoga4lyfe@eemail.com: Is there another animal that sometimes lives in the room?

rhysnorland@eemail.co.uk: The room itself is animal-free, but the surrounding rooms are not. People with allergies have not done well here in the past.

yoga4lyfe@eemail.com: In that case, we will get along smashingly.

That was a British thing, right? Wasn't everything just smashing over there?

rhysnorland@eemail.co.uk: Grand. See you Friday, then. Cheers.

Friday. Oh, my. He would be seeing me Friday because I would be in *England* on Friday. And not just England, but the Cotswolds, where some of my ancestors had come from. I could walk across the very same floors they did. I could sit on a pew they probably sat on, or look through a window they once looked through.

I didn't get into genealogy the same way my granny had, but I still thought it was pretty cool. If those couples had never gotten married in the 1600's, I wouldn't be here today.

My stomach fluttered anxiously, and I could not dim my grin. I flipped tabs to book my flights, my body growing more and more fluffy with excitement until I felt round and giddy like Frosty the Snowman. From the animated film, of course. By the time *White Christmas* ended, I had flights—super economy, but does anyone ever change their tickets anyway?—a place to stay, a car booked, and had ordered outlet adapters and a compatible blow dryer.

"This is happening," I said quietly.

Mom slipped her arm around my back. "Just remember, Lu, you can come home at any time. No one in this house will make you go to that wedding."

"I know." But it didn't matter, because I wasn't going to chicken out. I was using my big old nest egg on this trip to begin my grand adventure.

"And your life is not a Hallmark movie, so no falling in love with handsome strangers under the Christmas tree lights, please."

I laughed. "You don't have to worry about that."

THE SAN FRANCISCO airport was bustling with harried travelers and intermittent PA announcements while I sat at a white table in the middle of the food court and took a bite of my overpriced, under-pickled burger. My video equipment was safely packed in a padded bag and resting on the chair beside me, and I pulled out my laptop to double check the car rental information, careful not to drip mustard on the keys.

My phone rang. I hurried to swallow so I could answer it.

"Hey, Cal." I took a swig of Dr Pepper.

"You're really leaving?" my sister asked, her wistful tone breathing static into the speaker. "I wish I could go with you."

"You should."

"No, I have finals," she grumbled. "And I promised my friend I would stick around for a week and take care of her dog before I head home for Christmas."

"Has she never heard of Rover? If you change your mind, I'm not opposed to sharing a bed."

"Consider it noted. Hey, listen, I called you for a reason." Her tone grew serious in a somewhat worrisome way.

I put my burger down in the cardboard container. "What's up?"

"You know how my friend runs that yoga studio I told you about?"

"Yes." I nodded even though she couldn't see me. Callie had a handful of fitness friends, and I'd chatted with some of them through my Instagram account. "He does Bikram, right?"

"Yeah, that's it, among other things. So, his studio is getting to be too much for him to manage while he's trying to finish his MBA. But he doesn't want to shut down any classes. You should see the kind of money he makes, Lu. It's insane."

I looked at my burger longingly. "That's great."

"Well, he wants to hire another teacher to offload some of his work, but his studio is full of more elite clients than average, so he can't hire just anyone. It would be part time to start, but I mentioned you as a possibility. He's seen your videos, and he is super interested in meeting to discuss working together."

I didn't know whether to be flattered or offended. Callie meant well, of course. She didn't think the YouTube thing was making me happy, and I'd made the mistake of telling her recently that I missed being in the room with people sometimes while instructing. I needed to find a better groove with my channel so it didn't feel like such a slog anymore, sure, but I wasn't ready to give up on it yet.

"I'm actually hoping I can film enough videos in England to do a whole new segment. I'm not sure I can jump to another job just yet." It would also mean moving down to LA where Callie went to school, and I wasn't sure I wanted to leave Mom and Dad or northern California.

"That's the best part," Callie said. "He doesn't want to chat until the holidays are over. I wanted you to know the offer is essentially out there so you have time to really consider it."

"It was nice of you to think of me, Cal."

"Give it some thought, okay?"

"Yeah, of course." I lifted my burger and took a bite.

"And find me a hot British guy while you're over there."

"I'm planning to find myself one first."

She laughed, but we both knew I wasn't serious. I still had to get over Jake. The obnoxious schmuck had a hold on my heart, unfair as that was. But I was going to pry his grip from my love organ one blasted finger at a time until he was well in my past and I could finally heal.

"You know," Callie said, as if she'd heard my thoughts. "It might not be such a bad idea. Maybe a little vacation fling is what you need to get Flake out of your system."

Her pet name for my ex was fitting, even more so after he had broken up with me.

"You want me to kiss a hot British guy to help me forget about the wedding? I specifically told Mom I wasn't planning to recreate *The Holiday*."

"I mean, don't fall in love or anything. Having half a state between us is hard enough. I don't think I could handle an entire ocean." She hummed a thinking sound. "Just, you know . . . kiss someone. You *are* single, Lu. You need to push Flake out of your head some way. Might as well do it with an accent."

I took another bite of my burger while choking out a laugh. "They might sound different from us, but I doubt their kissing is."

Callie snickered. "I guess there's only one way to find out."

THREE

IT TURNED OUT SNOW WAS MUCH COLDER THAN IT looked on TV and even harder to drive in. Movies made it look like innocent, pillowy powder, all soft and magical. The reality was more like a half-melted Slurpee poured all over the roads and a bitter, stabbing cold.

My tiny two-door Kia took the narrow roads well enough, but it slid around a bit, and I found myself driving fifteen below the speed limit so I wouldn't lose control.

The guy behind me wasn't pleased with my careful approach to driving, if his constant beeping was any indication, but with the snow banks built up so high on either side of us, there wasn't anywhere to pull over and let him pass. Thick forest lined both sides of the road, all covered in a blanket of undisturbed, heavy snow.

"Hang on a minute," I called, gripping the steering wheel with white-knuckled ferocity. He answered me with another beep as though he'd actually heard me. I rolled my eyes. The horn was unnecessary. His tailgating proved how badly he wanted to pass.

A break appeared in the forest ahead by way of a turn-off

lane, and I pulled cautiously into the opening to allow the guy to pass, avoiding the small ditch between the lanes. He sped past me, spraying melted, muddy snow over the side of my car.

Rude. But I couldn't expect better from a bright yellow sports car that had been practically kissing my bumper for the last three miles—even one with an ironic peace sign sticker on the top corner of the back windshield. So far the report Callie was going to get on British kissing was this: road-ragey.

I looked over my shoulder to make sure the way was clear. I wasn't too far from my destination. Only a mile or so further and I would hit High Street, which was where the address for my apartment was. Just a few more minutes and I could find myself wrapped in a blanket before a fire.

Only, the car wasn't moving forward. It was sliding slowly to the side.

I gave it more gas, and it slid faster, so I slammed on my brakes. Evidently, that was the wrong thing to do. My car slid on the ice like one of those oversized puck things they use in curling until the back wheels started tipping down into the ditch behind me and the front slanted upwards.

"No, no, no!" I yelled, as though my pleas would put the car back on the road. My foot pumped the gas and brakes intermittently, but it only aided in moving me back faster. I clutched the steering wheel with both hands and waited for the car to stop, the air around me going still.

This was it. I was already failing. I'd only been in England for half a dozen hours and I'd already ruined my car and gotten stuck in a ditch.

I pulled up the roadside service number I'd gotten from the rental place and dialed, waiting until someone answered.

"Hello!" I said brightly. "So, I ended up in a ditch."

"Registration number?"

I opened the glove box, but nothing was there. "It's not in the car."

"It's *on* the car, ma'am," he said, and I could not get used to hearing an English accent.

I looked for a sticker. "What do you mean, *on* the car?"

"Big, tin rectangle on the back? Should be obvious."

"The license plate?"

"Sure."

I got out of the car and trudged through the shin-deep snow to read the number to the guy, and he looked me up in their system. My feet were cold, and I was suddenly aware I had not brought adequate shoes for this weather.

"No one is nearby to pull you out?" he asked on the phone.

I looked from one end of the deserted lane to the other. "Nope."

"The soonest we can have someone out to your location is Monday."

Two days away? "I'm partially blocking a lane." What if it led to someone's house and they needed to get past me?

"Sorry, ma'am. Monday at the soonest. Our trucks are all busy. You aren't the only tourist in a ditch."

What was the point of roadside assistance if it wasn't even available?

I hung up and looked at the car. It was tiny. Like three of these little guys could probably fit in the bed of Dad's truck alone. I was a fitness professional. If I gave it a hard enough shove, maybe . . .

Crawling down the small ditch proved more difficult than it looked. I braced myself behind the car, got a solid hold on the bumper, and heaved.

Nothing.

Drawing in a deep breath, I turned around and wedged my back against the trunk and tried again. My feet slid on the icy ground and I went down, banging my elbow against the ice and landing hard on my back with the wind clean knocked from my lungs.

Oh, sweet heavens. I pushed myself up and admitted defeat. The Kia might be small, but it was heavy. It was still a car.

No one would ever learn of this shameful moment.

Cold snow had seeped through my leggings and down into my socks, and a chill swept through my body. I certainly couldn't stay here. My place was only a mile away, right? I could walk that in fifteen or twenty minutes easily enough. I got my suitcase out of the trunk and pulled my camera bag from the front seat before making sure the car was locked up. It felt reckless to leave the vehicle here, but I didn't know what other choice I had. No cars had passed me in the last fifteen minutes, and I hadn't passed any cars going the other direction in miles.

I was no more than five minutes down the road, my rolling bag bumping along behind me, when I came to an abrupt halt in the center of the lane. This was *exactly* how Cameron Diaz's character had begun her English vacation in *The Holiday* as well —walking down a snowy lane to her cottage and dragging her suitcase along. If my apartment host's brother showed up tipsy tonight and looked extremely kissable, all bets were off. I fully intended to embrace the possibilities England wanted to offer me.

Maybe Callie was onto something, and kissing an Englishman would remove Jake from my mind altogether.

My stomach twisted at the thought of my ex-boyfriend. Jake the Flake, as my sister lovingly started calling him during the last year of our relationship. It began as a jokey way for her to vent her irritation when he seemed to find a lot of flimsy excuses for bailing on dates or events at the last minute. It became a star-tlingly on-the-nose label when he failed to uphold any of the things he'd promised me—a house, a ring, a couple of miniature Jake and Lunas—and then flaked on our relationship completely.

And now Jake was with Aubrey, and I was ankle deep in dirty slush and unable to feel my nose.

Lugging a suitcase down a snowy road was harder than it sounded. I questioned the wisdom of my choice when twilight set in and my jet lag started to make the edges of my brain—and the snow-covered, admittedly magical-looking forest surrounding me—feel a little fuzzy.

The trees opened up to a wide view of white, rolling hills and stone buildings. Snowshill's lights shone through the dimming sky, and I followed the GPS instructions until they brought me to a pub door. The Wild Hare was engraved in green on the sign above me, and I pushed my way inside. This couldn't be right. A cozy fire burned in the stone hearth and a smattering of tables held dinner guests, while a lone man sat at the bar, a dog laying at his feet. It was a small establishment, and it smelled like absolute heaven, but it wasn't an apartment building.

"Can we help you?" the barman asked, tossing a dish towel over his shoulder and bracing his hands on the counter before him. It had a way of tightening the plaid shirt around his arms and defining the muscle on his biceps, making him look like a British lumberjack. I dragged my gaze up before I could be caught staring. At least he looked nothing like Jude Law, or I would be in massive trouble.

He lifted his dark eyebrows over equally dark pools of brown irises. His eyes were—no joke—striking. They were the very definition of broody, complete with a stony expression and a stubbled jaw.

Oh mercy, if this was the sort of man England offered up as eye candy, I was in for a few cavities.

"Yes, hi. I'm looking for a place." I pulled up the address and set my phone on the bar between us. "I got this from my Airbnb host, but I think our wires got crossed somewhere because it led me here."

Hot Lumberjack Barman looked up from the phone. "No confusion. This is the place."

I looked around me. The room had not changed, still only

boasting a dining area and a bar. It was small, and there certainly weren't any hidden beds.

Though I did notice, on my second sweep, three more dogs dining with their owners, happily eating beneath the tables and none of them wearing service dog vests. Dogs *in* a restaurant? We're certainly not in America anymore, Toto.

"Luna Winter, yeah? There's a car park around the back if you need to move your car from the street." Hot Barman leaned down to get something out of a drawer.

He knew my name, so that confirmed I'd reached the correct place at least. Everything else still didn't make any sense. "My car isn't here. Not in Snowshill, I mean. That is, I walked."

His gaze swept from the snow-covered window to my body, dragging down my thick coat and leggings in a heavy way. Were his dark eyes attached to actual x-ray machines? His gaze felt like a force and only further frazzled me. The warmth from the pub was unthawing my body, and my fuzzy vision was hard to keep from blurring.

Maybe this was an atmospheric reaction. It was normal for your head to get really heavy in England, right? Like altitude sickness, but a result of a barman's perusal.

"Walked from where?" he asked.

"From the ditch down the road." I hooked a thumb over my shoulder. "I moved aside to let a jerk pass me, and I couldn't get back onto the lane."

"You hear that, Hamish?"

The guy who was seated at the bar with a pint and a sandwich lifted his glass. His cheeks were sunburned and his dark blond hair well-trimmed. His beard was long but groomed, and he didn't bother sparing me a glance. I'd probably classify him as handsome if he looked even remotely polite. "Aye. I'll get it here in a trice."

How very convenient. I faced the man. "Oh, do you run the tow truck?"

Hamish looked at me like I'd sprouted elf ears and asked for a ride to the North Pole. "No."

He dug into his sandwich again as Hot Barman came around the counter. A short, curvy woman slipped past him, her red ponytail swinging as she carried a tray full of stacked plates with half-eaten dinners. She looked about my age and gave me an appraising look.

"Tenant's here. I'm showing her the room," Hot Barman said.

The woman nodded, sending me a perfunctory smile before she kept moving toward the kitchen around the corner. Hot Barman reached for my suitcase, and I let him take it.

"Just over here." He led the way past the bar and to a narrow staircase hidden by the wall near the toilets.

Yep. It didn't say *restrooms*. The sign actually said *toilets*. Because that's a mental image we all needed.

I stood on the lowest step. "I thought the listing mentioned it was on the first floor."

He looked at me again like I'd said something strange, then pointed up the stairs. "First floor."

"What's that, then?" I asked, pointing below us to the main dining room. The brown dachshund who had been sleeping beneath Hamish's barstool now scurried past me and paused at Hot Barman's feet.

His brow creased further, not bothered at all by the canine addition. "The ground floor."

"Ah."

"I'm Rhys," he explained, carrying my suitcase up the stairs like it weighed nothing. I prided myself on my own strength, and it had been a beast for me to lug all the way from the car. It looked like Rhys's muscle wasn't just for show.

"Oh, we spoke a few days ago," I said, recalling his name from the email conversation. Had I known the specimen of man I had been speaking to then, I might have chosen a different apartment with a much less intimidating host. If Callie saw him now, she'd be reminding me of my semi-new goal to kiss an Englishman. "This is your place?"

"Yes."

I cleared my throat. "I was under the impression I would have my own entrance."

He shot a puzzled expression over his shoulder. "You do."

We stopped before a door halfway down the narrow hallway and Rhys put the key in the lock and turned it. He pushed the door open and set my suitcase down, then stepped back. The dog circled his feet before lying down in the middle of the hallway.

The room looked exactly as it had in the pictures. It was cozy with a little kitchenette, a bed, and a modest bathroom. The fireplace on one side was small but charming, with room enough for one chair in the "sitting area." The appeal was overall lovely. But also *small*. There was hardly enough room for a yoga mat, let alone space to set up my video equipment.

"Is this the biggest room you have?"

Rhys looked surprised. "It's the only room we have. That's me"—he pointed to the door almost directly across the hall—"and that's Ruby down on the end."

"Ruby," I repeated, clocking the lavender-painted door at the end of the hallway.

"My cousin. She runs the pub with me, so I'll introduce you later. We're both around if you need anything. Just give us a knock."

If I stayed around, that was. This was far less private and much smaller than I expected, and I wasn't sure if it would suit my purposes at all. I needed to read the refund rules before I said anything to him, though.

"Great."

"Pub's open for dinner, and you're welcome to bring dishes upstairs so long as you return them to the kitchen."

I nodded. I could smell whatever they'd been cooking already, and it was making my mouth water.

He hovered in the doorway, his thick arms crossed over his chest. The dish towel still hung over his shoulder, and despite that domestic quirk, this man was a vision. I would need to somehow snap a sneaky picture of him to send to Callie. Maybe it would entice her to join me out here.

"The laundry is down in the kitchen, and if you give me your car keys, we'll have your car in the park tonight."

A record scratched through my daydream. "Give you my car keys?" I asked in disbelief.

"Yeah." He waited, not seeming to understand what was strange about his request. "Hamish can't bring the car here without the keys. I'm guessing you locked it."

"Of course I locked it."

He gave a flutter of a smile, but there was no humor on his face. He was a solidly patient man, it seemed, which gave me the absurd desire to ruffle his feathers a bit.

He held out his hand. "Then I'll need your keys."

"That's a lot of trust you expect me to put into a complete stranger."

"Yet you're staying in my house."

I scoffed. "House? I am staying in a small room above a pub, and I feel extremely misled in this situation, so you can't expect *that* argument to work to your advantage."

He shrugged. "You want the car picked up or not?"

Ugh. He had a point. It was either blind trust in these strangers—who could have orchestrated the whole thing with the rude yellow sports car just to steal my Kia, for all I knew—or wait until Monday and leave my rental at the whims of the drivers on the country road. The *unstable* country road, from my limited experience maneuvering in that snow.

"Fine." I pulled the car keys from my pocket and curled my fingers around them. "But I need something from you in return."

"Something from me?"

"Yeah. Collateral."

He ran a hand over his stubbled jaw. "You Americans are weird, you know that?"

"*We're* weird?" I threw my arms out to the sides. "*You* call this the first floor!"

He walked out of the room, his shoulders and head shaking in sync, and crossed the hall to disappear into his own room. I hoped his humor was a result of laughter and not shock. I thought he might have left me there for good, deciding not to even bother anymore, but he returned a minute later, his hand behind his back. Rhys stepped directly up to me with widened, serious eyes. He dipped his head and lowered his voice, and I had to fight not to lean in a little. "If I am to trust you with this, you must guard it with your life."

I swallowed. Why did his accent make that command sound much more serious than it likely was? My body tensed in preparation to receive the secret that would win me World War II or a message for the queen. My England experience in life thus far was limited to what I'd seen on TV, and yes, it showed.

Rhys took my hand and uncurled my fingers. He set a mass of curly, artificial white hair in my palm and it ran over my hands like a synthetic hairy waterfall. He took my keys and closed my fingers back over the hair so it wouldn't fall.

"What the—"

Rhys looked me severely in the eye, and while this seemed like a joke, his expression made me wonder if he was entirely genuine. "I am trusting you."

He couldn't be serious. A mass of white hair that appeared to have yellowed a bit with age in exchange for my *rental car*? It really was a shame when the hot ones turned out to be insane. I fought the impulse to chuck the stringy wig. "What is it?"

His lips quirked into a smile. "Father Christmas's beard."

He walked away, leaving me with nothing but silence and artificial hair.

FOUR

JET LAG WAS A BEAST. I'D ONLY EVER HEARD PEOPLE TALK about it before, and I never paid much attention to it then. I tended to scroll past those complaint posts on social media. So what if you woke up at a weird time? You're in *Paris*, Madi, so I'm having a hard time feeling sympathy for you.

Well folks, I got it now. This was my California body clock's first time on the other side of the world, and it did not appreciate the six o'clock bedtime I'd accidentally given myself the evening before. After Rhys left me with the beard, I locked my door and laid down on top of the bed . . . and didn't wake up until a little before five in the morning. What a waste of my first evening in Snowshill.

The travel blogs I'd scoured in preparation for this trip recommended staying awake all day upon arrival so I would get a full night's sleep and reset fairly quickly that way. I did the math and figured out that it was almost nine at night back home.

I'd passed dinnertime in my sleep, so I was wide awake and starving. My stomach growled, the empty chamber echoing irritably.

"Fine, I'll feed you," I whispered. I had no food, but there was a pub downstairs. People probably came in early for breakfast, right?

I crawled off the bed and unzipped my suitcase. I needed a shower more than anything else. The bathroom was—yes, you guessed it—small, and it had a weird capsule shower thing with a bunch of buttons and a timer on the outside. The knobs made no seemingly direct correlation to what was happening with the water, and thirty minutes later I'd had an arctic shower and a really wet floor.

The two towels they'd provided were, embarrassingly, not enough to sop up the mess, so I left them on the floor and got dressed.

Whispers of continued failure licked at me. Maybe coming to England alone had been a mistake. I allowed myself a hot second to wonder if I was better off eating the cost of a new ticket and just flying back home. I could drive out to Linscombe, pop into the church, then return to Geyserville and hide out until Christmas and the wedding both had passed.

I hadn't checked the return policy on this room yet, but I had a feeling I'd missed the window for getting my money back. Maybe I could consider it a donation and suggest Rhys look into upgrading his hot water heater with the money.

My stomach rumbled again. I brushed through my wet hair and scrunched it so it wouldn't dry weird, then let myself into the darkened hallway. The building was so old I felt like I was walking around the set of an Elizabethan movie. What did people do before phones? Carry candles around? I flipped on my flashlight and flooded the narrow stairway with light.

The dining room was quiet and dark, but light spilled from the kitchen at the back, along with the sounds of someone moving around inside. Hallelujah. Maybe I could order a hot breakfast after all.

Not that I had planned to rummage through the pantry . . . but it had definitely been an option.

"Hello?" I called hesitantly, waiting at the counter.

No one answered, but there was definitely someone in the kitchen.

"Hello?" I tried again. The little dachshund I'd seen last night perked up at this and trotted toward me from the dark fireplace. A low rumble in his chest conveyed his disapproval of me before he trotted back to his resting place near the empty hearth. Apparently he wasn't a fan.

I slipped around the counter, feeling like I was crossing a barrier into forbidden lands. The kitchen was narrow and lit overhead—a contrast to the dark taproom. Rhys stood at the counter, mixing something in a large bowl, a bottle of dark liquid on the workspace beside him. I had to admit the kitchen itself was much too modern for my taste. Stepping into it after being in the low-ceilinged, stone-covered dining hall felt like walking out of a Jane Eyre film into a spaceship.

"Rhys?" He didn't seem to hear me, so I said it again louder. "Rhys?"

Still, he ignored me.

I took the opportunity to admire his wide shoulders from behind and the way the muscles in his back moved through his dark gray t-shirt as he worked. I was not a woman prone to ogling men, since I had been in a committed relationship for five years and then had spent the subsequent months mourning the loss of that relationship. I hadn't *needed* to look at other men. I'd loved the one I was with.

But I didn't have Jake anymore. I wasn't with anyone. I could admire Rhys from afar and it hurt no one but my own pride— were I to be caught.

I shook myself. Ogling wasn't classy. Rhys was hot, but that didn't mean I had a right to watch the muscles in his shoulder move or the way his arm definition changed and flexed as he worked whatever was in that bowl. He probably had a girlfriend —or a string of them—and even if he didn't, he was way too far out of my league. There was an odd safety in that feeling, though, and I waded into it. I wouldn't try to flirt with the guy, because he would never be into a tourist like me anyway.

Not that I was into *him*. I was only here for a vacation. He was an attractive man. I switched the flashlight off and pulled up my camera, snapping a picture of his back and texting it to Callie.

Luna Winter: This guy runs the pub where I'm staying. Are you still sure you have to watch your friend's dog? I will buy your plane ticket. Just say the word.

I slid my phone into my pocket. Rhys's head had moved enough to reveal the earbuds blocking me out, and I reached forward to tap him on the shoulder.

To say that he jumped would be a massive understatement. Rhys startled, throwing his arms into the air along with the large bowl of whatever he'd been stirring. It bounced off the white painted wall and tipped down, splashing thick, brown goo all over Rhys, the counter, and the floor.

I was completely unscathed.

Rhys surveyed the mess, then looked at me, pulling the earbuds from his ears.

"Good morning," I said with a grimace.

He blinked at me. "It's hardly past five. What are you doing?"

"I was hungry."

Rhys shook out his hands and thick batter flung from his fingers. Guilt crept over my arms.

"I'm sorry," I said quickly. "Tell me where the rags are, and I'll clean this up."

"It's not your mess."

"It *is* my fault, though."

"I can't argue that," he muttered.

I shot him a wry face. "Rags?"

He indicated the cupboard on the far wall. "Everything's in there."

I retrieved the necessary supplies and got to work wiping the walls, counter, and floor, wringing my rag repeatedly in a small bucket of hot water. Rhys scooped globs into the bowl and took it to the sink to wash out.

My stomach rumbled. I'd passed the point of hunger and moved onto a barren wasteland. The mixture smelled sweet, and I was tempted to lick a little off the counter while Rhys's back was turned. The thickness of the batter could coat my stomach and save me from further pain. "What was that meant to be?"

"A Christmas cake."

Mmmm, cake. "So like sugar and spices and that sort of thing?"

A little lick surely wouldn't hurt.

He eyed me over his shoulder. "Brandy, butter, eggs. Typical cake ingredients."

Eggs. Drat. "How many times have you *actually* gotten salmonella from eating raw eggs? I'm convinced it's just a myth."

"Never." He turned off the water and dried the bowl. "But I've also never consumed raw eggs."

My mouth fell open. "You cannot seriously mean you've never tried cookie dough or cake batter from the bowl?"

His dark eyebrows drew together as he turned around and leaned against the counter, crossing his arms over his chest. A light danced in his brown eyes. If I wasn't mistaken, Rhys was amused. "I can seriously mean it. It's foolish, which is why it's a practice for children."

I sat back on my heels where I was kneeling on the floor and shook my head slowly. "What a sad childhood you must have led."

He cocked an eyebrow. "My childhood probably had more biscuits and cakes than you've had the chance to eat in your life-time, Luna. I just didn't eat them before they were cooked."

"It's not the same thing at all." I stood up and crossed to the sink to empty my bucket and rinse my rag. Rhys didn't move, so my elbow knocked into him while I worked. "That's like telling me you ate a donut so you don't need to bother trying a soft pretzel. They're both fried dough, but they couldn't be more different."

"Agreed."

I smiled at him triumphantly.

His dark eyebrows rose. "Because they are different. Soft pretzels are boiled, not fried."

Shoot, I had forgotten that. I pressed my lips together. "Are you determined to be a Grinch?"

He bent his head a little to look down at me, and I wondered if the smell filling my nose was the Christmas cake or Rhys's essence. Either way, I wanted to eat it up.

"Don't you mean grouch?" he asked.

"No."

He shook his head. "Forgive me. I was a little frustrated that the cake I've spent three days nurturing is now in the bin."

"I'm sorry . . ." I shook my head, fairly positive I hadn't heard him correctly. "Did you say *three days*?"

"Yes."

"And . . . *nurturing*?"

Cake was food. It wasn't a tomato plant or a puppy. Food wasn't meant to be nurtured; it was meant to be consumed.

"Yes," he said. "Christmas cake is a process."

I shook away my judgy thoughts, and remorse seeped into my stomach. This cake had been a process that apparently required the dedicated attention typically attributed to raising a child, and he'd done it for three days. The sense of loss was evident in his brooding eyes, and it was all my fault. "I'm sorry. I didn't mean to startle you. I really was just looking for something to eat."

He ran a hand over his stubbled, perfectly sculpted jaw. Callie would definitely appreciate this angle much more than the last. Maybe if he kept his eyes closed long enough . . . Nope. He opened them before I could successfully get my phone out of my pocket.

"Kitchen isn't open."

"Oh." My hollow stomach rolled, as if arguing in its own defense.

He sighed. "I need to get started on remaking that cake, but I can heat you some beans on toast first."

That sounded strange. "Just toast would be fine. I'm happy to make it myself—"

"You aren't insured to cook in this kitchen, Luna. I'm not letting a guest touch the stove."

"Well, maybe I can get the cake started for you, then—"

"Absolutely not." He moved around me, swirling the scent again. It was warm and sugary and simply delightful.

Exactly the opposite of Rhys, as far as I could discern from our short acquaintance so far.

Yeah, it had to be the cake I was smelling. The man was too grumpy to smell like cinnamon and sugar and joy.

He laughed as though the idea of me mixing a cake was humorous.

"Hey," I said in defense, crossing the floor to toss my rag into the small washing machine at the end of the room. "You don't have to be a professional to know how to mix batter."

"It's an old family recipe, and I will not let your American eyes come near it. We all know what happens when a Brit trusts a Yank."

I rested my hands on my waist. "If that's a jab at the American Revolution, then it's about two hundred years too late."

"Still happened."

"I'll be sure to include your prejudice when I review your apartment," I teased.

He lifted an eyebrow. "So you're allowed to call Brits weird for referring to the ground as the ground, but I'm not allowed to protect my grandmother's recipe from your traitorous eyes?"

Okay, he had a fair point there. I dropped my superhero pose. "I'm not interested in caretaking my food into old age, Rhys. I'd rather eat it. I can promise your recipe is meaningless to me."

He chuckled, turning away, and the sound of his laugh went straight to my stomach. *Whoa.* He started gathering what I assumed were the ingredients for beans on toast, and I noticed brown batter had dried over his arms. I got a new rag from the cupboard and rinsed it, wringing out the excess water.

I approached him carefully, and he shot me a funny glance over his shoulder. "Why are you walking like that?"

Tiptoeing like the Grinch about to nab a fully decorated tree? "I didn't want to startle you again."

He turned back to finish working at the stove, and I offered the rag to him. "For your arms."

He looked surprised, but he took it and wiped the crusted batter from his corded forearm. Arms like that could not be sculpted in a kitchen, right? Surely Rhys side-gigged as a logger. He had the scowl and the plaid already.

"Are you always awake at five in the morning nurturing your cakes?"

Rhys's grumpy mouth fluttered with a smile. "Depends on the time of year."

I surveyed what I could see of the empty dining room from where we stood. "Is the pub always empty this early?"

He shrugged. "Like I said, we aren't open yet."

Oh, yeah. He'd mentioned that. I swept my gaze from the alien ship kitchen to the rustic, Elizabethan dining area and snagged on the stairs. "My own entrance, huh?"

He looked confused. "I thought we spoke the same language, but there's no understanding you half the time."

I ignored that remark. "The posting for the apartment said my room had its own entrance."

"It does," he argued. "You have a door and a lock."

"But I have to go through the pub to reach it. I'm assuming you lock those doors at night?"

"Yes." So he wasn't completely insane, then.

"What happens if I'm out late and you lock the door? I'll need to get into my room, but I can't. I'm assuming my key doesn't open the pub."

"You would give me a ring, and I would let you in." He spoke so easily, as though my arguments were invalid.

"But if you were asleep?"

"How late are you planning to stay out?"

"It isn't a plan. It's a what-if. I'm trying to demonstrate the importance of having my own entrance to my apartment, or how someone could be misled in this situation after reading that on your posting."

He rolled his eyes and put two pieces of golden toast on a plate, then scooped beans over the top. "Like I misled you?"

I lifted a placating hand. "Not intentionally, I am coming to learn."

"I'm glad you reached that conclusion. Go sit at the bar, and I'll bring out your food."

"I can carry it—"

"It's fine."

He waited for me to walk ahead of him while he carried the plate. When I sat on the stool, he flipped on a dim light over the bar and slid breakfast in front of me. Two slices of thick, toasted bread sat on the plate, covered in what looked like somewhat soupy pinto beans. Where was a McGriddle when you needed one? This looked the opposite of appetizing. Would it be rude to nibble the untouched edges of the bread and throw the rest away? Maybe when Rhys left I could whistle the angry dachshund over and sneak my beans to him.

"Can I see your mobile?" he asked.

I slipped it from my pocket. "Why?"

He stared at me a beat too long, his dark lashes fringing very serious eyes. He was a Grinchy Scrooge of a man who nurtured cake and most likely moonlighted as a lumberjack. He also thought it made sense to pour soupy beans over nicely toasted bread. Enter: Rhys, the British alien. I would never understand him.

"So I can put my number in it in case you stay out too late and need to ring me to unlock the pub door."

"Ah, smart."

"Though I would like to point out that this has never been an issue before."

I ignored him and faced my phone to unlock it, then handed it over.

Rhys paused, staring at the screen, and I took a tentative bite, beans and all. Hmmm. Not bad, actually. The beans had a slight Spaghettios taste to the sauce, but better. Over toast, it was actually pretty good.

Or that was my poor, hungry stomach clamoring for food and grateful for whatever foreign thing I could feed it.

When Rhys failed to move, I glanced up. "Having trouble with my American phone? It's an Apple product. You might not have them here yet."

He looked at me, his face a mask of stone, apparently not appreciating my joke. "What's this about, then?" He turned the phone to show the message thread between me and Callie, the picture of his back front and center.

I dropped my bean-soaked toast on my plate, cold embarrassment washing through my body. "Nothing."

"That's me," he said.

"Yeah. Um. It's really not as creepy as it looks."

He waited for an explanation, his eyes never leaving my face.

"My sister told me to find a hot British guy while I was over here, so it's really just a joke."

Or maybe it was exactly as creepy as it looked.

He turned his attention back to my phone, and I watched his pupils move as he read the message I'd sent directly after the picture. He looked up at me again, raising his eyebrows. "So I'm a hot British guy?"

I scoffed ridiculously loudly. As if he wasn't already aware of this fact. "Psh. No, of course not."

He chuckled, his fingers swiping over the screen. I hoped he was finally putting his number in so I could get the phone back and slide down to hide behind the counter. He handed it back to me, his smile lingering, and my skin prickled with embarrassment.

"If you wanted a photo, Luna, you only needed to ask."

He went back into the kitchen, and I opened my phone to check my message thread and re-read what I'd sent Callie. My eye caught the most recently sent message, and I clicked on it. Rhys had evidently sent himself a text so he could have my number. He either thought he was pretty funny or wanted me to always remember the colossal level of embarrassment I'd reached, because he'd sent a fire emoji to the newest contact in my phone: Hot British Guy.

FIVE

Finding the pub room empty so early in the morning had given me an idea for my yoga channel, but I needed to run it by Rhys sometime later when my mortification had drained a little further and I was brave enough to step foot downstairs again.

Which had to be soon. My stomach ran off a very steady food clock that was evidently stronger than my body clock, for it was now noon and I wanted lunch. Badly.

Sounds from customers downstairs drifted up to my room, and if I wasn't sure before how I would film any videos in this tiny room, I now knew it would be impossible. But the deserted taproom early in the morning just might work.

Snow continued to fall on the other side of my window, and a chill ran through the air. I slipped a sweater over my shirt, gathered my courage, and left my room. My utter embarrassment had kept me holed up for far too long, cutting into the Snowshill exploration I'd planned to do. I also still had to meet Ruby, my other temporary landlord, and I *needed* a sandwich.

Dramatic? Maybe. But it was acceptable to be dramatic about food. Food in general was literally a life-or-death situation.

I also had the right to be just as dramatic about water, sleep, or Cadbury mini eggs. My body would expire without all those things.

A few of the tables in the dining room were occupied, and an older man sat in one of the tufted leather armchairs set before the fire with Rhys's dachshund at his feet. Hamish was perched on a stool at the bar, and the short, curvy woman who had been waitressing last night was seated beside him, curling the end of her long red ponytail in her fingers.

Rhys was—somewhat blessedly—nowhere to be seen.

I crossed the room and took a seat at the bar a few stools down from Hamish and the waitress. She looked up and set a wide smile on me. "You're our tenant, then?"

"Yes, I'm Luna. You must be Ruby?" I hazarded a guess.

She flicked her red ponytail. I wondered if the hair or the name had come first. "The very one. Can I get you a menu?"

"That would be great."

Ruby stood on the bottom rungs of her stool and reached over the counter for a coaster with a QR code, then plopped it in front of me. "Scan that with your mobile and the menu should pop up." She turned back to say something to Hamish. "Yeah, Tamsin *could* work if we didn't want someone jolly."

I tried to ignore them and scanned the menu. The bottom had a little section of dog delicacies, and I laughed out loud. Was all of England this canine-friendly? Or just The Wild Hare inhabitants?

I chose a sandwich and waited until Ruby finished listing the finer points of each woman of her acquaintance and whether or not they were jolly enough to suit her purposes. She hopped off the stool, and I wanted to ask where she sat on the jolly-ometer so I could gauge each of the people she'd been talking about.

"You've decided?" she asked brightly. She was young—about my age, at least—and I instantly liked her energy.

I placed my order, and Ruby ran around to the other side of

the bar to take my money. She disappeared into the back for a second before returning, filling a glass with Dr Pepper and setting it before me. My first sip was heavenly, so I took another long one.

As a fitness professional, I did my best to maintain a mostly healthy lifestyle. But fully-leaded Dr Pepper was nonnegotiable.

Ruby watched me with amusement. Her ponytail swung as she talked, and her mouth was of that variety that always appeared to be smiling. She was, to me, the very definition of jolly. I was certain she would have been a cheerleader in high school. Or whatever the equivalent of that was here.

"What brings you to Snowshill then, love?" she asked. I adored her accent. It was hot on Rhys, but it was so quirky and lovable on Ruby.

"Just here for a vacation." I quickly corrected myself. "A holiday, you know?"

Her amusement grew, and she shared a look with Hamish. "We do know what vacation means here. Any particular reason you chose Snowshill?"

I couldn't very well say it was the name of the town that caught my attention, or that I was skipping Christmas with my family in order to avoid Jake and Aubrey's wedding. I might sound unhinged. Desperate. Pathetic enough to fly across the world just so I wouldn't be forced to say the word *no*.

I attempted a laid-back shrug. "I just needed a break. My ancestors came from Linscombe, actually, so I'm hoping to drive over and check it out soon."

"*Blergh*," Hamish said and made a spitting noise. He was younger than he'd looked last night. Probably not much older than me, either.

Ruby's eyes widened. "Don't mention them around here if you want to make friends." She leaned in. "They have to one-up us on everything. We go up against Linscombe every year for cricket matches, Christmas fairs, and rugby. There's a fair bit of rivalry between us."

Rhys carried a plate from the kitchen and set it before me. My cheeks warmed, and I thanked him before turning my attention entirely to my turkey sandwich. He seemed unfazed by my bashfulness, but I could not get the image out of my head of him standing across from me at this very bar and finding the picture I had taken *of his freaking back* and sent to my sister.

Mortification really didn't begin to cover the intense squirming in my stomach. Rhys undoubtedly intended to avoid the crazy girl staying in his pub, and I didn't blame him.

"What's this about Linscombe?" Rhys asked, pausing beside Ruby.

Hamish hooked a thumb my direction. Traitor. "She has family there."

"Not anymore," I defended. "My ancestors came from Linscombe a long time ago. They were in Kentucky by the 1800's, so it's been a while since they left."

Hamish made a spitting sound again. I desperately hoped he was not actually spitting.

Rhys wrinkled his nose. "I wouldn't brag about that around here, if I were you."

"It wasn't a brag. I was explaining why I chose Snowshill for my holiday."

"Why didn't you just stay in Linscombe?" Hamish asked, running a hand over his dark blond beard. I bet he was beginning to regret fishing my car out of the ditch.

Because Rhys's apartment on Airbnb was the best quality of the cheapest options that were remaining on such short notice. "I *can* stay there—"

"Don't be daft," Ruby said, clicking her tongue. "Hamish is only cross because he lost to Linscombe in sixth form. He was the rugby captain, so he takes it personally."

Hamish made a grunting sound.

Rhys wiped the clean counter with a hand towel and tossed it over his shoulder. "We would have won if they hadn't cheated."

"Can you cheat at rugby?" I asked, genuinely curious. All I knew of the game was that it was similar to American football, only much more physical.

Rhys and Hamish shared a look and broke out laughing. I returned my attention to my turkey sandwich, my cheeks probably glowing like the red lights on a firetruck.

Rhys left the room and returned with a snow shovel. "I'm going to clear the doorway."

Hamish left his stool and followed Rhys outside, and Ruby came to sit beside me.

"Don't take it personally, love. They don't mean any harm. The conflict between Snowshill and Linscombe runs deep, and this village can't seem to forget each time we've lost to them at anything."

"We have high school rivalries back home, too. At one of our last rallies when I was a senior, someone dressed up as the mascot for our opposing team, and our mascot made a huge show of pummeling him. It was a little . . . violent. But everyone gets so into it."

Ruby looked mildly disturbed. She shook her head as though removing the image from her mind, then lowered her voice. "Well, while they're out"—she nodded toward the door Rhys and Hamish had disappeared through—"I wanted to warn you of something."

"Sure." I picked up one of the chips on my plate and popped it in my mouth. *Mmmm*, parmesan.

"You seem nice, but Rhys isn't really in a position to date anyone right now."

"Oh, gosh, no," I said, leaning back and all but choking on my chip. What had he said about me? Had he told her about the picture? I shook my head. "I have *no* intention of making any sort of romantic connection while I'm here."

Yeah, I'd ogled. But that didn't mean I actually thought anything would happen between us. He was out of my league, remember?

Ruby looked a little startled. Probably by the intensity of my denial. *Cool it, Luna. You'll only make yourself look guilty.*

"Okay," she said. "It's just that I saw the way you were looking at him."

"No, that's just me being embarrassed. I stumbled on him this morning in the kitchen and ruined his Christmas cake—"

She winced. "I did hear about that."

Hopefully that was the only thing she'd heard about. "Then you know I have every reason to want to avoid the man."

"That's a relief." She let out a tired breath. "The last girl who stayed here kept trying to sneak into his room at night. He added an extra bolt to his door just to be cautious."

I chuckled nervously. "Does he think I would—"

"He said nothing to me. I don't know what he thinks. But he's pining for his ex, and it's not something you want to get yourself wrapped up in." She rolled her eyes dramatically. "Such a mess."

Her revelation was both a relief and a disappointment. Relief he wasn't dating someone, disappointment that he wasn't emotionally available.

Not that it mattered. I reiterated my earlier point sternly. I was not here to make a romantic attachment. I was here to avoid my past, and maybe kiss a Brit to forget that past—just not Rhys.

Super healthy of me.

"What about you?" I asked. I'd watched the easy way she bantered with Hamish earlier. "Are you and Hamish together?"

"Oh, no," she said, laughing. She hopped down from her stool. "Hamish? I've known him my whole life. He's like mine and Rhys's third Musketeer. You'll see him around quite a lot. He never goes anywhere."

"What does he do?"

"He has a farm down the road, but anytime he isn't needed there, he's here."

"Ruby," the man who was seated before the fire called. He lifted a teacup. "I need another one, darling."

"On it, Frank." Ruby went around the bar to make Frank another pot of tea. Another couple walked out and she got to work clearing their table. I watched the doorway when the couple left and caught a glimpse of Rhys outside laughing at something Hamish was saying. The environment here was cozy, comfortable, and made me want to curl up on the chair across from Frank with a book and a hot cup of tea to pass the afternoon.

How did people in England get any real work done?

Ruby lugged a few boxes onto a nearby table and started sorting through their contents, and the other people having lunch slowly vacated the pub. All except Frank.

By the time I finished my sandwich, Rhys came back in alone. I stood to take my plate into the sink—living here gave me a weird sense of ownership over my messes—and Rhys took it from my hand.

"I wondered if you would ever come down again," he said quietly, his deep voice running over me and sending chills over my neck. I purposefully ignored that ridiculous sensation. *He's emotionally unavailable*, I reminded myself. *I'm not even looking for a romantic fling.*

"You think a little firsthand mortification would keep me away?" I asked facetiously.

Rhys smirked. "You hid in your room all morning, didn't you?"

I would neither confirm nor deny that completely accurate accusation, so I changed the subject. "Did you get your secret cake made again?"

He looked like he was going to press the matter, but then let it drop. "Yeah, it'll be fine. Don't stress about it too much." He ran a hand absently over his jaw. Did he do that just to bring attention to how cut it was? Unkind.

"Knitters in twenty!" Ruby called. Rhys nodded to her.

"Hey, can I get my car keys?" I asked.

"Oh, sure thing. I have them upstairs."

"On the first floor."

He gave me a funny look and started toward the stairs. "Yeah."

I was still not used to the weirdness of them starting the first floor up a level. It was almost as weird as everyone around me speaking with an English accent.

I followed him but went into my room to retrieve his Santa beard. We met in the hallway. "Are you going to tell me the significance of this now?" I shook out the curly white wig.

"No. You have to earn that kind of privilege."

I laughed, curling my fingers around it. "Then maybe I'll hold it hostage. You can't drop something like this in my hand and not explain it."

"Actually, I believe that is exactly what I've done." He dangled my keys far above my reach. "Stalemate."

"You can't keep a car."

"I'm not. I'm just holding the keys. You're welcome to take them back."

He knew very well I would never be able to reach them. I was average height for a girl, and he was on the tall side of average for a guy, which made his arm span much longer than mine.

I took a step back toward my room and tucked the wig behind me. "Fine. Then I'll keep your wig."

"That's stealing."

"You're welcome to take it back," I said, mimicking his tone and his words.

He looked at me for a long moment, and I held my breath. Was he going to make a leap for the beard? I wouldn't mind if his arms went around me while he tried to reach for it. Oh, gosh.

Was I flirting with him? What had felt playful a moment before only felt desperate now.

"Knitters came early," Ruby said from the stairwell, startling both of us from our stalemate. She looked suspicious, and I felt my cheeks warm.

Rhys lowered his hand and held the keys toward me. I took them and tossed the beard at his chest, which he caught like a rugby ball. I wanted to chase Ruby down the stairs and insist that I wasn't flirting with Rhys, that I one hundred percent meant it when I told her I wasn't here for a fling. The very reason I had left California for the month made it obvious I wasn't ready for a romantic connection, just like Rhys.

I was still hung up on my stupid ex.

Maybe that was the cause for the tension running between us. It was a safe bet to flirt with one another, because on some deeper, molecular level, both of us knew the other person wasn't truly emotionally available.

My phone rang, and I pulled it from my pocket. *Mom.* "I need to take this."

Rhys nodded, and I slipped into my room. I shut my eyes, dropped my head, and expelled my shame.

No more playful banter with Hot British Guy.

SIX

THE WILD HARE BOASTED A STEADY STREAM OF consistent patrons from open to closing over the next few days. It never felt overwhelming in its occupancy, but there always seemed to be some group or other taking over the main seating area for a Mommy and Me group, knitting, or elaborate board games that included costume-wearing. Aside from me, everyone knew each other.

I kind of felt like I'd been dropped into the middle of a sitcom where all the regulars gathered at the same coffee shop and had *regular* orders and *regular* seats. I had nothing like this back home, and I came from such a small town we didn't even have our own elementary school. Kids had to bus a town over for that.

Geyserville wasn't Snowshill-small, but it was small enough that I couldn't get tacos without running into my exes.

I sat cross-legged in one of the tufted leather chairs near the burning fire, my laptop opened to my video editing program while my body defrosted from an attempt to walk one of the nearby country lanes *yesterday*. By the time I'd returned to the pub, my feet were popsicles and my socks wet through to the skin, but the views had been worth a little wet exploring.

Now I was getting ready to go outside again soon to shoot something for social media promotion, so my feet were encased in two pairs of wool socks to warm them up before trekking back into the snow. I sipped hot cider and focused on my computer. There were two videos I'd filmed in my zen-looking studio room prior to leaving California. I tried to post two videos each week on average, but sometimes I only got one. My following grew much faster in the beginning when I was doing daily videos, but I didn't have Jake to push me anymore. I couldn't seem to find the drive to film more than one or two, and a quarter of them were sponsored ads, so I couldn't avoid doing them.

Various fitness and nutritional food companies had reached out to me in the past few years to rep their brands, but the most I got out of the deals were free clothes or a supply of protein bars. I appreciated those collaborations, of course—I basically never had to buy clothes anymore—but they couldn't pay my phone bill or fill my car with gas, so maintaining my YouTube rankings was necessary.

I was still holding out for Dr Pepper to reach out and offer a rep deal. I would pay *them* for that kind of sponsorship. Maybe I needed to draft a letter about the importance Dr Pepper played in my daily diet.

Remember? It's non-negotiable.

Perhaps Instagram was my answer there. My page was growing daily, and I hoped to find a way to funnel people from there to YouTube.

Maybe if I threw on those Stella Fit jogger pants I'd brought and posed next to the red telephone booth across the street, I could put out a little teaser for the Cotswolds content I had planned. I'd been in Snowshill for four days now, and aside from venturing to the market to fill my little cupboards with cereal, granola bars, fruit, and sandwich ingredients, the only times I'd gone outside were for nature walks—and I stayed close because my feet would start to freeze and I'd need to return to the pub to defrost.

I wasn't sure if I could stress this enough, but snow was *cold*. I now understood why the only time Jake ever wanted to go to Tahoe was during the summer.

"What is it you're working on?" Frank asked, creaking a little as he lowered himself into the chair opposite mine. His white hair was neatly combed and his sweater was festive. He'd become something of my pal the last few days, and I liked spending a few companionable hours by the fire working on my videos or Instagram content. Even if Ned, the pub's dachshund, seemed to follow Frank everywhere, yet absolutely hated me. I'd grown up around animals, so I was taking Ned's rejection personally.

I turned the laptop screen so he could see it. "Editing a video. Though I think I just decided to go for a walk."

"Is that another one of those yogi poses? My granddaughter is always doing those yogi poses."

"Yes, yoga," I said, emphasizing the A sound. I had studied a few yogis, but I could never count myself among them. Not that Frank understood the difference. "I'm an instructor."

Of sorts. I didn't actually do any in-person training anymore, so using the title felt a little like cheating. I used to teach in a studio in San Francisco, but when Jake and I had moved up to Geyserville, he helped me funnel my focus into the LunaMoon channel, and I didn't bother looking for a new teaching job.

I closed my computer and slid it back into its case.

"She lives in London, so I don't see her much," Frank said sadly. It took me a moment to realize he was talking about his yoga-posing granddaughter still. "There never was a yogi pose she did not conquer, though. Fine talent, my little girl."

Wasn't everyone's grandchild simply the best at whatever they tried to accomplish? I imagined this one in particular was twelve and had taught herself. Frank's pride was endearing. "I am sure. Have you tried to do it with her?"

Frank looked at me with consideration before shaking his head and bringing his cup of tea to his lips. "No. I don't bend that well."

I made a sound of disbelief. My favorite class during my teaching years in San Francisco was at the senior center. "You can do yoga sitting down. All you need is a chair with no arms and a mellow environment to help you relax."

Frank looked at me like I had just claimed I was Santa Claus's niece.

I stood, swinging my bag over my shoulder. "I need to run outside for some pictures, but I'll probably see you later."

"You can bet on it," Frank said.

From my four days in Snowshill, I was half-convinced Frank lived in The Wild Hare's taproom.

The air outside was frigid. I'd thrown a heavy sweatshirt over my sweater, gloves, and a beanie, but still the cold bit at me like a pack of German shepherds. Smoke rose from the pale stone chimneys all along the road, and I circled around the side of the building to make sure my little Kia was still safely parked.

It was.

Not that I hadn't trusted Rhys not to make a copy of my keys, or something. I'd trusted him enough to let him take my keys, at least. I mean, the guy had given me *beard collateral*. I really had no reason to trust him yet. Except that I had lived in his pub for four days, and he had been doing nothing but respectfully keeping his distance. I kept waking up at five, but I avoided downstairs until I knew the pub was open and Hamish and Frank were already in their regular places.

Was I avoiding the prospect of being alone with Rhys? Me?

Of course.

I shuffled through the thick snow in my comfortable Stella Fit joggers and crossed the road toward the church on the other side. A low stone wall ran at a slight decline in front of the building. An iron bench was nestled in front of the wall with a bright red telephone booth beside it, and I wasn't sure if there was a more quintessentially British thing in all of the United Kingdom. The old and new together.

My tripod took an extra minute to set up due to my stiff fingers and the gloves, but I lined up the shot with the telephone booth, the snow-capped stone wall, and the ancient church behind it built from the yellow Cotswold stone.

Now, what pose to do? I ran through a few of them, loosening up my muscles and opening my chest. It was easier said than done in the cold, and I settled on a tree pose. Simple, cute, and easy to accomplish while freezing my tush off.

The streets around me were vacant, and I wondered if that was due to the cold or the time of day. I hit record on my camera, got into position, and filmed a brief video of myself getting into the tree pose.

Cold slush seeped through my leggings where my shoe was nestled against my thigh and I sucked in a surprised breath and subdued the reaction, hoping I hadn't just ruined the video.

"I'm in a holiday oasis, and I cannot wait to share what I have planned with you," I said in a gentle tone, the same way I spoke whenever teaching yoga or filming a video for Luna-Moon. "Any idea where I am? Place your guesses in the comments."

I held the pose a bit longer with a wide smile before releasing my breath and lowering my legs and arms. My foot had left a giant wet spot on my inner thigh, and I shuddered.

The snow around the telephone booth was thick and the ground below it dirty. My robin egg blue pants were now covered in a muddy Adidas footprint, and snow had seeped down my socks and was chilling my feet.

My footwear was clearly not good enough for the likes of England, and it was high time I got something more suitable.

"Mummy, what is that lady doing?" a little voice asked in the most adorable accent I'd ever heard in my entire life.

I looked up quickly to find a woman in a long coat and sensible boots pulling a child's hand toward the pub.

"I don't know, Finn, but don't stare. It's impolite."

Finn ignored his mother's direction and watched me, his tiny copper eyebrows pulling together as he followed her into the pub.

My phone rang while I was putting my equipment away, and I tucked it between my head and shoulder. "Hey, Mom."

"Good grief, Lu. The new horse is giving Dad trouble and I'm about ready to march down to the Johnsons' and demand a refund." She expelled a loud breath, but I was—not surprisingly—unmoved by her blunt greeting. "How are things going over there?"

"Good, actually. Really snowy, you know. Did you see those pictures I sent of the church yesterday?"

"Yes. Is that the one our ancestors were married in?"

"No. I haven't made it to Linscombe yet." In all honesty, I was hesitant to get back on the road after the incident with the yellow car and the ditch. "Oh, let me send you a picture of the pub I'm staying in." I snapped a picture of The Wild Hare and sent it.

"Pub? That doesn't sound safe, Lu."

Shoot. I forgot who I was talking to. I had purposefully not mentioned that part of my sleeping arrangement so Mom wouldn't freak out. "It's not like I'm sleeping in a bar, mom. Pubs are different here. It's more like a cozy little restaurant." A restaurant *with* a bar, but it wasn't the seedy environment she was imagining.

"Hmmm."

"Really," I said in a sing-songy way, folding up my tripod. "There's a guy who is always sitting at the bar. They said he's a farmer, but I *know* how much work goes into running a farm.

There's no way he really has time to sit here and run a farm at the same time. And there's an old man who drinks tea *all day* in front of the fireplace. And they have these little groups that meet in the main room for game board parties, mommy groups, and a knitting club."

"Knitting?" Mom asked. "Like with yarn?"

"Yes. It's mostly women, except for Frank."

"Frank?"

"He's my friend."

"Hmmm."

I was pretty sure I had her nearly convinced that my situation was completely fine. "I even saw a woman take her little boy in there a moment ago."

"Uh huh," Mom said.

"I don't like your tone, Mom. It really is safe, I promise. And Ruby—I told you about her, she runs the pub with her cousin—well, she's home all the time. In fact, the pub itself is never empty."

Except at five in the morning when the hot owner was downstairs nurturing his cake mixture. But Mom didn't need to hear about that.

"So long as you keep texting me every day, I'll sleep fine."

"Done."

"Luna . . . listen." Her voice dropped to a serious tone, and I could tell she'd stopped walking. "I ran into Sherrie this morning at Safeway, and she told me Aubrey has been having a really hard time with all the wedding prep."

So what? I swallowed my rude remark. Of course Aubrey was having a hard time when Michelle Riedman was her maid of honor. That girl couldn't go six seconds without thinking of herself. My feet stalled on the sidewalk outside the pub, my tripod under one arm and the camera bag over my other shoulder.

Mom spoke tentatively. "I know you don't owe Aubrey

anything, and heaven knows I struggled with whether I should tell you or not. But I've been thinking about this. You have a lot of power right now to help make Aubrey's wedding experience a better one."

Aubrey's experience marrying my ex-boyfriend? *That* Aubrey? The one who fell instantly in love with the man I was dating and made him fall right back in love with her?

I shook the image of them from my mind. "I don't think it's up to me how much she enjoys or doesn't enjoy her whole wedding experience. She chose this."

"I know, honey." Mom blew out a breath. I knew this was hard for her. She wanted problems fixed and dealt with, and me running off to the Cotswolds was exactly the opposite of fixing or dealing with anything. "Honestly, I'm not sure it's even a good idea for you to reach out to her. You are, obviously, my priority here. I've just been thinking about it since I saw Sherrie, that's all."

"How is Sherrie doing?" I asked, my body still frozen before the pub door and my feet slowly turning to icicles. When Aubrey stole my boyfriend, I cut her and her mom from my life, but I missed Sherrie's warm apple cobbler and ready smile. She had been a mother figure to me beside my own all through my growing up years, and I missed her.

"She is stressed, as can be expected."

Because she was throwing a wedding. Of course. Because the man *I* was supposed to marry was about to become her son-in-law. My body tensed with the reminder, and I wanted to hang up the phone and pretend this conversation had never happened. It wasn't my responsibility to make Aubrey feel better about her mistakes, about stealing my future. It wasn't my job to assuage her guilt.

Instead, I did the only thing I knew how to do. I laughed. "You should see my pants right now, Mom. I just did a tree pose for Instagram and my shoe was so wet it ruined them. I should have realized what was going to happen, but I didn't until it was too late."

Mom sighed. "That sounds awful, babe. I hope they have a good washer and dryer."

"I guess I'm about to find out."

Mom said goodbye, and I hung up the phone. The cold had turned my nose completely numb, but I stood there a moment to regain my bearings. I didn't like talking about my feelings, but I still felt them. They climbed up my stomach and made my shoulders heavy and my heart weak.

Aubrey needed me to absolve her before she could enjoy her wedding preparations, but that wasn't my responsibility. Absolve her from what, exactly? She and Jake had waited almost two weeks to start dating after he ended things with me. Almost *two weeks*. That buffer ensured no one had cheated, right?

Except I didn't believe that. I didn't intrinsically believe Jake did anything wrong here, except fall for my best friend while he was with me. He fell for her, and that was why he ended our relationship. But he and I hadn't been casual. Jake moved up to Geyserville to begin his law firm because we had a plan. We were going to get married and raise children together in my hometown. He was helping me grow my LunaMoon channel, we had a shared Netflix account, and we were happy.

The whole thing was messy. I shook it away, burying it deep in the cavity of my thoughts where I put things I didn't want to think about, like dental appointments and renewing my car registration. I pushed open the door to The Wild Hare and the thick scent of pie crust and seasoned meat assaulted me at once. I inhaled the smell and shut the door behind me.

Aubrey and her problems could stay in the cold. There was no room for that negativity in the inn.

SEVEN

AS PREDICTED, QUARTER-PAST FIVE IN THE MORNING rolled around and I lay wide awake, staring at the slanted ceiling. I was on my fifth morning in the UK, and it was clear that this early wake up was now a habit. A really annoying habit. But I'd been strong about eating breakfast in my own room so I wouldn't find myself alone downstairs with Rhys again.

Since Ruby had pointed out where the little market store was around the corner, I'd walked down twice to fill my cupboards with basic essentials—a double win to avoid both seeing Rhys and blowing all my money at the pub.

I could tell from last night's meat pie that the pub's proximity to my room posed a distinct problem for me. Rhys was a good chef, and his food made it really clear why people were always eating here.

Ruby had also been an angel, pointing out the pull cord in the bathroom that allowed me to access hot water. I felt much better, knowing I wasn't crazy when I'd taken an icy shower that first morning—none of the buttons I'd tried could have produced hot water without that cord activated. I had thought it was some sort of fire alarm. They really needed to rethink their system here, or at least label it better.

Now I stared at my bedroom door in the dark and weighed the possibility of running into Rhys downstairs alone against the need to make a video. The fact was, I'd put off filming long enough, and there was no way I could do it unless the pub was closed. I needed to pull up my big girl pants and hope Rhys was sleeping in today, because I had a video to film. Or that he would allow me to film while he worked in the kitchen.

After a solid effort—and failure—to try and fall back asleep, I rolled out of bed and dressed in a set of yoga pants and a long-sleeved t-shirt. I liked to go barefoot during my videos, but I could see how that was not going to fly here. I pulled wool socks up over my leggings, gathered my tripod, camera, and mat, and quietly snuck downstairs.

There was no light in the kitchen this time, and I breathed out my relief through puffed cheeks. I could film without an audience. Though the downside to no Rhys in the kitchen meant there was also no fire going in the hearth.

Today's video would have to be done in front of dark windows. Hopefully the stone walls would be charming enough on their own, and without the fire, for a soothing yoga tutorial. I found the lights and turned them on, then set up my camera and framed the stone wall behind me. The look was perfect for a holiday theme, and I unrolled my thin yoga mat and found my muscles relaxing as I began the video.

This was what I'd needed since running into Jake and Aubrey at El Azteca last week. A minute to calm my mind and remove the tension from my neck and shoulders.

Yoga had a way of soothing me one stretched muscle at a time until I felt pulled and molded and shaped into a calmer being, prepared to face whatever stood ahead of me.

When I reached the end of my twenty-minute segment, I looked straight at the camera.

"This time of year can be stressful for a number of reasons, but don't let those things deter you from enjoying the holidays. Take time when you need it to find a quiet place to breathe, run through a simple routine like the one we just finished, and reset your body and mind."

I smiled for a moment while a few seconds passed, and then dropped my expression and my head onto the mat in front of me, bending nearly in half. I would end the video in a minute and remove this part in editing. I stretched as far as I could, inhaled slowly, and then stretched just a little farther, crawling my fingers forward on the squishy mat.

I was good at giving advice as LunaMoon. Too bad I wasn't equally good at taking it.

"That was interesting," a deep voice said.

I jolted, sitting up so fast I tweaked my previously relaxed neck. Rhys was seated on the steps in the corner, his arms crossed loosely over his bent knees, swathed in shadows.

I rubbed my cricked neck, then pressed my palm to my racing heart. "How long have you been there?"

"Fifteen minutes or so."

"Gosh, Rhys," I complained, burying my face in my hands. "You could have told me."

"And ruin your video? I'm not that rude."

I lifted my face. "The opposite, actually. If I had known you were awake, I would've asked for a fire."

He chuckled. "Here I thought you were being bashful."

"I can't be that bashful. I post these on YouTube for anyone in the world to see."

"YouTube, huh?" His smile was practically audible.

I realized my mistake. "For *yoga* enthusiasts to see," I corrected. "You have no interest, so steer clear of my channel."

"I have an interest in yoga."

I snorted.

He looked a little hurt. "I do, actually. A friend of mine

taught me a children's pose thing, and I liked how it stretched out my shoulders."

"Child's pose."

"I guess." He shrugged. "Maybe I'll find your channel and learn a few more stretches."

"You do that," I said, getting up to turn off the camera.

Rhys stood, stretching his arms high above his head. The room was dim and quiet. It should have felt abandoned, but it still had the same homey, comfortable vibe it maintained during the day. Rhys wore faded jeans and a t-shirt that hugged his shoulders just right and hung down his waist. He looked soft and worn, and I yanked my gaze up to his face.

"Have you come down to nurture your cake?"

"As a matter of fact, I have." He went into the kitchen and flipped the light on. "It's baked now, but maybe you should stay out of the kitchen anyway."

I scoffed in pretended umbrage and started putting away my equipment. Secretly I agreed with Rhys about me staying out of the kitchen. I was bad luck around that cake. Besides, I had the tiniest kitchenette known to mankind upstairs in my room and enough milk and cereal to get me through the week.

"Hungry?" he called.

Well, twist my arm. "I could eat," I called back as though I'd hardly given the idea any thought. Forget the cereal. If Rhys was cooking, I was willing to be poor. "Is the kitchen open?"

"Not in an official capacity, no. But I could make you something." His voice was disembodied, lost somewhere behind the stone wall that separated the bar area from the twenty-first century kitchen back there.

"Beans on toast?" Which sounded sarcastic, but I would totally be happy with. It beat the Corn Flakes upstairs.

"Or a sausage, or an egg."

"I don't need much." His version of sausage or eggs made me

a little nervous. I wasn't an adventurous eater. The beans on toast had been a big step for me.

He poked his head around the corner and pointed to the bar. "Sit. I'll be right out."

I brought my camera with me and pulled up the video I'd just done, scrubbing through it to check the lighting. It was dark outside, so the mood was a little dim. I hoped that leant itself to relaxation and didn't just make it depressing yoga. That kind of defeated the purpose.

That was *it*. Relaxation. I could title this video something about relieving the holiday stress at the end of the day and capitalize on the dim, soft lighting.

Rhys returned a few minutes later carrying two plates. He surprised me by setting both of them on the bar and sitting beside me. Our banter so far had hovered between playful and testy, but I had a feeling underneath the broodiness was a bit of a soft middle. Rhys surprised me sometimes with flirtatious smiles, but his heart was closed off, so I didn't read into them. If I was reading the man correctly, it almost seemed like he wanted to be friends.

His shoulder brushed mine, but he didn't seem to notice. He wouldn't though, would he? He wasn't on the market. A man still hung up on his ex wasn't noticing the drooly, heart-eyed tourist.

"How did you make this so fast?" I asked. Half a tomato sat next to an egg, sausage, and a triangle of toast with beans on the side. This was a full breakfast. But how was I meant to eat the tomato? Plain? Just cut into the warm, juicy thing and eat it by itself? English breakfasts needed to come with instructions too, just like their showers.

"Most of it just needs to be heated." He shoved a bite in his mouth. "It's not hard."

"Says the chef. It would take me an hour just to figure out how to brown the sausage."

He lifted his eyebrows. "Has no one taught you to cook?"

"My mom's tried, but I'm mostly hopeless. My sister picked it up pretty well though. Which only proved that the fault is on me and not my teacher."

Rhys shrugged. "I think anyone can cook, but not everyone can manage to do it well." He pointed his fork at the low ceiling above our heads. "Ruby has tried to master the stove, but she can't get it quite right. It would be nice if she did, though."

"So you aren't stuck in the kitchen all the time?"

"No, it's not that." He piled his egg on the toast and took a bite before answering me. "I like being back there all the time, and Ruby is good with the customers. We have a few employees who come in sometimes so we aren't working all the time, and it's a good balance. But they're both gone for the holidays. I just wish she could hang out back there with me sometimes. I could pass on some of Nan's old recipes to her."

"You two are close."

"Yeah, we are. I was raised by my grandparents under this roof, and Ruby was here more often than not. Her parents weren't around much, and she ended up staying with us quite often." His lips had the whisper of a smile. "We are more brother and sister than we are cousins."

That was weird to think about. But I didn't have any cousins who lived even close to me, so this was a foreign concept. "Where are your grandparents now?"

"Grandad died a while ago, and Nan is in a care home."

I looked around the small pub anew. "So this is where little Rhys took his first steps."

He was being awfully forthcoming, and it was refreshing. *Hello, Rhys's soft, gooey middle. I like you.*

He gave me an indulgent smile and shoved the last bite of egg in his mouth. "In the cottage next door, actually. I didn't move in here until I was fifteen, when I thought I was a man and needed my own space."

"Why don't you live in the cottage now?"

"We rent it out. I might move into it someday, but the pub suits me just fine now." He eyed my nearly untouched plate.

It was normal food, all of it, but I didn't know how I was meant to eat it. His nearly empty plate made mine look rude. I guessed I could do what he did, maybe. I piled the tomato and egg on the toast and took a bite. Hmmm. Not too bad. Not exactly a sandwich, but kind of.

He chuckled softly, and his low voice wrapped around my skin and drove a shiver down my neck. "We'll convert you to our British food. Just you wait."

My stomach took a dive and flipped like a roller coaster while tingles danced down my spine.

I needed to rein it in a little. This physical reaction to Rhys was bordering on a crush, and I was much too old for crushes. Especially when I was only going to be in England for three more weeks. Time to lay a joke on him, to raise the volume of our conversation from quiet and intimate to playful and boisterous, or at the very least, jolly. "You can never trump tacos, but I do commend you for trying."

"Tacos, huh? I can make tacos."

I took another bite. The flavors were growing on me, but it could use some salt. "Doubt it."

Rhys's eyes took on a serious glint. "Challenge accepted."

"Not just any tacos," I explained. "But Mexican street tacos. Carnitas on a corn tortilla—"

"Say no more." He put a hand up. "I don't want you to believe you've given me any advantage here."

"You're competitive, aren't you?"

"Sometimes," he said quietly, clearly not picking up on my jolly, lighthearted cues. I was channeling *Christmas Vacation* vibes, not *The Holiday.* "Depends on what I'm fighting for."

"Your Santa beard. The ability to prove you can make Mexican food. Your high school rugby games."

He grinned, and his smile was so handsome and so close it was nearly blinding. Even in the dim light I could make out the way his brown eyes darkened towards the outer rims, which looked almost gold, and the way his nose bent just a little in the center. I became very aware of how alone and how quiet and dim it was right now, but my body was alert, my heart racing, my attention captured.

Teasing Rhys wasn't working to cut the tension; it only seemed to amplify it. Time to try another tactic.

I stuffed the sausage in my mouth to give my face something to do, something that wasn't staring at this handsome Englishman while I thought of a new strategy. The bite went too far, lodging itself in my throat. I slammed my hand against my sternum, but it did nothing.

"Luna, are you all right?"

I looked to him, unable to speak, unable to breathe. Panic rose in my chest, and I hit the top of the counter with my hand.

Rhys was on his feet at once. He put his arms around me and pulled me from the stool, pumping his fist against my belly in a precise, circular motion, until the sausage popped out of my mouth and flew over the counter.

"It's out?" He sounded panicked.

"Yeah." I sagged forward, the fear of choking fighting my mortification that Hot British Guy just had to do the freaking Heimlich maneuver on me.

Rhys's hands splayed on my stomach, as though he was hesitant to release me, as though he wasn't yet satisfied that I was out of danger. Silence pounded the air around us—or maybe that was just my pulse. He slid his hands around to my back, then squeezed my shoulders. The touch was jarring in its sweetness. I hadn't had a man touch me on purpose in almost a year, except hugs from my dad, of course, and I'd forgotten how it felt. Like the warmth of a fire's blaze with the comfort of a favorite hoodie. Safe, soft, and warm.

Jake's touch hadn't felt like this in a long time, and I couldn't actually remember the last time he'd made me feel cozy. I mostly recalled feeling like I needed to try harder, to reach farther, to hold on to him.

Rhys, conversely, made me feel heavy and weightless simultaneously. He hovered at my back, and I could turn right now to face him and would be in his arms, perfectly situated to steal the kiss that Callie joked I needed.

Another beat passed in heavy silence before I felt his breath on the back of my neck in a quiet sigh. "I know my cooking is amazing, but you need to pace yourself. That sausage isn't worth a trip to the morgue."

Thank the heavens for Rhys's apparent ability to lighten a heavy mood. I turned around and faced him. "Thank you."

"It was nothing," he said, reaching over me to take both of our plates.

"Kind of meant something to me." I moved in search of the sausage bit on the floor so I could throw it away. "You just saved my life."

"Nah, don't worry about it." Rhys rounded the bar and passed me to enter the kitchen. "Now you just owe me one."

EIGHT

IF THE WAY I RAN AWAY FROM JAKE AND AUBREY'S wedding was any clue, it was probably pretty obvious that two of my greatest talents were running and hiding. I was the kid picked first for hide-and-seek and never picked to be *it* in tag because I tagged people too quickly. To this day I could claim the ability to artfully avoid an uncomfortable conversation with a well-placed joke or a shift in the topic. Needless to say, I carried all my stuff upstairs shortly after the sausage choking incident and camped out in my room for a few hours under the guise of editing that morning's video.

Snow fell on the other side of the window all morning, creating a picture-perfect scene with the white-capped church across the street. I'd pulled a chunky rust-colored sweater on and wrapped the bed quilt around my shoulders, leaning against the headboard to edit my video.

I really needed to get my hands on some snow boots so I would be able to walk without soaking my feet down to the skin. I'd mostly stuck to the paths and hikes near the pub since arriving in Snowshill, but I was ready to go out further and explore more—proper footwear and weather permitting, of course.

There was a faint knock on my door, and I shoved aside my blanket to answer it.

A small boy stood in the hallway, looking up at me with a very serious expression on his delicate little features. I recognized him from yesterday, when he had come to the pub with his mother. A slouchy cap sat lopsided over his cherubic copper curls, and his widened eyes fell flat upon seeing me. "Oh," he said, disappointed.

Glad I had that effect on children.

I crouched a little, resting my hands on my knees. "Are you looking for someone? Ruby's room is down the hall—"

"No, not her," Finn said, a little furrow on his brow. "I was looking for Father Christmas."

"Oh." I blinked. That, I had not expected. Was there an English tradition with Santa hanging out in pubs a few weeks before Christmas no one had yet filled me in on? This kid looked massively discouraged, so I infused my voice with as much cheer as I could. "I'm afraid I haven't seen him up here today."

"The man said Father Christmas was upstairs. This is upstairs, isn't it?"

"That depends on where you are when you're asking." Who was *the man* and why was he filling this poor boy's head with nonsense? "Does your mom know you've come up here?"

He looked to the side, and I could see his little mind working through the problem I had just presented. I didn't know kids very well, but I knew this one was trying to think up a reasonable excuse for sneaking up a set of stairs that I could only assume were off-limits to most pub patrons.

I slid my feet into my still-wet Adidas from when I'd walked to the red telephone booth the day before. Gross. I offered the kid my hand. "Should we go downstairs and find your mom? I don't think Father Christmas is up here right now."

He let out a resigned huff. "I suppose so."

I had to fight not to laugh at the utter disappointment and resignation on his cute little angel face. He took my hand, and I locked the door to my room before leading him down the stairs. I spotted his mom at once, seated at a table and looking at her phone. She must have sensed my attention, because she looked up and caught my eye before her gaze slid down to her son.

"Oh, bloody—"

He let go of my hand and ran toward his mom, then climbed onto the seat opposite her.

"He came upstairs looking for Father Christmas," I explained.

That only seemed to confuse her further.

I put my hand out. "Hi, I'm Luna. I'm staying here for a few weeks."

"Nice to meet you," she said, shaking my hand. "I'm Florence, but everyone just calls me Flo. And this is Finn." She shook her head and gestured to her phone. "I was so wrapped up in this article I didn't even know he wandered off. I'm sorry he bothered you."

"He's no bother at all." I'd expected a man to be with them— whoever told Finn Santa lived upstairs—but the only man in the room right now was Frank, and he was dozing by the fireplace, his fingers laced over his thin belly.

"Usually Finn's little friend meets us here, but they moved down to Kent a few weeks ago, so now he doesn't have his play-mate to keep him distracted."

"I'm not judging you," I said, smiling. "I don't have kids, so I don't really have a right to."

Her demeanor relaxed a little. "You're from the States?"

"Yeah, California. No, I'm not a surfer, and no, I've never met a celebrity. Our northern beaches are nothing but ice water and great white sharks."

She grimaced. "I've never been, but I've always wanted to see the redwoods."

"We have loads of those. Actually, there a few in my backyard."

Flo's eyebrows lifted. "That's amazing."

"I don't think it tops five-hundred-year-old churches, but our ancient trees are pretty cool."

She laughed. "Someday I'll make it out there. In the meantime, I'm busy chasing around this little guy."

I looked at Finn and tried to suppress the deep yearning in my chest. It was unfair, but I couldn't help looking at his red, curly hair and imagining myself chatting with Flo under different, more balanced circumstances. If I'd had it my way, Jake and I wouldn't have waited the whole year to get engaged after moving to Geyserville. We would have been married already, and I wouldn't be in England hiding from his wedding, I'd probably be mooning over my own kid instead of a complete stranger's.

Good gracious, I needed to get a hold of myself.

"Things all good here?" Rhys asked, pulling me from my spiraling what-if scenario and images of tiny little baby Jakes with his golden hair and my sloped nose.

I blinked at Rhys. "Yeah. Actually I was going to head out in search of boots." My feet squished against the damp soles, and I suppressed a shudder. "Do either of you have recommendations for me? I don't know where to go. The closer to Snowshill, the better."

Rhys took the dish towel from his shoulder and started folding it. "I'm actually heading to Primark now if you want a lift."

"Is that a boot store?"

Flo laughed. "No, but they carry boots. That's probably your best bet if you don't want to drive too far. I think the storm is supposed to continue through tonight."

I definitely didn't want to drive too far. I didn't want to have to drive anywhere at all. I looked at Rhys, the man who ran this pub. "Can you even leave? It's the middle of the day."

And spending time alone together was not going to help me suppress the crush I'd been explicitly warned by Ruby to not develop.

"Lunch is over," he said. "I'll be back by dinner. Ruby can manage the interim if people stay."

Such a strange, slow way of life. I thought as a yoga instructor who lived on a farm that I knew slow, but The Wild Hare took slow to a whole new level. Rhys's brown eyes watched me, waiting, and I relented. Letting him drive meant not having to drive in this snow myself, and that trumped managing my crush on him. "Okay. Let me grab my purse."

"I'll be out front."

Anytime I was not forced to drive on these tiny, winding lanes—and on the side of the road I wasn't accustomed to, at that—I'd take it.

Rhys waited in front of the pub with the defroster on and the seat warmers blazing. I slid into his car, which was not quite as small as my rented Kia but certainly smaller than I was used to seeing in the States. Though, to be fair, it did make sense to own a compact vehicle when every road around here was a narrow snake. Especially when the snow made the two-way roads more like one and a half.

Rhys rested his elbow on the center console as we took off, so comfortable in his own skin that it was hard not to admire him. There was something about the way he didn't need a super masculine car that was appealing.

What? Appealing?

I stomped that thought down, poured lighter fluid over it, and tossed a match. I could not allow this stupid crush to develop further.

It was just plain embarrassing.

"So, you met Flo," he said softly.

His voice had a way of grabbing me in the chest and making me want to lean into it just a little. So much for dousing my reaction with flames. That seemed to only have heated me more. Where was the music? We needed something to make this silence less loud and his voice less intimate.

I raised my volume to compensate. "Yeah, Finn is adorable. He went upstairs looking for Father Christmas though, which is just weird—"

"Oh, bloody he—"

I looked at Rhys sharply. "What? The jolly red elf isn't actually up there, right?"

He rubbed a hand over his jaw and sucked air through his teeth. "Finn must have heard me talking on the phone."

"About the old man you have hidden in your room?"

"No." He rolled his eyes. "About the *suit* I have hidden in my cupboard. I'm glad he misunderstood me though."

I turned in my seat to face him better and cocked my head to the side. "I think you need to explain this further."

Rhys hesitated, and it was the first time I noticed him looking unsure of himself.

"I play Father Christmas for the village fair."

Images of Rhys being good with children ran through my head and squeezed my uterus. Why was it that men who were good with children were so attractive? "You play Santa Claus." It was all clicking together. "Like, with a long, white beard."

He winked at me, and I was pretty sure my entire insides melted into a puddle on his clean leather seat. Not just any white beard, I guessed, but the one he'd put up as collateral. "Is this something you do often?"

"Once a year, ever since my grandad died."

"Oh." I didn't ask the obvious. Like, could they not find another believable old man in town? Frank, for instance, seemed like he would do the job well enough and already had white hair and authentic facial wrinkles.

"It's kind of a family tradition." Rhys shrugged. "When I have the whole suit on, no one can really tell that I'm not seventy-five. It was passed down to me, so the suit is pretty old. It looks authentic."

Which explained the significance of the beard. It was his grandfather's.

"Do you enjoy it?" I asked, curious. It was such an odd thing for a man who looked like he stepped out of *Hot Loggers Monthly* (not a real magazine, but I'm thinking that it should be, and it doesn't need to have any actual trees in it) to have in his repertoire.

He eyed me from the side. "I'm not answering that. You're judging me."

"Am not," I lied.

"Oh yes, you are. I can see it in the wrinkles on your nose."

I smoothed out my expression at once. "I think it would more accurately be said that I'm surprised by this revelation. I think it's cool that you want to bring ultimate joy to kids during the holiday season. That's a pretty wholesome ambition and not very cool of me to judge you for it."

"Then why are you?"

I scoffed. "I thought my speech was pretty good."

"It was fine." He nudged my shoulder with his arm. "But you didn't fool me."

"*Judge* is too harsh a word for how I'm feeling about this."

He eyed me momentarily before setting his attention back on the road. "Then how are you feeling right now?"

Hot, stuffy, like every time he looked at me my temperature rose another degree. "Like I don't really know anything about you, Mr. Rhys. You just keep surprising me."

"Mr. Rhys?"

"I forgot your last name. I would have put it in my phone, but someone was really awkward and gave you a super unrealistic title instead of your actual name. Trying hard, much?"

He chuckled. "That's Mr. Rhys Super Hot British Guy Norland, to you."

"*Super* hot, huh?"

Rhys kept his attention on the narrow lane. "I thought the Father Christmas thing just gave me bonus points by the way you became speechless."

A warmth bloomed in my chest that had nothing to do with my innate physical attraction to Rhys. The amusement playing on his lips was at odds with the serious nature of his dark brown eyes. I sort of wanted to crawl across the center console and see what he would do if I kissed him, but that would certainly incite a car accident and I didn't want to die today.

I sat back, nestling my shoulders into the soft leather seat. "Touché, sir. Wanting to brighten kids' days? Ten points to Gryffindor."

"I actually think I'm a Ravenclaw."

I frowned. Jake was a self-proclaimed Ravenclaw, too. "Don't ruin it."

"What house are you in?" he asked.

"Hufflepuff, hands down."

He looked as though he was considering this. "Yeah, I could see that."

I sat up straighter. "Because I'm a pushover?"

"No. I didn't know that about you, but consider it noted. Because you seem kind and helpful. You have a good heart."

I laughed to ease my discomfort. "Is my heart really that easy to read?" Our acquaintanceship had almost hit a week. That wasn't long enough to know much of anything about each other yet.

"I watched one of your videos. I can see how golden your heart is from there."

I was deeply affected by the praise and equally concerned that he'd seen a LunaMoon video. "Which one did you watch?"

"Toddler Time. The Chair Yoga for Seniors one was pretty good too."

"Hmm." Neither of those were geared toward healthy, adult males. "Not Lumberjacks Unwinding?"

"Blimey, you have that too?"

I laughed. "No." But I was beginning to think I should. It could be a whole untapped market just waiting for me.

We pulled into the Primark parking lot, and Rhys stopped the car and turned it off. He set his dark eyes on me.

I blinked. "Do I have something on my face?"

"No. You ready?"

Funny. The last time someone asked me that, it was my dad at the taco shop. Only two weeks had passed since that moment, and I realized with startling surety that until Rhys had mentioned Ravenclaw, I hadn't thought of Jake once this entire car ride.

Maybe I was finally starting to move on.

NINE

PRIMARK HAD A DECENT SELECTION OF BOOTS, AND I found a pair to fit my needs. They were tan with thick soles, went just past my ankles, and claimed to be fully waterproof. Perfect for tromping around a snowy winter wonderland—I mean, a Cotswolds town.

I found Rhys near the checkout stand staring at a selection of Haribo gummy candy.

"What I wouldn't give for a good chocolate bar right now," I said, staring at the yellow Haribo bear.

"I can make that happen," Rhys said.

I faced him. "Don't tease me."

He shook his head, chuckling. "Pay for your boots, then we'll go." Rhys grabbed a bag of gummies, and we went to the checkout.

I eyed his treat. "That's all you need?"

He rubbed a hand absently over the back of his neck. "They didn't have what I needed. It's fine."

"Shoot. What a waste of a trip."

He looked at me. "It wasn't a waste."

I was sure he only meant to put me at ease, but a squiggle in my stomach proved my feelings were only growing. I felt like an idiot.

Ruby had specifically warned me away from this very thing, and the more time I spent around her, the more I learned that she was mostly kind with a bit of snark, but altogether genuine. She had only warned me in an effort to be helpful—and probably to save her hot cousin from another crazy tourist looking for a fling.

I would *not* be looking for a fling. All joking with Callie aside, I'd never been the type for casual hookups. It just wasn't in my nature.

Rhys led me outside and into the store next door with a large sign calling it Poundland. He stopped in front of a row of candy bars, and Cadbury's trademark royal purple caught my attention. There were more flavors than I had expected. "I think I haven't had the full English experience until I've tried each one of these."

He looked up at me, amused. "Our yoga enthusiast is also a chocolate consumer?"

"I'm not sure what you mean to imply here, but yes. Cadbury Mini Eggs make up an entire food group in my diet." I stepped closer and read the different names. Wispa, Flake, Twirl, Caramel, Double Decker, Crunchie. "There are so many different ones! I don't know where to begin."

"Here, start with this." He reached for one called Marvellous Creations, and I read the description. "Hmmm. Not sure this sounds even a little bit appetizing. Jelly bits? Pop rocks? *Inside* my chocolate?"

"Yeah, I don't go for them myself, but people love them."

"I better get a few backups." I selected the Flake, Crunchie, and Caramel just to be safe.

We made it to the car again and Rhys pulled onto the road.

"Thanks for driving. I have never driven in snow before and after sliding into that ditch, I'm happy to avoid it."

"You don't get snow in California at all?"

"Not where I live. I've never even touched snow before last week."

He did a double take. "Seriously? None? Not even on a ski trip?"

"None. My family runs a farm, and it's not the sort of thing you can easily leave behind for vacations. We've done a number of short trips growing up, but neither of my parents ski, so that was never a priority for us."

A slow, delicious smile curved his lips. "A farm girl, eh?"

"Yes." I straightened a little in my seat. I was proud of my roots. I had legit boots back home that would have kept the snow out of my socks as well as they had the muck in our barn stalls, but I hadn't thought to bring them with me. My vision of this trip had been all cutesy snow bunny pictures in my puffy marshmallow coat for yoga marketing.

"So that's why you came alone?" he asked. "Your family couldn't leave the animals?"

"No. I came alone because I didn't invite them. Well, I invited my sister, but she couldn't make it." We passed a big house set back away from the road a bit. I only got a glimpse of it, but it struck a chord within me that strummed the theme of *Downton Abbey*. Whatever the building was, it was clearly grand. "Wow. What was that?"

"What?"

"The museum-looking place back there." I turned, craning my neck to try and see it, but the snow-covered trees lining the road made it impossible to see much of anything.

"Brumsworth Manor."

I waited for Rhys to say more, but apparently that was it. "Brumsworth Manor. What is it?"

"A house."

"You mean a mansion?"

"Sure."

Someone was a bit grumpy. "Like, someone *lives* in that beastly building?"

"Yes."

I couldn't contain my awe. I'd watched a behind-the-scenes video about the making of *Downton Abbey* a few years back. The family who owned the building where they filmed was still in residence in part of the house, but had kept the other half open for visitors when they weren't using it to make popular TV shows or movies. Brumsworth only appeared to be a quarter of the size of Downton, but it looked just as old and Jane Austen-y. "Is it one of those grand houses that gives tours?"

"I think you can take a tour, but not every day," he grumbled. "I'm sure the website has more information."

"I know what I'm doing first thing tomorrow," I sing-songed.

"If they're open."

I ignored his surliness. "I can't wait to walk the rooms and pretend like I'm a guest at Downton. I'll need to learn how to curtsy properly."

He shot me a very disapproving, yet mildly amused, expression. "You're free to do whatever you want, but I'm not taking you."

Salty much? "Is it located in Linscombe or something? I better make sure I see the house and the church on the same day and return before the sun goes down so you don't lock me out for bad behavior. I wouldn't want to pass on any negative vibes." I wiggled my fingers at him. I truly had no idea where we were right now, so it was a legitimate question. Rhys could have driven me to Wales and I wouldn't know it. Until we saw a castle on every corner, of course.

"Brumsworth is in Snowshill, actually. But let's just say that manor and Linscombe carry the same bad luck." He looked at me wryly. "I cannot remember the last time I've been in that house. The only time I cross Brums's land is to reach the skating pond just past their fields."

"Ice skating?" On a *pond*?

His dark eyes widened. "Don't tell me you've never skated, either?"

"We have an indoor rink not too far away from my house, thank you very much. I've gone a handful of times. But I've never ice skated outside."

"We ought to fix that."

"Yes, we ought to." I couldn't help but mimic him sometimes. I wondered if he noticed it, or if I just sounded like I fit in better. "But I'm guessing you can't rent skates at a pond."

I watched the long dry-stone wall on the side of the road, covered in lichen and snow. It never seemed to end, and there were narrow, ragged rocks on top of the wall that looked as though they were meant to keep people from climbing it, though the snow softened the look.

"You can borrow my cousin's skates."

I guffawed, then looked to see if he was joking. He wasn't. "They would never fit me."

His eyebrows drew together. "What are you? Like twenty-five? So is Ruby."

"Twenty-four, actually. But age has nothing to do with foot size." I laughed harder, bending over in the seat. "I've got like six inches on Ruby, *at least*. She probably has tiny elf feet, and I'm a solid eight-and-a-half."

Rhys looked at me like I'd switched over to French halfway through my sentence.

"Trust me," I said. "There's no way your petite little Ruby's skates would ever fit my feet."

"Okay. Well, someone will have skates you can borrow."

"I'm not canvassing the town for a pair of skates, Rhys."

"Well, you can't have a proper country Christmas in England without skating on a pond."

He made a valid point. I could picture it now—us skating hand-in-hand, cute fuzzy earmuffs keeping my ears warm, mittens on my hands. I didn't own mittens or ear muffs, but there was no sense in ruining a perfectly good daydream with reality.

I wouldn't be holding his hand, either, but that didn't stop me from imagining how it would feel.

"Speaking of Christmas," Rhys continued, "I know your reservation goes until the twenty-ninth." He cleared his throat, and I could see that he was uncomfortable asking me whatever was on his mind. But clearly he'd been thinking about it, and I liked the idea that he might have been thinking about me, even if it was purely in a host-guest capacity.

"I wanted to be home in time for New Year's Eve. We have a tradition I don't want to miss."

"You and your boyfriend?"

Oh. My. Gosh.

Rhys had just used the oldest, most overused trick in the book to find out if I was single. I stared straight ahead, wondering what to do with this information, when it hit me with a jolt. Maybe he didn't want to know for himself. He was likely asking on behalf of someone else.

Ruby was a reputable source when it came to Rhys, and she had mentioned he was hung up on his recent, messy break up. There was no way he was ready to bounce back—fling or not.

Snap out of it, Luna. This hot British lumberjack pub owner was not going to kiss me.

"No, me and my family. We watch *Lord of the Rings*, which is my sister's favorite, and eat Mexican food."

"You and your tacos."

I grinned. "Nothing beats a good street taco."

"You sound really close to your family."

"Oh, I am. I'm really lucky in that regard."

"Yet you're here for Christmas, without them."

Ah. I saw where he was going with this. He was curious, and I didn't blame him, but I definitely wasn't going to unload the greater embarrassments of my life, like the way Jake left me for Aubrey, or how fast I ran when Aubrey had asked me to be part of the wedding.

I still couldn't really get over her gall.

We passed the church and pulled into the narrow lane that led to the car park behind The Wild Hare. "Someday my mom wants to come to Linscombe to see that church, but not this time around."

"Which is your way of telling me to mind my own business?" he asked, putting his car in park. It got incredibly quiet in the small car and my heart pounded.

"I ran away from home." The words slipped out without intention, but Rhys's dark brown eyes bored into me with such intense focus that they basically pushed the truth out of me. So much for keeping my embarrassing past to myself. But I supposed once someone did the Heimlich on you, that broke down barriers.

"Like . . . without telling your mum and dad?" he asked.

"No. My parents are fully aware. My mom requires nightly texts to reassure her I'm still alive. I ran from . . . other things." Not a lie. But still, it was cryptic of me. "I'm hoping to reset my mind and film a lot of good content for my channel while I'm here."

"I see."

We got out of the car and trudged around the building toward the front door. Rhys paused before we turned the corner and put a hand on my arm, effectively freezing me in place. His touch permeated my layers of sweaters and filled my chest with warmth. "You are welcome to film your videos in the mornings as often as you wish. I can do my best to stay away from the kitchen before six if that's better for you."

"Thanks, Rhys. You don't need to stay away though. Just avoid slamming pans around and we'll be good."

"Do I often slam pans?" He pretended to look thoughtful. "I've never been told before that I'm a particularly noisy chef."

We started toward the door again, and Rhys held it open for me. When I stepped inside, I heard him draw in a sharp breath.

"Speak of the bloody devil," he muttered. His gaze was stuck on a man leaning casually against the bar, dressed as though he had just left an important board meeting in a high-rise office and not at all as though he fit in with the charming crowd that typically patronized the pub.

The man turned a wide smile on me. His brown hair was impeccable, his suit looked as though he'd rolled through lint paper on his way into the pub, and his stance easily proved how comfortable he was in any environment.

To put it plainly: the man looked like he was dripping in money. He had an ease and self-confidence about him that only came from a life of comfort and privilege, and the designer suit to match.

Rhys expelled a breath and moved behind the bar.

"It's been a long time, Rhys," the man said, but Rhys kept walking until he disappeared into the kitchen without so much as a nod of acknowledgment. "Cheers," he called to Rhys's back.

The man turned the weight of his attention on me, and I felt a shift in the room, as if everyone gathered in the dining area was just as aware of his attention on me as my racing heart was.

"And you," he said with a devilish grin, "must be LunaMoon."

TEN

HOW IN THE SWEET BABY GOATS DID THIS MAN KNOW who I was? Follow-up question: how did he know *where* to find me? Both of these answers better be forthcoming quickly, or he was getting a firsthand glimpse of exactly how fast and how far I could run away.

Well, all he had to do was watch one of my YouTube videos to know who I was, I supposed . . . but as far as finding me? My potential creep alarm was going off.

"Forgive me," he said quickly, "that was impolite. Allow me to introduce myself."

"Yeah, that would be good." I stepped further into the pub but left a good distance between us. Rhys had disappeared completely, but Frank sat in his usual seat with his cup of tea and Ned snoozing at his feet, an older woman sitting across from them. Ruby leaned against the bar, eyeing us, and Hamish was at the far end of the bar, not paying us any attention.

"I am Edward Brumsworth, and my sister is a huge fan of yours."

"Brumsworth?" I asked, finding myself taking a step closer. "Like the manor?"

He straightened his posture, and I wondered briefly if it was automatic or if he knew he did it. He gave a crisp nod. "Indeed."

"How funny. I was just about to look up your website."

"May I ask why?"

"To find out how to take a tour of the manor." I crossed further into the room and leaned against the bar a little, facing Edward, with Ruby and Hamish in my line of sight behind him. Ruby still watched me closely, and Hamish still did not seem to care that we were here.

"Don't bother booking a ticket," Edward said, flashing me a row of white, if a little uneven, teeth. "I'd be happy to show you around myself."

That was an extremely tempting offer, but he was still a stranger. Although a tour from a member of the family likely meant I'd be able to see more than just the rooms they left open to the public. "You mentioned your sister?"

"Ah, yes." He gestured for me to be seated beside him, and I set my shop bags on the floor before settling onto the bar stool. "My sister runs an athletic apparel company, and when she saw your post in front of the church, she recognized it at once and called me straight away to come down here and find you."

"You came to The Wild Hare on a whim?"

He gave a little smile, like he could see I was not about to easily lap up every word he spoke. "No. She didn't narrow her search to the pub until she saw the video you filmed here."

Ah, that was fair. "Well, you've found me." I gave a little uncomfortable shrug. I didn't have people stopping me all the time for autographs or anything, but occasionally someone recognized me, and I was too awkward to navigate the interactions like a normal human. I'd felt thrown off my game since the moment he had called me by my username.

"My sister is a huge fan, and she wants to set up a meeting if you have any interest in a potential collaboration. But first, I must ask how long you intend to remain here. She is out of the country until next week."

The only people privy to my travel plans were myself and the hosts who booked my apartment. "I will be here that long," I said, going for vague but not annoying. "What sort of collaboration does she have in mind?"

He gave a quick wave of his hand. "I haven't a clue, but likely something to do with your channel and her clothing. Can I buy you a drink?"

"Um, sure. That would be fine." A drink wasn't like a date or anything, right? This wasn't a date anyway. It was a business meeting. Or a pre-business meeting, I guessed, since his sister was the one who wanted to do business with me.

Edward snapped to Ruby, who looked up at him through the closest thing to a scowl that she was likely capable of producing —though it was mild by anyone else's standards.

"What'll you have?"

"A Dr Pepper for me," I said.

Edward looked at me strangely, but I didn't bother giving an excuse. So what if I preferred soda to whatever uber fancy drink he was likely about to order? I was entitled to my preferences, just as he was.

"I'll take a lager. Whatever you have on tap."

Ruby turned away to get the drinks.

"Speaking of your sister's company," I said, trying to bring the conversation around. "Will I recognize the name?"

Ruby slid my beautiful Dr Pepper in front of me and turned away to fill Edward's glass. I took a long sip from the straw.

"You might do. It's called Stella Fit."

Stella Fit?!

I spit the large mouthful of Dr Pepper all over the bar in front of me and doused Ruby, who was leaning over the counter to push Edward's drink toward him.

She sucked in a surprised breath as she knocked over the beer, spilling it all down the front of Edward's designer pants.

Edward jumped to his feet, backing away from the stool and cursing mildly.

"Sorry, guys!" I said, coming around the counter. "I'll grab some rags."

I didn't give Ruby time to protest. Dark Dr Pepper that had previously been in my mouth was now all over her face and the front of her light pink tee. I ran around the bar and into the kitchen, nearly colliding with Rhys, who stood right around the corner.

"You aren't meant to be back here," he said.

"I need rags." I passed him and went to the cupboard. "I just spit all over Ruby and she poured beer on Edward."

"You spit?"

"Not intentionally." I tossed a look at him over my shoulder before gathering a few rags and a small bucket to fill with water. "You mean you didn't hear what happened while you were eavesdropping?"

Rhys watched me, but his face was a work of stone. "You've misread the situation."

"You aren't cooking, so you're either hiding or eavesdropping, right? Or maybe both."

He shook his head. "I don't need to hide from that pretentious piece of—"

"Right," I said. I didn't know how well the people in the bar could hear into the kitchen. They really weren't too far away, only separated by a wall and an open doorway.

I filled the bucket halfway with water and passed Rhys to go clean up my mess.

Ruby was a step ahead of me. She'd used the bar rag to start on the counter, and I tossed her a clean one, then handed a rag to Edward. "I'll take care of this if you want to go shower, Ruby? I'm so sorry. I was totally caught off guard."

"Rhys?" she called.

It was a moment before he stepped out, pretending he hadn't been waiting right near the doorway, by my guess. "Nice," he said, surveying the Dr Pepper droplets everywhere. His gaze flicked to where Edward was dabbing at his pants and then away again to the soda-covered wall. I wasn't proud or anything, but it had been a pretty big mouthful, and I gave a wide spray.

Ruby tossed her long ponytail over her shoulder and scrunched her nose. "I'm going to shower."

"I have this," he said, gesturing to the bar.

She snuck away, and I caught Hamish's amused gaze following Ruby from the room. At least someone found it all funny. I was worried I'd just blown my chance to collaborate with the biggest name in designer yoga wear *in the world*. I owned one set of Stella Fit yoga clothes—they were so pricey I couldn't justify more than that—and they were the most comfortable, soft-like-butter athletic wear that had ever graced my skin.

Some things were overpriced fads, and some things were priced high because they were exceptional quality. In my experience, Stella Fit fell into the latter category.

"I best be off, too," Edward said apologetically, setting the rag on the counter. "But is it too forward of me to ask for your number, Luna?" He paused. "May I presume to call you Luna?"

Rhys scoffed quietly where he'd bent to wipe up soda from the wall behind the bar.

"Yes, you may." What was I, a Jane Austen heroine? It felt a little grand granting permission for this posh British guy to use my first name. Though, since he'd called me by my YouTube username earlier, it was entirely possible he wasn't aware of what my last name even was.

I recited off my number, and he sent me a text so I would have his.

"I will contact you to set up that tour, and perhaps we can

video in my sister. She's eager to hear about your interest." He drew a set of car keys from his pocket. "Can I tell her you're interested?"

"Oh, yes, very," I said, a tad too eagerly. I cleared my throat. "I look forward to hearing from you."

He smiled softly and left the pub, and I suppressed the excitement ringing through me. Stella Fit was the cutest, most comfortable fit wear in the world, and I was going to get some for *free*. Possibly. Probably. I mean, what else could they mean by collaborate?

"Don't let him fool you," Rhys said, his grumpy tone puncturing my perfectly happy cloud-nine and floating me back down to earth. "He doesn't give anything unless he gets something back."

"You know him pretty well, then?"

"I've known the toff my entire life. It's not worth getting mixed up with him."

I dipped a rag in the bucket and started wiping the floor. "What about his sister?"

"Stella?" Rhys leaned back, sitting on his heels. "She's grand. You can trust her, at least."

"But not her brother."

"I would not trust Brum with my dullest set of knives."

"Ah, but you hardly trust *me* with anything in your kitchen."

He gave a ghost of a smile. "That is an unfair comparison. This is me trying to warn you. You need to protect yourself."

"He offered to give me a tour of his house, Rhys. I hardly think I'm in any danger here."

"He has a certain reputation—"

"Let me stop you there." Oh, good grief. So Edward was a player, then? I had even less of a chance of succumbing to his charms than I did the Prince of Wales. "I'm here on vacation, and I'll only be in England for a few more weeks. I'm not here for a relationship."

Rhys held my gaze for a minute. Did he not believe me? "That is logical."

"I mean it. I'm only here to shoot some videos and get away from—" The words lodged in my throat. I couldn't speak about my shameful escape out loud. I was twenty-four years old. It was embarrassing that I had struggled so much with the idea of telling Aubrey I wouldn't be able to be her bridesmaid.

Rhys waited a minute, but I stood, mentally distancing myself from what I had almost revealed.

"Yeah?" He stood beside me, and I couldn't help but feel like Hamish, Frank, and the older woman were all listening intently to our conversation. My cheeks warmed, and I turned away to dip my rag so I could wipe up straggler drips on the wall Rhys had missed.

"Yeah. Thank you for the warning, but you don't have to worry about me. I'm not a woman on the hunt."

"Good."

Good? Was he relieved?

I took his dirty rag and the one Ruby had left behind, carrying them in the bucket back to the kitchen to rinse and toss in the laundry. I needed to catch my breath. For a man who was so hung up on his ex, Rhys certainly sent a lot of mixed signals my way.

When I turned away from the sink to put the rinsed bucket back in the cupboard, I was startled to find Rhys standing against the wall, his arms crossed over his chest and his gaze on me like he was a fierce hunter and I was the doe.

He looked like he wanted to say something, but I didn't want to hear what it was. If a deeper warning was dancing on his tongue about Edward Brumsworth, I didn't need it. I wasn't in danger of falling for the guy's charming smile. I could see right through it to the swanky frat guy beneath.

If, on the other hand, Rhys could sense my budding crush for him, and he was gearing up to warn me that his heart was still fractured and unavailable, things were about to become too awkward for my taste. I needed to head off the conversation from the start.

No emotional explanations today, please.

"Hey," I said, as cheerfully as I could. My enthusiasm had the magic ability to dispel the thick tension in the air. "Thanks . . . again . . . for driving me today."

He paused. I held my breath and hoped he would follow the detour my chipperness had taken us toward.

Rhys let out a small sigh. "It was no trouble at all. I needed to go anyway."

"What took you to Primark?"

He tilted his head to the side. "What are you planning to do if it snows until the twenty-ninth?" he asked, missing my question. "Extend your trip?"

I hadn't thought of that, but surely he was being facetious and no storm would last *that* long. Besides, I planned to attempt driving in the snow again, but not until the weather calmed, things mellowed out, and it wouldn't be as bad on the roads as it was now. Google had explained that with a few sunny days after snowing, the sun usually melted it and the plows would clear it, and when had Google ever steered me wrong?

"I guess I'll just be hoping for a Christmas miracle."

ELEVEN

NED MET ME IN THE HALLWAY THE FOLLOWING afternoon with a frown and a disapproving bark, then followed me down the stairs. He stayed close to my heels, and it was mildly concerning. The dog hadn't become fond of me yet, so his sudden attachment was reason enough to be cautious.

Or so I thought. My dogs at home stayed outside. They had jobs, and their jobs were with the other animals. So having canines following me around the house was new.

Ruby sat on a barstool, and I pulled out the one beside her, setting my gloves and hat on the bar. The boxes she'd brought out days ago were still sitting on the back counter. I wanted to ask what they were, but I didn't want to be nosy.

She looked down at Ned, who barked again before taking his customary seat before the fireplace. "He really doesn't like you, does he?"

"Heaven knows why." I pulled out my chapstick and applied a layer. "You've got him well-trained. I've never seen him go in the kitchen."

"Wasn't me. He's a pub dog. We all kind of pitch in where he's concerned."

"Then he must know I'm an outsider." I put my chapstick away.

"Heading out?" she asked.

"Yeah. I want to get more shots of the town." The teaser I'd posted in front of the red telephone booth had been a big hit, and the segment in the dining room as well. I wanted to capitalize on the snowy perfection that was Snowshill, so I needed to find a few more places to snap photos of myself in different poses— ones without my snowy, wet foot resting on my leg, like a normal person. I hadn't heard from Edward yet, but he had mentioned his sister was out of the country until the end of the week, so I was going to give him another four or five days before reaching out to him myself.

I wanted to tour his house, and I would find a way to do it, whether I had to pay for a ticket or not. It would not be a trip to England without walking through at least one fancy manor house. My Austen-loving mother would probably be ashamed of me if I failed to see one.

"You ran out of here pretty quickly last night," I said to Ruby, unwrapping the end of my granola bar and taking a bite. After her shower, she had all but sprinted out the door and disappeared for the evening.

"Yeah, I didn't mean to be rude. I was running late."

"Hot date?" I asked. Did I sound like an old woman? Did people even have *hot dates* anymore? It had been more than five years since I was young and single, and sometimes I felt like being in a steady relationship had aged the coolness out of me. I was like a Tamagotchi that had been left without food and water for too long. Wait. Was that an outdated metaphor?

Ruby laughed. "Who has time to date?"

A scoff ripped out of my throat. "I do."

She looked up quickly, and I hurried to backtrack. "Not *here*. At home I have time. I don't do much outside of filming, editing, and posting."

"It sounds like so much work to keep it all up."

I shoved another bite of the granola bar in my mouth. "It is a lot of work, but it doesn't eat up *all* my time."

She slouched forward. "We should put you to work while you're here, then. I could use a bit of a break."

"I've never waitressed before, and I don't know if I'd be any good at mixing drinks." Though the idea of working alongside Rhys made my stomach clench in anticipation. I could picture us passing each other in the tight doorway and the fizzy energy running between us. Really, this crush was getting to be a little embarrassing. It was a good thing no one else could see into my thoughts.

"There are so many other things you could do. Rhys and I do pretty well, but there never seem to be enough hours in the day." Ruby pointed to the boxes stacked on the back counter. "Like those Christmas decorations. We're over a week into December and they're still packed away. Nan would be ashamed, but it's such a project that I can't ever start it because I know I won't have time to finish."

Decorations? *Christmas* decorations? That was the one thing missing from this pub, and it would bring the holiday spirit into the space. "I'll do it."

"I was only joking. Or complaining, rather."

I shrugged. "I don't mind helping out." It was too far into December not to have decorations up. I'd been missing my family a little more every day, but I had a feeling this would help keep me strong in my determination to finish out my vacation here.

Don't tell anyone, but I checked return flights home last night for the week before Christmas. They were outrageously priced, which was the only reason I hadn't bought one. I needed to find a way to keep myself firm when the temptation hit me again. A place to stay that actually looked like Christmas would be a huge step in the right direction.

Ruby looked uncertain. "If you put those decorations up, you can have free dinners the rest of the week."

Since it was already Friday, that wasn't as much of an incentive as she'd made it sound, but it was a fair trade. Especially when I selfishly wanted the decorations up anyway. "Will Rhys be upset if I do it? You don't have any special holiday decorating traditions or anything?"

"Not really, no."

I looked at the boxes and a bit of red popped from the bent cardboard opening, calling to me to liberate it from the Scroogey confines of the storage box. I was tempted to begin now, but I really needed to keep up my work too. If I didn't, I wouldn't be able to afford an apartment down in LA—I mean, *if* I decided to move there. "Okay. I'm gonna go for a quick walk, then I'll decorate your pub."

Ruby leaned over and kissed me on the cheek. "You're a gem!"

I pulled on my gloves and hat and finished zipping up my coat. The toasty warmth of the pub clung to me for half a second when I stepped outside, then quickly dissipated under the onslaught of the frigid air. The snowstorm had stopped last night and slush already lined the lanes. The thick banks to the sides of the roads were receding, and the darkening sky was mostly blue with tints of orange where the sun was sliding behind the row of yellow buildings. White-capped Cotswold stone lined the image with smoke billowing from the chimneys and mixing with the sky. Pops of color broke the yellow-stone scene, like the red telephone booth and the occasional turquoise door. How did anyone leave this place? It was idyllic and homey, touched with a hint of magic from the odd wreath or fairy light-laced greenery hanging above a door.

I passed the church and walked up the hill along another row of houses to find a good vantage point for a photo. I wanted to catch a large portion of the village behind me and maybe the setting sun would give me a mostly silhouetted look. It started getting dark so early here. It wasn't even five, and the sun was already disappearing.

It took a minute to get the buildings framed behind me in the camera, but I got the tripod set up and the camera angled exactly how I wanted it.

An older woman opened her door to my left and stood in the doorway, watching me fiddle with my camera settings. She looked familiar, and if I wasn't mistaken, I believed I'd seen her sitting with Frank in the pub a few times before.

I sent her a smile, and she returned it briefly, but said nothing.

As an internet personality, I was used to others watching me online and commenting about my yoga or my videos or even my altered hairstyles (I had chopped everything off after Jake broke up with me because he'd loved my long hair so much and I'm just contrary enough), but having others watch me in the flesh outside of a yoga studio was jarring and uncomfortable.

Thankfully, she went back inside and closed the door, so I moved in front of my camera and reached to the sky to stretch my arms. I shook them out, then shifted into position, leaning forward and wrapping my hands around my ankles to find my central balance. I had a standing split pose in mind, only modified so I wouldn't have to rest my gloves on the dirty, melted-snow ground.

If my actions were slow and smooth enough, I hoped to use the video instead of stealing a still shot from my recording, which would be cool with the smoke billowing from the rows of homes and businesses down the hill. Given the position of the sun, I was certain me and the town would mostly show as darkened silhouettes against a stunning sky, and I hoped it would look as pretty as I envisioned.

I continued to move slowly, keeping my eyes closed to visualize my central gravity and maintain my steady breathing. My hamstring felt tight, so I rested my forehead against my shin and bent my knee to move into the split a little slower.

"Do you need help?" the older woman called. She was back. I shifted my head to better see the doorway of the old woman's house again. She was upside down now, and she appeared confused, holding a blanket in her arms.

Was it embarrassing to be caught doing a yoga pose in front of an old woman's house? Yes.

I tried to keep still. If I didn't move and the camera didn't catch my mouth moving, I could probably still use this video without the sound. "I'm all right, but thank you!"

"Oh, an American," she said with surprise. "I do love America. Have you come for a holiday?"

This conversation was evidently going to continue. I straightened, lowering my foot to the ground and rolling up into a standing position. I'd try again when she left. "Yes."

"Hmm." The woman gave a shiver. She gestured to her blanket. "It's much too cold outside for a chat. Come in and warm yourself. I want you to tell me why you were standing in front of my house like a flamingo."

Had she brought the blanket to me on purpose? That was thoughtful. I supposed I could spare a minute to warm my frozen Californian bones.

I retrieved my tripod and ended the video on the camera before following the woman through her narrow door. It was a shorter opening than I was used to, and I ducked to avoid scraping my head on the beam.

"I love America," the woman repeated.

I set my tripod down near the door and paused. It was evident from the decor in her narrow sitting room that her statement was true. Union Jacks lined the ceiling in a patterned bunting, alternating with American flags. The two were represented in couch pillows and on stuffed bears resting on the mantel, and the only thing more present in this room than country flags were *birds*.

"Do you love birds as well?" I asked. It was a safe assumption. Chubby stuffed birds, bird wallpaper, and bird decor slammed into me from all sides.

"I do," she said, as though impressed by my intelligent guess. The bureau against the wall with what looked like a hundred little bird figures made it the opposite of clever, though. "Come on through, love."

I followed her into the sitting room and left my tripod near the door. I sat on the other end of the sofa from her. She was still a stranger and a little space between us was probably a good thing.

"My George took me to Texas a dozen or so years ago," she said wistfully. "The Gulf Coast. Have you been there?"

"I haven't."

She clucked her tongue. "Shame. We saw a roseate spoonbill and altamira orioles. Oh, the colors were so vibrant. Though the beach left a little something to be desired."

"I don't think most people go to Texas for the beach."

"You're all too right, love. They go for the birds."

I wasn't sure that was the case, either.

She stood, her spry motions impressive for a woman with that caliber of wrinkles. "Tea? I can have a pot heated in a jiffy."

"That would be lovely, thank you."

"Why are you in our little village, then?" she asked on her way from the room.

I could hear her moving about the small kitchen, and I spoke up to be heard. "I'm just here for a holiday for a few weeks. I'm staying at The Wild Hare."

"Lovely place, the pub," she said, pottering around in the kitchen some more. "I thought I recognized you."

A cupboard shut and it occurred to me, belatedly, that I probably ought to be a bit more cautious about entering stranger's homes and accepting their tea. I didn't know this woman. What if she was crazy? She seemed sweet enough, but so did the old women in *Arsenic and Old Lace,* and they had gone around killing bachelors.

I could probably just verify that she was harmless with a quick text. I pulled out my phone and messaged Rhys.

Luna Winter: Do you know the woman who lives at the end of the houses at the top of the hill? She was sitting with Frank in the pub yesterday.

His reply was almost instantaneous.

Hot British Guy: You mean Maggie

"Your name, dear?" the woman called, making me jump.

"Luna Winter." Should I not have told her?

"I'm Maggie." She sat again on the sofa and looked at me expectantly. "Maggie Fulton, but you can just call me Maggie."

Luna Winter: Yes. Do you trust her?

Maggie blinked at me, so I searched for something to say. "I love your birds, and your . . . flags."

"Oh, thank you." She blushed. "That means a lot coming from a real Yank."

There was a compliment in there somewhere, I believed. "It must have taken a long time to amass such a collection." The mantel looked like something out of a Texan gift shop. American themed spoons, bears, tiny pillows, bowls, shot glasses and thimbles were arranged between items sporting the Union Jack. It was really something to behold, and I wanted to send a picture to Callie.

She beamed at me. "I have more upstairs if you'd like to see."

And risk an arsenic cocktail? "Oh, maybe another time. I really should get back to the pub soon. I promised Ruby I would help her this evening. Ruby is the—"

"Yes, yes. I know Ruby. Have done since she was this high." She held her flat palm about two feet from the floor. "What are you helping Ruby with? Poor girl has had to run the whole pub for too long now."

"Well, she and Rhys—"

Maggie scoffed. "Rhys was nothing more than a nuisance for the last few years. He's only just returned to cooking, and mighty glad we are about it." She leaned forward to impart her secret. "Ruby doesn't have the same touch with the scones as he does. Or the pies. Or the roast."

"I heard he had a bad breakup," I offered. I *hadn't* heard that it had kept him from working, though. That had to be a pretty intense split. Maybe like steal-your-best-friend-then-invite-you-to-the-wedding intense. Rhys and I could probably understand one another's heartache, swap war stories and commiserate.

Not that I intended to attempt any sort of understanding with him. This was a vacation, not my real home, and my crush aside, hooking up with a stranger was too emotionally complicated for me.

As much as I wanted to be, if only for the sake of replacing Jake completely, I just wasn't that sort of girl. I was envious of the ones who could make out with handsome British strangers and walk away unscathed.

"A bad breakup?" Maggie said, tipping her head to the side. "I suppose you could call it that. A year of bad pies, that's what I would call it."

Man, Maggie really loved her pies.

The kettle screamed in the kitchen and Maggie hopped up to attend to it.

"Can I help you with anything?"

"No, love. You sit right there and rest a minute. Your legs must be tired from all that faffing about like a bird."

No wonder Maggie seemed to like me. I embodied two of her favorite things: birds and America.

My phone buzzed.

Hot British Guy: Ha. Maggie is about as dangerous as I am.

Luna Winter: So, quite a bit then?

My fingers flew and sent the text before I could consider what it sounded like. They froze over the keyboard in stunned stillness while the three dots on his end appeared. The dots disappeared, then came back, all the while driving my nerves through the roof.

Hot British Guy: I'm only as dangerous as you want me to be.

Um, *what*?

Maggie returned with a small tray containing two teacups, a pot, and a small plate of little rectangle cookies. Shortbread, maybe? They looked slightly browned and buttery.

"Biscuit?"

My hands trembled as I reached for the tea. Rhys had affected me more than I realized. "Thank you."

"You'll need the warmth. Now, what were you doing out there?"

"I was filming a segment for my YouTube channel." I took a sip. Before his cryptic flirting, Rhys had made me feel better about being in here with Maggie. But I still surreptitiously brought it to my nose for a sniff. What did arsenic even smell like? Could old women get their hands on it anymore, or had the

Broadway play made that avenue too obvious now for senior murderers?

"YouTube is wonderful," Maggie said, crunching the end of a cookie. "There are so many bird videos available."

"And videos of America," I quipped.

She stilled, her cookie lingering just before making contact with her teeth again. She lowered it. "You're correct. Why had I not thought of that?"

"Of America?"

"Yes. Watching videos on YouTube." She set the cookie on the tray again. "My George and I dreamed of taking a trip to see the various natural wonders in America—the Grand Canyon, Niagara Falls, Yellowstone, that sort of thing—but we never made it."

I wouldn't burst her happy memory bubble by explaining just how far away each of those places were from each other.

"I can see them on the internet."

"It wouldn't be quite the same," I warned.

"No, I imagine not." She looked contemplative. "But if I wear my George's old coat, perhaps it will feel like he is with me."

I meant that it wouldn't be the same as seeing the sites in person, not that it wouldn't be the same without her husband. My heart warmed that she had thought of him. That he had been the thing on her mind.

Someday I wanted a man in my life that I felt this way about, that I wanted to wear his coat because it made me feel closer to him, that I would travel across the world to look at birds with merely because it was something he enjoyed doing.

Jake was supposed to have been that man for me. He was supposed to start his law practice, build up a name for himself in Sonoma County, then propose. We were going to buy the sweet Victorian house at the base of the mountains in my hometown and raise our kids on wild land and fresh milk in the heart of the wine country.

I had *a plan*. I hadn't known my best friend would ruin it.

My eyes stung, and I blinked rapidly before tears could form.

"Is the tea too hot, love?"

Sure, let's go with that. I nodded and set my cup on the tray. "I should be getting back to the pub. Ruby is waiting for me."

Not strictly true, but, you know, *arsenic*.

"It was good to have a chat. Come by any time, Luna."

"I will, thank you."

She walked me to the door. "What are your YouTube videos about, love?"

"Oh, just yoga." I pulled my boots on and tucked my tripod under my arm. "I have a channel for yoga instruction."

Maggie brightened. "I know yoga!"

She probably had a granddaughter like Frank did who had shown her a pose or two.

"Do you?"

"Oh, yes. Rhys's ex used to perform yoga in the pub."

"She did?" That left a weird, metallic taste in my mouth. It was such an odd way to phrase it, too. Yoga wasn't really something a person performed—it was something they experienced.

"Jenna, that's her name. She was quite the holistic little thing. Very taken with herbs and fancy yogic practices."

But could she stand like a flamingo and get herself invited into a stranger's house for tea? I shook the thought. Why was I even comparing myself to this woman?

Oh right, my ridiculous crush.

"Poor Rhys." Maggie sighed. "It is really such a good thing he is back in the kitchen. Nothing will heal that broken heart like a good dose of distraction."

I had the same plan for myself. So far, it seemed to be working. I thought of Jake holding Aubrey's hand in the taqueria, and my body tensed. Well, working a little.

"We all benefit from having Rhys in the kitchen," I agreed.

"Indeed. You should have seen the food we endured after his

divorce. Soggy pies and mushy sausage." Maggie cringed. "Ruby did try her best, though, poor love."

I stopped listening after *divorce*, the Union Jacks and American flags swirling in my vision around a plethora of birds, all with Maggie at the center innocently blinking up at me.

Divorce? Not a break-up, not a girlfriend he didn't love anymore, a *divorce.* The end of a marriage, for heaven's sake.

Rhys wasn't healing from a bad breakup. He was recovering from trauma. If my resolve had begun to soften even a little bit, I could now confirm that it was as rock solid as a slab of concrete.

Rhys and I were never going to sit in a tree, K-I-S-S-I-N-G.

"Take a biscuit for your walk?" Maggie asked.

I took a handful of the square cookies and dropped them in my coat pocket. My feelings were shouting to be fed, and at the moment, disappointment sharp and potent, I was only too happy to oblige.

TWELVE

YES, I WAS HIDING IN MY ROOM LIKE A TEENAGER WHO needed to avoid her parents after a night of sneaking out. And yes, the only things left in my little kitchenette were a handful of granola bars and half a box of dry cereal. It should come as no surprise to anyone when, two hours after leaving Maggie's little cottage and sneaking past the diners in The Wild Hare and up to my room, the smell of roasting meat and buttery crust followed me upstairs and made me salivate like a basset hound.

I craved one of those dinners Maggie had praised, but I was terrified of how I would react to Rhys now that I knew about his divorce. Obviously, I couldn't face him.

He wouldn't want pity. Which was fair, and I *didn't* pity him. But I did think my face might say otherwise when I saw him again. It was so awkward I couldn't take it. So I did what I was best at . . . I hid.

But food. I needed food.

I pulled out my phone and sent a text to Ruby's number.

Luna Winter: Any chance you do room service here for an extra charge?

Ruby Norland: Not usually, but we can make an exception if you need it.

Luna Winter: Bless you, sweet Ruby!

Ruby Norland: What do you want?

Luna Winter: That meat pie from last night would be great. Or a cottage pie. Or even just chicken and potatoes. I'm easy, just hungry.

Ruby Norland: I'll let Rhys know.

Panic shifted through me, shaking my fingers as I hurried to type back.

Luna Winter: NO! Don't tell Rhys! Just bring the food yourself. I'll explain later.

Ruby Norland: Did something happen between you two?

Luna Winter: No, nothing.

Ruby Norland: Why don't I believe you?

This was the problem with texting. I had no idea if she was mad, annoyed, frustrated, or even cared at all. She gave me no emojis to help me decipher her mood.

Luna Winter: I'm just avoiding the dining room tonight.

Maybe by tomorrow my hesitation and concern would dissipate a bit, my awkwardness would be a wisp of an idea and not fully in control of all my faculties. Or maybe that would happen after I got some dinner in my belly. I needed to decorate downstairs like I'd promised Ruby, but not until I'd eaten something and everyone (read: Rhys) had gone to sleep.

With the promise of food on the way, I sat on the chair next to the empty fireplace and went back to editing my video. I was able to crop the end off when Maggie had come out to speak to me, and it still made for a good enough promo piece to add to my Cotswolds segment online—even if I hadn't completed the pose.

A light knock rapped at my door, and I put my computer on the chair and went to answer it.

"Ruby, you are an angel," I said, swinging the door open. I jerked in surprise to find Rhys standing in his cousin's place, and the knob slipped from my hand. The door flew back and banged against the wall.

"Not excited to see me?" he asked, his dark eyebrow raising slightly.

He'd noticed my awkwardness. Of course he had. It spilled from me like a pot of pasta boiling over.

"I just expected Ruby." A weird laugh poured from my lips. "Thanks."

I reached forward, but he pulled the plate back a little, his brown eyes narrowing.

"What happened?" he asked, reading my face as well as I'd feared.

"Nothing." I spoke too fast. He was going to see right through me. I had the distinct impression that if he looked at me long enough, he would sense that I knew about his divorce and how it altered my opinion of him—how it made him off-limits. I could not have a holiday fling with a man who was healing from a dissolved marriage. It was too deep a wound, had the potential to be too messy. I would not be responsible for slowing his healing with a rebound he would undoubtedly regret.

If he read my mind, he would know about my crush and why

I had to talk myself into considering him off-limits in the first place. A point made even worse by the fact that Ruby had warned me away from *this very thing.*

Good grief, I felt like I was in seventh grade again, navigating the very first time a boy told Aubrey he liked me and we had to pretend I didn't know.

Except this was even worse, because Rhys had never told anyone he liked me, and my crush on him was only growing by the minute.

I did awkward finger guns toward the pie he held. "I think my dinner is getting cold."

"Yeah, it is." He didn't sound remorseful in the least. "You better tell me what's going on so I can deliver this and leave."

I scoffed, the sound a little too forced. "Nothing is going on."

"Then why can't you eat downstairs?"

"Didn't you tell me I could eat in my room if I returned the dishes to the kitchen?"

"Yes, but I imagined you would walk downstairs and pick up the dinner yourself. Have you hurt your foot so you can no longer navigate the stairs?"

"No. My foot is fine."

"Are you trying to avoid someone?"

"Wow, aren't you a nosy man?" I laughed to soften the joke.

His thick brown eyebrows pulled together, his dark eyes scouring my face. "I guess this is not an entirely appropriate line of questioning, but I feel responsible for maintaining the safety of my guests, and I would like to know if there is someone making you feel unsafe."

Well, *that* was attractive. My heart beat wildly from the concern in his eyes, and I wanted to invent a mysterious stalker just so Rhys would take it upon himself to be my own personal bodyguard.

I tucked my hair behind my ear. "My safety is not in question."

"Then who are you avoiding?"

I reached for my plate, the golden crust of the half-moon pie making my mouth water. "I'm so hungry."

He moved it about a little, wafting the rich butter and saucy meat in my direction. "Does it smell good?"

"Yes."

"Guess you better hurry up and tell me why you're being weird so I can give it to you then."

I scoffed. "Isn't that illegal or something?"

"You haven't paid for this yet."

True.

"And," he continued, leaning closer, "you've been weird ever since I saved your life."

"Well, hold that over my head, why don't you."

"I'm trying to."

My mouth broke into a smile. I couldn't help it. He *had* saved my life. But I couldn't tell him this.

He dipped his head a little, holding my gaze. "You said you came here to get away from something or someone. I just can't help but worry after that."

So he *did* think I had some sort of stalker on my case? "I came to England because I run from my problems," I said quietly, shame seeping into my words, matching him tone for tone. "That's all. I'm a runner. It's what I do. There is no danger of that problem following me here at all."

"Is that problem a man?"

I glanced up sharply, confirming without saying a word. "That problem is a whole mess of a situation." I cringed. Why was it so difficult for me to make myself vulnerable? To share that I had been passed over for my best friend, then begged to stand near the freaking podium while they got married as a bridesmaid? I shook the thought and focused on Rhys. "It's more than just a man."

He stared at me for a minute, the thick silence full of secrets I was too scared or ashamed to admit to.

"I'm running from a wedding," I blurted, unable to keep it in any longer under the weight of his gaze. "I just . . . I couldn't stay."

"Your own wedding?"

"Someone else's."

After another minute, Rhys handed the plate to me, and I accepted it quietly, the hot air immediately diffused from my outburst. "Thanks."

"What are you working on?" he asked, nodding toward the open laptop on my chair.

I was grateful he didn't press the issue further. It was a lot for me to say what I had, and I needed a moment to recover from that bit of vulnerability. "Just a video for social media. It's kind of lame." I had to stay here for two more weeks, so I wanted us to at least be on friendly terms. What was more friend-zone than talking about work? I shifted my mouth into a smile and hoped he didn't see my lips tremble. "Do you want to see it?"

"Sure." He followed me into my room, and I set the plate on the small table next to the chair, pulling my computer onto my lap. Rhys sat on the edge of my bed and leaned forward, resting his forearms on his knees and clasping his hands loosely together.

"Don't laugh," I said. I turned the computer and hit play, and the music Jake had made for my LunaMoon channel started pouring through the speakers. I cringed a little, like I always did, and Rhys looked up at me before dropping his gaze to the video again. It showed me at the top of the hill, my body a dark silhouette against the background of a dimming Snowshill, the yellow Cotswold stone bleeding down the hill, the smoke from various chimneys blending with the darkening sky. It looked cool. I moved slowly through my yoga pose, my leg tightening and bending down toward my body.

It paused on a still shot of my head turning a little when I'd been talking to Maggie. "I couldn't finish the move because I got interrupted, but I'm going to use the video anyway because the sky in the background was too good to ignore."

"For what it's worth, it isn't obvious you didn't finish the move."

"It will be to most of my followers who do yoga."

"Well, good for them. I like it the way it is now."

I reached for the hand pie he'd made and took a bite, the flaky, buttery crust melting on my tongue. "Mmm, so good."

"You returned from your walk a few hours ago. Have you been hiding up here that whole time?"

"I've been *working*," I said around a mouthful.

Rhys's skeptical look proved he didn't necessarily believe me. With my request to have Ruby bring my dinner upstairs, I couldn't really blame him. "Is it *me* you're trying to avoid?"

I stilled, the pie turning gluey in my mouth. I reached for my water bottle and took a swig to clear my throat.

"It is," he said, tilting his head to the side.

"No, of course not. I don't know you well enough to want to avoid you."

"Oh, good." He didn't appear entirely convinced. "I was just wondering what I could have done to make you want to run from me. Usually when you save someone's life, it has the opposite effect."

I narrowed my eyes, fighting a smile. Opposite effect? "I don't know you well enough to run toward you, either."

"That's fixable," Rhys muttered, so quietly I didn't know if I'd heard correctly. He ducked his head and ran a hand over the back of his neck. "I should get back to the kitchen."

That was an end to our somewhat flirty banter, like a door slammed in my face. Which was a good thing, since the man was recently divorced and still hung up on his ex. That wasn't the kind of situation I should insert myself into. Regardless of how much I kind of wanted to.

"Thanks for the dinner," I said brightly, trying to cover the awkwardness flowing through me.

"Don't forget to pay for it. I can't be handing free meals out to every beautiful woman who walks into my pub."

WHAT.

He had called me beautiful. I floundered, forgetting how to smile normally. "Add it to my tab," I said, like a dork.

Rhys's lips turned up in a smile, and I was hit by the force of it. What woman would walk away from this rugged GQ logger? He wasn't just outrageously handsome, he was kind and generous as well. The breakfasts he'd made me, the ride he'd given me to pick up boots, the way he brought me dinner—Rhys was a thoughtful man.

Jenna, his ex, was an idiot.

"Where's Ned?" I asked, standing to walk him to the door.

"Napping in front of the fire."

"Ah, keeping Frank's feet company?"

"As usual."

He hesitated in the doorway.

"I promise I'll pay for my dinner."

Rhys's lips quirked to the side. "I'm not really worried about it."

Then why was he hovering in my doorway while the rest of my pie was getting cold?

His head bent a little, giving me his full attention, and his voice was low. "Whoever this guy is that you left behind, he's a fool."

"That's a bold statement to make when you don't know what he's done."

"If he made you run, he's a fool," Rhys said with perfect, calm confidence.

From the cadence of his voice and the intensity of his stare, there was absolutely no debating that Rhys Norland was sending me a message right now, and it conflicted heavily with what I knew about him. First off, he was not a player, as evidenced by the added locks he'd put on his door after his last female boarder hit on him, so he would not be hitting on me unless he had somewhat good intentions. Second, he was still supposed to be reeling from his divorce, so he couldn't possibly have any interest in pursuing anything beyond a fling.

And yet, those eyes. They were dark brown pools of Dr Pepper above perfectly kissable lips. The kind of lips that smirked as easily as they smiled. I wanted them to wrap around me and test Callie's theory about whether or not accents would change the way a person kissed.

"What are you thinking about?" Rhys asked. "Your forehead just became very serious."

A blush rose to my cheeks, and I shook the thought of accents and kissing and Rhys's beautiful mouth. "I'm thinking about my cold pie."

"Really?"

No. "Yeah, well, it is waiting for me." But I made no move to leave the doorway. Cinnamon and sugar and a hint of Christmas wafted from Rhys in warm waves, and I wanted to lean in and inhale.

"Could you step away from work after your meal is finished? I happen to know that tonight's group is not something you'll want to miss."

"Tonight's group?" Neither he nor Ruby had mentioned anything about it. Not that they'd felt inclined to warn me about the knitters, gamers, or Mommy and Me groups, either. "What is it?"

Rhys grinned. "It always starts as a book club. Usually about murder mysteries."

Which implied that it ended in a different manner. "Oh yeah? And how does it end?"

Rhys leaned a little closer, bringing that cinnamon sugar smell closer to my nose and making me wobbly like a jellyfish. He lowered his voice, not moving his eyes from mine. "You'll have to come to find out."

THIRTEEN

I COULD NOT HELP BUT FEEL UNDERPREPARED FOR AN evening with the Snowshill Book Club. A variety of ages and genders—though the majority were women in their fifties—were represented in the circle of less than a dozen avid lovers of all things Agatha Christie. They had spent the better part of an hour debating the differences between the book and the movie versions of *Death on the Nile*—and heaven help us all after Maggie brought up the 1978 film and sent Frank into a fit. Maggie was prepared to argue in favor of what she deemed a classic, but Frank insisted that Gal Gadot was a stunner, and he was prepared to die on that hill.

The argument rolled the little group into shouting for more drinks, which Rhys quickly provided while I watched the entire thing from a barstool at the counter.

Rhys returned from delivering the fresh round of drinks and pulled out the seat next to me, setting his tray on the bar behind us. The room was otherwise empty, but we sat on the stools facing the group in their circle of chairs fighting over whether or not Gal Gadot was worthy to play her role—um, hello? Of course she was—and shooting glares across the circle at one another.

"Where is Ruby tonight?"

Rhys shrugged. "Other plans, I guess. She doesn't find this as entertaining as I do."

"A group of old people arguing?"

He scoffed in quiet umbrage. "The best part is yet to come. Don't worry, they'll make up." Rhys sent me a wink and my insides melted into puddles and gathered in my feet.

He leaned back against the counter and stretched his arms out, his fingers brushing along the skin at the nape of my neck. A volley of chills ran down my melted spine. I was molten lava over a *finger brush*. That was what he did to me. At what point was I going to erupt?

"You all know what we need now, don't you?" a woman asked, getting unsteadily to her feet. She had a short, round perm and clothes I was convinced were vintage 90s. I liked her saucy smile, too. She looked up at us. "Oh, Rhys darling. Could you be a dear and fetch the mic?"

"The mic?" I whispered.

He hopped up, his fingers brushing my neck again—was he doing it on purpose now?—and grinned while he disappeared into the kitchen. He came back carrying what looked like a karaoke machine and started setting it up near the fireplace.

The group became rowdy. Men and women in their late forties to early seventies were moving their chairs out of circle formation and turning them to face the fireplace, which I assumed acted as their stage area. The woman in the 90s windbreaker and neon swishy pants took the mic and plugged what looked like an older iPod into the jack before bringing it to her lips. "All right ladies and gentlemen, who would like to go first?"

Every hand in the room shot up, including both Frank's and Maggie's, and Rhys returned to my side with a smug grin.

Apparently he could see how utterly delighted I was by this turn of events.

"If I'd known how this evening was meant to turn out, I

would have brought some popcorn," I said. Karaoke was one of the finer enjoyments of life. There was something about people singing their heart out, tone deaf or not, and the utter confidence and joy they exhibited that made karaoke pure, smile-inducing entertainment.

Rhys stood. "I don't have any on hand, but I can fetch a bowl of crisps."

"That's good enough for me."

Rhys returned after the first song—*My Heart Will Go On*—came to a close and the next person, a man in his fifties, took the stage. Rhys moved to a table at the back of the room behind all the book clubbers. He set down a dark glass of bubbly soda, a glass of water, and a bowl of crisps. His gaze lifted to mine and he gave a little jerk with his neck, inviting me over.

"I don't know how Hamish sits there all day," I whispered, stretching my back before joining him at the table. "My back could not survive it."

"In his defense, he's really only here at mealtimes. He does have a farm to run."

"With a hundred little minions? My parents could never take the time away from their animals the way Hamish does." I picked up the soda he gestured to and took a swig. Aww, Dr Pepper. He'd remembered.

"He has a few minions," Rhys said lightly.

Feedback from the mic screamed through the room before Maggie bent and turned it down. We'd passed through an entire song, and I hadn't even recognized what it was due to Rhys's attention and the delicious parmesan crisps he served every day. Maggie waited pleasantly for her music to begin, then closed her eyes and sang, in an admittedly lovely voice, *Blackbird* by the Beatles.

"Did you know Maggie's husband?" I asked quietly, leaning closer to Rhys purely so I would not disrupt the mood in the room, and for no other reason at all.

He nodded. "Bird enthusiast."

"American enthusiast."

"He was a loyalist, too," he said, bemused.

I grinned. "I saw an equal ratio of Union Jacks and American paraphernalia in their house."

"When did you go to Maggie's house?"

"This afternoon." *Where she fed me non-poisoned tea and told me about your divorce.* My throat clammed up, and I sat back in my seat, facing Maggie, a mic in her hand and her eyes still closed. Was Rhys hung up on his ex because she was the one who ended things and he still wanted her? The woman who used to *perform* yoga in the pub? It hit me with a sudden jolt that Rhys must have been shocked to find me performing yoga to my video camera that morning, but he'd seemed so quietly unmoved. Though, by the time he had spoken to me, he had been sitting there for fifteen minutes or so. He must have gotten over the majority of his surprise by then.

Rhys leaned closer, his arms crossed over his chest and his shoulder pressing against mine. I waited for him to speak, but he said nothing, his body just resting close to me and sending my brain into an overload of overthinking. So, analyzing in double time, pretty much. Why was he doing this when he wasn't a player and he wasn't interested in other women? One of those observations was wrong, obviously, but which one?

Sometimes I wished I had the nerves to be blunt. I wanted to straight-talk with the man and ask him if he was just looking for a quick holiday fling. That certainly made more sense of the two options . . . and the way his body was barely touching mine but still sent me into a flutter of constant tingles probably meant that kissing him would be, at the least, enjoyable. At the worst . . . setting me up for disappointment in the next guy I kissed.

But right now, I was thinking the future disappointment would be completely worth it.

Besides, Callie was right. Kissing a hot British guy was bound to push Jake from my head completely. Rhys already had a habit of pushing Jake the Flake from my thoughts.

Blackbird came to a close and the room erupted in friendly applause. Rhys's arms shook beside mine as he clapped, and we settled again to listen to the rest of the songs, making jokes about the choices and overall enjoying the goofy book club who didn't seem to care that no one had mentioned anything of a literary nature in the last hour.

The 90s woman—whose name happened to be Katherine—took the mic and speared Rhys with a cheeky smile. "I think we all know who we'd like to close us out tonight, but I think he'll need a little help. What do you say, Rhys? Do you and your friend want to take the final song?"

He froze beside me. "Not tonight, Katherine," he said pleasantly, but I could feel the undercurrent of discomfort rippling from him in steady waves.

"I can't sing," I said with an apologetic shrug. "Sorry!"

"Oh, come on," Maggie called, her cheeks flushed. "Give us a song."

"You don't want my voice wrecking your evening."

There was a general murmur of disappointment. Frank took one for the team, rising to sing *Don't Stop Believin'* to a mournful crowd.

The patrons soon after wrapped their necks in scarves and pulled on heavy coats before filing from the pub. I set to correcting the chairs and gathering used glasses to put in the kitchen while Rhys stood at the door to wish them all farewell and locked it behind the last book clubber.

"Did you forget that you don't work here?" he asked, pushing a few of the heavier chairs back onto the stage area.

"No." I kept gathering glasses and taking them into the kitchen a handful at a time. A full tray might have been more efficient, but I didn't trust myself not to drop them all on the floor.

Rhys stood near the dying fire, wrapping the microphone in its cord. "You don't need to do this."

"I know." I shrugged, taking the last of the dishes into the kitchen. I retrieved a rag and ran it through hot water. Rhys passed me and disappeared into a storage closet at the end of the room.

We worked side by side in relative silence, cleaning the tables and righting everything so it was prepared for patrons in the morning. Once the floor had been swept and mopped, Rhys hovered near the counter and watched me wash my hands in the sink.

"Why do I have the feeling that you aren't just helping to be nice?"

"Because I'm not just helping to be nice," I said. The added time spent with Rhys was a bonus, but I had to get the room cleaned so I could put out the decorations. It was nearing midnight, and Ruby still wasn't home, so I understood why she needed the help.

From the tired set to Rhys's broad shoulders, he likely needed the help as well.

He stepped around the bar and into the doorway of the kitchen, then leaned against it. "Why are you helping me, then?" His voice was low, a suggestion or a promise . . . I couldn't quite tell which. But it made my throat go dry.

And I realized my mistake. He thought I was flirting. I wouldn't mind that he thought that and seemed to respond favorably to the scenario, but I didn't have time to kiss him with those three boxes of decor screaming at me and the bare pub in desperate need of some holiday cheer.

"I'm really helping *Ruby*."

That made his eyebrows rise.

"And," I continued, "I know this is going to sound strange, but if you have hot chocolate on hand, I would really love a cup before you go up to bed. I can make it myself if you will allow it, my liege."

"My liege?"

"You're the king of this kitchen, right?"

"I'll make you a cup. But what are you doing for Ruby?"

I drew in a breath and slipped past him, inhaling his Christmassy scent and sounding far more breathless than the situation warranted. "I told Ruby I would set up the Christmas decorations tonight."

"You what?"

"I'm not doing it for free." I shrugged, opening the first of the boxes to find a plethora of greenery and red ribbon. "She said I could have free dinners the rest of the week."

"It's Friday. So . . . like two free dinners?"

"I like helping out. And I like decorating. I missed it this year at home."

He watched me rummage through the boxes a little bit longer before disappearing into the kitchen. By the time I had everything inventoried and my general plan in place, he still hadn't reappeared. I took that as permission to begin.

Soft music came on the speakers mounted in the corners of the room and Bing Crosby crooned about snow. I stood on the stone fireplace and gently laid greenery around the picture frames already situated there. I hummed along to the song, and when I turned around, Rhys was watching me with great amusement.

I passed him and went to the box for more greenery. If he wasn't going to get me a cup of hot chocolate, he could make himself useful in other ways. "If you plan to stay down here, you might as well help."

FOURTEEN

Rhys picked up the box of greenery and followed me to the windows. Not gonna lie, I was pretty happy he opted to help. But if he intended to use that to finagle me down to one free meal . . . I would still take the deal. I *liked* setting up Christmas. It was the gateway to the holidays, transforming regular homes into warm vessels that shipped you straight into coziness and joy, where it was socially acceptable to build a small house out of candy and immediately eat it.

I selected another strand of greenery and stood on a chair to hang it above the window, humming along to the song. I felt a pang about missing Christmas with my family. It wasn't going to be quite the same.

Rhys stood next to the box, holding another strand of greenery toward me. When I reached for it though, he did not release it. "You lied to Katherine during karaoke."

I stopped humming right away, and a blush bled into my cheeks. "*Lie* is such a strong word." I yanked, and he let it go. "You looked like you really didn't want to sing in front of the book clubbers, so I improvised."

"I don't think *clubbers* is a real word."

"It's a noun: people who live for book clubs. Which I think epitomized the group you had in here tonight."

"Fair enough."

We worked quietly together through the next few songs of what was apparently a Bing Crosby Christmas playlist. Rhys disappeared when I went to add red velvet bows to the greenery, and he returned with a large wreath that he affixed to the front door. Within an hour, the boxes were emptied and the pub had been transformed into a warm Christmas haven. The fire roared with fresh new logs and the windows and mantel were draped in green and red velvet. Gold figurines forming a nativity gathered in the center of the mantel, lit by the glow of the fire underneath. Greenery hung behind the bar, and it was tasteful but very obviously Christmas decor.

"You don't have a tree?" I asked, surveying the room with happy satisfaction. Though my evening was missing the most important component of decorating night: the hot chocolate.

Rhys paused behind the bar. "We usually cut one down, but I haven't done it yet this year."

"I love real trees. I grew up with them, too." I leaned my elbows on the counter. "But then my parents invested in a nice fake one a few years ago and we've used it ever since."

"It's certainly more convenient," he agreed.

"But doesn't smell quite the same."

Rhys's mouth turned up into a smile. "Oh, hang on." He disappeared into the kitchen and returned a few minutes later with two steaming cups of hot chocolate.

"Yes!" I accepted the mug from him and took a drink, feeling the warmth travel down my throat and solidify this as the best day I'd had on vacation yet.

Rhys stood next to me at the bar and sipped his own cup. "Thanks for your help."

I took another drink and lifted my eyebrow. "I didn't do this out of the kindness of my heart."

"No, of course not. Two free dinners is worth an hour of manual labor."

"When you're cooking them? One hundred percent worth it."

"Right."

The music changed, and *Silent Night* came on, setting the mood brilliantly. Too bad there wasn't any mistletoe in those boxes or I'd be able to finagle an accidental meetup beneath it.

"Thanks for getting me out of singing, too," Rhys said, his voice lowering, matching the change in the mood of the music. "I haven't sung with the book clubbers—"

"The name sounds good, doesn't it?"

"—since before my ex left."

I set my mug down with a soft thud, regretting my levity. "Ouch. Sorry. My timing could have been better." But now I knew that *she* had left *him*, and it made this all the more depressing.

Rhys shot me a self-deprecating smile. "It's fine. It's been a while. I need to move past it at some point."

"You're still hung up on her?" I asked gently.

"No . . . and yes. It's hard to forget about a relationship that lasted as long as ours did."

A long relationship like a *marriage*. Why wouldn't he call it what it was?

"It's never easy to move on." Look at me: eight months after being dumped and I still ran straight to the airport to avoid my ex. A woman who was well and truly over her ex would not have needed to escape.

"But she moved on with other men before our relationship had even ended, so I really need to get her out of my head." Rhys ran a hand through his hair, shaking it out a little.

She moved on with other men? So not only had she left Rhys, but she cheated on him? My heart reached for him, yearning to comfort away his past pain.

He looked at me. "I don't know why I'm saying that. I'm not

hung up on her in a way that keeps me from thinking about other women."

"So you've dated again since she left?"

"No." He regarded me closely. "I've been waiting for the right woman." The way he murmured and locked his gaze to mine like a vise grip was suggestive, and my body froze in place, fighting the gut reaction screaming at me to flee. The heat in my body wanted to stay to find out what was going to happen. Could blood reach a boiling point over a guy's stare? My body was certainly testing that theory.

"It's been over eight months for me," I said, volunteering information he had never asked for. I wondered if his hesitance was because of my cryptic explanation earlier about how I ran from my problems and I'd run from a mess back home. No man heard the word *mess* and didn't think *Mayday! Mayday! Emotional baggage alert!*

I might as well open up my huge roller bags and let him see what kind of baggage I carried with me. "I dated a guy for five years, and he left me for my best friend."

Rhys gave an appropriate grimace. "Ouch."

"Yeah. The bigger ouch was getting their wedding invitation a few weeks ago and then being asked to stand up with them as a bridesmaid." I took a sip of my hot chocolate, glad it was no longer hot enough to scald my tongue. "I don't know how to say no, clearly, so I told them I had a trip to England planned during the wedding. If I had known the wedding was planned for Christmas Eve, I would have come up with a different excuse."

"But instead, you corroborated your story with a plane ticket?"

I shrugged. "I've always wanted to come here, and I thought the distraction would be useful."

He nodded. "Distractions can be very useful, I think. They get you out of your own head at least."

"Oh, yeah? You've found success with distractions?"

"I have lately. By throwing myself into running the pub. I mean, it hasn't removed my problems, but it has helped me forget them for a minute."

I cleared my throat. "My sister thinks that's just what I need to get over Jake. Date around and distract myself with men until one of them sticks."

"Maybe your sister is onto something."

I gave him a flat look. "She also wondered if men with accents kissed differently than Americans, so I'm not sure I can take all of her advice as solid and reliable."

Rhys looked down at his empty hot chocolate mug. "From my experience, different accents haven't changed the kissing experience a whole lot."

"Have you kissed a lot of women from different countries?"

"A few, and they weren't mind-blowingly varied or anything." He looked at me from under his thick, dark lashes and stared into my soul. "But I'm willing to test that theory again."

My heart thudded. The room had gone quiet, Bing Crosby's playlist at an end, and I was sure my pulse was pounding loud enough to give us a steady beat if he suddenly felt like dancing. "Purely for the sake of science?"

"Science. Of course," he said, taking a step closer until he stood flush with my barstool, my knees on either side of his waist. Rhys was at eye level, thanks to the stool, and his dark brown eyes looked black. His large hand slid behind my neck, and he dipped his head, keeping eye contact. "But only if you want to."

Woah. His words whispered over my lips, and I felt them move. I didn't bother thinking beyond this moment—I would allow myself to experience it now and overanalyze it tomorrow in minute, anxious detail. An early Christmas gift to myself. *Merry Christmas, Luna! A hot British kiss.*

"For science," I agreed. I gripped his shirt and pulled him closer, until his lips touched mine and the entire room erupted like Vesuvius. Rhys's hands moved and didn't stop, splaying across my back and neck and running down my arms, touching me everywhere and pulling me closer while his mouth explored mine. He kissed like he dealt with his Christmas cake, with nurturing affection, and I mapped the tender, gentle care of his fingers and his lips while I grew weightless.

He pulled back, looking me in the eye, but I wasn't ready for it to end. I ran my hands through his hair and brought him back to kiss me again, his hands on my waist and an urgency about his movements that wasn't there the first time. He tasted faintly of chocolate and parmesan, and he smelled of Christmas. As a woman representing my country, I tried to make America proud.

I leaned back when it became necessary to breathe again, but my hands were still around his neck, my fingertips grazing his skin. Goosebumps spread below his ears and sent satisfaction through me. He swayed closer and leaned his forehead on my shoulder for a minute, as if his legs had gone weak and he needed a break.

He straightened. "Marks out of ten?"

"Hmmm." I pretended to think about it, scrunching my nose.

He kissed the tip of my nose and the wrinkles went away at once. "Don't tease me," he murmured.

"As far as accents go, I would say yours is far better than anything I've had back home."

He grinned. "On behalf of my fellow countrymen, I would like to thank you for partaking in this experiment."

"Science wants to thank me, too?"

"Yes, of course. Science is extremely grateful for your help. You've proved that Americans certainly kiss the best."

My stomach flipped again, and I grinned like a kid on Christmas morning. "I'm the first American you've kissed?"

"I don't make it a habit of toying with tourists."

A little of my joy deflated at the reminder that I was on a vacation and this could never be serious, but I was glad for the confirmation, too. Rhys wasn't a player. He wasn't *completely* hung up on his ex—just a little. It was a relief to know that now.

A key in the lock made a scraping sound and Rhys stepped back and hopped on the stool next to me as the door opened to admit Ruby. She flew inside with excited energy. "Wow! You're both still awake? It's nearly one."

I liked her a lot, so I tried not to feel disappointed that she'd arrived and cut short any more possible scientific research Rhys had felt like doing. "I had to wait for the book club to leave so I could put up the decorations."

She stepped further into the room and unwrapped her scarf, turning in a slow circle to take in what we'd done, a giddy smile on her face. "I love it. All we're missing is a little Bing Crosby—"

"We had him on earlier," Rhys said, scoffing. "You missed it."

Ruby stepped up to me and threw her arms around my waist in a brief hug. She smelled of garlic and sautéed onions, as though she'd just come from dinner. "You're the best. I wish California wasn't so far away. I want to keep you."

I glanced over and caught Rhys's eyes before they cut away from me. "Yeah, I wish it wasn't so far away, too."

FIFTEEN

I WOULD NOT CALL MYSELF A FLIRT OR A PLAYER, BUT I had kissed enough guys to have a solid baseline for comparison. Rhys had blown them all out of the water. Thinking about the kiss made it difficult to fall asleep that night, and I spent way too long staring at the ceiling, dreaming about the man who was asleep—or maybe staring at the ceiling too—across the hall. By the time morning rolled around, I was exhausted and turned away from the bright windows to try and fall back asleep.

At least the kiss was good for helping me kick the absurdly early mornings jetlag had thus far gifted me. My phone buzzed on the table beside my bed, and I reached for it, unhooking the charger and answering it as soon as I saw Mom's name flash across the screen.

"What time is it there?" I asked groggily, aware that my morning was her middle of the night.

"Almost one." Mom sighed. "It's been a doozy. Dusty got loose. The Garcias called Dad to let him know they saw the stupid horse walking down Moody Lane."

"Moody?" I sat up and rubbed my eyes. "So like on the other side of town?"

"We have no idea how he got so far. It was a pain to hunt him down. But he's home, and he's safe now."

"Dusty's lucky you love him so much."

"Yeah, or we'd be talking glue."

I cringed. My mom never meant that joke, but it still didn't hit right all the same. "But since we both know you would never do that . . ."

"So, Dad and I were spread thin trying to track Dusty down," she continued, her voice deceptively light. "You'll never believe who jumped in to help."

Judging by how Mom's voice went a little higher than average and the measured way she spoke, I assumed it was someone I wouldn't want to hear about. "Probably Jake or Aubrey."

"How did you know?"

"Because you're calling me instead of going to sleep."

All pretense slipped from her voice. "Dad was out looking on the four-wheeler. Jake passed him and pulled over to ask what was going on. Dad didn't ask for help, but Jake offered. He took his car up River Road so Dad could go up Moody, where the Garcias had seen Dusty. Anyway, Jake found the horse on River Road, so we were glad for the help. We could have been going in circles all night."

It was too early in the morning to discuss ex-boyfriend hero-ics. "Mom, you're going to make me lose my breakfast, and I haven't even had it yet."

"He's not a bad man, Lu."

"I never said he was. But he is the man who broke my heart, and I don't really want to hear about how much you love him before nine in the morning."

She was silent for a minute, and I knew this was hard for her. Her brain was probably screaming *must-fix-must-fix* robotically on repeat while she was actively computing that I was an adult and holding grudges was my prerogative. I could admit Jake wasn't a bad guy; he was just a guilty one. But I didn't want to analyze it. I wanted to shove all thoughts of him under a pillow and let them die naturally.

As much as I found myself the villain in Aubrey's romantic comedy, I knew Jake wasn't the typical terrible ex-boyfriend who deserved to have rotten tomatoes tossed at him or a barrage of insults to his manhood. He was a nice guy. I had dated him for five years, so I would know.

He had also been—when he was with me—afraid of commitment. Since he jumped into a life commitment with Aubrey after only a few months, it was safe to assume the lack of marriage proposals hadn't been because Jake feared marriage. It was me.

My stomach tightened, and my inner AVOID alert button was flashing bright red lights.

"We stopped loving him when he broke your heart," Mom said sternly. "But he helped us out tonight and Dad really enjoyed—"

"I can't, Mom," I said, my chest burning and my eyes closing against the daylight streaming through the drapes. If the universe was trying to ruin my happiness after the best kiss I'd ever had, then it was succeeding. Jake was a wet blanket over that smoldering fire, and just thinking about him made my entire body clench in discomfort.

She was quiet for a minute. "So you're still planning on missing Christmas?"

Her question was like a knife to the heart. "My return ticket is for the 29th, remember?"

"I have it on my calendar." Her resignation was obvious though. What had she been holding out hope for? That home-sickness would win over my grudge and I would return early for the holidays? I didn't want to spend another thousand dollars just to move my already-purchased ticket, and I didn't want to be home during the wedding, sitting in my house and knowing that down the road Jake and Aubrey were swearing to love and cherish each other through influenza and 5k races for the next sixty years.

I swung my legs over the side of the bed and planted my feet firmly on the cold floor. "I will be here until the 29th. I'm glad you got Dusty back, too, but I should really go shower, and I don't want to keep you up anymore."

"Okay, good night honey. I mean . . . good morning?"

"Yeah. Good night to you."

A soft knock rapped on my door. I set my phone down and padded across the chilly floor. I swung the door open, and Rhys's dark brown eyes waited on the other side. His appearance was only minorly troubling. If he had come for a Define The Relationship talk, then I would happily report I had no designs on committing him to anything that outlasted the month of December. We'd talked about distraction, right? How good it could be for not thinking about exes? That's all we were for each other—a little distraction.

It certainly didn't feel as cold and heartless as it sounded, but either way, I hoped he didn't want to hold that conversation right now. I was putty in his dark, broody gaze, and I couldn't be sure the explanation would sound as rational on my early morning tongue as it did in my head.

Sudden awareness over the state of my pajamas fell over me, and I crossed my arms over my chest to hide the words on my oversized T-shirt. At least my cat-themed leggings were Christmassy with their alternating feline Santa hats and elf ears, which made their tackiness somewhat acceptable for the month of December. The shirt my dad had gotten me as a joke for my birthday last year emblazoned with *FEED ME & TELL ME I'M PRETTY* didn't send as cute of a message.

By the look of Rhys's amusement, he'd already read the words on my shirt. "I think I've already done both of those things." He nodded down to my shirt. "So what do I get?"

"You've done neither of them today, and this is more of a direction for daily gratification than a checklist."

"Daily, huh?" Rhys leaned one shoulder against the door jamb and crossed his arms to mirror me, accentuating his biceps in a way that made it difficult to keep my eyes on his face. "Consider it noted. Hey, I was wondering if you have plans this afternoon?"

My calendar for the next few weeks was empty except for a small asterisk that said *visit the church in Linscombe and maybe tour Brumsworth Manor at some point.* Basically, my schedule was wide open. Irritatingly wide open. Though if Rhys and I both knew that whatever blossoming fling was developing between us had a bit of a time limit on it, did that mean I didn't need to temper my enthusiasm for spending time with him? Following Christmas, I wouldn't see him again.

Or at least I hoped it was a blossoming fling and not literally a science experiment that was one and done.

Normally I would try to avoid seeming too desperate. But with a pulse-rising, organ-melting smile like Rhys wore now, I couldn't find it in me to care about looking too cool. One glance at my wild hair and raccoon eyes in the bathroom mirror had made that abundantly clear.

"I am wide open today. Though I was hoping to film a segment downstairs after everyone cleared out for the night if that's okay? I want to take advantage of the Christmas decor."

"That'll be fine." He unclamped his arms and ran his fingers down my forearm until they reached my hand, then tugged it free. Okay . . . so definitely more than just one science experiment. His touch was soft and sent goosebumps over my skin as his fingers laced mine. "Be ready to leave at half past three, then? Wear all the winter clothes you have."

"Like, layer my shirts on top of each other?" I had an image of the kid from *The Christmas Story,* except it was me walking down to meet Rhys with my arms out to the sides because I was too bundled to lower them.

"No, just wear your coat and scarf. That sort of layering."

"Got it." His calloused fingers were doing something to my heart the way they played with my hand, and it was not good for my concentration. I expected there to be a bit of awkwardness after last night, or at least some mention of it, but we had fallen into a comfortable rhythm together. There was no elephant in the room. It was just Rhys, me, and my overactive heart. His touch had to have been infused with drugs of some sort, because I was slowly losing the ability to focus. I dropped my gaze and grimaced. "I need to change out of this before anyone else witnesses the monstrosity that is my pajamas."

"I like them," he said, his fingers unrelenting in their quest to turn me into jelly.

"And I like my pride."

"Pride is overrated."

"Overrated? I thought the same thing about full English breakfasts, but you turned that opinion around."

"I'm glad you aren't too set in your American ways. That would make something like kissing an Englishman intolerable."

"How do you know it wasn't?"

He lifted an eyebrow at me, as though his expression was saying *you really want to go there?* Spoiler alert: yeah, I really did.

"By the way you kissed me, Luna."

"Maybe I'm just a good actress," I said, a grin splitting my face nearly in half. Was the world tipping, or was I just leaning toward Rhys? I blamed his magnetic pull.

He lowered his voice. "That is quite obviously not the case. I'll see you at half-three."

"You'll see me much earlier than that. My appetite is screaming for real food."

Rhys grinned. "Even better."

Whatever happened between us last night, it wasn't the start of a relationship or anything of that nature, which was why I perfectly understood when Rhys leaned back and released my hand, stepping away without so much as a cheek kiss. Nothing. His lips didn't even enter the vicinity of my face. But my purely mature understanding of where we stood did not mean I wasn't disappointed. I watched Rhys walk away before I closed the door and leaned against it, emitting something of a sigh. I mean, he still hadn't mentioned his divorce, so it was pretty obvious he didn't want to dive to that level of depth with me. Which was fine. I was totally fine with that.

I pulled my phone out to text my sister.

Luna Winter: Fly to England? Check. Kiss an Englishman? CHECK.

She responded so fast I was half-tempted to tell her she should be asleep right now.

Callie Winter: That text is severely lacking in details.

Luna Winter: You would approve. That's all I'm saying.

Callie Winter: So he's hot. Are we talking Idris Elba/Tom Hiddleston hot? Or more like the royal princes hot?

Luna Winter: None of the above? I wouldn't say he had distinguished gentleman or royal vibes. More like rugged and broody.
Luna Winter: OH! You already have a picture of his back. I'll try to be covert later and get a picture of his face.

Callie Winter: You mean you kissed that guy from the picture you sent me last week? You kissed the cook!?

Luna Winter: He's the pub owner, cook, my neighbor, and I'm pretty sure he has a side gig chopping trees somewhere due to his excessive plaid and biceps.

Callie Winter: Excessive biceps? Or are they juuuuust right?

Luna Winter: Gross. We will no longer be objectifying my landlord.
Luna Winter: Well, not until I get another picture for you.

Callie Winter: Is he on Instagram? Send me his handle! I need to stalk.

Why hadn't I thought of social media until now? I opened my Instagram app and went to the search bar. My fingers stalled, hovering over the keys. If I did this, I could potentially see things I wouldn't like. His ex-wife, for example, or other women from his past. But he wasn't even that forthcoming about the nature of his relationship with Jenna Who Performed Yoga, so obviously I couldn't rely on learning much else from him firsthand.

The curious side of me won the moral debate, and I typed in Rhys Norland into the search function before I could talk myself out of it.

One account popped up with his name. *One*. The little profile picture was of a man in plaid, but it was so small I couldn't quite confirm if it was my Rhys or not. Well, not *my* Rhys . . . although that did have a bit of a ring to it.

I clicked on his picture and went to his page. It wasn't set to private, thank the heavens, and I confirmed immediately that it was my Rhys. His profile picture was him behind the bar, laughing. From the angle, I was sure it had been taken by Ruby while she sat on a stool beside Hamish or somewhere in that vicinity.

He had a brilliant, wide smile and a clear disinterest in social media. The photos that popped up most recently on his feed were shots of the pub or Ned or a cute image of Rhys and Ruby flanking an older woman who was most likely their Nan, with a Christmas tree in the background. I double checked the date to confirm, then sat back. One of the most recent images he shared was from Christmas last year.

My thumb hovered for half a second before scrolling down. I immediately regretted it. Images of Rhys with a tall, lithe blonde woman with a dusting of freckles and an Insta-Perfect vibe filled the feed, broken up by the occasional food post.

He was married to *that*? Of course he hadn't kissed me good morning. I was a good couple of inches shorter than her, my rounds were rounder, and my brown hair lacking her luster. She was probably a model. No one who looked that good in a bikini deserved to go unpaid for it.

I tossed my phone on the bed and fell face down, burying my head in my pillow. Checking Instagram had been a mistake. An utter disaster of comparison. I wouldn't be able to face Rhys now without comparing the ways I lacked to the woman he'd last loved. He'd said himself how he was still kind of hung up on her, so obviously he was making comparisons too.

My phone buzzed, and I picked it up.

Callie Winter: Insta??

I screenshot a picture of Rhys in front of the pub, alone, and cropped out his handle so Callie wouldn't stalk him online, then sent it to her.

Callie Winter: Mmmm. I can see why you chose to stop the man drought with this guy. Just try not to get hurt, okay?

Luna Winter: Says the girl who told me to kiss a Brit in the first place.

Callie Winter: I stand by my words. I just don't want you to get hurt.

I sighed. Neither did I.

SIXTEEN

I WENT DOWN TO THE TAPROOM AT THREE-THIRTY decked out in long underwear, a layer of clothes, a sweater, and a coat. I was taking no risks with this cold. I even doubled up on socks, fairly positive Rhys had an outdoors excursion in mind. My kerfuffle with the rental car in the ditch had taught me to be prepared for snow drifts that reached higher than my boots. Nothing in the world was as sickeningly uncomfortable as wet socks.

The pub was empty, except for Rhys waiting by the front door. It was eerily silent, except for Ned's tail thumping on the floor at Rhys's feet.

"Ready?"

"Why is it dead in here?" I asked, passing through the open doorway while Rhys held the door for me.

He was—praise the logger gods—wearing exactly what you'd expect a man to wear who was standing on a porch in Vermont or surveying the wild marshlands of Scotland. A plaid flannel beneath a quilted navy vest and heavy boots. "I'm locking up. I close the pub every day from three to six."

I stopped. I'd been in that taproom many times between

those hours over the course of the last week and never once had he closed or left the pub, even when it slowed or mostly emptied out.

I thought back to the early dinner I'd eaten a few days ago because my body was still not used to the new hours I was forcing on it. "When you made that sandwich for me a few days ago . . ."

"I was being nice," he muttered, pulling the door closed and locking it. Ned pawed the ground behind him, testing the snow. "Kitchen closes every day from three to six, but I don't bother clearing out unless I have to leave."

"Oh." A blush spread up my cheeks. "I'll remember that."

Rhys shrugged. "I don't cook unless I want to." He nodded toward the road. "Ruby and Hamish are waiting in the car."

He left me a little speechless while he moved toward a blue Range Rover idling on the street, and he paused halfway across to look back at me. His expression asked *are you coming?* but his eyes were screaming *kiss me again, please.* Or maybe that was just what I wanted to see. Either way, I planned to answer both of those questions favorably today, if I could manage it.

It was hard not to compare myself to the tall blonde he'd previously been married to, but since this was just a fling, there was no sense in ruining it with unsavory comparisons.

Now that I'd had a taste of what kissing Rhys was like, I craved more. More kissing, maybe some canoodling. I'd be happy with any time spent together before I left for the States. Rhys was not an object, and neither was I, but we were two people who'd had our hearts broken and discovered that kissing each other was one way to stem the pain. His affection didn't heal me, but it did throw duct tape over the cracks in my heart and hold it together a little better.

Rhys had MacGyvered my heart.

He opened the back door of the Range Rover, and I slid onto the seat. Ruby was there already waiting for me, and Hamish was in the driver's seat, a blue cap pulled over his blond hair. Rhys went around back to let Ned into the trunk, and the dachshund trotted over to Ruby to lick her ear before settling comfortably in the center of the trunk.

"You ready?" Ruby asked, her eyes sparkling as she rubbed the dog's slobber from her ear. She took a pair of shoes from the floor and handed them to me. "I borrowed them from Flo. You seemed about the same size. Want to try them on?"

It took a minute for the gleaming metal below the shoes to register. Ruby had handed me ice skates. I glanced up at Rhys when he got in the passenger seat. He shot me a look over his shoulder that screamed insecurity, then bent to secure his seatbelt, his eyes darting from me to the window and back.

"We're going ice skating?"

"If those things fit you, then yes," Rhys said.

Hamish hadn't said a word, but he pulled onto the road and started driving away from Snowshill. I tugged off my boots and slipped the ice skates on. They were snug, but I'd rather have them a bit tight than too loose.

"They fit," I said.

Ruby cheered and Rhys smiled. He leaned back a little, relaxing in his seat while Hamish took the narrow country roads like they were a wide motorway. I admired his bravery. I would be driving at least half this fast and probably with white knuckles if my California self was forced to take such winding, slushy lanes. We pulled onto a smaller lane not too far out of Snowshill and past a farm. The road bent away from the animals and up a mountainside studded with snow-capped trees. White, rolling hills spread out in every direction as far as I could see, making it feel like we were in the middle of a secluded, winter wonderland.

"Ice skating it is!" Ruby said. "But first . . ." She dragged out the word, looking expectantly at me like I was supposed to already know this.

"First, a tree," Hamish said, bored.

My head jerked toward the front of the car. "Really?"

"Really," Rhys confirmed. "Well, two trees. One for Hamish and one for the pub."

Hamish took us a little further up the mountain before pulling sideways on the road and putting the car in park. Everyone but me got out of the car quickly—I joined them belatedly. Wasn't it rude to leave his car in the center of the lane? No one else seemed bothered by it.

Ruby shot me a questioning glance.

"We're blocking the road."

"It's Hamish's property," she said, pulling Ned from the trunk and letting him jump to the ground.

Well, that explained things.

We trekked through the woods, the snow hitting above my ankles. The cold up here was crisp, cutting into my nose and chilling my exposed skin. Blue sky peeked through the tops of the trees, spreading wider as the forest thinned. Rhys paused and gestured for me to precede him. He rested the ax's handlebar against his shoulder, and I did a double take at the image he presented, rugged and refined, like a GQ Paul Bunyan. I itched to pull out my phone and snap a photo of him in his natural habitat.

"What?" he asked.

Could you blame me for staring? "I was just thinking about how natural you look holding an ax."

"Am I feeding into your Thor fantasies?"

"Now you are." He didn't have much in common with Chris Hemsworth except that they could both smolder with the best of them, but that didn't stop me from imagining Rhys wielding the Stormbreaker ax, wearing tight leather and a red cape.

"Stop imagining me in a costume, sicko," he murmured, passing me on the path.

I grinned. "Now I'm only gonna imagine it harder."

Rhys shook his head, walking ahead of me. We moved deeper into the woods until Ruby stopped at the perfect tree, and Rhys started hacking at the base of the trunk.

I pulled out my phone for real this time. The power behind Rhys's whacks against the trunk reverberated through the air, and I lined up the camera and took a shot. I would hold onto this memory forever. He looked up and smirked at my camera, so I took another picture. Callie was going to love that one.

"Signal's dodgy up here," Ruby said with a grimace.

"That's okay. I just want pictures. We should get one of the two of us."

Her eyes lit up, and she smoothed her ponytail. I framed us together on the screen and snapped a selfie. Our cheeks and the tips of our noses were red. It was charming on Ruby, but I looked like Santa's preferred reindeer.

Ruby gestured to Hamish, who then looked away, pretending he hadn't been watching her. I didn't care what Rhys or Ruby said—a man did not look at Ruby as much as Hamish did unless he had feelings for her or wanted to draw her later.

Hamish really didn't seem like the artistic type.

"Come on. Let's get one together," Ruby said, taking him by the arm and pulling him toward us.

"Without Rhys?" Hamish grumbled.

"I got one of Rhys already."

Ruby looked up at me with suspicion, but I was glad she didn't say anything. We posed again.

"You're making me do all the work *and* cutting me out of the photos?" Rhys asked. I hadn't realized the chopping had stalled until he spoke.

I lowered my phone. "I'm happy to chop the tree if you're tired of it."

His eyebrows shot up, and he held the ax toward me. "Be my guest."

There was a challenge in his raised eyebrows I definitely

wanted to accept. He'd already done a good portion of it. How hard could it be?

"Picture first!" Ruby called.

Rhys pretended to roll his eyes, but I could see he didn't really mind. He joined us, sliding his arm around my waist and leaning in. I could feel his heart pound where his chest pressed against my shoulder, even through the layers that separated us. Why didn't I take more of an opportunity last night to admire him? With the way we were steadily marching along friend territory, it wasn't looking like I would necessarily get a repeat opportunity to kiss him, which I was doing my best to be okay with. It was undoubtedly better for me if we ended the physical relationship now. I wasn't naïve enough to think I could kiss a man like Rhys for two solid weeks and walk away completely unscathed.

"You gonna snap the picture?" Ruby asked, holding her smile while pressed against my other side. Hamish probably didn't mind the extended pose with his arm around her, but I hadn't meant to let my mind run away from me.

My cheeks flushed, so I threw on a wide smile and took a few shots.

I slid my phone back into my pocket and Rhys held out the ax for me. "Fancy yourself better at chopping down the tree?"

"Not *better*, maybe."

"We'll go find the second tree," Ruby said, taking Hamish's hand. "I'll call you when we find it."

"I thought you said the signal wasn't good?"

"It's rubbish," she confirmed. "I meant yell. We'll literally call out when we find it."

Hamish whistled, and Ned obediently scurried after them, jumping through the snow.

I gripped the wooden handle of the ax, waited for Rhys to take a few steps back, then swung. The blade hit the tree trunk . . . about six inches above Rhys's massive dent.

"Take your time," he called to his cousin's retreating back, a grin flavoring his words. "With the way Luna's hitting, this might take us a while."

I squared my shoulders, widened my stance, and swung again. Darn. Didn't hit it that time, either. "I'm just getting a feel for the ax."

"You realize you hit way too low, right?"

"Yeah. And too high the first time. So now I know how to find the middle." *Please, please hit the middle.* I swung back and hit the tree again, striking it right in the center of Rhys's cuts. I spun, grinning in all my victory.

He shook his head lightly. "Lucky hit."

"Wanna bet?"

His gaze dropped to my lips. "Sure."

My stomach flipped. I pulled the ax out of the tree like I wasn't fazed by his attention. "What's the bet?"

"Best out of five gets to make dinner for the other person. *Best* meaning the most accurate hits."

"You say that like winning the chance to *make dinner* is a desirable outcome."

"Fine. You win, and I'll make you dinner."

"So . . . either way, you're making me dinner?"

"You make it hard for a guy to ask you out, Luna."

My stomach flapped with the wings of tiny turtle doves who seemed to like the idea of Rhys feeding me very much. "Okay, how about dishes, then? Loser cleans up."

"Sounds fair to me."

I swung the ax. Three of my five swings hit close enough to the mark to count, and I passed it off to Rhys. He squared his feet, pulled back the ax, then let it fly. Five times, five hits directly in the middle. *Bam. Bam. Bam. Bam. Bam.*

Obviously this had a great effect on my ability to keep my mouth closed and my eyes in my head. All of my lumberjack fantasies were coming to life before my eyes while watching Rhys in a thick flannel shirt and vest attack a Chritsmas tree with zeal. It toppled slowly, the last of the trunk cracking slightly as it broke.

"Shouldn't we call timber?" I asked.

"Not necessary in this situation." He grinned, his lips stretching over white, slightly uneven teeth. "It looks like I'm cooking for you."

"Oh, good, because I haven't had your cooking every single night since I arrived."

"Cheeky." He rested the ax against the fallen tree and stepped toward me. "This will be different."

"Because I won't have to pay you?"

He slid his arm around my waist, effectively making me forget how to breathe. "Because Ruby will be out, and the pub will be closed, so we will be alone. Does Monday work?"

"Alone." Like we were now. I liked the sound of it. I leaned into his hold and tipped my head back to see his eyes. "That could be fun, I guess."

"I'll be sure to avoid going to too much effort if you're going to exhibit such a lackluster response."

"What you call lackluster, I call trying to not appear too eager."

"You don't have to worry about that with me," Rhys said. "I know you aren't angling for a serious relationship."

My hands froze. "Of course not. Because there is an ocean between our houses, so how could I?"

His smile turned a little funny. "Did I say the wrong thing?"

"No, it's the truth." I scrunched my nose to soften the distaste that was probably evident in my expression. "I guess it just isn't fun to be reminded of it."

"You could extend your trip."

I scoffed. "My parents would love that. My mom has already been asking if I would change my plans and come back before Christmas."

His hands tightened on my waist. "Are you considering it?"

My chest swelled with longing for him, even though he was right in front of me. "And be there during the wedding? Not a chance."

"Because you could never be there and just choose not to attend the wedding?"

I scoffed comically loudly. "Of course not. That would require a level of maturity I haven't mastered yet." I closed my eyes. "It's a miracle I've held out against my mom and her efforts to bring me home early. If I go home, Aubrey will guilt me into attending the wedding, and I won't be able to say no."

"Who is Aubrey?"

"The bride."

His eyebrows shot up. "Gutsy of her to even ask."

"I understand that she wants to put the negative feelings behind us, but she stole my future. I'm not going to watch them vow to love each other for as long as they both shall live."

"She stole your future," he said slowly, as though considering the words. "If she hadn't met your ex-boyfriend, you think you would be the one marrying him in a few weeks?"

In a *few weeks*? Would I? We had moved up to Geyserville to start a life together, and I had waited a year for the ring he had given her after only a few months of being together. But that ring wasn't the one I'd pinned and absently looked at when he was around. Jake had never wanted to marry me, did he? If he'd wanted to marry me, he would have proposed. Clearly he was capable of bending one knee and saying the words, complete with a sunset at the beach.

I'd pegged Jake as a commitment-phobe to explain his hesitancy with getting engaged to me, but he'd known he wanted to commit to Aubrey in a matter of months. All he'd known in our five years together was that he wasn't *quite* ready.

My mind whirled and my stomach was sick anew, like I was just learning these facts for the first time. In a way, I was. In my running away from all things contentious, I hadn't given myself any space to face Jake or Aubrey's betrayals beyond hating them both. It made my stomach ill. Ugh. This was why I avoided these things, because peeling back my anger and looking at the situation objectively was painful and made me realize things that hurt.

I extricated myself from Rhys's hold and took a step back, but he reached for my hand. "I'm sorry. I said the wrong thing."

"No, not at all." I tried to smile, but I probably looked like a grimacing sloth—sorrowful eyes and slow movements. "I just hadn't thought of it that way really. I mean, Jake and I talked about marriage. He moved to my hometown because we wanted to build a life together, and that's not a small thing."

"That sounds pretty serious to me."

"Oh, we were definitely serious." I lifted one shoulder. "I just wasn't *the one*."

Rhys froze, like I'd tripped his breaker and he no longer functioned. Then he blinked at me. *Phew! Evidence of life.* "There are no such things as soulmates, Luna."

I gave a humorless laugh. "That's a little all-or-nothing, don't you think?"

"It's just a fact." He shrugged. "I thought I'd found my soulmate, too, but I was proven wrong."

"Because things didn't work out?" I couldn't deny the zip of displeasure flashing in my chest. He'd thought his wife was his soulmate. That wasn't an easy thing to come back from.

"Maybe. If she was my soulmate, then I'll never find someone to love like that again, and I don't want to think that's an indisputable fact."

"Because you loved her so much," I said. It wasn't a question. I understood. I had loved Jake with my entire heart at one point, and I didn't think the way things ended negated the feelings I'd really had for him—and him for me.

"Yeah, I loved her so much. Love isn't really a switchboard, where you can flip it on and off at will. And 'soulmate' is singular, which implies there is only one. I don't want to believe I missed my one shot already because my soulmate walked away."

"Maybe you didn't miss your shot with your one soulmate. Have you considered that she just wasn't *the one*?"

Rhys shook his head. "No, but lately I've been reevaluating my beliefs. I think love is too giving to be bogged down by particulars and forced into a box like that. I don't believe there's only one person for everyone. Do you?"

"I don't know." I lifted one puffy-coat clad shoulder. "But I'd like to believe there's someone out there for me."

"There is," he said with a simple confidence that surprised me. "I can't imagine a world where there aren't a hundred guys who'd love to be yours."

Mine. "You're being nice. Right now, I'm too much of a mess for anyone."

He gave me an appreciative sweep—layers of winter clothes and all—that brought a blush to my cheeks. "Beg to differ."

I smacked his arm playfully. "I meant *my life* is a mess, Rhys. Vacation Luna is carefree. Real Luna is depressed, dumped, and nobody's idea of a good time."

"Because you have more stress at home?"

"Not so much stress as just more memories and feelings," I said, as if it was a disturbing truth.

He shrugged. "Maybe it's not Vacation Luna that's carefree then. Maybe it's Snowshill Luna who has figured out how to let her past stay in the past and enjoy the present moment."

"Is that not the very definition of my problem? I'm a runner? I'm happy here because I ran from conflict and anything remotely uncomfortable and let it stay back in California?"

He looked at me for a long, hard moment. The snow around him was a stark contrast to his dark features and those brooding brown eyes I could so easily lose myself in.

"Rhys!" Ruby's voice yelled faintly. She must've been fairly far to sound so distant. "Found it!"

Rhys picked up the ax and took my hand, pulling me along the path.

"We're leaving the tree?"

"We'll come back for it." He snuck me a glance. "I don't let anything go easily once it's mine."

SEVENTEEN

RHYS AND RUBY TOOK OFF WITH EASE ON THE ROUND, frozen pond in the center of the clearing, giving me the impression ice skating was a somewhat regular staple in their winters. They both fumbled a little initially but each got their bearings quickly enough. Hamish, however, was the most surprising of all —an utter natural on skates, gliding about the small circle with his hands in his pockets like he was out for a stroll checking his cows or something else equally mundane. I hadn't expected such a quiet, perpetually bored man to be so graceful.

"Bump," Hamish said, pointing to the ice, and the other two avoided that particular section of the pond after that.

I sat on a folding chair just off the ice, pretending to tie my skates for the fourth time and avoiding nature's rink. Cold wind whipped over my hair, pulling loose strands over my face, but Ned didn't seem to mind the weather at all, happily lounging on the chair beside me. The laziest dog I'd ever met. At least he'd stopped growling at me.

"You want me to come hold your hand?" Ruby teased.

"Just so I can bring you down with me when I inevitably fall?" I did a quick sweep of the quiet countryside, the frosted trees encircling our small, open field. It was a veritable winter wonderland, completely at odds with the industrial indoor rink I was used to, the one that always played *The Hokey Pokey* at some point with flashing colored lights. "There's no railing."

"It's a pond," Ruby said.

Exactly. "How do you know it won't crack? We could all fall in."

"No one has fallen through the ice in at least four years," Hamish said.

Rhys looked at me quickly, probably realizing this answer wasn't what I wanted to hear. "The last accident was caused by stupidity, anyway. It wasn't nearly cold enough to keep the water frozen. Come on." He slid to a stop in front of me like a hockey player, and I was very pleased by the image. Until he held his hand toward me expectantly. "I'll help you warm up."

"Yeah, you will," Ruby muttered, passing us with effortless elegance. She shot me a look that I struggled to interpret. Her initial warning to steer clear of Rhys hadn't been subtle, so why was she so hard to read now?

Rhys shook his hand a little, stealing my attention again. "Come on. I won't bite."

I stood on shaky legs and slid my gloved hand over his. Rhys pulled me onto the ice, and my footing was wobbly. He put an arm around my waist. "Just until you get your bearings," he murmured. His voice in my ear sent chills over me that had nothing to do with the temperature outside.

We started slowly on the perimeter of the pond while Ruby and Hamish lapped us repeatedly. Within a few rounds, though, I was getting the hang of it. I pushed away from Rhys, and his hand dropped from my waist, but he stayed close.

"Truth or dare!" Ruby yelled, her long, red ponytail flying out behind her.

Hamish growled. "We're not children anymore, Rubes."

She glared playfully at him. "It's a time-honored skating

tradition, and now you're up first because you complained. Truth. Or. Dare?"

"Dare."

"Do a jump!"

Hamish rolled his eyes, and Rhys grinned. He tugged me to a stop and we moved back out of the way. Hamish circled the ice a few times, then did a sort of jump spin thing like they do in the Olympics.

"What the—"

Rhys leaned in. "Hamish's mum forced him to take lessons all through school. She had a thing for ice skating."

Ruby hollered her support, and we each started skating again. Hamish's cheeks were splotched with a blush, but he ducked his neck and continued as though he hadn't just wowed us all.

"Your turn," Rhys said.

Hamish looked at him. "Truth or dare?"

"Truth."

"Oh, come on, mate."

"Truth," Rhys reiterated. "I'm not licking the ice again."

Hamish grumbled and skated away.

"I'll have a go then," Ruby said, eyeing her cousin. "Truth: if you could have *anyone* play your jolly elf for the fair, who would you choose?"

His eyes cut to me and then away quickly. "We've gone over this."

"But you won't give me a clear answer. This is truth or dare, so you can't lie."

"Why can't you do it, Rubes?" Hamish asked. "You're elfy."

"I'll have to leave halfway through to go run the pub."

"You can't close the pub?"

"That's a lot of revenue lost if we do," she countered. "We're always busy on the night of the fair. It's probably our highest earner of the month, counting New Year's Eve."

Rhys frowned. "You aren't going to cook, though, right?"

Spots of color formed on her cheeks, and I recalled what Maggie, the old woman who hadn't poisoned me with arsenic, had said about the quality of food at the pub when Rhys had to step away from the stove for a time.

Ruby threw her arms out to the sides. "Why can't you just trust me?"

The silence was complete. No birds called across the sky. No other noises infiltrated this moment, the cousins squaring off in the center of the ice.

I glided away to give them more space, but my skate snagged on an uneven bit of ice and I lost my footing. I tried valiantly to regain my balance, my arms flailing and feet striking the ice for purchase. My feet shot out in front of me, and I went down hard on my back, the air knocked clean out of my lungs.

Blue sky stretched across my vision, unmarred by any clouds or structures. I was faintly aware of the hurried scraping of blades over ice. Rhys's head popped into my line of sight, concern evident in the bend of his eyebrows. "Are you hurt?"

"No." I sucked in tightly, my breath no longer choking, but slowly returning to normal. "Just struggling to breathe."

"I think you hit the bump," Hamish said helpfully from the other side of the pond. The bump he'd warned us about, of course.

Rhys took my hands and pulled me up, and I went into his arms easily. With his face only inches from mine, it was hard to regain a normal pulse. My heart beat out of my chest, pounding as though shouting that it wanted to be closer to Rhys—that any distance was too great.

Hamish came to a halt just before us, and I was ultra-aware of how we looked. Rhys holding me, his arms around my waist while I gazed with adoration into his smoldering eyes. I gave an awkward chuckle and tried to skate out of his arms to prove I was well, but held his hand to keep from falling again.

"You could do it," Hamish said, gesturing between us.

Do what? Be together? I didn't allow myself to voice the thought, but I couldn't help noticing the way my entire body seemed to nod in agreement to Hamish. Rhys was different. He was careful, thoughtful, giving. He enjoyed senior karaoke for the pure joy of watching others in their element, and he made sure foreign tourists who drove their car into a ditch were safely restored to their vehicles. He was a good man.

"She isn't a local," Rhys argued, cutting my daydreams to a stop.

Wait, what?

"She *will* still be here for the fair," Ruby said, frowning. "It's not the worst idea in the world."

"Not ideal, but she beats Tamsin," Hamish muttered.

Ruby narrowed her gaze. "How are you with children, Luna?"

Children? "I'm sorry, but what are you all volunteering me for?"

"To play Father Christmas's elf at the fair with Rhys."

Oh. Right. Because Rhys was always Santa Claus. Three pairs of eyes blinked at me expectantly, and I slid back a little. "Don't you think Flo fits the part better? She's a local," I asked, wiggling my toes in her snug ice skates.

"Who would bring Finn to see Father Christmas if his mum is playing the elf?"

"Right." Based on the way Finn had snuck upstairs looking for Santa, there was no way the kid would miss this opportunity.

"You do have the correct disposition," Rhys said gently.

"For a jolly little elf? Gee, woo me first."

Ruby skated to the edge of the pond and sat on the chair next to Ned before she bent to unlace her skates. "You don't have to do it, Luna. But it might be kind of fun."

They all waited expectantly, and I didn't miss the irritation still playing on Ruby's face. Was she still smarting from her disagreement with Rhys? I wanted to make her happy again.

"When is it?" I asked.

"Friday."

"Okay, I'll think about it."

Rhys nodded. "That's fine. Just let me know."

The ride back into town was quick and a little tense—things between the cousins didn't seem fully resolved yet. Hamish pulled in front of The Wild Hare and got to work untying one of the trees on the roof of his car while Rhys unlocked the front door and left it wide open. Ruby slipped inside, carrying Ned, and they disappeared upstairs. I stayed behind and helped the men get the tree inside and into the tree stand that waited for us in the taproom.

Hamish closed the door behind himself and left us in utter silence, which was thick and a little stifling. Rhys slipped past me to fetch water from the kitchen and returned to pour it into the base of the tree stand.

"Do you think the people of Snowshill will be annoyed if I play your elf and I'm not a local?" He'd mentioned as much earlier, at least.

He looked up at me from where he bent at the tree base. "No. Why would they care?"

"You said it earlier."

"Only because you shouldn't have to work on your holiday. You don't owe us anything, and you certainly don't need to work while you're here."

"I *am* an American. I won't be faking any British accent. I don't know . . ."

He smiled. "I'll just be happy to have help. Last year I did it alone, and it was chaos trying to keep the kids in the queue."

"Who used to play the elf before last year?"

Rhys's face went stonily blank, and I knew at once it had to have been his ex. Why else would he be weird about it? The number of similarities I shared with Jenna were beginning to be a bit much, almost like I was just trying to step into her shoes, with my yoga and kissing Rhys and hanging out with the karaoke book clubbers and now playing the elf to his Santa Claus. At some point it was going to get weird, wasn't it?

No, not at some point. It had already gotten there. The weirdness was upon us.

The silence in the room was proof, and my limbs were all itching for me to slowly back away. Maybe I could moonwalk from the room like Nick always did in *New Girl* when he didn't want to confront the situation, and Rhys would be so bewildered by my oddness he would let me leave.

"It's okay," I said breezily. "You don't have to talk about it. I'm just gonna—" I hooked a thumb over my shoulder, backing away from Rhys and still considering the moonwalk option. Was it heel-toe, or toe slide then heel up?

"Maybe it would be good to talk about," he said.

My stomach clammed up. My heart started racing. Talk? About his ex? About his feelings? I simultaneously desired and feared this conversation, and it created a weird flight response in me. Okay, so not *weird*, exactly. More like my go-to response.

"Pssh," I spit out, literally. "That's fine. I don't need to know."

But also, if I wasn't lying, I wanted him to *want* to tell me. I just didn't want to face the difficult situation.

"Luna, wait." Rhys straightened and ran a hand through his hair. "I was married."

I waited for him to continue, then realized he thought this was a bomb of new information. He was completely unaware Maggie had already dropped that bomb days ago. As much as I didn't like imagining Rhys and the blonde supermodel cutting a tall, white cake together or dancing beneath strings of fairy lights, it was part of his past.

I forced my feet to stay where they were. "How long ago did you get divorced?"

"Almost two years."

"So when I was warned to give you space because you were hung up on your ex . . ."

"Then Ruby—I'm guessing it was her that warned you at least—probably just wanted to spare you."

"Spare *me*?" It had really sounded more like she was trying to spare him.

"Yeah. I haven't dated much since Jenna left."

I don't let anything go easily once it's mine. Hadn't Rhys said that earlier when we were chopping trees? He'd let Jenna go, though, hadn't he?

"Until now," he whispered.

"Dating? Is that what this is?" I asked, trying to make a joke. It fell flat, unsurprisingly.

"I'm making dinner for you tomorrow, aren't I?"

He was. It was a date. He'd plainly said he was trying to ask me out. Wow, I hadn't realized I was the first person he'd dated after his divorce, or that it would feel like so much pressure. Or maybe that was why he'd chosen me. There couldn't be a lot of pressure with a woman who had a ticking clock on her time left in your life, right? Two more weeks and I was gone. Kaput. Our relationship: finito.

That must have been why he wanted to date someone who was about to leave, practice getting his feet wet with women again. Those deep, soulful brown eyes watched me with trepidation, like he was nervous about my response to all this. This man, who I might or might not stalk on Instagram for years to come, who kissed like a supernatural being and cared about little kids getting to sit on Father Christmas's knee, would probably never see me again after I left Snowshill, and we both knew it. His careful handling of my feelings was proof of his good heart.

"Well, you won a bet," I said. "Does it really count as a date?"

"Yes." He crossed the room and stopped before me. "I fancy

you, Luna, and I want to take you out. Will you go on a date with me?"

He *fancied* me? Swoon. "To the pub."

"Yes."

"Take me out on a date to *this very room*."

His mouth tipped into a smile. "It has some significance for us, doesn't it? We can choose to see it as romantic and not shabby, right?"

"True. It's where we met." I started ticking things off on my fingers. "Where I ruined your Christmas cake. Where you saved my life from a rogue bite of sausage. Where you kissed me for the first—"

"Excuse me, but I think you have that last one wrong. It was *you* who kissed *me*."

My mouth dropped open. "No. I specifically remember your hands around my waist first."

"But it was your lips on mine first."

"Does it really matter?"

He shrugged. "To me, it does." It was silent for a minute before he added, "I don't ever want you to think you were taken advantage of by the Hot British Guy."

Was that why he hadn't kissed me again? "What about the Lonely American Girl who was taking advantage of the grieving lumberjack pub owner?"

"Lumberjack?"

Oops. That part should have stayed inside my head. "You have a way with trees."

"I don't think you can consider me grieving anymore." His fingers curled around mine, lacing together much like they had at my bedroom door earlier that morning. If Rhys had a sign for desiring intimacy, I was starting to think this might just be it. "I felt ready to start dating again at least six months ago, but I just haven't found the right woman yet."

I tugged on his hand lightly, and he stepped closer. "I'm going to pretend that means I'm the right woman."

"There's no pretending on my end."

I closed the distance, my lips finding his easily as though they'd done so many times before. Rhys held me with sturdy strength, his hands sure and strong. My fingers tripped down his chest, feeling the hard planes of his stomach beneath his thick shirt and eliciting a groan from his throat. Rhys deepened the kiss, and—

Bark! Bark!

We both pulled back abruptly to the yapping sounds of Ned at our feet. Ruby stood at the bottom of the stairs, her copper eyebrows high on her forehead. "So, that's happening now, is it?"

Embarrassment rushed through me, splotching my neck and cheeks with heat, and I stepped back from Rhys, putting more distance between us. "I never lied to you, Ruby. I really had no intentions—"

"Save it," she said, shaking her head. She looked at Rhys. "My cousin is a big boy, and he can apparently take care of himself. Because heaven knows I'm not good enough to take over the kitchen if he gets his heart broken and everything falls to rubbish again."

Rhys's jaw ticked. "I don't need you mothering me."

"You sure? Because I'm kind of all you have."

"Not anymore." He ran a hand over his face. "You're gone more evenings than not, which makes it a little difficult to depend on you now."

She scoffed. "Well, forgive me for trying to have a life of my own *outside* this pub."

They stared at one another, their eyes saying far more than I knew or could interpret at this point.

I stepped toward the stairs. "I'm just going to change. I'm still wearing like seventeen layers."

Rhys nodded.

Ruby left, slamming the front door on her way out.

"Give Nan my love," Rhys yelled to the door, bending down to pick up Ned and rub him behind the ears.

I was halfway up the stairs when I finally let out a whoosh of breath. This thing between us was a holiday fling, regardless of how much I'd wanted to avoid that, and I would do good to remember it. I didn't want my heart broken at the end of this, either.

EIGHTEEN

WHEN I WENT DOWN TO THE DINING ROOM AT THE END of the evening for something to eat, I was surprised to find the knitters gathered in a circle near the fire. Hamish sat at the bar, eating a savory pie that smelled like heaven, but everyone else was working away with their needles and yarn, discarded plates and half-full glasses sprinkling the tables around them.

"Didn't they meet in the morning last week?" I asked Hamish, leaving an empty stool between us. He seemed like the kind of man who appreciated his space. Unless it was Ruby—then he probably wanted zero space at all.

"That was the morning crew." He jerked his head toward the knitters. "This is the evening group."

I looked at them again. "Except it looks like the same people."

He shook his head. "There was drama a few years ago. Some people couldn't make it in the morning because of their work schedules or something, but not everyone could do evenings. They split, and each group meets every other week."

"So some of them meet every week."

"Yeah."

"Luna!" Maggie called, waving enthusiastically.

I waved back, then greeted Frank and a few of the other familiar faces.

Rhys must have heard her call my name, because he came out of the kitchen a moment later, wiping his hands on a towel. "You hungry, Luna? What can I get you?"

"Cottage pie, extra chips?"

He nodded, and his gaze cut to Hamish. "Are you keeping the knitters in line?"

"No outbursts yet, boss. Unless you count undue excitement after seeing Luna."

"Undue?" I asked, scoffing. "I think it was a perfectly reasonable level of excitement. In fact, I'm going to hang out with them while I wait for my dinner." I slid from the stool.

"Careful or they'll recruit you," Hamish muttered.

"It's fine. I don't knit."

Somehow, though, that minor fact didn't deter the members of the Snowshill Knit-Owls from attempting to make me join their ranks.

"Don't worry, dear," Maggie said, pulling an extra set of knitting needles and a ball of yarn from her oversized bag. "I can teach you."

"My dinner will be out soon," I said, as she thrust the needles and yarn into my hands. "I just wanted to say hi. How are you?"

"I've been better. The cold weather is never easy on my joints." Her fingers deftly moved the yarn around her needles as though they meant to belie her point. Clacking of plastic or metal needles around the circle moved at varying speeds and continued uninterrupted.

"I hear that," a man said across the group, shaking his bald head. "Nothing like the winter to remind your bones just how old you are."

Nods joined from around the circle in general murmurs of

agreement, except from the woman who looked closer to forty than sixty.

"Have any of you tried yoga?" I asked. "It can be really good for mobility and keeping your body from growing too stiff."

The bald man laughed. "You mean the stretches Rhys's wife used to do? Don't think you could get me off the ground if I tried that." His laughter grew wheezy until he took a drink from his cup and resumed his knitting.

Wow. Did everyone know Jenna? I couldn't help disliking the present, inaccurate descriptor of *Rhys's wife*. I pasted a smile on my face. "Not floor yoga. Chair yoga."

Blank stares met me around the circle.

"None of you have tried it? I used to teach a chair yoga class at a senior center in San Francisco, and my students showed a great response to regular stretching. It's such a simple routine, you could do it every morning when you wake up."

"Chair yoga?" Maggie repeated. "So I would sit the entire time?"

"Yes." I nodded. "No need to find someone to pick you back up from the floor if your joints are weak. You need a chair without sides, and that's it."

The Knit-Owls looked at each other's chairs and came to the same conclusion at the same time, apparently, because they lifted their aging faces toward me.

"You can teach us, then?" Frank asked. I wondered briefly why he didn't offer his granddaughter for the job. Proud grandpas like that were usually so confident in their posterity's skills.

"I could, if you want me to. We need a location first and a good time to meet."

"Here," the bald man said. "Now."

"Not *now*," Maggie complained, her eyes wide. "I'm not dressed for it."

"We'll need to clear it with Rhys first, anyway," Frank said.

Rhys materialized at my side, a steaming plate of food in his hands. The smell of thick cut fries and savory pie made my mouth water. "What are they trying to rope you into?"

I met his gaze, and all thoughts of cottage pie left my mind at once. "Just a little yoga class. I offered."

"But can't they just watch your videos online?"

I shrugged. That was true, but I enjoyed teaching. I looked forward to the possibility of this chair yoga class far more than I was willing to admit. "Can we use this space? What are the steps for securing a club in the taproom?"

"I need to check the calendar," Rhys said. "And everyone has to agree to order something."

There it was—the way Rhys made the clubs financially worth holding in the pub. I handed Maggie her yarn and needles so I could eat. "I'll work out a time with Rhys and let you know."

She beamed at me, and I couldn't help feeling the warmth of reciprocating joy. The Christmas decor around the room and the blazing fire in the hearth created such a cozy atmosphere that I thought I could probably never leave this taproom again and be completely satisfied. Snow fell lightly on the other side of the dark window, and merry chatter and tinkling knitting needles made up the din in the background, meshing with the soft holiday tunes playing on the overhead speakers.

"The only thing your pub is missing is a *decorated* tree," I said. "It's basically Christmas personified. My parents would absolutely love it here."

"You could invite them to come out," Rhys said easily, lifting a shoulder.

"I wish." I sat on the stool and was surprised when Rhys sat on the one beside me. We still left an empty space next to Hamish. "There's no way my parents could leave their animals so last-minute. They have no one set up to watch them. Lately, one of their new horses has been getting out, so I doubt my dad would be willing to take a vacation right now, even if he could find someone to help."

"It's the sort of thing they plan much in advance?"

"Like a year in advance," I joked. Though it wasn't that far off. "I'll just have to send them all the pictures."

I pulled out my phone to snap a few of the dining room and the knitting group when I noticed a text message on my phone.

Edward Brumsworth: My sister will be in town on Friday. Lunch at the manor? She cannot wait to meet you. x

I let out a quiet sound, somewhere between a shriek and a yip, startling the men on either side of me.

"What was that for?" Rhys asked, his brown eyes wide.

"I get to meet Stella Fit."

"You mean Stella Brumsworth?" Hamish asked, then made a gross spitting sound.

Why did he *always* do that?

"I guess so. She's Edward's sister." I went to reply, then looked up at Rhys, who was watching me through a stony mask. "What time is the Christmas fair? Will I have time for lunch that same day?"

"You'll have time for whatever you'd like," he said crisply.

I lowered my phone, sensing the great rivalry between the men hadn't calmed much in the days since Edward was in The Wild Hare. "I would like to do both, if it works out."

"Then do both."

"Rhys, what time does the fair start?"

"Five."

I set my phone on the counter and picked up a fry. "It's a business meeting," I said carefully. "Stella Fit is one of the biggest names in yoga wear, and she wants to meet about a collaboration. Which means I'll rep her products on my page and she gets some free advertising to my viewers."

"I do comprehend the meaning of a collaboration. But I wonder if you realize you're doing business with a snake."

"I'm not really doing business with Edward, though. He's just the liaison connecting us."

Rhys shrugged, his body saying he didn't care, but his face saying he did. Hamish studiously ignored us. I dug my fork into the pie and took a bite.

Rhys got up and rounded the bar before disappearing into the kitchen.

Hamish stood as well and wiped his mouth before putting the napkin on the counter beside his plate. He looked at me for a minute, and I wondered if he was trying to decide whether or not he wanted to speak to me. He sucked in a long breath before letting it out again. "You know, I don't think he was talking about just Edward."

He walked away before I could question him. Rhys had told me Stella wasn't that awful, but was that who he meant? I was descended upon by a flock of aging knitters as Hamish made his escape.

"Arthur can't make it to yoga if it's to be on Monday," Maggie said, pointing to the bald-headed man putting his knitting away in a canvas bag. "Wednesday would be best. In the evening, if Rhys has the place free."

Rhys appeared at the bar and tossed a hand towel over his shoulder. "Wednesday," he said, clearly having heard Maggie. "Time?"

"Eight."

He nodded. "You'll all have to order dinner."

"Don't we always, love?" Maggie asked, as though his stipulation was the silliest thing in the world. It was rather brilliant of him, actually, to create a space people liked to use for their functions and clubs. It gave him a steady stream of revenue each week that could be relied upon, and he didn't close the pub to other patrons, so he always seemed to have more than just the clubs anyway.

Then there were the regulars, like Hamish and Frank, who likely kept Rhys in business with their habits alone.

I finished my free dinner—thanks to my decorating work—and slid off the stool. The taproom was empty, but Rhys was still back in the kitchen, and I felt I shouldn't go back there and bother him during business hours. It just seemed unprofessional. I opened my phone instead and typed out a quick text to Edward.

Luna Winter: Lunch sounds great. I can't wait to meet your sister, too!

Edward Brumsworth: Brill. See you Friday at two. x

I stared at the phone. What was with the x? I thought the first time around it was a typo, but unless Edward had a compulsion to end his messages like this for the sake of OCD, I didn't understand it.

Rhys came out of the kitchen and paused when he found me looking at my phone. "I'm about to lock up," he said. "Want to watch a film?"

A wide grin spread over my lips. "Which one?"

He spread his arms a little, the sleeves on his plaid shirt rolled up to his elbows and displaying nicely shaped forearms. "Anything you want." His mouth curved into a wider smile. "As long as I have it already."

"Do you have a favorite Christmas movie?"

"Probably *Elf*. Or *Home Alone*."

"Oh, yes! That one. I love watching a child fend off a couple of grown convicts with intelligent little pranks."

Rhys's head tilted a little to the side. "I can't tell if that was sarcasm or not?"

"It's a completely unrealistic premise, but I love the movie."

"*Home Alone* it is, then. Stay here and I'll fetch the telly."

"You'll what? Is it mobile?" I asked, following him to the stairs.

"I figured you would prefer to watch the movie downstairs, beside the fire. We still need to decorate the tree, too."

I had plans tonight to film another segment for the Luna-Moon channel, but that could be put off for another day if it meant a Christmas movie in front of a fireplace with the resident lumberjack pub owner. Or *any* time spent with Rhys, if I was being honest with myself. I was starting to feel comfortable around him in a way that made me nervous and content simultaneously. He was easy to be with, and his hand seemed to fit easily over mine without any prompting on my part.

Rhys carried his television downstairs and set it up against the wall on a table. It only took a minute to find the movie on his cloud system and start it while I dragged the two most comfortable chairs in front of the screen.

"I guess I didn't think this through," he said, looking from me to the chairs. "At least upstairs the telly sits in front of my bed. It would have been much more comfortable."

I swatted his arm. "And yet, you brought it down here. You're such a gentleman."

"Yeah, for now," he murmured, leaving the room. My heart jumped up to follow him but I commanded it to calm the heck down. He came back with a box of tree decorations, and we spent the next hour setting up the tree, then sitting in front of the movie with mugs of steaming hot chocolate. I looked at Rhys on the tufted leather armchair beside mine. His dark eyes were rimmed with charcoal lashes, and his face was set into a consistent, small smile while Macaulay Culkin ran around his house setting up bricks on ropes, dancing mannequins, and fixing a Michael Jordan cutout to a small train to make him glide.

"Is it boring you?" Rhys asked, not removing his eyes from the screen.

I had a sudden surge of affection for him that squeezed my chest and pushed all the breath from my lungs. I leaned against the side of the chair and looked at him. "No. I was just thinking about how nice it would be if Christmas wasn't so soon, and we could stay in this little magical holiday world for a little longer."

He went really quiet, and I immediately regretted my words. What man wanted to hear such a blatantly longing exclamation from their holiday fling?

I sat up straight in the chair and put my hot chocolate on the table to my side. "Not that I expected this to go anywhere, obviously. You live in Snowshill and I'm from Geyserville. So *clearly* we aren't pursuing a relationship or anything." I cringed. "Not that I'd want a relationship."

"Good to know," he said.

Had I offended him? His voice was so quiet, and his eyebrows were doing that funny thing where they bunched together softly. Rhys's lack of speaking was like a serum that forced me to fill in the space and try to fix my misspoken words. I laughed lightly. "I mean, in any other universe, if we weren't both reeling from past breakups and didn't live on opposite sides of the world, then maybe I'd consider it."

"Reeling, huh?"

"You did mention you were still a little hung up on your ex."

"And you flew across the world to escape the wedding of yours."

"So, like I said. Reeling."

He watched me quietly for a minute, then reached across the small gap between our chairs and laced his fingers through mine. "Tell me something no one else knows about you."

I half-expected him to run for the front door and out into the snow to escape the train wreck that was this conversation, so his request surprised me, and it took a moment to recalibrate. "No one?"

"Not the ex, not the ex-best friend. Something about you no one knows."

"Hmmm. Okay. If I share this, do you promise to keep my secret?"

"Of course."

I received strength from his hand squeezing mine. My body screamed *run away! Do not engage in personal conversation!* but I fought the impulse to flee. I understood on a logical level that the better I got to know Rhys, the harder it was going to be to leave him behind after Christmas, but it wasn't enough to stop me from wanting to be near him now.

His thumb ran over my skin lightly, and I quit caring about how hard it would be later. That was a problem for the Luna of December 29th. The Luna of today was going to enjoy Rhys's company.

I cleared my throat. Okay, something about me that no one else knew. "I love doing yoga, and I really love sharing that love with the world."

He smiled. "Something they *don't* know, Lu."

My chest constricted. Lu. Only my friends and family called me that, but I think I loved hearing it in Rhys's voice most of all. "Right. What they don't know is that I don't think it's something I want to do forever."

"You want to quit your channel?"

"No. Yes. Maybe? I don't know." I shrugged. "My sister has picked up on my feelings a little, actually. She's going to school at UCLA, and she has a friend who runs a yoga studio down there. He's looking for another teacher and kind of offered me the job. I have to meet with him, of course. But it would mean teaching in a classroom again instead of on the internet."

"Would that make you happy?"

"I don't know. I'd love to be near my sister, but then I'd have to move to LA." I pulled a face. I enjoyed visiting Callie down there, but the traffic alone was reason enough for me to not want to make it my home. I was used to the winding two-lane roads and plenty of land and sky we had up in the wine country.

"Which is far from your parents?"

"Yeah, but that's not the part that bothers me. My parents are busy, but I would still see them. I've been leaning toward taking the job because I think it could be good to get out of Geyserville for a while. Everywhere I go reminds me of the life I thought I was going to have with Jake."

"So maybe it's a good move until you're over him."

My stomach tightened, and not because of my feelings for Jake. I squeezed Rhys's fingers and looked into his broody brown eyes. "I don't think I need to get over Jake anymore. I'll always hate what he did to me because of how it made me feel. He couldn't commit to me after five years, but like four months into dating Aubrey, he popped the question. That has done a number on my confidence, and it's pathetic that it's taken me this long to get over it—"

"It's not pathetic," Rhys said calmly. "It's how you're feeling, and that's valid."

I closed my eyes and sank my head back against the chair. "I don't know how to come back from feeling like something is so unequivocally wrong with me. Because I can attest that Jake isn't a major scumbag. He didn't cheat on me. He wasn't rude or degrading. He didn't always listen . . . he pushed me to make my channel more than it was, that wasn't something I wanted initially. But I'm not upset with how that turned out, either."

Rhys watched me quietly, and I sat up tall again. Now that he'd opened the door to conversation, it was like I couldn't seem to get enough off my chest. "If my life was a romcom, I would be the girl left behind because the hero and the heroine finally met and fell in love. But there's nothing wrong with the hero in those movies. He's lovely. Which makes it hard to hate him, but it also makes me hate him more."

"I don't watch enough romcoms, I'm afraid, so I'm lacking context here," Rhys said. "But I think I understand what you mean. Moving out of Geyserville would be good for you."

"I think it might," I said, my voice small and unsure. Not to escape a man I loved, but to move forward with my life. The distinction was important, because one of them was running away and the other was running toward something. The problem was, I didn't know if living in LA and teaching yoga to low-key celebrities was really the answer I was looking for, either. "I just don't know what to do."

Rhys tugged my fingers until I stood. "You have time to decide." His hands slipped around my waist and pulled me down onto his lap, and I sank back against him, my body and mind exhausted from opening up when it was something I so rarely did. His arms tightened around me and his lips pressed a kiss into the skin below my ear.

"But for now," he whispered, driving chills down my neck. "You get to stay right here with me."

NINETEEN

DATING A MAN WHO OWNED A PUB AND THEN GOING ON A
dinner date to that pub looked a lot like a couple having dinner
in early retirement years. It was four o'clock, the sun was still
shining brightly through the windows, and we were sitting down
to a romantic, candlelit dinner in the center of his taproom. I'd
thrown on the red dress I'd brought on the off chance that I
would choose to see a play or an opera in London. I hadn't left
Snowshill—or the pub—much since arriving, but at this
moment, I couldn't quite be mad about that.

"It smells heavenly," I said, inhaling scents that were both
familiar to me and foreign for this setting, though I couldn't
quite figure out why.

Rhys came around the bar in a button-down shirt tucked into
slacks, carrying a platter of food. He set it on a nearby table
before unloading the dishes in front of me containing meat,
onions, cilantro, tortillas, and salsa.

I laughed. "Tacos!"

"We probably should have worn casual wear."

True, tacos were messy. "Where did you get the recipe?"

"Google. I did some research though. You'll have to tell me how these compare to what you miss from home."

I took a corn tortilla and loaded it up on my plate. I sank my teeth into the folded taco and moaned.

Rhys's smile beamed light like a flood lamp. "You mean they're okay?"

"*Okay*?" I scoffed, then took another bite. "I can live here. There is absolutely nothing keeping me in California now that I know you can cook carnitas like this."

"Next stop: carne asada."

"Oh, stop there or you're going to get a marriage proposal."

Rhys looked up from where he was assembling his taco. "Noted. The way to Luna's heart is through tacos."

I wasn't going to burst his bubble by sharing that I had a shirt announcing that very thing to the world. It wasn't exactly a state secret.

Rhys's phone vibrated loudly on the table, and he reached for it and hit the silence button. We returned to our tacos, but his phone started buzzing again immediately.

"You can answer that." I had a firm belief that since almost no one enjoyed talking on the phone, if someone called twice in a row it *must* be an emergency.

He reached for the phone and slid it on. As soon as the person started talking, Rhys's eyes cut to me and away.

"Have you called 999?"

Silence.

"Of course, I'll take you. Are you in a position to give me five minutes to shut down the kitchen?"

More silence. Rhys stood and looked around, like he was trying to find the phone in his hand. He stilled again. "Yes. Of course. See you soon." He clicked off and looked at me. "I need to go."

That sounded like an actual emergency, and I didn't like that I'd been right in my prediction. "What can I do to help?"

Rhys cupped his hand around the flames on the tall, white tapers and blew them out. "Frank fell. I need to drive him to hospital."

Rhys started gathering plates, and I put my hands on his wrists. "You go. I can manage things here."

He looked up and nodded. "Yes. Good. I'll go, then." He retrieved his keys from behind the bar and ran for the door without further hesitation, out into the snowy cold. I couldn't help the anxiety that fluttered in my stomach for Frank and what sort of injury his fall had created.

Rhys likely felt the same degree of stress, since he hadn't even stopped for a coat.

It didn't take long to clear the table and put the food in the fridge for later. My stomach had lost its desire for more tacos—which was saying something—so I pulled out the mop and set to cleaning the floors (after I changed into jeans and a t-shirt, because cleaning in a dress was simply impractical). I filled a glass with ice and Dr Pepper, drinking it between chores. My mind fretted less when I was busy, so I seamlessly shifted to dusting the mantel and the window frames, clearing a cobweb from the light fixture in the center of the taproom, and wiping down all the tables and countertops.

I brushed the loose strands of hair from my face and pulled out my phone to see a text had come in.

Hot British Guy: I won't make it back in time to open for dinner. Can you put a closed sign in the window of the front door? They're stacked beneath the register.

Luna Winter: Absolutely. How is Frank doing?

Hot British Guy: He hit his head and broke his arm. His arm is set now and dealt with, but they want to keep him overnight for monitoring.

I "loved" his text message and set down my phone.

Ruby let herself into the pub while I was rummaging beneath the till. I looked up and waited to see if she was still angry, but she smiled. If anything, her beef with Rhys was concentrated on him, and I knew better than to get in the middle of someone else's family drama.

I grimaced. "Rhys told me where to find the closed sign, but I'm not having much luck."

I moved aside a stack of receipts again as if the sign would materialize on a second sweep of the space, and my fingers caught on the edge of a torn paper. I pulled it out and stilled. It was a photo ripped down the side, clearly with the intent of removing the bride. The groom—Rhys, in a stellar tux that fit him like a hand-sewn glove—was missing the arm that was likely slung around his wife's waist. Ruby and Hamish stood to his other side. Rhys beamed at the camera, a fact which tore through my stomach with neon green envy, but neither of the other two faces showed as much joy.

Ruby stomped the snow from her shoes at the door and unwound her scarf. She came to my elbow and looked down at the photo in my hands. "Before you go thinking Rhys was some sort of angry dumpee, you should know I tore the photo."

"Why?"

"Because I was angry on his behalf." She grimaced. "He didn't appreciate it, though. He didn't want to be petty, but after I tore up the photo he couldn't keep it on the register anymore."

Why would he want a photo of his wedding on display after the divorce? Unless he was more concerned with what the ex-wife would think than any desire to look at her day after day. "Do you mean when Jenna came back and found it missing, he was worried she would be hurt to find it gone?"

"I don't really know what his thought process was. He was really silent in those days. Just a total wallowing wreck."

The neon green envy thickened. Not sure why I hated so much that Rhys had had such deep feelings for his ex. He'd married her, so of course he'd loved her. I knew him well enough now to know he wouldn't toy with a woman's emotions. He certainly wouldn't marry anyone he didn't love entirely.

I ran my finger along the frayed edge of the photo. Maybe I was more worried he loved her still—which shouldn't affect me since I was only a fling and nothing could come of such a long-distance relationship.

Ruby looked from me to the register. "Why do you need the signs?"

"You haven't heard from Rhys?"

She shook her head, ducking to pull out a red sign that read CLOSED. Where on earth did she find it? "My phone's dead."

"Frank fell and hit his head, so Rhys ran him to the hospital."

Ruby straightened, her gaze widening. "Why didn't you lead with that?" She pulled out her phone, then remembered it was dead and swore. "Can I use your mobile?"

"Of course." I fished it from my pocket, found Rhys's number, and handed it to her.

"Hey. Yeah, it's Ruby. He hit his head?" Ruby was silent for a minute. "But he'll be fine? What about . . . is she coming?" She let out an irritated groan and rolled her eyes. "Sure. Okay. Love you."

Ruby hung up and handed my phone back before sweeping past me. "I have to go. I should be there with them. I need to call a cab or something. I drank too much during my class. We're meant to pour only a *small* portion of wine into the dish, but I'm not about to waste an entire bottle, am I?" She leaned in and whispered. "I've always been a bit of a lightweight. But I don't drink that often really." She paused and looked to the ceiling in thought. "Or Hamish owes me a ride—"

"I can give you a ride if you tell me where to go." She had to be sober enough for that at least. She didn't seem too tipsy. "My rental is in the car park already."

Ruby looked at me shrewdly. "Okay, yeah. Let's go." She stopped and pointed right at my face. "But make sure you don't veer onto the wrong side of the road, American woman."

"I'll do my best," I muttered, hoping her verbiage wouldn't lodge the Lenny Kravitz song lyrics in my brain for the rest of the week. Some songs just had extra staying power, didn't they? *American Woman* was one of those for me.

We got into my little Kia, and Ruby directed me pretty effortlessly to the hospital. We only missed our turns twice, and with my slow driving it was kind of a feat that we missed any roads at all.

"What class are you taking?" I asked while we got out of the car. I reached into the back seat for Rhys's coat and the paper bag of tacos I'd assembled and individually wrapped in foil for Rhys and Frank. He'd left without a proper winter coat or dinner, so I hoped to rectify both of those things. We started walking toward the entrance.

She looked at me quickly. "I can't tell you."

"Why not?"

"Because I don't want Rhys to know."

"That you're taking a class, or what you're learning? It's cooking of some sort, right?" Either that or a wine pairing class. Was that even a thing here?

"Don't tell Rhys." She pressed her fingers to her temples. "Oh, I can't think straight. Just don't tell Rhys. I can explain later."

When I had said almost the exact same thing to her, she hadn't listened and told Rhys I wanted dinner delivered to my room. But I could keep a secret better than her. I wasn't really mad about that anyway, since it had worked out favorably for me.

So, Ruby was taking classes she didn't want her cousin to

know about. Interesting. Was that what she'd been doing on all these late nights out? No, because it was early afternoon now and she was just returning.

We found our way inside and to the waiting room. The nurses wouldn't let us back into Frank's room when we said we weren't close kin, and Ruby pouted. "Call Rhys, maybe?"

I sent him a text instead.

Luna Winter: I've brought Ruby. We're in the waiting room and she'd like to speak with you if you think you can get away for a minute.

Hot British Guy: Be out soon.

I sank onto the vinyl chair beside Ruby, clutching the aromatic carnitas on my lap, Rhys's coat flung over the seat next to me. "He's coming. But why did they let him back there and not us?"

"Because he's family. Well, sort of. I mean, he must not have explained the divorce or they wouldn't have let him in the room, probably. They can be so strict here about family rules. But with Frank's age, I guess it's not a bad thing to be extra careful, right?"

I really didn't hear much of what she said beyond the first little bit.

She looked up at me sheepishly. "Oh. You probably didn't know, did you?"

"Know what? That Rhys and Frank are related? Nope."

"Frank is Jenna's grandfather." Ruby's eyes widened to a comical degree, and she grasped my arm. "Oh my gosh, I forgot to tell you Rhys called her. Her parents live in Australia, so Frank doesn't have anyone else close by."

My mind was reeling with this *fun* new piece of information when Rhys stepped through the glass doors into the waiting room, still in his slacks and blue button-down shirt, though he'd rolled up his sleeves and undid the top button of his shirt.

"You're dressed up," Ruby said, her gaze narrowed. "Why?"

Rhys's eyes cut to me, then back to his cousin. "Just a date. Frank called me in the middle of it."

Or the very beginning, if it was meant to last as long as I'd been hoping it would. I cleared my throat and handed him his coat. "How is Frank?"

"Thank you." He looked from the coat to me. "He's going to be fine," Rhys said, but his tense shoulders spoke to his discomfort. He must have been much more worried than he let on, because his back looked stiffer than a stale baguette.

"They won't let us back there," Ruby said. "Give him our love."

"Only two guests in the room at a time, I believe."

"I'd thought it was because I wasn't kin." Ruby looked up. "Two guests? So she's already—"

The doors opened into the waiting room again and a tall woman with long, perfectly wavy blonde hair stepped out in a sleek olive romper that probably cost more than the entire contents of my closet combined. Her heels clicked across the floor with purpose, the sort of woman who knew she was beautiful and couldn't be bothered by us lesser mortals.

Except, she was walking directly toward us, her sharp eyes on Rhys. Not that I blamed her for staring. He was so perfectly disheveled, like GQ gone rogue.

And why did Ruby stop talking? Her eyes were narrowed into slits.

Oh, gosh. Recognition dawned on me like a cool sluice of water down my back. This was the woman I'd seen on Rhys's Instagram page. Jenna, the ex-wife. Ruby's dislike was nearly palpable, and I could see why. It wasn't enough for Rhys to be super-hot and single and a little hung up on his ex. His ex had to be Jessica freaking Rabbit personified, with platinum hair and blood red nails that landed lightly on Rhys's bicep posses-sively, despite how *she'd* been the one who cheated and left him.

"They took Grandad back for the MRI."

Oh, *gosh*. Even her voice was velvety smooth. She must sing like a goddess.

Rhys nodded. When his gaze swung back to me, it was hard, his brown eyes reaching a whole new level of brooding I'd yet to see on him. If men could level up in broodiness the way we used to level up in Mario on the N64, then Rhys had reached Bowser status. I just wanted to take my unassuming Toad self out of the picture completely.

Or at least out of this waiting room.

I wasn't a proponent of comparison in general. Like I taught my students all the time back when I was teaching in a studio, there was no sense comparing your level to the person on the yoga mat beside you. You don't know how long they've been practicing or if they were a once-a-weeker or a daily participant. But *this*? Man, this comparison was out of my control. We were like a Souped Up Barbie standing next to a Cabbage Patch Doll. I had the round cheeks and soft dimples, even. It was impossible to guess what Rhys ever saw in me when he had *that* to compare me to.

Ugh. Was Rhys comparing us as terribly as I was? Just swallow me up now, dirty linoleum floor, I beg you.

"You're staying around, then?" Ruby asked.

"For a while, yeah," Rhys said. There was something off about his voice, and I didn't want to analyze it too closely or try to figure out why seeing his ex had such a great effect on him. In my perfect world, Rhys wouldn't even be bothered by Jenna, because his heart had slowly filled with me. But this wasn't my perfect world. It was real life.

Real life was the worst sometimes.

"We brought you dinner." Ruby nudged me in the side with

her elbow, and I lifted the paper bag as if her elbow had hit a switch that controlled my arm.

"Tacos."

Jenna made an *awww* sound like I was a sweet kitten and not a full-grown woman. "That's so thoughtful. Rhys ordered in from that Thai place down the road. But Grandad might want to try this."

Rhys finally took the bag from my outstretched hand. "I'd love a taco. Thanks, Lu."

Ruby looked at me with widened eyes and mouthed *Lu?*

I took her by the arm and smiled too broadly for the situation. My Cheshire Cat grin was breaking hospital waiting room etiquette, I was sure of it. It was too sober a place for so many teeth. "We'll get out of your hair."

Jenna looked from Rhys to me, a small, nearly inconsequential line marring her perfect, otherwise smooth forehead. A look flashed in her eyes that I couldn't quite pinpoint. Her grip seemed to tighten on his arm, and I saw fresh possessiveness wash over her like a tidal wave. "You aren't going to introduce me to your friend, Rhys?"

He pointed the bag of tacos at me. "Luna." Then waved it toward his ex-wife. "Jenna."

If an introduction could scream how loudly he didn't want to perform it while simultaneously shouting he'd like to be anywhere but here right now, that was it. We hadn't even earned titles to go along with our names—maybe because Rhys didn't know how to classify his relationship with me. *Ex-wife, meet my temporary holiday fling that I'm using to get you out of my system.* Insecurity washed through me anew, and the blush that accompanied Rhys's dismissal flooded my cheeks. I ducked my head, but not before noticing Jenna's triumphant smile as she perused me from head to toe.

"LunaMoon," she said. "I thought I recognized you. Welcome to Snowshill."

"Thank you." I didn't know whether to be disturbed or flattered that she knew who I was. But Maggie had mentioned that Jenna used to perform yoga at the pub, so it shouldn't have been a major surprise that she'd recognize me, I guess. I couldn't help but feel she had a leg up, though.

"We should be going now," Jenna said again. "I don't want Grandad returning to an empty room."

No, she wanted to be in that empty room right now with Rhys and the tacos he'd made for me.

Ruby took my arm and pulled me toward the exit before I could gawk any longer. When we reached the car, she let out an exasperated sigh. "Don't take that personally, Luna. He always becomes putty when she's around."

Like that explanation made the situation any better? I slid into the driver's seat and dropped my forehead against the wheel. Ruby rubbed circles on my back. Her comfort was saying everything she was too nice to speak out loud: that she'd told me so when I first arrived, and I would have done better to listen to her.

"I know," I said, my voice garbled from being face first in a steering wheel. "I shouldn't have ever let a thing start between us."

"Rhys might be confused," she said softly. "But he's a good guy. He wouldn't use you, and he wouldn't say or do anything he didn't mean with his whole heart."

He was also just a man. Like a hot blooded, human *man*, and he couldn't be blamed for kissing a tourist who all but threw herself at him. He'd given me outs. He'd told me he didn't kiss me first intentionally, that he didn't want to take advantage of me. I'd taken that to mean he was a gentleman—and I still thought that was the case—but more than that, it had been Rhys's way of making sure I knew we were a fling. A blip. A tiny dot on the graph making up the relationships in his life.

Jenna had an entire plotted line with dips and curves

—*perfect* curves, unfairly—and breaks surrounding their commitment to one another.

I was going to protect myself from here on out, because that was the wise thing to do. And I was a yoga lady, so I was nothing if not wise.

(Feel free to laugh. I just did, too.)

TWENTY

RHYS MUST HAVE GOTTEN HOME AT SOME POINT DURING the night, because he was up early the next day cooking breakfast. I could smell it from upstairs, and despite the way my stomach screamed for beans on toast or even a bite of the sausage that had once tried to kill me, I forced down a bowl of Corn Flakes and a banana in my room.

My phone buzzed, and I picked it up to check the message. My stomach clenched when I read the name that lit up my screen.

Flakey Jakey (Do Not Call): Can we talk?

Um, hard pass. Such a hard pass, in fact, that I wasn't even going to bother responding. Not only had he reached out to me privately—something I couldn't help but feel was a bit sketchy a week and a half before his wedding—but he'd led with the absolute worst text in history. *Can we talk?* was the kerosene of fire starters. It was the best way to incite anxiety in even the most zen people. Why did anyone ever start with that? Why couldn't they just start with the actual talking?

I clicked off my phone and layered up. It was time to drive out to Linscombe and see the church of my ancestors.

Hamish was seated on his regular stool. I sent him a little wave when I passed. Ned lounged in the chair Frank typically inhabited, but otherwise the dining room was bustling with people I vaguely recognized or strangers stopping through town on their way to somewhere else. The vibe in the pub was so familiar now. Walking through the taproom felt like pulling on a cozy, well-worn sweater. It was crazy how quickly this little pub had come to feel like a second home to me, and it was depressing to think I might not ever make it back here.

What reason would I have to visit again?

I hurried outside before Rhys could come out from the kitchen and try to talk about the icy conversation we'd had with Jenna. I didn't want flimsy explanations, and he didn't need to provide them. He had been really clear that he was still a little hung up on his ex. It would have been unfair of me to expect differently now.

The drive to the hospital had given me a little more confidence behind the wheel, and I set up my GPS on my phone and pulled out of the car park—slowly, of course. It hadn't snowed in a few days, but that didn't stop England from looking like a settled snow globe. I turned onto the road, and a man stepped away from the pub door and slapped my window.

I screamed, slamming on my brakes out of sheer reflex. The roads weren't icy—thank the heavens above—so I didn't slide or crash into the cottage that butted up to The Wild Hare's side. I gripped the steering wheel with two hands, waiting for my blood to properly distribute through my body again.

It was a good thing this road was completely empty and I'd been driving so slowly. What kind of person hit a moving car?

A soft tapping on my window brought me back to the present, and I pushed the button to roll it down. Rhys.

Okay, so desperate-looking British men hit moving cars. He

hovered above me, a worried light in his brown eyes. "You're leaving?"

"Yes." Was it not obvious? I was in the car driving away. "You could just call next time, you know. No need to scare me into having an accident."

"Sorry about that. I panicked." He looked pained, then stepped back and ran a hand over his face. "I didn't mean for it to be so awful last night in the waiting room. Can we not talk before you go?"

I stared at him. I'd never met a man before who was so eager to fix things between us after an uncomfortable encounter. Given Rhys's creased frown and the way he looked so desperate for my forgiveness, you'd believe he had done something unspeakable to me. But he hadn't. He'd stood in a hospital waiting room beside his ex-wife and hadn't treated me any differently than he had Ruby. But why should he? We weren't in a relationship. He had been under no obligation to claim me.

"You don't owe me anything, Rhys," I said, trying to soften my words with a slight lift of my shoulder. After witnessing the British goddess that was Jenna, I no longer felt the need to put my inadequate body in his arms. She was a quick fire extinguisher to my flaming feelings for Rhys. I mean, come on. Jessica. Freaking. Rabbit.

I shook myself. I *really* hated negative self-talk in other people, so I needed to quit doing it to myself. Our bodies were different, and that was okay. She was no better than me simply because she was drop dead gorgeous and I was on the short end of average and severely lacking in curves. I took stock of how I was feeling. Did it work? My stomach felt lighter, so that was good.

"Maybe I want to, though," Rhys finally said, his breath clouding before him. He wasn't even in a coat. The man must've been freezing. "Can't you wait, Lu? Just . . . don't leave yet. I can't talk right this second. I have the lunch rush in there, and I really need to be in the kitchen."

I held his beautiful gaze. I craved the warmth of his arms around me—so maybe that positive self-talk had worked after all —but I was still unsure about where we were, and he needed to get back inside. Linscombe wasn't too far away, and I didn't plan on staying there long, but the way Rhys was acting, this conversation seemed really important to him. "Can it wait a few hours?" I asked. "I don't plan to drive in the dark, so I won't be gone too long."

"Wait. You're coming back?" He took a step toward the car, his mouth open in hope. "Today?"

"Yes . . ."

OKAY. Did Rhys think I was *leaving England* because of what went down with his ex at the hospital? And his response to that misguided assumption—perhaps from Hamish, who was in the taproom now—was to run into the street and flag down my car? My entire body thawed into goo, and I lost speech capabilities. This was Hallmark movie status. I'd never had a guy chase me down before, let alone *this*: a man trying to stop me on my way to the airport.

Yes, I wasn't actually going to the airport. But that was what he *thought* I was doing.

Rhys let out a breath and his shoulders relaxed.

I just wanted to clarify. "You thought I was running back to California?"

"Hamish told me you'd left."

Nailed it. Hamish might be the quiet type, but there was a gossipy old woman buried deep within him. "Yeah, but not leaving for good. I'm just going to Linscombe to see the church."

"Your ancestors' church? Well, maybe you shouldn't come back, then," he teased, the twinkle in his eye a thousand times better than the hurt he'd worn earlier. "Maybe we can talk when you return."

The briefest hesitation slowed my words. His coolness last night needed to be explained—but he clearly wanted a chance to do that. But I'd been so humiliated, and I'd felt so invisible beside Jenna.

I swallowed my reservations. "Sure, we can talk later. How is Frank?"

"He comes home this afternoon. Jenna is handling his transportation."

"Should he be at his house alone?"

"He won't be. I imagine Jenna will stick around for a bit." He gestured to the cottage sharing a wall with the pub—the one his family owned and rented out. "He lives there, so I'm close if he needs me. I told him not to worry about dinner for the next bit. I'm planning on taking it to him."

"Him and Jenna." Frank wasn't the only person who would now be extremely close to The Wild Hare.

"Well . . . yes. Is that a problem?" His tone was void of challenge. It was a genuine question, and the anxious way he held his breath meant he cared about the answer.

I drew in a sustaining breath and released the negative comparisons. Facts: Rhys wanted to talk to me. He was upset to mistakenly learn I was leaving the country. He chased my car down *while* I was driving in order to keep me around. His ex-wife's proximity might not be my favorite thing in the world, but Rhys clearly wasn't going to let it get in our way too much. I could either get used to Jenna, or I could just see myself out of this friendship-where-sometimes-we-kiss-but-also-I'm-leaving-in-two-weeks situation. "No, it's not a problem."

He gave me a soft smile. Before I could overanalyze his actions, Rhys pressed a kiss to my cheek and straightened again, but his touch left a heated mark. "Drive safely."

"Of course."

"And stay away from Linscombe's pub. It'll give you food poisoning."

I was about seventy percent sure Rhys was making that up, but I would avoid their pub anyway. Just to be safe.

I pulled away from The Wild Hare with confusion, warmth, and anticipation all bubbling in my stomach. My phone rang as I pulled off High Street, flashing **Flakey Jakey (Do Not Call)** across my screen, and I hit the red decline button straight away. Flakey Jakey and his problems were not going to derail me or my holiday fling.

THE CHURCH in Linscombe was easy to find. I got out of the car and walked the perimeter, my boots sinking into the marshy grass. Headstones were slanted from age and the soft ground, some tipping almost parallel to the ground. I scanned the legible names for any of my ancestors but didn't find any. I tried to Face-Time my mom, but she didn't answer, so I made sure to take a lot of pictures and videos to send to her. It was a gorgeous building with a long, pointed spire and rows of gothic windows that each came to a point.

A couple walking past the churchyard were complaining angrily, and I overheard pieces of their conversation. "The entire thing was chewed up by mice. It's a shame really."

"What does it mean for the Christmas fair?"

The man let out a long sigh. "I guess we'll have to figure out something else. The tents are completely unusable."

They went on their melancholy way, and I returned to my car.

Despite the animosity between the towns, Linscombe looked lovely. Green wreaths and twinkling lights decorated the windows and doors of the buildings along High Street, and the war memorial in the center of town was framed before a tall building that must have been their town hall.

A banner hung between the rows of shops on High Street announcing the Linscombe Christmas Fair. I slowed my car when I passed it and squinted to read the bold red words lining the bottom of the banner. *Much better than the Snowshill Christmas Fair. Rated Number One in the Cotswolds!*

Oh, good grief. Rated by whom? The makers of this sign? I kind of understood Hamish's impulse to spit.

Mom returned my call as I was driving away, and I answered it remotely while the navigator continued telling me where to turn.

"I just left Linscombe," I said. "I have so many pictures to send when I get home."

"Home?" Her hopeful tone was like a snowball to the chest.

"Well, back to the pub." My cheeks warmed. I was glad this phone call wasn't FaceTime or she would've picked up on my discomfort.

She laughed like she was in on the joke. "Don't go feeling too homey there, Lu. I don't think I could bear it if you lived so far away."

My laugh was far less authentic. "Well, it is a different country. There are rules for moving overseas."

She paused for a beat. "You say that like you've looked into it."

"I haven't." Not yet . . . but I did wonder how difficult it was to move. Just for a short period of time, obviously. And only if Rhys asked me to. Not that I expected him to ask me, or anything, but his grand gesture of flagging my car down had begun the wheels of "What If" turning in my head. Then I had gone directly from the Hallmark movie gesture to a church where my ancestors had been married in the past, so it wasn't really a crazy leap for me to be thinking about relationships.

But out loud, I only said, "It would take a soulmate or something to drag me away from California." Which was a bit of a downer, since Rhys didn't even believe in soulmates.

"It would take a soulmate to make me feel okay with you leaving California, too," Mom said. "Tell me about this church."

So I did. I filled her in on all the details I could recall, both small and large. "It's so sweet how churches here are often right in the center of town. It's a physical representation of the importance of religion, historically, I think. The church across the street from the pub in Snowshill is the same way. It's so old and so beautiful. People who live there get to open their windows every day and see gorgeous architecture from their bedrooms."

"It makes for a lovely vacation, I bet."

I didn't miss the emphasis Mom put on the word *vacation*.

"Have you put any more thought into coming home before Christmas?" she asked. "We would help you avoid even thinking about the wedding, you know. You wouldn't have to attend it."

My heart did a weird twist, and I pulled the car into the Poundland car park so I could think. Primark was in my rearview mirror, and I thought back to the day I had bought the boots and Rhys had chauffeured me around. It felt like a lifetime ago. I turned off the car and leaned against the headrest.

At least Mom had moved on from trying to convince me to contact Aubrey.

"I'm not coming home before Christmas, Mom. My flight was cheap because it's unchangeable. I'd have to buy a completely new ticket, which could be up to a thousand dollars since it's last minute and right in the middle of the holidays."

"No amount of money is too much to keep you from coming home for Christmas. You say the word, and Dad will buy you a ticket."

"I have a ticket." My voice was growing weary. I knew she could hear it, too. "I want to see this through."

Neither of us mentioned my knack for running away when things grew scary or tough, but I was sure she was thinking about it as much as I was. How would I be challenging my faults and growing as a person if I ran home? Besides, I *wanted* to stay.

Mom needed to see that I wanted it, too, and that my trip wasn't lacking in holiday spirit. "They have a Christmas cake here that they spend a month baking. Sometimes longer, even. It's a whole process, and it's fascinating. I'm surprised it doesn't mold."

"That sounds . . . interesting." Read: disgusting.

"Yeah, but it's totally normal here, and I think the amount of alcohol involved probably keeps the cake from going bad. It smells amazing, but they won't cut it until Christmas. I don't think I can leave Snowshill until I've tasted it, Mom."

She was quiet for a minute. "Fine. I'll let it go. It's just not the same here without you. We've already made caramels and delivered them to the neighbors, and when Callie gets home we're going caroling with the church choir. I'm just used to doing these things together, and I feel like a piece of my heart is missing because you aren't here."

My stomach clenched in a strange way. I missed doing those activities too, but I didn't feel like my holiday experience was lacking just because I wasn't home. I had a feeling my mom needed to hear that. "I'm having a good Christmas season here. We decorated the pub where I'm staying with greenery and red velvet bows while listening to Bing Crosby. We watched *Home Alone* and drank hot chocolate, and we even cut down a Christmas tree on the mountain and decorated it with tinsel and old homemade ornaments. I helped cut down the tree, Mom. Like with *an ax*."

"Wow."

"It was all safe. Then I borrowed ice skates from a woman in town, and we went ice skating on an actual pond in the middle of a field. It was a nature rink, I'm not even kidding. The friends I was with promised it was totally safe, but I still waited until everyone else skated before I tested it myself." I sighed. "It was magical."

"I bet, honey."

The more I spoke, the more animated I became. I could hear

the smile in my voice, feel the way my cheeks stretched with the creases of contentment. "The guy who cooks at the pub made carnitas yesterday because I missed tacos. They were heavenly. Snowshill has a book club that meets once a month in the pub, and their meeting turns into karaoke nights of mostly seniors— which was *great*—and there's another group who wants to take a chair yoga class, so we set it up for this week, and I'll get to teach real people for a minute again. I just . . ." I paused, trying to find the words to put to the experience I'd had so far. I sat up and shook my head slowly, unable to explain how utterly filled my heart was.

"It sounds like you've had a really good time."

"I have," I said. "Honestly, I haven't really thought about Jake or Aubrey very much. I know I shouldn't run from my problems, and I know that's how this trip started out. But Mom, I'm also finding out how to be on my own again. I can't run away again. I'm seeing this through."

After living with my parents since the break up because I didn't know how to be alone, I knew my mom understood the importance of this. I cleared my throat and closed my eyes. "I think I needed this."

Mom sighed. "I hate to say this, but I agree." She laughed, the sound genuine and sweet. "I guess I was hoping you'd miss us so much that you'd come home. But I can't really be sad if your trip has been so rewarding and fruitful. Your growth is important to me, Lu."

"It's important to me, too."

"As long as you know our door is always open. Always. Even though I know you won't be here forever, just know Dad and I will always want you around. It's not a hardship on us to have our baby girl in the house."

"I know."

"Okay. I better go. Dad is walking in from the yard with that determined look of his. Love you, babe."

"Love you, Mom."

I hung up the phone and let out a long breath. It hadn't registered before exactly how much I'd grown since I considered all of those things. Despite the way Jessica Rabbit had made me feel yesterday, Rhys had done nothing but stay upfront and kind to me. I owed him the chance to talk through what he experienced yesterday and to be his friend without any expectations.

But first, I was running into Poundland for some chocolate.

TWENTY-ONE

I WASN'T EVEN ASHAMED OF MY GROCERY BAG FULL OF chocolate when I walked into The Wild Hare. I'd grabbed one of everything from the chocolate aisle, and a few extras of the ones I'd enjoyed from my last trip to Poundland. I'm looking at you, Crunchie Bar. Honeycomb dipped in chocolate? There was nothing wrong with that.

My newfound skill behind the wheel on English roads had been tested by an extended drive home when my GPS wasn't quick enough to tell me to turn and I had a bit of a detour. It was dark when I'd pulled into the car park at The Wild Hare and hefted my Costco sized bag of candy bars and Haribo Starmix and these little cat-faced gummies that looked too cute not to buy.

Ruby sat on one of the leather chairs in front of the fire, her legs folded beneath her and a notebook on her lap. She chewed on the edge of her pen and looked up when I helped myself to the empty chair beside her.

"I have enough chocolate to feed a small army. Want something?"

Ruby's eyes brightened. "You have any Wispas in there?"

I dug through the bag and pulled one out for her, then snagged a Marvellous Creations bar for myself.

Ruby bit into her chocolate, staring at her notebook paper again. "You any good at maths?"

"Maths?" I asked. "Plural? Like . . . all the types of math?"

She cocked her head and shot me a funny look, like I was the one losing my marbles and pluralizing school subjects. "Yes. Maths. You any good?"

"Not really." I took a bite of chocolate loaded with pop rocks. Rhys was right about the combination being weird, but I liked it anyway. "I didn't fail out of algebra or anything, but it's not my strong suit. What do you need help with?"

"Just altering a recipe so it will yield more. I can figure it out."

"Fractions were *never* my thing. I think they were invented to make kids hungry in school with all the pepperoni pizza and cherry pie charts."

She grinned and took another bite of her Wispa bar.

The front door opened to admit Hamish and a wave of cold air with him. He went out of his way to pass behind our chairs, reaching down to flick Ruby's ponytail as he made his way toward his customary barstool. She swatted his hand absently, never removing her eyes from the notebook on her lap.

I watched Hamish take his seat, but when Rhys came out of the kitchen, I dragged my gaze back to Ruby. I didn't feel ready to face him yet. My comfort zone was purely in the *ignore the awkwardness* realm. Talking to Rhys about what had happened at the hospital with his ex-wife would be awkward. It also didn't seem like a necessary step for two people who were determined to remain in the friendship zone. He didn't owe Luna-his-friend anything. He *did* owe Luna-his-romantic-partner an explanation, though, and that distinction was the only thing keeping my butt in this chair when my feet were antsy to run upstairs and hide.

Hamish looked at us over his shoulder when Rhys left him again. I scooted as close to Ruby as I could get and leaned forward. "Psst."

She looked up. "What?"

"After that"—I gestured vaguely between her and Hamish—"you really want me to believe there is *nothing* between you and the Scottish farmer?"

"Hamish isn't Scottish."

"Then why does he have a Scottish name?"

"His mum is Scottish. He was named after his grandfather."

"Okay. Are you telling me there is nothing between you and the half-Scottish farmer?"

Ruby looked back at her paper, but her cheeks pinked and she fought an embarrassed smile. "He's going to hear you."

"Doubtful. I'm whispering really quietly." I took a bite of my candy bar. "I have only been here a few weeks, but it's painfully obvious that he watches you. Like, all the time."

"Um, creepy."

"Now you're just deflecting."

"Maybe I am."

"Fine." I leaned back. "Let's talk about math some more. You know what I really hated more than fractions back at school? Trig. Oh my gosh, it's the worst. Sine, cosine, tangent . . . *blegh*. It's a really good thing I only have to smile and film myself in soothing tones because if my career required math—"

"Okay, I get it." Ruby let out an exasperated laugh. "You are relentless."

"No, I'm romantic. Seriously, Ruby. Everywhere you go, he watches you when you aren't looking. Try to catch him at it and you'll know what I mean."

She looked at me thoughtfully. "It's not what you think it is. Honestly, Luna, I would know if there was something there." She leaned closer and lowered her voice more. "I kissed him once."

"What?!" Well, no wonder he was silently pining for her. "When?"

"New Year's Eve, last year. We threw a party here. I was a little tipsy, and the guy who came with me left early with someone else." She stopped to roll her eyes. "At midnight I grabbed Hamish because he was the closest unrelated man to me and we snogged."

I found myself scooting closer. "And?"

She shrugged and leaned back in her chair. "The next day he acted like it never happened."

"Well, did you say anything about it?"

"No. It would have been awkward. Besides, trying to be in a relationship could ruin our friendship, and *that* isn't really worth jeopardizing."

"It could be worth it if you fall in love. Maybe he was waiting for you to say something and you never did, so he wrote it off."

She shook her head. "I was pretty obviously into him. I'm the one who kissed him, Luna. Even a little drunk, it was the best kiss I've ever had in my life."

I lowered my voice. "Maybe that's why he never said anything. If you were tipsy, he might have thought you didn't mean it."

Ruby opened her mouth to argue, then said nothing. She stared at me, a line forming between her red eyebrows. "I never thought of that." She glanced again at Hamish. "You see him watching me?"

"Yeah. I thought you guys were a thing when I first got here."

She grew really quiet. Her brow furrowed, and she stared down at the fireplace. If I was right, then Ruby would give Hamish a chance if the situation presented itself. *Someone* deserved to have their romance outlast the holidays, even if it wasn't going to be me. Given how hard Ruby worked, she probably needed a little help getting from single to wrapped in Hamish's arms.

"I have an idea."

"Hmm?" she said, though her focus was on her notebook again.

"Ruby." I whispered, and she looked up at me. I kept my voice quiet so we wouldn't be overheard. "Maybe we need to recreate that kiss, only sober this time."

Her chin dipped. "On New Year's Eve?"

"Or sooner. All we need is a little mistletoe in the right spot."

Her eyes focused. "I can get some mistletoe."

"Then I can hang it up. All we'll need to work on is our timing—"

A shadow appeared over us and Rhys said, "What are you two whispering about?"

I screamed, startled, and threw my candy bar in the air. Ruby screamed too, and chucked her notebook at me. It bounced off my nose and fell with a splat on the floor. My eyes stung from the immediate reaction, but I shook the prickling sensation away. My nose didn't hurt, but I probably had a nice red mark on it now.

Rhys stepped back, his hands up in surrender. "Sorry. Food's ready, Rubes."

"How much did you hear?" Ruby asked.

"Nothing. But now I wish I'd listened better."

Ruby scowled at her cousin, but he didn't seem to notice. He was watching me.

I went to retrieve my candy bar. "Hey, can I order dinner? Whatever you have is fine."

"Sure. I can get you something." He pointed to Ruby, gathering her attention. "Hamish has the bags." Rhys left, and I tossed the other half of my chocolate bar in my grocery bag. I couldn't help but notice that the cousins seemed to be on good terms again.

"I've never seen the pub this empty," I said.

"There's a planning meeting happening over at Frank's

tonight. They moved it next door so he wouldn't have to walk over here."

"Planning what?"

"The Christmas fair. We need to take the food over." She looked at her phone. "Yeah, we need to go. It started at seven." Ruby stood and gathered her things together.

"We?" I asked.

"Me and Hamish." She looked at me sharply. "No saying anything."

"You do your part, then I'll do mine," I promised. I watched her hike her purse over her shoulder, then take a paper bag of takeout from Hamish. He carried the other two bags, and they left with a wave. Did they not realize how much they already acted like two people in a relationship? Hamish had clearly come to the pub to meet up with Ruby and help her carry the food next door. It was such a normal thing for a boyfriend to do. And the way his hardened, too-cool-to-talk self softened around Ruby was the stuff of romcoms. They were the grumpy-sunshine trope personified.

A thud stole my attention from the door. Rhys set a plate of food on the small table before me. "What is going on here?"

"I don't know what you mean."

He pointed between me and the chair Ruby had previously occupied.

"Nothing," I said, taking a fry from the plate and popping it in my mouth. Ouch. Too hot. "Don't you need to be at the meeting, too? You're kind of a big part of the fair."

"I show up in a red suit and smile at the children. Not much planning in that." He watched me expectantly, but now that I found myself alone with him, I wasn't sure I was ready for the discussion he wanted to have.

I ate another fry. This was a chance for me to prove I wasn't going to run away from every uncomfortable situation anymore, but it was really hard. How were you supposed to begin these conversations? I had avoided them so thoroughly throughout my life that I definitely didn't know how to start one.

"Christmas is a week away," I said. "Will the whole town show up to eat the moldy cake?"

Rhys untied his apron and tossed it over the back of the leather armchair beside me, then sat there and leaned back. "It's not moldy, remember?"

"I remember you *claiming* that, yeah."

"You can remember it after I prove it to you on Christmas Day, too. Ruby and I will go have lunch with our nan while the pub's closed." He hesitated, looking from me to the fireplace. "You're welcome to join us."

He was inviting me to lunch on Christmas with his grandmother? Why did we bypass the conversation about Jenna and jump to the next level of a relationship that was about to end? I wasn't sure I could stomach meeting the woman who raised him if I was never going to see Rhys again after I left Snowshill.

"I've scared you," he said.

"No." Yeah, he did. But not in the way he thought. "I just don't want to intrude on your family time."

He was thoughtful, his brown eyes tracing the lines on my face. I wanted nothing more than to push aside the plate of steaming fries and cheese and onion pasty, crawl onto Rhys's lap, and have him hold me.

My phone buzzed, and I pulled it out of my pocket.

Flakey Jakey (Do Not Call): Luna, I swear I am not contacting you for any selfish reasons. Please just give me a chance to explain. This has nothing to do with us. You have every right to ignore me. I get it. I'm just asking you to set aside your anger for five minutes and hear me out.

Of all the selfish things to say.

"Who is being selfish?" Rhys asked.

Apparently I'd spoken aloud. "Just my ex. He wants to talk about something."

"The ex getting married next week?"

"Yes." I shook my head and put my phone face down on the table beside my pasty. Directing my full attention at Rhys, I pretended my phone wasn't buzzing again. We'd avoided talking about the hospital situation thus far. Probably because a person could walk into the pub at any moment and it seemed better to wait until we wouldn't be interrupted, but I needed the distraction right now. "You said earlier you wanted to talk?"

"Yeah. Yes. I do." He cleared his throat and looked to the pub door. Still silent and unmoving. "I wanted to thank you for bringing tacos and my coat and for driving Ruby. It was nice of you, especially when you aren't comfortable on the roads."

"I'm getting better, actually. I think that drive was what I needed to get back out there again."

"Which helped you see the church in Linscombe," he finished. He seemed to hesitate, as if he wanted to say more, then ran a hand over his face and trained a soft smile on me. "How was that?"

I had a feeling Rhys wasn't saying what he wanted to, and the church was just a distraction. But if that's what he wanted, I'd oblige. "It was cooler than I expected, standing in the place where my ancestors had been married. I mean, they don't know me. They didn't know that four hundred years later a girl was going to be born because they'd chosen to get married, and then she would make herself into a low-grade YouTube yoga star and travel the world to avoid showing her face at a wedding."

"No," he said carefully, "but if they did know all of that, they would have a lot of questions. Like, what's YouTube?"

I smiled.

Rhys continued. "I bet they would be proud of you. We probably have different definitions of what it takes to be considered a low-grade YouTube yoga star, but I don't think you qualify. Are there any other yoga channels on YouTube with a bigger following than you?"

"There's a few. One in particular is certainly bigger, but we have such a different vibe that I don't consider him competition. We're reaching different audiences."

"So you're at least a middle-grade star."

"Sure. Fine. I'm a better-than-subpar YouTube yoga instructor who lives at home. Really impressive."

"I'm impressed by you." He ran a hand over his chin. "Listen, last night in the waiting room I wasn't myself. It's been a while since I've seen Jenna. It was unexpected, and I think when you showed up I was still in a bit of shock."

"You don't need to explain yourself."

"But I do. I want you to know I wasn't ashamed of you or trying to hide whatever this is." He waved his arm between us. "Jenna has moved on, and I have too. We were both there for Frank, and that's all. It was the first time I've been around her with another woman I have feelings for, and it felt weird."

Feelings? I tried not to sound too affected by that revelation. "That's fair, Rhys. You were married to her."

"More than that, though. I'd been with Jenna since we were eighteen. She was a huge part of my life for years."

"And you're still a little hung up on her," I said helpfully, though inside my stomach was tying itself into a system of Eagle Scout-level knots.

"No, I don't think that's true. I realized the other night I'm not hung up on Jenna herself, but more what she represented to me. The marriage and relationship we had—that's what I can't quite let go of. I just . . . I guess I realized I don't need to have it with her anymore, but that doesn't mean I can't still have it with someone else. That was a little shocking to discover."

Someone else. Not *me*, but not Jenna either. Maybe if I was a native, we'd be having a different conversation. One about us instead of Rhys's self-discovery. I was happy for him, but it hurt a little, too.

Rhys reached across the space between our chairs and took my limp hand. He squeezed my fingers until I looked into his dark eyes. Why was this happening to me? It was unfair. It was the first time I'd ever felt such a deep connection to a man, and he didn't even live on the same side of earth as I did. Come on, universe. You could do better than that.

My phone buzzed again, and he looked pointedly at it. "You want me to answer that?"

"While that sounds extremely entertaining, I think completely ignoring him is the best thing to do."

"Maybe if he knew how you felt, he would stop bothering you."

I stared at Rhys. "How can he *not* know how I feel? The man left our five-year relationship for my best friend and got engaged to her within months."

"He probably knows you have a right to be hurt. But he might not understand the anger." He ran his thumb over mine. "Maybe he wants you back."

"He doesn't." There was no question of it. "You haven't seen the way he looks at Aubrey. It's like she carries the sun."

"Did he ever look at you that way?"

Cold washed over me. *Had he?* I tried to think back on our earlier months, the times when we were blissfully happy, or before we had decided to move up to Geyserville and the way that level of commitment had made me feel. He'd loved me, I knew he did. But even then, I didn't think I ever carried the sun for him. If I was being honest, he didn't carry any massive stars for me, either.

We could have been happy. But would we have had joy? Fulfillment? Contentment? I didn't want to be placated in my relationship. I wanted to give and take in equal measure and find a man who cared for me exactly as much as I cared for him. I wanted someone to stroke my hand the way Rhys did, with care and delicacy like he was holding something special. Like *I* was special.

Like I carried the sun.

"No, I don't think he ever looked at me that way." I owed Jake nothing. I picked up my phone and typed out a text.

Luna Winter: Please stop trying to call me. I'm not interested in speaking to you.

Flakey Jakey (Do Not Call): This isn't about me, Lu. It's about Aubrey. Please, just five minutes.

I slid my phone into my pocket and closed my eyes.

"Can I take your mind off of him?" Rhys asked.

"I don't . . . I mean, just to be clear, I'm not hung up on Jake." I held Rhys's brown eyes so he would know I meant it.

"That's something of a relief. I don't know how I'd feel about it if you were thinking of another man while I was trying to woo you."

"Woo me? What are you, Romeo?"

"Only if you're Juliet." He cringed immediately. "Okay, that sounded better in my head. I definitely don't want a *Romeo and Juliet* relationship."

But he wanted a relationship?

"I do," he murmured, standing and pulling me up beside him. I really needed to stop saying the things out loud that were meant to be thoughts in my head.

He pulled me into a hug.

"A two-week holiday fling."

"Three weeks," he said, "if you count the rest of the time we have together."

Three weeks. But it felt like a year. Or at least a few months. I

221

felt like part of his life, part of this town's community. I could see myself staying here forever and being with him and being content—but that was just plain unrealistic.

"Three weeks," I confirmed.

Rhys grinned, then he bent to kiss me.

TWENTY-TWO

THE SENIOR CLASS FOR CHAIR YOGA WAS REMARKABLY difficult to keep under control. They reminded me of the Mommy and Me class I'd facilitated a handful of times in San Francisco: easily distracted and much more interested in the prospect of snacks after class than the yoga itself. I struggled to hold my smile as I sat before the group. We'd had a turnout of eight people, which was more than I'd expected, and already our peaceful meditation had been interrupted twice by mentions of how good the roast beef smelled.

It was as if Rhys knew that particular meal was a senior favorite and had chosen it to purposefully disrupt my class.

I spoke softly throughout the entire session, avoiding the bar where Ruby and Rhys both watched me with amusement. When we reached the end, I instructed the seniors to inhale deeply.

"Now let it out slowly and inhale another breath. Feel free to make audible sounds. Inhale, relax, release. Now, on your next release I want you to bend forward, lengthen the spine, feel the stretch in your shoulders."

I waited, moving through the motion slowly. "Now bring it

up, long spines, shoulders back, inhale. And release." We moved on to rolling our necks and shaking out any remaining tension, and I looked up and smiled at my motley, somewhat disinterested class. "That's all for today."

No one moved.

I bent forward to pull my shoes back on. I hadn't needed to take them off, but I'd wanted to. No one else in my class had. When I looked back again, they were still silent. Maybe they thought there was more to the class?

"Do you have any questions for me?" I asked, hoping that facilitating conversation might segue into the class disbanding for their dinner.

Maggie raised her hand. "Are we going to be on your YouTube channel now, love?"

"Oh, um, no." I grimaced. "I don't put videos of entire classes on the channel, just the instruction part. Just me."

"But how will we manage to keep it up when you're gone?"

"When I'm gone," I repeated. Eight sets of eyes blinked back at me. Oh, she was serious. Apparently my distracted class had enjoyed themselves more than I thought. It gave me a warm feeling of accomplishment. "I have some chair yoga videos on the channel. If you want to follow along with those, they're very similar to what we did today. I try to post new routines every so often so you don't get bored with the same video over and over again. I'll show you how to find the chair yoga playlist I've made, if you want."

"Yes, please."

Arthur stood and stretched his arms in the air. "Do I look five years younger, Maggie? I feel it."

"You sure do," she said without even looking at him.

He shuffled toward the bar to order his dinner, and the other members of the class meandered that way as well.

Maggie approached me. "I am so eager to learn the flamingo

move you did near my house, or perhaps other aviary positions might be easier in a chair. Do you think you could do one more class before you leave?"

"If Rhys approves it, I'm more than happy to. It all depends on the pub's schedule."

She nodded. "I'll work it out. Rhys adores me. I shouldn't have any trouble there." Maggie sent me a wink, approaching the counter with the rest of her friends. I suppressed my laugh and started moving chairs back to the tables where we'd taken them from.

Ruby slipped out from behind the counter and helped me convert the makeshift yoga studio into a dining room again. "I might join you next time. It looked restful."

"I'll do a routine with you sometime if you want," I offered. "Chairs or no chairs, your call."

"Ooo, yes please." She looked over her shoulder to check for something before talking again. "I got the stuff."

"What stuff?"

Ruby widened her eyes at me like I should be able to read her mind. She pulled a bit of greenery from her pocket and nodded to it discreetly like she was offering me something on the black market and didn't want anyone else to notice.

It was mistletoe.

"Give it to me," I whispered. "I'll hang it above the door. You'll just need to walk through it with him."

"Okay." She looked around again to see if we were being watched before taking it from her pocket and shoving it at me like an amateur drug dealer. I didn't have pockets though, so I curled my fingers around it. It was bigger than I had expected, and there was no hiding all the leaves.

"I'll distract Rhys after everyone leaves," she whispered. "You can find pins beneath the register. Just stick it in a beam."

"Got it."

We walked away from each other like our covert meeting had never happened and finished straightening the dining room. I tucked the mistletoe into my bag and gathered my things from the corner table where I'd camped out for most of the day.

It had been almost twenty-four hours since Rhys and I had had the conversation about our relationship and decided to be something until I left for home again. An entire day where all I wanted to do was follow him around the kitchen while he worked, but refrained from the stalkerish behavior. I'd sat in the taproom for most of the morning, sipping hot chocolate beside the Christmas tree while carols played softly overhead and editing the segments I'd woken up early to film.

Except when Rhys and I had taken advantage of the pub closing between the lunch and dinner rushes. We took a walk in the snow, and he showed me where some of his ancestors were buried in the church's cemetery and told me stories of his childhood in Snowshill.

Hamish hurried into the pub, slamming the door against the wall. He didn't seem to notice the way his brash actions had gathered attention from all of the patrons eating dinner, his gaze scanning the room until it came to a stop on Ruby. Ned jumped to his feet from where he'd been lounging in front of the fire and trotted over to Hamish, who ignored the dog and crossed the room toward Ruby.

"We have a problem," he said softly.

Her widened eyes looked from him to me, and I could see the panic lacing her gaze. "How did you find out?" she asked, stress radiating from her in waves.

"They called me. Wait—" He shook his head, his confusion understandable. "How did *you* find out?"

Before Ruby could ruin our mistletoe plans, I stepped in. "What's the problem, Hamish? Are your animals okay?" Because he was a farmer, so that was a safe question, right?

"It's the fair," he said. "Linscombe stole our tents."

I took a step back before he had time to make a spitting sound. You know, just in case there were any strays.

"What do you mean?" I asked.

"The tents for the fair," Hamish said.

"We set them up to keep out the elements," Ruby explained. "If we don't have tents, then we're just mingling outside in the cold."

Hamish looked furious. "They weren't delivered yesterday as planned. When I finally got someone on the phone today from the company we use to rent the tents, she told me the address they were delivered to. Freaking Linscombe had the order changed."

A faint memory of the conversation I'd overheard in Linscombe came back to me. "When I was there a few days ago to check out the church, I heard people talking about the tents."

Hamish turned his attention on me, and it was a stronger force than I was prepared for. Man, he really cared about this fair. Or he really hated Linscombe. Probably the latter. "What did they say?"

I shook my head. "I only got pieces of it, but they mentioned something about mice chewing something and not having tents anymore."

"So they stole ours," Hamish spat.

"Then we'll go get them back," Arthur said from his chair at a nearby table. "Did we pay for them?"

"Yes," Hamish grumbled.

Rhys came out from the kitchen carrying two plates of steaming food. He gave Ruby a look that said *quit chatting and help me*, but she ignored him.

"We don't know where they're keeping them, though," Arthur mused, running a hand over his bald head.

"I have the delivery address written down at home. I doubt they moved them far."

"We are *not* going to steal them back," Ruby said, guffawing.

"Just because you're still miffed about Thomas Fielding winning that rugby—"

"I am *not* miffed about Thomas Fielding. That was ten years ago. I don't care that he's on the council now for Linscombe. I just don't want him sabotaging our fair. So why not take the tents back?" Hamish's steady eyes didn't move from her. "We paid for them, and they stole them first, so we aren't doing anything wrong."

"What tents?" Rhys asked, setting the plates in front of Maggie and another woman who'd attended my chair yoga class.

Ruby filled him in, and he chewed on his bottom lip for a minute. A look passed between him and Hamish, some silent communication where they hatched an unspoken plot.

"You can't really be considering it," Ruby said.

"Better to do it yourself than to get the law involved," someone said from a nearby table. "It'll be much quicker that way."

Rhys went back toward the kitchen. "Rubes, help me with these plates."

Hamish left the pub entirely. Whatever nod passed between the men, it was probably an entire *Mission: Impossible* plot, subbing themselves in for Ethan Hunt. And here I thought this degree of small-town rivalries were a product of television and romance books. I never knew people were actually this spiteful in real life. To steal the tents from another town's fair? I wouldn't have believed it possible if I hadn't seen their sign myself.

A town who would print something so boldly on their banner and then sabotage their neighbor town's fair by stealing their tents was repulsive, and they didn't deserve to get away with this.

If Rhys and Hamish were going to silently retrieve all the tents that had been taken, then they would need help.

I CHANGED into all black clothes while the chair yoga group was finishing their dinners and lingering over drinks. The only black t-shirt I'd brought with me had a bright white Snoopy wearing a Santa hat on the front beside Woodstock in elf ears, but my coat would be covering most of that anyway. I still looked ready to slink in the shadows and bring justice to Snowshill's Christmas fair.

I slipped down the hallway and knocked on Ruby's lavender door. It took her a minute to open it. When she saw my outfit, she raised one copper eyebrow. "You can't be serious. You look like a Snoopy ninja."

I tried to seem nonchalant when I shrugged, like adventuring to neighboring rival towns was part of the norm for me, but I wasn't good at acting cool. "I think they'll need help."

"They could report the guy and have the tents delivered without doing anything reckless and possibly illegal, you know."

"But will they? You saw the way they looked at each other."

She frowned. "Probably not."

"So we should go to make sure they don't do anything too stupid then, right?" And to carry poles and canvas—or whatever the tents were made out of.

"I can't." Ruby hesitated. "I have a thing tonight, and I can't miss it. Go with them if you want to."

"Okay." She started to close the door, and I put up a hand. "Wait, Ruby. Is your thing tonight the cooking class?"

"Shhh!" She took my hand and pulled me into her room before closing the door behind me. "I don't want Rhys to know."

"Why not?"

"Because it might not work, and I don't want to let him down again. I could be rubbish at it, even after all these classes. I need to test my skills before he finds out."

"How are you planning to do that?"

She hesitated a second, then lowered her voice. "During the fair, he has Father Christmas duty, and I'll be coming back here to open up for all the stragglers who want to keep the party going. I'm going to offer a few things I've been learning and test them on the patrons while he's gone."

"So if it doesn't work, as you phrased it, then he'll never have to know?"

She gave a quiet scoff. "He'll know. There's no keeping secrets like that around here. But I can ask for forgiveness later instead of begging for a chance to prove myself again. Last time didn't go so well."

As I'd heard. Rhys had told me on one of my first few days in Snowshill how he wanted Ruby to cook with him so he could pass on their grandmother's recipes and keep the family traditions alive for another generation. I wasn't sure if Ruby realized how much he wanted this, but I could understand why she kept it a secret. Managing expectations and all that.

"Okay, I won't say anything. But is that where you're going tonight? Or are you just ditching us because being around Hamish turns you into a stress case now?"

Her cheeks pinked. "You noticed that? Do you think he did, too?"

"He might have if I let you keep talking." I grinned. "We need to get that mistletoe up quickly so you don't blow it."

She smoothed back her ponytail. "No, just throw it away. I'm done trying to be discreet. All this sneaking around to cooking classes has stressed me out and the whole Hamish thing is going to throw me over the edge."

"Or relax you. Kissing has a way of making all of life's problems disappear."

She shook her head. "No. Can't do it. Just bin it." Ruby shook her hands out and placed them on her waist with what appeared to be resolve. "Yes. That's the best thing to do. Bin it."

"If that's what you want," I said.

"It is." She pulled me in for a quick hug, her long ponytail swinging behind her. "Be safe tonight, and don't let my cousin do anything too stupid."

"I'll do my best."

TWENTY-THREE

RHYS WAS BANGING AROUND IN THE KITCHEN, DRYING and putting away clean pans while the dishwasher ran in the background. He looked up at me and straightened, his eyebrows rising. "Are you dressed like a Christmas ninja for any particular reason, Lu?"

I threw my arms to the sides and did a spin. "For our covert operation tonight."

He laughed. "I don't remember discussing a covert operation with you."

"Not with me. You and Hamish talked about it with your minds, but it was pretty obvious you both planned to go. I want to help."

He crossed his arms over his chest, highlighting the muscles he'd gotten from chopping wood on the sly. "It might not be safe."

"You'll protect me."

"You have a lot of faith in someone you've only known for a few weeks."

"Are you telling me not to have faith in you?" I asked, leaning against the door jamb and mirroring his crossed arms.

"No. I like it." His simple words were serious, void of all humor. The raw tone of his voice called out to me, clawing for me. I crossed the floor slowly, pulled by an invisible tether to where he leaned against the counter.

"I like it, too," I said. It was probably reckless to feel like I knew Rhys, but I *knew* him. In the last two weeks I'd heard more stories about Rhys's childhood than I had gotten in the five years of being with Jake—and I knew a lot about Jake, so that was saying something. This was more than just knowing about the time Rhys fell from his bike and got a moon-shaped scar on his knee, though. I was confident with Rhys like I'd never been confident with anyone before. We were comfortable around each other in that way that you get with someone after dating for months. It was going to make leaving harder, but for now I wasn't going to let myself dwell on that.

Again, that was a problem for the Luna of December 29th. The Luna of today just wanted to hold Rhys's hand and be a Snowshill Crusader, rescuing the stolen tents and saving the Christmas fair.

Rhys's plaid flannel was buttoned all the way up, and he'd rolled down his sleeves to his wrists. I liked the laid-back Rhys, but this Rhys was nice, too.

"Your village deserves to have its fair in warm tents," I said, "and we're going to get those tents back from the Linscombe jerks who stole them."

"My village?" Rhys took my hand and pulled me flush against him. He brushed a strand of hair from my cheek and smiled down at me, his dark brown eyes warming until the edges looked rimmed in amber. "It could be your village too, you know. You've already been accepted by the majority—"

"Canoodle later," Hamish said from the doorway, silencing Rhys at once.

His hands tightened around me, and I surreptitiously inhaled his warm, gingerbread cookie scent. Come *on*, Hamish and his awful timing. Rhys had been so close to professing himself and saying the words I would probably die to hear. My heart hammered like an elf in the toy-making assembly line, and I could feel Rhys's sigh of annoyance on my neck.

He pressed me closer, then released me. I frowned, but he took my hand and pulled me toward the door.

"We can discuss that later," I said.

Rhys smiled.

I pulled my coat on and followed Hamish outside. Rhys bent to scratch Ned on the neck, then closed and locked the door.

"I think Ruby is still going out tonight," I said when his key slid into the lock. The mistletoe was still in my coat pocket, waiting for its banishment to the trash. Later. I didn't want to be questioned about it, so I would wait until I was alone to get rid of it.

Rhys looked up at me. "She has a key."

We approached a faded red truck, and I slid into the center seat. "Why didn't we take this thing to get the trees?"

Hamish looked at me. "There are only three seats." He moved his attention to the windshield and turned the music down. "Ruby is going out tonight?" he asked. Or at least I thought it was a question. He was a man of so few words that I hadn't quite mastered reading him yet.

"I think so." I tried to sound noncommittal, like: she *could* be, but who knows?

Well, me. I knew.

"She's been gone a lot lately," Hamish muttered. "New friends?"

"She'll never replace you, don't worry." Rhys sounded distracted. "Okay, the address is taking us down Old Mill Road. Who lives out there?"

Hamish shrugged.

I leaned a little into Rhys's side and he put his arm around my shoulders. "So we're going into the lion's den, but you guys don't know who the lion is?"

"We might know the lion," Rhys said. "But we won't know if we know who it is until we get there."

"Enough tongue twisters," Hamish said.

It wasn't normal to sneak onto someone's property to retrieve stolen rented tents, but I reminded myself it also wasn't normal to redirect another town's tent rental. Linscombe people were sneaky.

But I guess we were, too.

After we reached Linscombe, we pulled onto Old Mill Road. Hamish slowed the car and dimmed the lights.

"It's just around the bend up here." Rhys pointed. "You know it?"

"No."

"Let's go then," I whispered when the truck came to a stop.

Rhys's arm tightened around my shoulders. "You aren't going."

What? I turned to face him, breaking the connection, and his arm dropped. "Yes, I am. I came, didn't I?"

He turned in his seat to fully face me. "You can stay here, Luna. I'm not putting you in a position to get into legal trouble over the sake of a village fair."

"That wasn't what I meant by needing your protection, Rhys. I came to help."

"You can be our getaway driver."

"Um—" Hamish said.

"You want your getaway driver to be fast, right?" I said.

Rhys hesitated. "Well, yeah."

"Then it's not me."

He ran a hand over his face. "Then you can be the lookout girl."

"Looking out for what? Owls and mice? They're probably hibernating now anyway." I was fairly sure neither of those animals actually hibernated, but my point was made. "If there are any headlights coming, you'll see them. You won't need me to look out." I unclicked my seatbelt.

"If she gets thrown in jail, she'll have to stay around longer," Hamish muttered.

Rhys ignored him. "Fine. But you stay with me and stay quiet. If we're caught, go hide and call Ruby to pick you up or something. I don't want you getting nabbed for this."

We all got out of the car and trudged quietly through the snowy field toward a barn set back from the road. "Is this where they have their fair?" I asked.

"Don't know," Hamish said. "We've never been to it before."

"The center of the village is just on the other side of the tree-line, so it would make sense to hold it here."

I chafed my arms. "Why don't any of you celebrate with indoor fairs? It's so cold."

"Don't have anywhere big enough for all the people," Hamish muttered.

We rounded the edge of the barn and both men slid to an abrupt stop. Three white tents filled the space, one long one in the center and two smaller tents flanking it. The middle of the roofs were peaked, the long sides covered and flapping lightly in the wind.

Hamish swore.

I didn't see the problem. "Aren't these what we came for?"

"Yes, but no," Rhys said. "They've already been set up."

"Can't we disassemble them?"

Hamish shot me an incredulous look. "The three of us? In the dark?"

I guessed that meant *no*.

"It's too complicated. It usually takes us most of the day to get them up, and that's with extra help." Rhys ran his hand over his face again. I could monitor his stress levels rising by how often he did that. He'd now reached the point where his scruff was going to give his palm a beard burn if he wasn't careful.

"What can we do then?" I asked.

Hamish shook his head. "Nothing. We can report them for redirecting our order, but by the time the police do anything about it, the fair will be over."

"It's too bad." I gestured to the wide barn beside us. "They don't even need the tents. They have this."

Hamish and Rhys were silent. They looked at each other, then turned toward the barn in unison as though they'd never seen one before. It was almost creepy how in sync they were.

"Okay, no more of this silent bro communication. Include me, please."

"You can't read my thoughts?" Rhys asked.

"She's not a bro," Hamish said, and I thought I detected the most miniscule edge of amusement.

"Definitely not." Rhys stepped behind me and wrapped his arms over my puffy coat, immediately providing a wall of warmth. I sank back against his chest and rested my hands on his crossed arms. I could feel him looking at Hamish. "So, is it possible?"

Hamish ran a hand lightly over his beard. "It'll take all day to clear it out."

"Clear what out?" I asked.

Rhys said, "His barn," at the same time Hamish said, "My barn."

"There could be a mice issue," Hamish said.

"We won't know until we look. We'll be thorough when we get it cleared out."

"*If* we can get it cleared out," Hamish emphasized. "There's a fair bit of junk in there."

"But it's huge, and it could even be warmer than the tents. We could have the vendors and the crafts and the food all set up in the same space."

"And Father Christmas's Grotto?" Hamish asked.

"We'll figure that out."

I squeezed Rhys's arms a little. "If we're not stealing tents right now, could we have this conversation in the nice, warm, heated truck?"

Rhys chuckled, his chest vibrating against my back. "Sure."

We turned back for the car when Hamish's foot collided with something metal, and it skittered across the frozen ground. He bent down and lifted a can of spray paint. "I have a few ideas for this. Maybe some choice words about Linscombe over the flaps on the tents." He shook it. "It's pretty full."

"So children can come visit Santa Claus and receive a lesson in sailor speak instead?" I asked.

Hamish grunted, but he must have agreed with me, because he tossed the can.

It felt massively unfair to leave without the tents when they were the ones who had stolen them from Snowshill. They hadn't even tried to hide their blatant rudeness toward us . . . I drew in a quick gasp. "Wait, don't lose the paint! Can you find it again?"

Both men looked at me.

"I have an idea."

WHEN I SUGGESTED MEDDLING with the rude banner that hung in the middle of Linscombe's High Street, I hadn't expected to be the person to see the task through. But here I sat in the middle seat of Hamish's truck, the offending can of spray paint in my hand, the men arguing on either side of me.

"It has to be her," Hamish said. "Or we can't do it."

"She's not putting herself in jeopardy like that. What if old Hankins catches us? I'm not letting my American girlfr—" Rhys coughed and turned his gaze toward the window. "I'm not letting Luna get put in jail."

It wasn't a crazy leap to believe he was about to call me his girlfriend, right? It felt that way, at least. My heart raced, a shot of adrenaline straight from Rhys's slip up and into my left ventricle. I would do anything for this man right now. "It's not a big deal. Are you afraid of dropping me?"

"I wouldn't drop you. It has nothing to do with that. Like I said, Linscombe hates us. If we're caught—"

"Then let's not get caught." I bumped Hamish with my shoulder. "Besides, we have an actual getaway driver."

"She's not wrong."

Rhys muttered under his breath. "Fine." He opened the door and helped me out, and I got into the bed of the truck behind him. "Crouch," he whispered.

We needed to be fast in case anyone looked outside and spotted us. I bent my head closer to him, my grin wider than a Cotswolds road. "Bet you're glad I wore all black now, huh?"

"Yeah, because that makes you completely unrecognizable."

I pushed lightly against his chest. "No more sarcasm. You're gonna ruin the best part of my trip."

"And here I thought *I* might be considered the best part of your trip."

"Nah, so far my favorite English person is Ruby. Sorry."

His hand slid around my waist and he dropped a kiss on my lips as Hamish slowed the truck to a stop just beneath the banner. I tore away, but my body was more relaxed now than it would've been after an hour-long yoga session.

"Climb on," Rhys said.

He stayed crouched, and I got on his shoulders. When he rose slowly, I bent forward a little and rested my hand on his chest to ground me. He held my thighs securely, and I felt safe.

I held tightly to Rhys, shook the can, and raised it to cover *Linscombe* in cream-colored paint. It really just looked like I was using Wite-Out to accurately edit the sign. Rhys moved where I directed him so I could reach better, and I proceeded to cover a few extra words on the bottom of the sign.

"Okay, I'm finished."

"That was fast." He crouched low, and I started to climb from his shoulders.

"Oy!" a man yelled. "What are you doing?"

I jumped from Rhys's crouched shoulders and slid into the slick truck bed on my knees. Rhys's arm went around me and he hit the back window. "Go!"

Hamish didn't wait for a second command. He took off to the sound of an angry man screaming at us to return. Rhys pulled me against him, and I nestled myself between his knees, up against his chest, while the metal ridges of the truck bed dug into my legs. Icy wind whipped at us, tugging at my hair. It was in no way comfortable, but I did not want it to end.

Once we pulled out of Linscombe and it was clear no one was chasing us, Hamish slowed to a stop.

We jumped down from the truck bed and into the warm cab. I leaned against Rhys, and he flung his arm over my shoulders and pulled me closer.

"Did you get most of it done?" Hamish asked, maneuvering through the roads easily.

"I got the whole thing done. I covered *Linscombe* on the top, and I covered *Much better than the* on the bottom."

Hamish grinned, a whole entire smile that covered the bottom half of his face. It revealed two shallow dimples, and I could see why Ruby was into him. He was handsome. A laugh rumbled from him, and he hit his knee. "I can't wait for everyone driving through tomorrow to read it."

"*Snowshill Christmas Fair. Rated Number One in the Cotswolds!*"

Rhys laughed harder. "I'm glad you think it's funny, mate. Because you know they'll be coming for you tomorrow."

Hamish nodded through his continued glee.

"How?" I asked. There was more bro communication going on. They knew more than they were letting on.

"It won't be hard to put two and two together. Hamish is the only person in Snowshill with a truck."

TWENTY-FOUR

WHEN HAMISH HAD EXPLAINED THAT HIS BARN WAS FULL of junk, he had not been exaggerating. It was only noon on the day before the Christmas fair, and so far all anyone had managed to do was move the tractors out of Hamish's storage barn and park them behind his gorgeous stone farmhouse. His property was a dream. It was exactly the sort of house I imagined the Bennets living in from *Pride and Prejudice*, and Hamish was out here all alone with his beautiful home and massive working farm. He was practically screaming to be the hero in a Hallmark Christmas movie who hires a down-on-her-luck city girl who is trying to escape her hectic life and falls in love with the small-town country boy. Or, you know, he could skip all that and just finally tell Ruby how he felt.

Some of his workers were coming to help us clear the barn after lunch, because they'd had too many tasks in the morning to come any earlier. For now it was just me, Ruby, Rhys, and Hamish clearing out the barn. Dust motes floated through the shafts of sunlight streaming from the cloudy windows to the dirt floor. Support beams punctuated one side of the huge barn, holding up a loft that spanned one-third of the space, leaving the rest of it with tall, vaulted ceilings. Regular divots lined the stone of one open wall, showing where a floor had once been situated, making it look like the loft had once extended through the entire space.

I'd spent the morning clearing out the loft rooms and sweeping away dust and cobwebs with Ruby. So far, no sign of rodents, which was a massive relief. "What is this place?" I asked.

"The old stable rooms," Ruby said, leaning against the top of her broom handle. "Back in the day, the servants slept there. But it's just been storage for as long as I can remember. I don't think Hamish's family ever used this barn for anything else. They have the newer one closer to the house that's better for the animals."

"This will be perfect for the Santa area," I said.

"Yeah, if we can get the rest of the barn cleared today."

We piled our brooms near the door. Ruby tossed dirty rags into a bucket while I gathered the mops. "Are you nervous about tomorrow at all?"

"I'm dying," she said, eyes wide. "Can you tell?"

"No." Yes, it was extremely obvious. She'd been jittery all morning with a perpetual frown turning down the edges of her lips. "I just wondered. What can I do to help?"

"Distract Rhys tomorrow night so he isn't worried about me being in charge of the pub." She rolled her eyes. "I swear, you mess up one time in this village and you're forever branded as dangerous in the kitchen."

"I still don't understand why the pub is opening at all. Won't everyone be here?"

"It's our best moneymaker of the quarter. No one wants the night to end, so everyone leaves the fair and heads straight to The Wild Hare. We're sort of like the afterparty for most village events. Rhys will premake a lot, I'm guessing. But it's a chance for me to prove myself and I think that alone is going to make me puke."

To me, it felt like a high-stakes night to test out her updated cooking prowess. But Ruby clearly had faith in herself, so I did too. I hefted all the brooms and mops to carry downstairs. "You can do this, Ruby. I'm here for whatever you need."

"Thanks, Lu." We reached the bottom of the stairs. Ruby set down her buckets and tugged lightly on my ear.

"Okay," I said, stepping out of her reach. "Is that a British thing? We boop each other on the nose sometimes in America, but it's kind of reserved for children."

She pulled on her sagging ponytail to tighten it. "I was just checking for elf ears or something. I'm half convinced Father Christmas sent you to me."

"Get in line," Rhys said, coming up behind us with his arms full of old ropes and rusty tack. His long, plaid sleeves were straining against his arms where his muscle was clearly being called to action. "I was thinking the same thing yesterday."

"Maybe he sent her to Snowshill for everyone," Hamish called from behind a stack of boxes. "Who hasn't been helped by Luna in the last few weeks?"

What? I looked between them, but they were serious. "Um, a lot of people."

"Name one," Ruby challenged.

"Hamish." I planned to help him get with Ruby, but that hadn't happened yet, so I couldn't count it.

He stepped out from the mountain of boxes, eyebrows up. "What do you call last night then?"

"I don't think you adequately understand Hamish's relationship with Linscombe if you're going to discount your heroic banner activity," Rhys said.

I recalled Hamish's spitting habit. "Okay, I'll concede that point." Two men darkened the doorway in heavy coats and muddy boots. "Them. I haven't helped either of them."

"You cleared the loft so now they can focus on the stuff down here," Hamish deadpanned. He was serious.

I looked from him to Ruby, then to Rhys, whose poor, beautiful arms were still straining against the heavy metal and rope. He dropped the junk to a heap on the ground, apparently tired of carrying it nowhere. "She *is* a Hufflepuff," he said.

I glared at him playfully. "Maggie," I challenged.

"Chair yoga," Rhys shot back.

"Frank."

"The tacos you brought to the hospital."

"Ruby."

"Decorating the pub," she said.

"Ned." The poor dog still hated me.

"You're reaching now," Rhys said. "I don't think he counts."

Ruby grinned. "Admit it. You're an elf. Our very own elf!"

"An elf never admits her secrets," I said.

Hamish had apparently had as much of this conversation as I had. He passed us, heading for the men in the doorway. "Richard, Chris, you can both start in that corner. Junk goes in the back of the truck and everything else to the east shed."

They headed off, and Ruby carried the cleaning implements away.

Rhys had a look in his eyes that could melt an entire snowman in one go. "They aren't wrong, you know. It seems like you've done nothing but step in as a reliable person willing to help since you got here. It's going to be hard to say goodbye."

"Ugh." I scrunched my nose, and not because Rhys carried a cloud of musty rope and leather scent with him from all the junk he'd moved. "I don't like that word."

"I've been thinking about that." The fire in his eyes only seemed to intensify. I would be frightened away if I didn't feel the same warmth reciprocated in my chest. "What if we didn't have to say goodbye just yet? You don't *have* to be in California, right? You can work from anywhere."

"Technically, that's true. But I don't know how long I can stay in the UK without a visa or—"

"Six months."

Someone fetch a defibrillator, because my heart just stopped. This wasn't the most romantic of settings for an invitation to move across the ocean to potentially be together . . . if that's what was even happening here. But he'd just implied that he wanted me to stay. He'd done research on the matter, and that alone was the hottest thing ever.

He stepped closer. "You can be here without a visa for six months in a twelve-month period."

"Oh."

"Oh?"

"Well, like wow. That's . . . a lot."

His eyebrows rose. "A good lot or a bad lot?"

"Not sure." I swallowed, the light, fuzzy feeling in my stomach intensifying the longer Rhys looked at me. This was real. *He* was real. And I was stunned. This wasn't how I'd felt with guys before. It wasn't even how Jake had made me feel. Like my entire body was smiling, not just my face. Like the warmth from the sun was permeating the snowy atmosphere and centering me in its rays. Like Rhys could kiss me and I just might spontaneously combust.

I wasn't ridiculous. I didn't think I *loved* the man yet, but I was seriously falling for him. Hard.

"If this conversation is giving your feet the desire to turn and run away, I will gladly hold them in place," he said.

"Oh, yeah? How do you plan to do that?"

"Using my lips."

"That's a pretty gross mental image."

He grinned, leaning toward me. "I was thinking more like my lips on your lips, but yeah, it came out wrong. I just don't want you to run away."

"I don't think I have reason to run away," I whispered, because I couldn't find a way to say it at full volume. Also, there were still other people around.

Rhys trailed his fingers down my arm and brushed the back of my hand. "You could pretend for a minute, just so I can practice giving you a reason to stick around."

"You've given me plenty of reasons so far. But I was always taught practice makes perfect, so I won't stop you." I took a fistful of his shirt, the soft plaid folding easily in my clenched hand, and pulled him toward me. He bent down, pressing his lips to mine in a familiarity we'd easily achieved over the last few days.

His hands didn't touch me. No part of his body touched me except his mouth and where my knuckles pressed into his abs, but heat sliced through me all the same. When I leaned back, he gave me a lazy, kiss-drunk smile, and I knew with immediate certainty that I wasn't ready to let whatever this was between us come to an end yet.

"Wow." A silky voice cut through my warm euphoria. Blonde Jessica Rabbit stood in the doorway, her arms crossed over her chest and a small smile playing across her lips like she was enjoying herself. "This is really weird for me."

Weird for her? She looked downright pleased. Rhys stiffened beside me, and I felt it like a physical force. "What can we do for you, Jen?"

"I came to help. I saw the text from Hamish on Grandad's phone."

"I think that was only meant for the council." Rhys was cool and collected, like he hadn't just been spotted kissing the American tourist by his ex-wife. But there were signs that he'd rather be huddling in an Alaskan igloo or floating on a door in the Atlantic ocean than standing here in this barn with us. His mouth was pinched, his knuckles white, and his eyes darted everywhere but at me.

"Well, Grandad shouldn't be doing manual labor right now, so I'm here in his place."

My stomach clenched uncomfortably. "That's nice of you," I choked out.

Jenna offered me a smile that said *why are you talking to me, orphan?*

I didn't know why I made myself parentless in this scenario when I had two perfectly loving parents at home, but it felt fitting.

Rhys pointed in the general direction of where Hamish was explaining something to Richard, Chris, and Ruby. "He's in charge."

Jenna gave him a soft, familiar smile. "It's good to see you again so soon, Rhys."

He nodded once.

Her retreat was so seductive I had to force myself to look away. Honestly, what was she trying to do? Make Rhys chase her?

"I guess I'll join them," I said.

He squeezed my forearm. "Or you can help me with these ropes."

My smile was as soft as our words. "I want to be helpful."

"And I want to keep you away from her." He frowned. "I don't know what she's playing at, but I think it's got to do with you. This isn't normal for her."

"I think not appreciating the visual of your ex-husband moving on is actually pretty normal."

He dipped his chin and held my gaze. "Maybe. But I don't want her back. I haven't for a while."

"Hold up. *You* were the one who said you were still a little hung up—"

"Hung up on the relationship. Not on Jenna. I should have explained better."

"Yeah, that might have been helpful."

Rhys dropped a kiss on my lips again, in full view of everyone. "Now pick up some rope, Lu, and help me get out of this barn for a minute."

"You've got it."

THE REST of the day was an exercise in extreme self-control. Jenna found a way to be involved with each of the projects Rhys was assigned to, and I found myself slipping further and further into the shadows. He tried to include me, so I wasn't feeling like he preferred her or any of that self-conscious garbage. But their past wasn't about to disappear, and the years they had spent together had produced many, many, *many* inside joke opportunities for them today. When Jenna got a real laugh out of Rhys after bringing up something about a one-eyed pirate called Smithson, I felt my insides crumble a little.

It was all going to be okay though, because jealousy aside, I was the one he looked for when Hamish called everyone up to the house for pizza in the late afternoon.

"I need to get to the pub," Rhys said. "You want to stick around for a while here?"

"No, I'll come back with you."

He smiled, then nodded to where I'd left my things. "Don't forget your jumper."

Rhys spoke to Ruby for a minute while I took my time gathering my purse and the extra sweater I'd brought. Then everyone cleared out of the barn, leaving us behind. Which was exactly what I'd wanted. I had a plan.

I felt in my pocket for the mistletoe, and it was still there—though maybe a bit crumpled.

"Ready?" Rhys asked.

"I need your help first."

He shook his head. "You aren't getting me alone in a barn to have your way with me, Miss Winter. It's unsanitary."

"No, I'm not." I pulled out the mistletoe. "I want to hang this above the door."

"I'll get the ladder."

Rhys carried it toward the main doorway and held the bottom while I climbed up to the second-to-last rung. The mistletoe was so small and difficult to discern against the dark beam of the door frame, but it was there, and that was all I needed. It was probably better if no one noticed it until I could position Ruby and Hamish just so, and then conveniently point it out . . .

"What are you doing up there?" Rhys asked, pulling me from my plan-hatching.

I looked down at him from my perch. "Just scheming with my elven Christmas magic, obviously."

"You don't have to scheme with plants to kiss me, you know. I've been doing it willingly for a while now."

I clicked my tongue. "So self-centered, Rhys. Who says I'm thinking about you?"

He looked a little taken aback. "Who are you thinking about?"

I climbed down the rest of the ladder and hopped to the ground. I reached up, booped him on the nose, and said, "Hamish."

"Not so fast." He took my hand when I started walking away and pulled me toward him. "Explain, please."

"I want to set up Ruby and Hamish, and I plan to use this mistletoe to do it."

He looked uncertain. "I told you, they—"

"No, I know. But there's something there. Ruby as good as admitted it herself. I think they just need a little nudge."

He hesitated. "I don't know if this is a good idea."

"It might not even happen." I pointed above our heads. "But I made it *possible*."

"Okay, Christmas elf." Rhys slung his arm over my shoulders and led me out to the snowy field toward the cars. "Just be careful."

TWENTY-FIVE

MY MOM ALWAYS TOLD ME THE BEST THING TO DO WHEN I was stressed was to sit on the floor and meditate. The second-best thing was chocolate. Thanks to Poundland's fabulous variety and my yoga training, I had both of those stress-relievers available to me in spades. The morning of the Christmas fair and my meeting with Stella Fit, I utilized both of them.

After I woke up way too early, did an hour-long calming meditation, and took a hot shower, I got ready, opened a Curly Wurly bar, and checked the clock. It was only half past six. The pub wasn't even open yet.

But that didn't mean something wasn't already cooking down in the kitchen. I opened my door as I took a bite of the chocolatey caramel goodness. Scuffling sounds came from Rhys's room across the hall, then the little yap of Ned at the door begging to be let out. His paw clacked on the wood. I waited a minute so I could greet Rhys when he opened the door, but he wasn't coming, and Ned was only growing whinier.

I knocked softly. "Rhys?"

No answer except Ned barking louder.

I knocked harder.

The door swung open and Rhys stood in the open space, a towel wrapped around his waist. His wet hair was all over the place, water droplets clinging to the ends of the glossy strands and rolling down his bare chest. For a man who received the bulk of his exercise rolling out pie dough and chopping logs for the pub's fireplaces, he was nothing short of a work of art.

Ned ran past my feet and would probably be yapping at the front door shortly, but I couldn't be bothered by things like bathroom needs when there was a veritable Greek statue in the flesh standing before me.

"Mmm . . ." I said, because apparently I equated Rhys's toned abs to the Curly Wurly bar now melting in my hand.

"Mmm?" he asked. His amusement knew no bounds. He crossed his arms over his chest because he must have felt that I needed to be further tortured by the accentuation of his biceps. Have I ever mentioned how much wood the fireplace downstairs needed to keep it going all day? Well, it was a fair amount. This guy had ample experience chopping logs.

"Yes. Mmm-*muy caliente*. It's a normal morning greeting in California."

"Very hot?"

Shoot.

"Yeah. I mean. Sometimes we wake up hot. So, you know . . ." I grinned. I wasn't fooling him, and we both knew it.

"Right."

I pointed what remained of my Curly Wurly down the stairs. "I'm gonna go help Ned with the front door. You go ahead and do whatever it is you were doing."

He shook his head, laughing. "I'll see you down there in a minute."

My internal body temperature had risen at least four degrees and the chocolate caramel bar was now a mess all over my palm. I let Ned outside, then went into the kitchen to wash my hands . . . after eating what I could save of the bar. I wasn't a heathen.

Rhys came up behind me while I was drying my hands. He slid his arms around my waist and pulled me toward him. "What do you want for breakfast?"

"You serious right now? Because I swear if you kiss me and look like that *and* cook for me today, I don't think I'll be able to contain myself. It's bad enough I know I'll have to see you in a Santa suit later. You're going to throw me over the edge here."

"Are you afraid that the costume will turn you off me?"

"No, I'm worried that watching you with little children will force me to get on one knee and propose, and a Christmas engagement is way too Hallmark for me."

He laughed. "I think I'd like Hallmark."

"You probably would. It's excellent."

My phone buzzed in my back pocket, and I pulled it out. **Flakey Jakey (Do Not Call)** was flashing across the screen. I could tell when Rhys noticed it by the way he released me.

"You can take it," he said.

"I don't want to."

"How many times has he called?"

"Four hundred, give or take."

He waited, looking at me with the sweetest, most careful expression. "You know I'm here. I'll get started on breakfast if you want to take care of that so he'll stop bothering you."

It wasn't bad advice, but Rhys didn't know the half of it. In the last few days, I had missed calls with voicemails from Callie, Mom, and Jake. Because I was afraid they were calling to make me face something I wasn't ready for, I'd studiously ignored every one of them. The beautiful part about having an ocean between us was that no one was forcing me to talk. They couldn't drive to my house or go up to my room and corner me with loving, compassionate stares until I broke and spilled. I had run away from them, and for the first time, they couldn't reach me unless I wanted them to.

Unread messages both in text and voicemail form from

Callie, Mom, and Jake were bolded, and they all said about the same thing.

I keep missing you! Phone tag, you're it.

Luna, we need to talk.

Hey, have you thought about that job offer?

When are you coming home?

Just call me.

Lu, you okay?

And the single message from Dad: *Love you, Lulu.*

They were all well-meant. I knew that. Well, maybe all except Jake's. I didn't know what he wanted, but I knew it had to do with Aubrey, and I didn't know how to be okay with hearing him fight for her. Hadn't they done enough to me? Why couldn't he just let things lie?

Rhys lit the stove and started pulling ingredients from the refrigerator. He was right, though. The sooner I spoke to Jake and told him in no uncertain terms to leave me be, the sooner he and everyone else would let it go. I was in England, anyway. It wasn't like I was going to change my flight for him.

I dialed Jake back and paced to the Christmas tree to plug in the lights.

He picked up after one ring. "Hey."

Really? A little sparse on greetings. "It's got to be after ten there."

"Yeah. Sorry for those middle of the night calls. It took me a minute to figure out the time zones."

But he thought it was okay to call before seven in the morning? "Don't worry, you never woke me up."

"Cool."

Not to sound like a broken record, but *really*? I pinched the bridge of my nose. "What do you need, Jake?"

"It's not me, it's Aubrey. I just . . . she's broken, Luna."

Kind of like I was when he left me for her. And then again when he proposed to her before I'd even reached the final stage of grieving our lost relationships. And then *again* after that, when they poured salt over my haphazardly stitched together wounds and tried to make me part of the bridal party. My stomach twisted.

"Come on, Jake. You and I both know you don't really want me at your wedding."

Silence. I was right. It was almost sickening how obviously he loved Aubrey. It would take a great amount of love for Jake to beg me to attend his wedding for the sake of his bride. We were together for *five years*. We weren't one of those short college relationships that had fizzled. We carried on to the point of moving to my hometown together. We were going to be married. He knew me, and he knew how hard this would be for me.

"She needs you," he said.

She should have thought of that before taking my boyfriend. "I'm in England, Jake."

"I'll pay for your flight."

"You're kidding." I scoffed. "Have you looked at prices for one-ways out of Heathrow right now? They're astronomical this close to Christmas."

"I don't even care. If you'll agree to come to the wedding, I'll pay for everything. You don't even have to be a bridesmaid. Just be there." He paused. "You know how important this wedding is to Aubrey. I know you do."

That was a bit below the belt, using mine and Aubrey's twenty-year relationship against me. The amount of money he was willing to spend for this was absurd. I almost couldn't believe it. Or maybe I didn't want to believe it. Would anyone? Aubrey missed me, sure, but she hadn't really tried to reach out in the last eight—no, nine now—months either. It was a little late in the game to suddenly alter course and fix our relationship. The wedding, however important to her, was less than a week away.

My lawyer ex-boyfriend was too logically minded to ignore all these things, too. There had to be a reason for this phone call beyond Jake's intense desire to make his fiancé happy. I knew this man intimately, and this was a huge ask, even for him.

"Why are you doing this, Jake?"

He blew out a breath that sent static through the phone. "It's not about me or you or even Aubrey. I'm just stressed out of my mind, and Aubrey's a wreck. She's an absolute *mess*."

That sounded like it was very much about both Jake and Aubrey and not about me at all. Why couldn't they let me get on with my life, and they could get on with theirs? "So it's my job to make sure she has a good wedding day?"

"No. I don't expect you to come for her, or even for me." He sounded pained. "I really didn't want to tell you this."

"Tell me what?" My voice was so flat and full of uncertainty I could hear the trepidation myself. The kitchen lights blared in my peripheral and Rhys stood beneath them, watching me with a furrow on his brow. He set two plates on the counter that looked like a full English breakfast again. I was really hoping for beans on toast somewhere on that plate.

It was a testament to how many awkward pauses this conversation had had that Rhys could whip up a meal in the amount of time I'd been on the phone. I could sense the impending bomb about to drop, but I had no earthly idea what it could be.

"Aubrey's stress levels are through the roof." Jake's voice remained level, but I could hear how uncomfortable he was. "Which is normal, she's a bride. But it's putting strain on the . . . on the baby. It will become dangerous for the baby's development if it's not managed soon."

You know how sometimes in movies when the character is shocked the camera tilts a bit? I always thought that was kind of kitschy, but it turned out it was actually realistic. Either that, or I suddenly gained the ability to see the earth turn. The phone slipped from my suddenly weightless hand and hit the floor with a thud. I stared down at it. *Baby*. It was an extremely powerful word for something that was probably smaller than my hand.

I bent to pick up my phone and found I didn't have the desire to get back up again, so I sat on the rug.

"Luna?"

"Yeah, I'm here. Just dropped my phone."

Silence. He was really good at that. But this time I was going to wait. It was his turn to talk.

It suddenly made a little more sense why they rushed the engagement and the wedding. For a woman who had planned her wedding—dress included—meticulously for years, I could see how she would want it to take place before her baby bump showed too much. Or maybe this was a recent development and the rushing was truly just a testament of their love.

"I wouldn't ask you to do this for me, or even just for Aubrey," he finally said again. "Do it for the baby, Lu. Stress is really not good for Aubrey or for him, and you could ease it if you came. Otherwise the doctors are talking bedrest if we can't get this under control."

Him. Oh wow. I didn't think Jake could make things worse, but that certainly did. Jake and Aubrey were going to have a miniature baby Jake, complete with curly golden hair (most likely) and a cherubic smile. My stomach twisted over itself and the Curly Wurly bar from earlier was threatening to make a reappearance. When I had told Rhys that Jake looked at Aubrey like she carried the sun, I hadn't realized she was actually carrying his son.

Do it for the baby, he'd said. *The baby.* So *now* if I stayed in England, I was a baby hater. Just line me up with the Grinch and Ebenezer Scrooge. You know, pre-heart changes.

"You've given me a lot to think about," I eked out.

"Can I buy your ticket? Just tell me when you can get to the airport and I'll arrange—"

What? "No."

"Sorry?"

White twinkle lights glowed in front of me, out of focus. His assumption that I would jump on a plane was a driving force in keeping me grounded right where I was. "No, Jake, you can't buy my ticket. I'm in England. I'm on vacation, but I'm also here for work. I have an important meeting today, and I will not—I *cannot* think about this right now."

He blew out another breath, and I could sense how difficult it was for him to rein in his frustration and not argue further for what he felt was a justifiable request. The man was a lawyer, for heaven's sake. "Okay. I'll give you time. Will you at least promise to think about it?"

I wasn't sure I was going to be able to think about much else. "Sure."

"Great. Thanks, Lu. You know, for what it's worth—"

"Don't. I just . . . don't. It's not worth anything right now." His sad attempts at making me understand were only going to make this worse. *Anything* he said right now would make this worse. I needed food to balance the sugar coating my stomach and to hear the voice of a man who did not want to force me to attend my exes' wedding.

"Fair enough."

Really? Nothing was fair anymore. I sucked in a breath. "Goodbye, Jake."

"Goodbye."

I hung up the phone and dropped it on the floor between my bent legs. Rhys watched me from the counter, but I couldn't face him. I dropped my forehead onto my knees and focused on slow, even breaths. I wasn't a baby expert, but I knew you had to be fairly far along before you learned the gender. Far enough that this wasn't brand new information. Had Aubrey been showing when I saw her at the taco shop last month? She had been wearing a big coat, so even if she was nice and volleyball-sized, I wouldn't have noticed it.

She was more than likely not even showing yet, because everything in life seemed to work out so perfectly for her. She would want to fit into her dress.

"Is it over?" Rhys asked, his voice hovering just above me.

I tilted my head back to look at him and was surprised to feel cool air hit the wet tears on my cheeks. Gross. Why was I crying about this? "They're having a baby."

"Oh." Rhys got down beside me on the floor and wrapped his arms around me, pulling me close. His large hands ran up and down my back in soothing rhythm while his chin rested on the top of my head. "I'm sorry this is hard for you," he murmured.

"I don't know why it is," I said into his shirt. I leaned back so I could see him, but he didn't loosen his hold on me. "I don't want that baby to be mine. But this was my future, so it hurts to see them having it without me, I guess."

"You're grieving. Grief isn't solely for death; it's our response to loss."

Loss. That was exactly what I'd experienced with Jake and Aubrey over the last nine months. Over and over again, it had pelted me with changes to my future. Things I'd been led to believe I would have someday had been ripped away and given to someone else.

"When did you get so wise?" I asked, trying to lighten the dark mood orbiting us.

"Therapy."

I leaned back further and could see the pain reflected in his dark eyes, echoing the loss and grief Rhys had worked through over the last few years. "I'm really impressed."

"I didn't have much of a choice. I was in a pretty dark place after Jenna left, and Ruby forced me to go. I'm grateful now, but at the time I wanted to disown her."

"She's a smart woman."

"Yeah, I think so too."

"The therapy helped?"

"Immensely. I learned things about myself and gained wisdom and understanding about loss and grief. I needed it in order to process the changes in my life and the changes in my expectations for my future." His hands didn't stop moving on my back, and I wanted to melt into him. His voice, when he spoke again, was soft. "I think sometimes the hardest thing to get over after a lost relationship is the alteration of what you expected your future to look like. But even if we'd stayed with them, Luna, and had the children or, in your case, the wedding and all those things we'd expected and hoped for, life still wouldn't have turned out the way we imagined it. It never does."

I sat with that for a minute, letting his thoughts penetrate my stubborn frustration and settle on my heart.

The words rang true. I had struggled more with losing my future than I did losing Jake. Not in the beginning, of course—that was pure sadness because I missed *him*. But his quick ability to move on had also put a damper on my desire to have him back in my life.

My future was still unknown. I didn't know if I'd take the job and move down to LA or amp up the LunaMoon channel or stay in Geyserville and finally get my own place or maybe even spend a little more time abroad. My five-year plan had been wiped clean and given a fresh slate, and maybe that was part of why I couldn't seem to let my anger go. I wasn't happy on YouTube, and I wasn't dying to keep building my brand. I wanted to help people, like I had with the chair yoga class here in the pub. I'd gotten more joy from that thirty-minute session than I'd gotten from anything in months—even if the seniors had acted like a group of toddlers for half of it.

"Are you hungry?" Rhys asked.

"Yes." I let him pull me up and lead me toward the counter, but I couldn't seem to get his words out of my head. My mind was a jumble of pregnant Aubrey, the Stella Fit meeting, my brand, my job, my room in my parents' house. It was a lot to process, but I had a feeling Rhys was onto something, and it was time for me to let go of the old future and determine what I wanted my new one to be. Maybe if I figured that out, I could finally move on with my life.

I reached across the counter and took Rhys's hand. He put his fork down and swiveled toward me.

"Thanks for being here," I said.

His mouth curved into a small smile. "It's *my* pub."

I rolled my eyes. "You know what I mean."

"Yeah," he said, his voice a little hoarse. "I do. And it's too soon for either of us to think much about a serious change in our futures, but I like that you're open to it."

With the Christmas lights on the tree in the background and the dim lighting in the pub, I felt cozy and warm, despite the way Jake had just figuratively ripped the rug out from beneath me.

"I'm open to it," I said, acknowledging that I thought whatever was going on between us was real.

"Good, because you're the first woman I've been able to see myself with in a long time, and I don't want you to break my heart."

I laughed. Break *his* heart? If anything, it would obviously be the other way around.

TWENTY-SIX

RUBY CALLED HERSELF MY FRIEND, BUT APPARENTLY SHE was just trying to torment me. I picked up the green, shimmering tights like they were a used diaper, pinching the slippery Spandex between my fingers. "You want me to wear *this*?"

"It's not that bad," she said, lifting the short dress. "It's a normal elf costume, just made out of Lycra."

"Because elves wear miniskirts and low-cut dresses while they're assembling toys."

"You would know," she said.

I held the costume against me and pivoted to face the mirror above the dresser in my room. "This looks more like something you'd find in the women's section of the Halloween store beside the sexy nurses, and less like Santa's wholesome helpers."

She stood behind me in the mirror and screwed her face into an apology. "Jenna got this outfit. She wore it the last few Christmases until . . ."

"Until she didn't wear it anymore?"

"Yeah."

I spun to face her. "Won't it be weird for Rhys to see me

wearing it, then? Maybe we can come up with a different costume before the fair starts tonight."

Ruby lifted an eyebrow. "Because we both have so much free time today?"

I looked at the clock on my phone. I had less than an hour before Edward would be here to pick me up for the lunch meeting at Brumsworth Manor. "Just don't be surprised if I leave my coat on while I'm helping Santa out tonight. I have a feeling I'll freeze in this."

"Hamish has space heaters up in the loft now. I saw them this morning."

Great. Of course he did. "How does the barn look?"

"Festive," she said. "The tables and everything fit well enough. It looks more like a bazaar than it has in years past, but I like it. It's nice having the kid crafts and shopping and hot chocolate booths all in the same place instead of separated in different tents like usual."

"Maybe the Linscombe tent mishap is a blessing in disguise then."

"I wouldn't go that far," Ruby said, laughing. "Especially not to the men. Don't say that around Hamish or you won't be permitted in his barn."

Speaking of the men . . . "Do you have everything ready for your cooking coup tonight?"

"Rhys isn't the government, and I'm not trying to overthrow him . . . but yeah, I'm ready for it." Her eyes were bright with anticipation. "I don't know how I'll manage to get through the whole fair. I might duck out early just to breathe a little."

"Want me to show you a quick routine you can use if you need to calm your heart rate tonight?"

Ruby blushed. "I've actually been using your videos the last few days, so I think I have that covered."

An unaccountable degree of pleasure bloomed in my chest. "You watched my channel?"

"Well, yeah. I know you said you'd do it with me sometime, and I'm sure it's much easier with you in the actual room, but your videos are good. You give the right amount of instruction and show me what I need to do from the right angles. Anyway, my free time for yoga is always way too early in the morning or too late at night to ask for your actual help, so YouTube was easier."

She had probably been upstairs practicing yoga while I was eating breakfast at the bar with Rhys. But I wouldn't tell her she could have just come downstairs and joined us.

"Besides, after you leave, I won't have you here anyway. I'll have to use YouTube." She picked up my elf hat and toyed with the pom-pom on the end of it. "You should be proud of what you've accomplished. You've done a good service for a lot of people who probably can't get to a studio or don't have the money for classes."

I lowered my flirty Spandex elf costume and hung it on the back of the chair. A lot of people couldn't afford extra things, but most people still had the internet. "I hadn't thought about it like that before."

Ruby shrugged. "I never wanted to do yoga before because Jenna used to set up downstairs and do these long routines that were probably designed to make people look at her butt. I mean, seriously, she would pull her mat out in the middle of the day, and it was never random. It was always when we had male tourists stop by."

"Um, gross."

"Yeah, and Rhys had to watch it all. I can't stand her. She cheated on him for like two years, and he just kept giving her chance after chance to fix things. They would be good for a minute, and then she would get bored again."

That left a sour taste on my tongue. "I thought she'd left Rhys."

"She did. It was messy, but I think he'd had enough and told her to choose him or leave. So, she left."

My heart sank to the floor. I couldn't imagine the hurt Rhys had gone through. "No wonder therapy helped him so much."

Ruby looked a little surprised by my admission, but she nodded. "Jenna and Rhys had been having problems for years, so once he got into therapy and worked it all out, it took a year for him to get back to his old self again. He's so much happier without her. Even if it doesn't look that way when they're near each other."

"I'm glad he found the help he needed."

She looked up at me. "Are you finding the help you need?"

"I think so." Jake having a baby with Aubrey had thrown me into a bit of a tailspin, but the reality was that it kind of finalized things for me in a weird way. Now nothing between us would ever change again. They were irrevocably connected, and if some tiny part of me had been holding out, hoping Jake would change his mind at the last minute—not that I would have taken him back, mind you, just that I would have had the *option*—then it was now safe to say the door had slammed shut on any lingering feelings I had for him.

It did something to my heart that was both painful and relieving. It made me crave Rhys.

"You know," I said, "when I first arrived and you warned me to stay away from your cousin—"

"Oh, gosh." Ruby lowered her head to her hand. "I was trying to spare *you*."

"I know. I'm not mad. I only wanted to say that I was being honest then, too. I'd told my sister I would try to kiss a British guy to get over my ex, but I hadn't targeted Rhys. If anything, I picked out right away that he would be a good one to steer clear of."

"Who'd you target then?"

"No one. I was just open to the idea." But my heart had

chosen Rhys the moment I stepped into The Wild Hare, and I couldn't take that back. The heart knew what it wanted, I guess.

Much like Jake's heart knew it wanted Aubrey. *Ugh.* Now I was becoming *understanding*? The whole baby thing had really put things into perspective for me. Sometimes being an emotionally mature adult was really annoying. I'd so much rather be a petty, angry, jilted ex. I couldn't deny how much lighter I felt, though. It might have been easier to be mad, but forgiving felt better.

"I need to go to my meeting soon. Is there anything I need to know about Stella Brumsworth?"

Ruby rolled her eyes. "She thinks she's amazing, and if you make her think you agree, then she'll love you forever."

"Sounds like a basic low-key celebrity."

"There is nothing basic about her," Ruby deadpanned.

We broke into laughter at the same time. I pulled her into a hug. "If I don't see you before tonight, then good luck."

"Pssh. I don't need luck. I need Valium."

"You don't need either. You're going to be great."

RHYS WAS ICING a cake when I leaned through the kitchen doorway. He must have sensed my presence, because he looked over his shoulder. "Stay where you are. This is a danger zone."

"Is that the Christmas cake then?"

"Yes, and if we're going to eat it on Christmas, it can't fall on the floor or be tipped into the bin or have a pretty American faceplant into it, or—"

I tried to look unamused, which was a struggle. "Okay, that's enough scenarios. Finish your cursed cake. I'll be out here."

"Wait, I'm almost done." He spread the rest of the white icing around the sides, then covered the cake and put it up in a cupboard, high away from me.

"Is it safe now?"

He cut me a smile. "Yes."

"You realize I have very high expectations for that cake now."

"Maybe lower them, then. My Gran was the master. I'm only the apprentice."

"I've had enough of your cooking to know you probably measure up to her."

"Sacrilege." He shook his head and dropped a kiss on my lips that tasted sweet, like he'd sampled the icing. "I'm excited for you to meet her."

My stomach clenched. I'd meet her someday, of course, but I didn't know if it would be Christmas Day this year like we'd planned. I couldn't get Aubrey's baby out of my head, and the more I thought about it, the more I wondered if I wasn't doing the right thing by staying here during the wedding. Letting go of my connection to Jake had felt liberating in the last few hours. Letting go of all my anger for both of them could be freeing on a completely new level.

But this brown-eyed pub owner with a habit of chopping firewood and smoldering unintentionally was staring down at me like I had offered him the world, and I wanted to give him the world. If I left now, would that be the end of us? Our holiday fling would come to a natural conclusion and we'd each get on with our regularly programmed lives?

I shook my head a little to remove the thoughts. It wasn't something I had to face right now.

"What's going on?" he asked, a little line forming between his eyebrows.

"I'm nervous about my meeting. I know she's a local, but Stella Fit is actually a pretty big deal."

Rhys's body grew rigid, his smile tightening. "I know, Luna. I think it's great that you made this connection and it could be good for you or whatever, but remember you're doing business with a shark. Don't forget that, okay?"

"I won't." I swallowed, his warning only proving to make me more nervous. "Is there anything else I need to know? Anything that might give me an edge in this meeting?"

He looked over my shoulder for a minute, his dark eyes glazing over a little.

"Rhys?"

His attention snapped back to me. "You're smart, Luna. You can handle this."

"Thanks. Edward is picking me up for lunch and giving me a ride to the fair." I lifted the grocery bag carrying my elf costume. "I won't see you until it's time to make little children's dreams come true."

Rhys's eyes flashed. "Edward's giving you a lift? You don't want to drive yourself?"

I shrugged. "He offered, and I figured I might as well take him up on it. I can catch a ride back to the pub with you tonight, right?"

"Of course."

I leaned up on tiptoe and pressed a kiss to his lips. "Good. I'll see you later, Father Christmas."

"You sound so American when you say that."

"Good." I grinned. "It's what I am."

TWENTY-SEVEN

BRUMSWORTH MANOR WAS EVEN BETTER UP CLOSE. THE stone exterior was covered in naked vines that probably teemed with emerald ivy during the summertime and turned red in the autumn. We crunched across the gravel driveway, and I carried my elf costume with me so I could change into it before going to the fair later. Edward was polite on the drive, though he took the roads in his slick black BMW much faster than I would have. But really, everyone here probably drove faster than I would have. I was used to winding roads, but back home we could easily fit two passing F-150s. I wasn't sure if snowy Cotswold roads could fit *one* American-sized truck.

"Tour first, lunch after?" Edward asked. "It was meant to be the other way around, but Stella is running behind. Her work associate is in town and they took a meeting in Cheltenham this morning, but they're on their way back now."

"A tour sounds great." I set my bags down on a wooden bench near the door. The walls were papered, the ceilings iced in intricate plaster work, heavily featuring roses.

Edward led me into the next room, a striking contrast to the previous one with its dark wood paneling but still filled with the same classic furniture that looked hand-selected to give the room an antiqued look. Or maybe the sofas really were two hundred years old. I stepped back just in case.

"How long have you been in Snowshill?" he asked.

"A few weeks. I only have a week left, and I am not ready to go home. I love it here."

"It's a quaint village. Did you spend much time in London before you came out here?"

How had he managed to make quaint sound like a bad word? "No, none."

"That's a shame."

I smiled politely. "I'm sure I'll get over there soon." I'd loosely planned to return to London a few days before my flight home so I could check out the Tower or ride through the city on one of those red double-decker buses. But now . . . maybe once Ruby proved herself in the kitchen, Rhys could take an entire day off and we could go see some of the city sights together.

If Ruby proved herself? Not that I doubted her, of course. But my opinion didn't matter here. Rhys had to be the one not doubting her.

We moved through the rest of the tour. Edward shared a surprising number of facts about the house and his ancestors' history with it. There had been many babies born in one of the upper bedrooms, and the story of a midwife fainting in the middle of one of the births and leaving the father to complete the delivery with only a servant girl to assist him plucked gingerly at my emotional chords.

It seemed impossible to go anywhere in this house without seeing a painting of an infant or a strategically placed ancient rocking horse in one of the tour rooms. Babies, just, *everywhere*.

My stomach tightened, and I stopped hearing the facts about Cromwell once sleeping in *this very bed*, because my brain snagged on a memory from high school. Aubrey and I had been in health class together when we had to do the baby assignment. My electronic baby survived it, no thanks to Tony Alvarez—I did not get to choose my "husband" for the assignment. But while most of us just fed the baby, changed the baby, did all the things we were supposed to do so the electronic thing inside the baby wouldn't report us as negligent, Aubrey embraced the assignment with zeal. She'd been a ready-made mom, and what's more, she'd wanted it. It was really a miracle she didn't have a motherhood goals scrapbook to go along with her wedding books, complete with babies cut from magazines or the strollers or toys she would buy.

While I was planning what I wanted to eat for lunch or what school I might attend after high school, Aubrey had had her next ten years mapped out. College, grad school, an interior design career she could manage on the side while devoting herself to her husband and adorable children, all before her thirtieth birthday.

It looked like she was about to get everything she wanted.

Since lunch was on the horizon for me, it seemed like I was getting everything I'd planned for, too.

"You all right, Luna?" Edward asked, yanking me from my high school memory.

"Just feeling a little off today. I heard from home this morning, and it's thrown me a little." I rallied, squaring my shoulders and offering a bright smile. "But I'm fine. It's nothing awful. What's next?"

The door downstairs opened and shut again to the sound of feminine laughter.

Edward turned an expensive smile on me. "Looks like it's time for lunch."

He led me through the last two rooms to the top of the stairs and we started down. Stella Fit and another woman were laughing together near the door, and when they turned around to face us, I stumbled on the steps.

"Jenna," I said shrilly, because my mouth apparently didn't know how not to do that.

"Oh, Luna." She moved to meet me at the foot of the stairs. "It's good to see you again. Let me introduce you to my friend and colleague, Stella."

The women stood like a pair of bored models, tall, lithe, and expensive. Stella was gorgeous on Instagram, but I'd attributed at least some of it to filters. Apparently, she defied natural laws because her skin was perfect, her hair looked freshly blown-out, and her clothes were immaculate.

I put my hand out to shake Stella's. She gave me a perfect smile and stepped forward for a hug. "Shaking hands is for old men in suits. I prefer to *embrace*." This she said while squeezing me, her cheek pressed to mine. We got real close, real fast.

Evidently, Jenna did not feel the same need to hug. After having to watch her ex-husband kiss me, though, I really couldn't blame her for wanting to keep her distance.

"How do you know one another?" Stella asked.

Jenna's mouth curved like the Cheshire Cat. "Luna is staying at the pub. She and Rhys are friends."

"Oh. Ohhhh." Stella looked at me appraisingly, her startlingly green eyes sweeping over my outfit. They *had* to be contacts, right? No one's eyes were that green. "Shall we eat?"

The table was already set for four, so I was the only one who hadn't known Jenna would be joining us. We took our seats, and Edward helped Jenna into her chair, his hand lingering on the back of her neck when he moved to take his own seat. The touch was familiar, and she didn't rebuff him. Interesting.

"You have quite a following," Stella began, ignoring the two women who brought food in and set it on plates before us. It all felt so *Downton Abbey*, but despite my adoration of the show, I was more uncomfortable being served than I expected. "Last I checked, you were one of the top yoga accounts on YouTube. But your Insta numbers aren't as high."

"I haven't focused there as much until recently, but I've seen a steady increase in the last few weeks. Mostly since I started posting when I arrived in Snowshill, actually. But Instagram has never been my priority."

"Still, it could be good for funneling new subs to your channel. You want to consistently increase in growth." Stella took a dainty bite of her salad. "Which is where we come in."

I forked a bite of salad to avoid having to respond right away.

Edward lifted a hand in a somewhat placating gesture. "Perhaps this conversation is best held after we eat, eh?"

"Of course." Stella blinked at me. Her eyes were so green and so round, I wondered if she'd spent much time before a mirror—or a front-facing camera—to perfect the innocent look. It was really close to authentic, but didn't quite ring true. Rhys's warning flashed through my head. Would Stella bear sharp shark teeth, too? He'd once said she was grand.

"Tell us about yourself," Jenna said. "I'm dying to hear about how you met Rhys."

So now we were getting personal. "At the pub."

"As a guest?" Her eyebrows shot up. "I just assumed you've known one another for a while, I suppose. He's not the sort to jump into a relationship."

He wouldn't be, would he? Not when he'd spent most of his life with one person and then the subsequent years healing from the trauma of that imploded relationship. When would he have had time to jump into anything? Over the last two years, I supposed.

And who said we were in a relationship? All she had done was seen us kiss.

Edward shifted uncomfortably.

"I don't think Rhys does anything without thinking it through," I said.

Jenna laughed a little forcefully. "Perhaps most of the time. I think our kiss at the hospital the other night was more what you would call spontaneous."

Edward's fork skid across his plate with a jaw-clenching screech.

She reached across the table and laid her perfectly manicured hand over his. "Oh darling, don't worry. It was nothing."

He looked up and gave her a tight smile, but I couldn't be so easily placated. I had specifically asked Rhys if there was anything I should know before going to this meeting, and he'd conveniently forgotten two major points here. First, that Jenna appeared to be Stella's business associate and, since she was local, it was highly likely she would be present at the meeting. Second, that *he'd kissed her* last week.

The balsamic vinegar dressing soured in my stomach, and I trained a polite smile on my face to get me through the rest of the lunch. When he'd warned me about the shark, had he meant Jenna? Her teeth were looking a little sharper than they'd been a minute ago.

The rest of the meal passed excruciatingly slowly, and we moved into a small sitting room to discuss business particulars. Edward, who had seemed more uncomfortable and annoyed than me, paced behind the couch instead of sitting.

He shot me a bland smile. "Since you all have business to discuss, I'll just leave you to it."

"Let's talk numbers," Stella said, her smile Barbie-wide again while her brother left. "My brand is only associated with the best of the best. We are very particular about who we partner with on collabs, as I'm sure you might be aware."

It was true that I'd only seen collaborations between Stella Fit and celebrities, for the most part. It wasn't a standard influencer ad. Quite a few influencers wore Stella Fit, but they didn't have the exclusive ad hashtag or call themselves ambassadors or anything of the sort.

"We have a new organic cotton line coming out in the

spring," Stella said, "and we wanted to offer you a place on our early ambassadors roster. You'll receive three outfits in the deal and we'll arrange how many videos and posts we'll need from you."

Three outfits? That had to be worth loads of money. Not that I was hurting for cash—my channel did fairly well—but I tended to be on the conservative side of the spending spectrum, and three outfits from a brand-new line would cost a fortune. "I'm honored you want to collaborate, Stella. I've loved your products for as long as I've been familiar with them."

"Thank you." She pulled out her phone and began tapping. "We require nine Instagram posts minimum and a correlating nine videos on your channel. The pieces we'll send you are easy to mix and match in a variety of combinations and I want you to showcase that specifically."

"Okay."

"You're in California, yes? Northern or southern?"

"Northern."

"Perfect." She tapped more, her nails clacking away on the screen so furiously I was impressed it didn't break. "Jax is my guy up there. I'll give him your info, and he'll set up a shoot with you. It will take the entire day, but trust me, it's totally worth it. That man works magic behind the camera. Jenna here is our content supervisor, so she'll grant post approval on anything before you actually post it." Stella looked up and sent each of us a smile. "But that'll be easy, since you already know one another."

My head spun with the information and the fast talking and the plans. I felt I was committing to things I didn't fully understand. Post approval? Photographer? *Nine* posts and videos based on three outfits?

I needed more information. "What sort of timeline are we looking at here for the nine posts?"

"Minimum," she reminded me. "Our soft launch is in April, so ideally I want them to span March."

"Nine posts and videos in the same clothes all in one month?"

"Minimum," Stella and Jenna said together, their faces Stepford Wives bland.

Good grief. What had I agreed to here? I wasn't sure I even wanted to continue the channel on a full-time basis, and this was basically throwing my social media work into turbo mode. I looked at the time on my phone and my stomach dropped. The fair began in a half-hour. I needed to get dressed and be on my way soon, or Rhys would be fending off toddlers and trying to hear their lists all on his own.

"I need to go now, but can we continue this later? Perhaps over email?"

Stella put her phone down. "Sure, but I would like an answer by Sunday. There are very few positions open on my early launch team, and if you cannot fully commit then I need to fill the spot with someone else."

Translation: I was expendable. But gosh, how much were free clothes and an exclusive ad deal really worth?

I stood. "I have been really honored to be considered, Stella. Thank you for taking the time to meet with me."

She stood as well and offered me a handshake. Whatever test she'd been administering over the course of lunch, I'd clearly failed.

"Can I use your bathroom? I need to change into a costume for the fair."

"Of course." Stella showed me where I could change.

"Stell, we need to go," Jenna said, sounding annoyed.

Stella shot me an apologetic look. "We have to be in London this evening. You can see yourself out?"

"Yes, definitely." It was her brother who would see me out anyway. He'd offered to drive me to Hamish's for the fair.

I retrieved my bag from the entryway while the women went out the front door and got into a bright yellow sports car. I watched through the window while Jenna climbed into the driver's seat and it spun away. The top corner of her back windshield had a peace sign sticker that I'd seen before on a yellow car just like this. I shouldn't be surprised that Jenna was the same person who'd run me off the road when I had arrived in town. It was rather fitting, wasn't it?

TWENTY-EIGHT

WHOEVER DECIDED THAT SANTA'S ELVES NEEDED GREEN shimmer tights and a short red skirt was probably never forced to actually put that outfit on. The long sleeves had white faux fur trim, and the low v-cut was blessedly not as revealing as I'd imagined it was going to be. I threw my coat over the top of it, snagged my purse, and tucked my hat away. I could put that on when I got to the fair.

The house was quiet. I checked the main rooms downstairs, but they were empty. Weird. It wasn't my house, so I wasn't about to check each room upstairs for the one Edward might be waiting in. I pulled out my phone and found a text waiting for me from Rhys.

Hot British Guy: Hope your meeting goes well. Don't be afraid to walk away if you need to. xx

My stomach constricted. X meant kiss, didn't it? That was the half of kisses and hugs that made up X's and O's. I realized this was probably a British cultural habit, but Rhys hadn't been kissing *only* me lately, if Jenna could be believed, and I couldn't help but think of that. While he might not have owed me anything, it felt slimy that he hadn't felt the need to tell me, either.

Or maybe he'd wanted to, and that was part of what he'd tried to say when we talked the other night.

I ignored his message and found Edward's number, who answered after a few rings. "Hello? Meeting go well?"

"Meeting's over," I said noncommittally. "I'm ready to leave."

There was silence for a few seconds. "Okay. It was good to see you today. Sorry if things were odd at lunch, but Jenna and I have been in a weird place, and—"

Cold slipped into my stomach. Why did he sound like he wasn't about to see me again? And what did he mean about Jenna? "I'm in your foyer, Edward. Are you still here?"

"No, I took off. Couldn't take any more of it, you see. Jenna can be difficult. But I suppose her fiery nature is part of why I love her so much."

Prickles ran down my spine. My voice echoed in the empty foyer—more empty than I'd realized. Was I in this house alone? "I need to go to the fair," I repeated. "Are you . . . that is, I was under the impression you would give me a ride."

Edward swore. "I forgot. Snag a lift with the girls?"

"The girls are gone."

He was silent, and I realized then that he wasn't turning around for me. If he'd left the house when he left us, he was at least forty minutes away. "I'll figure it out."

"Great. It was good to see you, Luna."

I hung up. Within about five minutes, I realized that letting Edward off the phone so easily had been a mistake. Neither Ruby nor Rhys answered my calls. Lyft didn't operate in England, evidently, and Uber wasn't out this far.

Too bad they didn't have a chauffeur waiting in the garage

like in *Downton*—oh, wait! The maids who served us lunch could still be around. I went searching for the kitchen and found one of the women washing dishes at the sink. When I explained my situation, she gave me an apologetic grimace. "Kristen just took my car to pick up her daughter for the fair. She'll be back to pick me up, but not for another hour."

I needed to be there well before an hour. I pulled up the walking directions on my phone, and it looked like it would take me thirty minutes to walk to Hamish's barn from here. Not terrible . . . especially if I did a light jog.

"Looks like I'm walking. Good thing the sun's out!" I said brightly.

The maid leaned in and pointed to a place on the map on my phone. "Might as well cut through the field there. Just pass the garden shed, you'll see the path. It'll cut off a few minutes."

"Thanks." I tightened my coat and pulled on my gloves. This would put me a little late to the fair, but it was better than being extremely late or missing it altogether. Gravel crunched angrily beneath my boots while cold air nipped at my nose and the sun shone overhead. It was such a lovely day, but the only feeling I could seem to process was frustration.

Frustration with myself, with Rhys, with Edward and Stella and Jenna. With this stupid, cold snow and my stupidity for not driving myself.

The shed door was open when I passed it, and I stopped and backed up a step. Right there, leaning against the wall inside, was a bright turquoise bike with a cute basket teeming with fake flowers. It was the bespoke bicycle I'd seen featured on Stella Fit's Instagram page a handful of times over the summer, and it gave the impression to followers that she was a down-to-earth country girl who rode about her family estate in her off time. After meeting her, I was fairly certain she only posed for those photos and probably never actually pedaled anywhere.

Which meant she wouldn't miss it now, would she?

I was probably emboldened by my irritation with Edward and the way Jenna had just casually been at the meeting and slipped in the news of a kiss she knew would crawl under my skin, but I didn't care that my actions were likely considered breaking the law. Was it really stealing when I didn't intend to keep the bike forever? Nah, that was just borrowing.

Santa needed me, so this was really for the kids, anyway. I was taking the bike in the name of elves everywhere.

I threw my leg over the side and hopped up onto the seat. The wet ground made it difficult to pedal, but I hadn't toned my leg muscles with hours and hours of yoga for nothing, and I quickly got the hang of off-roading on basic street tires. At least the gravelly path wasn't also covered in snow. It was slippery enough as it was.

My phone called directions to me from where I'd tossed it in the basket. I hadn't called my mom or sister back since speaking to Jake, but that hadn't stopped them from continually reaching out to me. My stomach clenched, the discomfort of knowing I'd left things too long with my family clawing at me. Jenna's revelation about the hospital kiss might have stung, but it also gave me really important insight into my situation: I had done *exactly* what my mom warned me not to do on this trip. I'd allowed myself to believe the romance was real and turned it into some Hallmark Christmas story of my own.

Those were great for fiction, but a holiday fling couldn't be real. I had been practically wearing vacation goggles the entire time I was in Snowshill, seeing the place and the people through the lens of a person not living their real, day to day life. Ergo, it could not be anything but a vacation fling. The electricity that hummed between Rhys and me was definitely there, but it was static-driven, not directly from a powerline. It was warm and sparked feelings, but they couldn't sustain a relationship. The idea that I would fall in love so quickly with a man I'd only known a few weeks was preposterous. Wasn't it?

I needed a voice of reason. I leaned forward and told Siri to call my parents' house phone, then hit the speaker button.

It rang a few times before Callie answered it. "Finally! She lives!"

"Very funny," I said, out of breath.

"You sound far away."

"I'm trying not to yell," I yelled, "but my phone is in a bike basket."

"You're biking?"

"I have to get to the Christmas fair on the other side of town, and my ride ditched me."

"A Christmas fair? How quaint!" When my sister said it, I knew she meant it as a compliment.

"You're gonna die when I send you pictures later. It's in a barn, and I get to play the elf and help all the kids sit on Santa's lap."

"Hot Santa or old Santa?"

"He's hot beneath the fake beard. I haven't seen the whole costume yet, though." My heart gave a pang, and I shoved the feeling away. I needed to be careful before I had a heart attack mid-bike ride. "Listen, is Mom there? I need to talk to her."

"She's out with Dad feeding the animals."

"Shoot, it's early there, isn't it?"

"Not too bad. What's up? You sound off."

I drew in a frigid, shaky breath. Suddenly talking to my mom on the phone wasn't enough. I knew the advice she was going to give, and I knew I'd only called her because she would tell me to do the right thing, and that was to go home and make things good with Aubrey. I could call Aubrey over FaceTime and clear things up between us, but that wouldn't put me in a pew on Christmas Eve, and if there was one thing I could do to prove I wasn't running away anymore, it would be to show up for her wedding and support her like I'd vowed to do when I was seven.

I hated what I was about to say.

"I need a plane ticket, Cal. For like tomorrow morning, if there's anything left." As soon as I spoke the words aloud, I felt the confirmation in my heart that it was the right choice. "I just can't do it myself right now because of the biking and the elf thing, so I wanted to ask Mom to look for a ticket for me." Ironically, I slowed to a stop, my breaths heaving. I didn't know why my heart was racing so fast—the amount of exercise I was doing didn't warrant my blood pumping quite that hard through my veins. Tears were screaming for liberation, but I fought their desperate cries.

"What happened, Lu?"

I leaned forward and rested my forehead on my bent arms. The time on my phone showed that the fair began in five minutes. I had to book it. But I couldn't seem to move.

I reached for my phone and held it closer. "I screwed up."

"Talk to me, Moon."

The sisters-only pet name unleashed a flood of tears that chilled on my skin the moment they hit my cheeks. "I think I fell in love."

She was quiet for a minute, and the winter wonderland around me only seemed to echo my foolishness back at me. "Like real love? With the hot chef/lumberjack?"

"Yeah. I've fallen for him pretty hard. And he is a few years out of being divorced, so he comes with some heavy baggage."

"You both do."

"Right . . . which is fine. It's manageable. But then Jake called—"

"*No*," she gasped. "What the actual—"

"It's nothing bad." I drew in a shaky breath. "Aubrey's pregnant."

"Shotgun wedding?"

"No. I don't know. Probably not? They're really in love, Cal, and it doesn't really matter. But I guess the stress of the wedding is getting to her. All she wants is reconciliation." I squeezed my eyes closed. "All I seem to do is run from everything. I run because I'm too scared to face it. I've been trying to change and be better, and I've made myself stay here and face some things, and I was so proud of myself for that. But really, I'm still running. Because Aubrey is there, pregnant, and trying to get married under a storm cloud with my face on it."

There was a little quiet before Callie spoke again. "That sounds like a pretty hideous storm cloud."

I spit out a laugh.

She gentled her tone. "Thus the plane ticket."

"Yeah, thus the plane ticket. I just . . . I need to stop running."

"Aren't you running from the hot—"

"He has a name. Rhys."

"Okay. Aren't you running from Rhys?"

"Not really. I'm just going home a week early to be mature and handle my stuff. It's like my real life is back in California on pause and my fantasy life is here, and if I want my Snowshill life to become real, I have to go back and face everything I ran away from. It's the only way to make it possible for what me and Rhys have to become real. If he wants to keep talking, we have phones, but I need to come home."

"That sounds mature," Callie said.

"It does, doesn't it?" Then why did I feel like I was breaking? I drew in a breath and put my phone back in the basket to pedal again.

Rhys had been the one to point out my grief and loss, and he was right. But it wasn't just the loss of Jake or Aubrey that had been hurting; it was losing the wedding I'd spent years helping Aubrey plan, losing the position as her maid of honor and best friend, losing the first stages of pregnancy excitement and ultrasound photos. All of these things were milestones I'd looked forward to sharing with her, and each one lost was another pelt to the heart with a paintball gun. They didn't puncture, but they left massive, painful bruises.

"I hate to ask the obvious," Callie said. "Especially when I want you home. But can't you just call her?"

"Yeah, I thought about that. But it's not the same. I mean, I can talk to her over the phone and clear the air, but being at the wedding—*that's* the support that's going to reduce her stress and the stress on the baby and let her enjoy her special day." A day I had personally helped plan over the years with various scrapbooks. I wasn't going home for Jake. I was going home for Aubrey. That distinction mattered, because he deserved nothing from me.

"Okay," Callie said.

"Can you have Mom get my ticket? Tell her to text me the total, and I'll Venmo her later. I have too much to do here tonight, but I want to be home as soon as possible."

"Consider it done."

"Tell her I don't care how much it costs. This expense is getting a write-off."

"You do know that means you still have to pay it, right?"

I laughed. "Yeah, Cal. I know."

"Okay. Mom will be out there for a while, so I'll get on it now and text you flight info when I have it. Any airline preferences?"

"Nope."

"I have to say, I'm sorry you're going through all this, but I'm not too bummed we'll get to have you home for Christmas."

"Good. You can pay me back by being my date to Jake's stupid wedding."

"Ugh. Fine."

She hung up, and I pedaled harder, reaching the road that led to Hamish's barn after a few minutes. Cars were lined up on an empty field, and I hopped off the bike and leaned it against the back of the building. Note to self: next time, drive myself to any foreign meetings.

It was warmer inside and the very image of a European Christmas market. People milled about the various tables selling wares while kids had started crafts in the corner and the smell of rich hot chocolate and coffee mixed together and permeated the space. It beat the musty odor we'd dealt with yesterday, and I thought setting the drinks up near the door so the smells hit straight away was smart.

Ruby appeared, grabbing me by the arm. Her bright green sweater was festive, and the red bow tied to her ponytail was a nice touch. "There you are! We were worried."

"Not enough to answer your phone though."

She grimaced. "I was just fetching it to ring you. Rhys is upstairs if you want to go now. We told the kids to start with the craft to buy you a little time."

"Thanks."

I climbed the steps, taking off my coat as I went. Rhys must have heard me coming because he appeared at the top of the stairs, his suit filled out with extra padding and the white beard that had begun our friendship hooked over his chin. But his dark, handsome eyes could not be hidden beneath an aged costume, and their twinkle was exactly the sort of jolliness these kids needed.

"Quite believable," I said, eyeing him as I passed into the room. I set my things down behind the set. There was a Christmas tree in the corner with wrapped packages and a large, wooden chair to the side. A red velvet blanket was thrown over the chair, and it looked much like what I'd grown up seeing in malls, only more rustic and less tacky.

He followed me over to the tree. "Are you okay?"

"Edward forgot he promised to give me a ride and left well before the meeting ended. By the time I got out of the bathroom all changed into this masterpiece"—I lifted my arms to showcase the ridiculous outfit—"everyone was gone."

"They left you? How'd you get here?"

"I stole Stella's bike. I might need help returning it tonight before anyone finds it missing."

Rhys let out a rumbling laugh that shook his padded belly. "That's gutsy."

"I didn't have another choice. No one was answering their phones, so it was either that or wait an hour for a ride from Stella's maid."

He stepped forward and wrapped his gloved hand over my cheek. "You're so *good*, Luna. I think most people in your position would have taken advantage of the situation and hung out at Brumsworth for a while."

"I made a commitment," I said simply. It was growing more difficult to hold his gaze, knowing Callie was scouring the internet for the best flight to get me out of here in the morning. Did I tell Rhys now? No, not when he was about to put on a jolly face for the next few hours.

I tried to smile, but his lingering touch left a mark on my jaw.

"Hey," he said softly, "what's going on?"

Wow, he could read me so well. Static electricity buzzed between us, and it didn't help that his concern was almost palpable.

Hamish poked his head through the doorway, surprising me with the vivacity of his bright red holiday sweater sporting a fuzzy puppy in a stocking. "Rubes is down there holding the line. You guys ready?"

"Just about," Rhys said. "Give me one minute, then send them up."

Was no one unfazed by Hamish in the puppy sweater? It was one of the types where the puppy was 3-D, like a stuffed animal leaning out a little from his chest. I shook away my amusement and leaned down to rummage through my bag for the elf hat, then plopped it on my head and tried to smooth out my wind-blown hair.

Rhys took his seat. "Thanks for doing this."

"Of course. I don't mind spreading a little Christmas cheer."

"You *are* Christmas cheer," he murmured.

Luckily, I was saved from having to respond by the sound of excited little feet running up the stairs. I crossed to the entrance and waited with my hands folded softly in front of me. First up was a little boy I recognized from the pub, Finn. His mom was just behind him.

"Good evening," I said brightly, my smile stretching authentically over my cheeks. It wasn't hard to feel the warmth in my heart reflected in the smile on Finn's excited face. He saw Rhys sitting on the chair, and his little eyes lit up. I crouched to Finn's eye level. "Are you ready to meet Father Christmas?"

"Yes," he said reverently. Then he tilted his head to the side. "But why do you sound so funny?"

I glanced up to his mom, and her face broke into a grin. "She's one of Father Christmas's elves, darling. They come from all over the world."

Finn gazed at me in awe, and I was glad he didn't seem to remember me from the pub. Thanks to my ridiculous outfit, no doubt. I suppressed the broadness of my smile and offered him my hand. He took it, allowing me to lead him at a sedate pace up to Rhys.

"Well, hello there," Rhys said, and his warm voice set all the liquid in my body to simmer. "Have you been a good boy this year or a naughty boy?"

"I have been so good, Father Christmas," Finn said seriously. "Even when I didn't want to be."

"I'm proud of you. Would you like to tell me what your Christmas wish is?"

"Yes." Finn leaned forward carefully and whispered in Rhys's ear, and I could see Rhys fighting a smile. They chatted for another minute before Rhys reached into the large red sack hanging from his chair and produced a peppermint candy.

"Thanks, Luna," Flo whispered before ushering Finn back down the stairs. I winked at her, then started over with the next little girl.

When I caught Rhys's eye over the girl's pigtails, my stomach constricted. It was going to be extremely difficult to leave him.

But what choice did I have?

TWENTY-NINE

FOR SUCH A QUIET GUY, HAMISH HAD THE ENTIRE FAIR surprisingly well in hand. He stood at the bottom of the steps beside me and hollered, "Father Christmas's Grotto will be closing in ten. Last chance for Father Christmas's Grotto."

He moved toward the doorway when Ruby ran toward us, her eyes wide. "I'm off. Rhys is staying to help with the cleanup, yeah?"

"That's the plan." Hamish slid his hands into his pockets and looked at Ruby.

"Good luck," I said, squeezing her forearm. Wasn't she supposed to be gone like a half-hour ago? "Not that you need it."

Hamish looked between us with suspicion. "What are you—"

"Oh look!" I said, before Ruby's nerves could give her cooking plan away. I stepped back and pointed above their heads at the beam that was not quite above them but close enough. "Mistletoe."

They looked up in synchrony and then to each other with matching sets of wide eyes.

"Come on," I heckled. "You can't leave from standing beneath mistletoe unkissed. That's bad luck."

Ruby shot me a look that was screaming as loud as Hamish's sweater.

"And you could really use the luck, Rubes," I said, using his nickname for her. Her face reddened further.

Hamish said nothing. He slid a hand behind her neck and brought her lips to his in a fluid motion. I would have been embarrassed to be standing there watching them kiss if I wasn't so utterly pleased with myself for orchestrating the situation. A man did not take control with a woman like that unless he wanted to kiss her. And she *obviously* wanted him to, as she'd told me herself.

When they broke apart, Ruby was a grinning, fluttery, ball of energy. "I have to go!" She ran from the barn, and Hamish watched her leave. Before another second passed, Ruby ran back inside and kissed Hamish again. She backed off. "Okay, now I'm really leaving!"

We watched her go, then Hamish returned to business as though nothing had happened, but I couldn't dim my smile.

The final ten minutes passed without a single kid arriving to see Santa at the grotto, so I sent Rhys a text. He'd waited upstairs in case I brought anyone up.

Luna Winter: We're done. No more takers for Santa tonight.

Hot British Guy: I'll start clearing out up here then. Thanks for your help tonight. It was fun playing Grotto with you.

Luna Winter: I'm an elf, remember? It's what I do.

I got a cup of hot chocolate from the table near the entrance and blew on it while I walked around the fair, still sporting my elf gear. People were selling everything from homemade crafts to bakery items and sweets. Jars of jellies and special dip mixes and hand-crafted soaps and jewelry filled the tables, and I found my arms filling with more and more bags of things to take home to my family for Christmas. No one seemed to want the evening to end, and by the time Rhys had changed out of his Santa costume —likely to preserve the magic for the kids—and joined us downstairs, there were still a few lingering patrons while the sellers began packing up their wares.

Rhys wore a hunter green sweater and jeans, and he had slung his hands in his pockets when he approached me. I wanted to eat him up, so it was a good thing I had hot chocolate keeping my hands and mouth occupied.

"You want to take off soon?" he asked.

"Don't we need to clear the tables?"

Rhys shrugged. "Hamish is eager to get over to the pub. He said we can lock up and worry about it tomorrow once everyone's out."

Tomorrow, when I wouldn't be here. I tipped the pair of handmade mittens I'd just bought into my bag and rummaged for my phone. A text showed on the screen from my sister.

Callie Winter: Got you on United. I emailed you the confirmation. Flight leaves at 9:04 AM
Callie Winter: Can't wait to see you! I'll be the one picking you up at SFO.

I clicked off my phone and slid it into my bag before Rhys could read it. It was going to be an early day for me tomorrow, but I wasn't going to stop that from letting me enjoy my last night as best as I could. I planned to leave things with Rhys in a good place.

"Ready?" he asked.

"Sure. Can we take the bike back to Stella's first?"

Rhys paused. "We can do that tomorrow."

Except I wouldn't be here tomorrow, and I promised Ruby I would distract Rhys for a little while after we were finished with the fair. "If it's not too inconvenient, I think I need to do it tonight."

He ran a hand over his jaw. "I did swear I'd never set foot on that property again . . . but I can take you." He gave a lopsided smile. "I just can't get out of the car."

"You won't need to. I promise."

We managed to secure the bike to the boot of his car, as he termed it, with some of Hamish's rope, but it was hanging out the open back and the resulting rush of air while we drove was freezing. Rhys reached across the center console and took my hand. "Is this okay?"

It was a testament of how weird things had felt between us this evening that he had to ask for permission. He must have sensed I was holding back, because we'd held hands a lot and he'd never asked for permission before now.

"Of course," I squeaked, then cleared my throat. I never was very good at pretending. We pulled to the back of Brumsworth's gravel driveway, close to the shed. I got out to untie the bike, and Rhys got out to help.

"I can do this. You're supposed to stay in the car."

"It's not that big of a deal. It looks like no one is even home." He started working on the knots.

Once the bike was on the ground, I rolled it toward the shed while Rhys wrapped the ropes into a coil using his arm. The ground was muddy and the pristine turquoise was no longer very clean, but Stella probably would never even notice. I pulled out my phone and sent her a text anyway.

Luna Winter: I was stranded at your house after the meeting, so I borrowed a bike to get to the Christmas fair. I just returned it. Wanted to let you know.

Stella Fit: Fab. Great meeting. Look forward to hearing from you. x

Again with the kissing. I'll never understand it. Maybe that was the British version of exclamation points, and everyone used it as a way to say *I'm happy! I'm not mad! My voice sounds light and positive!*

Notice that I didn't use any exclamation points in my last text to Stella? I still didn't know how her requirements made me feel.

I shut the shed door behind me, and a light near the car caught my attention. Someone was walking toward it with a flashlight out.

Rhys put up his hands. "I was just helping Luna return a bike, mate. No harm intended, I promise."

No harm intended? What was that supposed to mean? I shielded my eyes against the bright light when it lowered to reveal Edward standing in the headlights of Rhys's car. He looked angry, his face contorted in a frown and his eyes shooting lasers at Rhys. "You're not welcome here, *mate*."

"We were just leaving."

"I could call the police."

"But you won't, because I'm leaving," Rhys repeated, placating with a gently raised hand. "Luna borrowed Stella's bike because she was abandoned at your house, so we returned it."

The reminder of Edward's poor behavior earlier must have quieted him further, because he lost his angry edge, his glare diminishing when it swept to me. "Sorry, Luna. Plum slipped my mind."

I nodded. "I forgive you. It all worked out."

We each hovered where we stood, Rhys next to the driver's door, me at the passenger, Edward in front of the headlights. The yellow glow splashed over his face and highlighted the shadows of his heaving chest.

"She's moved on, you know," Edward said quietly. "She

doesn't want me anymore, either. She's trying to hide it, but I've already lost her. You were right."

There was a moment of quiet before Rhys answered him. "That doesn't bring me any pleasure. I'm sorry."

Edward shook himself. "No matter. Karma, eh?"

I was dying to know what they were talking about. I mean, it had to be Jenna, right?

Edward stepped out of the path of the car. "Don't come back."

"Don't plan to," Rhys said as he slipped into the driver's seat.

We pulled away from the house, leaving Edward in the rearview mirror. "*That's* who Jenna cheated on you with?"

"Yeah, and I decked him for it. Legally, I'm not supposed to step foot on his property."

It made sense now why Rhys seemed edgy whenever the Brumsworths were mentioned. And why he'd hesitated to take me there tonight. "But he can still enter the pub?"

"That's his choice. I wasn't in my right mind the night I found out about them, and I regret my actions heartily." He shot me a self-deprecating smile. "I've grown a lot in the last few years. Though I predicted Jenna wouldn't stay with him long. She never did like him when we were younger, but he'd always worshiped her."

"It appears things are over between them now."

"Not surprising. It was only a matter of time. Jenna was swept up in Stella's name and her brand for the last few years of our marriage, and the pub life wasn't enough for her anymore. Now she works for Stella and does whatever she wants because she's not tied to a husband any longer. I figured she wouldn't want to stay tied to him, either."

It sounded like she was doing whatever she wanted while she had still been tied to a husband, too. I reached over the console this time and took Rhys's hand, lacing my fingers through his.

"Were you and Edward close?"

"Not really. We had a lot of friends in common—a hazard of living in such a small community—so we were around each other a fair amount growing up. But we were never close."

"Still, that's awful."

Rhys nodded, then gave my hand a squeeze. "You're freezing."

"Fair warning, I plan to lay in front of the fireplace when we get back to the pub. I need to thaw."

"Good luck with that. It'll be a madhouse."

A madhouse full of people eating Ruby's cooking. My stomach clenched anxiously. I cut a glance to him. A warning now might be good so he could prepare himself mentally. It was too late at this point to change things anyway. "Hey, don't be surprised if Ruby serves more than what you left behind."

"What do you mean?" His low voice was steady. "She promised she would never cook in that kitchen."

"Well . . . maybe she didn't then." I'd wanted to set his expectations since we were about to arrive at the pub, but now I wondered if maybe that had been a mistake. His hand was squeezing mine like a vise.

"She's planned something, hasn't she?"

"Maybe."

Rhys swore.

I turned on the seat a little to face him, my defenses rising on Ruby's behalf. "Are you *that* opposed to her cooking? I thought you wanted her in the kitchen with you."

"I do. But she almost killed half the village last time she tried, because she undercooked the chicken and gave everyone food poisoning. She needs proper training."

"Oh." Ruby hadn't told me that part. I only knew about the burned crust. "Well, it's too late to change it now. So just don't get too mad. She's been really nervous."

"Understandably," he muttered. "We could have been sued."

We pulled onto High Street and into the car park behind the

pub. Rhys was in a hurry to get inside, but I took his hand and pulled him back toward me. "Hey, listen, can we talk later tonight when things have settled down?"

He immediately turned to face me. "I knew it. Something is up with you. You've been acting sad all night."

"Sad? I was the jolliest elf that barn has ever seen."

"Maybe on the outside."

My heart squeezed. He knew me so well.

Rhys's voice softened. "What is it, Luna? I don't want to wait to talk about this until the pub clears out. That could take hours."

I hadn't planned on doing this now. I dropped his hand and fiddled with my fingernail, unable to hold his gaze for more than a second. "Jenna mentioned something about a kiss at the hospital, and I know she was only trying to get under my skin, but I can't stop thinking about how little I know about you. Or how short a time I've known you."

He blew out a breath. "I didn't want you to read into it."

I dropped my hands to my sides, deflating like a popped bouncy castle. "So it's true, then." I'd thought she was making it up, or that it had been a chaste kiss on the cheek and that was why he hadn't felt the need to tell me. Something reasonable at least.

"It's probably not what she made it sound like, but yeah, it happened."

Breath fled my lungs, my chest constricting painfully. "I realize you don't owe me anything—"

"Don't do this," Rhys said. "That isn't why I didn't tell you. It was *nothing*. Jenna was distraught over her grandad, and she kissed me, and I didn't immediately push her away. But I did end the kiss, and I told her not to do it again."

He didn't immediately push her away? What did that mean?

I shook my head a little in a sad attempt to clear it. But there was too much mud to think clearly. For the first time since speaking to Callie, I was relieved I had the ticket to go home. While I knew I needed to fix things with Aubrey, I hadn't known if leaving Rhys was the right choice or not before. Now I couldn't help but think it was the wise, smart thing to do. Rhys wasn't my someone. He was an incredible man I had fallen for, and I needed to leave before my heart was irrevocably engaged to him. But if he was my someone, he would have been more upfront with me about everything. The kiss, the nature of Jenna and Stella's relationship, how Edward was the man Jenna had left him for . . . all of it. It was too much *not* to share. It made me question how well I knew him.

I cleared my throat and straightened my spine. "I'm leaving in the morning."

I'd shocked him. His mouth hung open, his eyes searching mine. "Because of the *kiss*?"

"No, not that. Not entirely. I just need to be home."

"Because of the phone call you had with your ex-boyfriend?"

"Sort of. Because of the baby he told me about. I'm not going for Jake—none of this has to do with him at all. I want to make things right between Aubrey and me before she gets married." My arms flew out to the sides. "I want to stop running."

Rhys ran a hand through his hair, disheveling it. "Is that not what you're doing right now?"

I took a step back, my arms dropping. "No. I'm not running away. I'm going home to face the problems I ran away from in the first place. I'm fixing it so *I* can move on, too."

"Or you're scared because I asked you to stay. You're scared of us. I swear it, Luna, that kiss was nothing. It lasted maybe two seconds, max, and I ended it."

He spoke so simply, so void of malice, that I believed him, and I could not lie. "I don't—it's not just the kiss, Rhys. It's also that you never warned me that Jenna would be there, that she worked with Stella, that Edward was the man Jenna had cheated with. There were so many things you *didn't* share. Of course I'm scared. How well do we truly know each other? I still have time to fix a relationship I've had almost my entire life, and I need to do it before her Christmas Eve wedding. If I don't, then it's over. She won't forgive me, and I won't forgive myself." I laughed, but there was no humor in the sound. "You don't know Aubrey. That woman has been planning this wedding her entire life. It's important to her, and because she knows I know that, whether or not I show up will mean something."

"But . . ." He shook his head. "Stella and Edward? I wasn't trying to keep anything from you. I didn't tell you those things because I don't think about them. It didn't cross my mind."

"A warning would have been nice, though, so I didn't feel so blindsided."

He rubbed a hand over his face. "I can see how you feel that way, and I can try to be better in the future. But why do you have to leave? Isn't *Aubrey* the one who needs to be forgiven?"

"Yes. That's why I'm going. She deserves to begin her life without a cloud of guilt hanging over her head."

"It's the twenty-first century. Can you not use video chat?"

"That's not the same thing as showing up and being there for her," I said. I was starting to get angry. My sweet, understanding Rhys had disappeared and this man didn't get it. How much clearer could I be? "I can't attend the wedding virtually, and being there is the right thing to do, whether you see that or not. I have a flight for tomorrow morning, and I just wanted to let you know I'll be gone when you wake up."

We stared at each other, our chests heaving. I simultaneously wanted to kiss him and run from him. His gaze kept falling to my lips, so I wondered if he had the same inclinations.

"The room was nonrefundable," he said.

"Keep the money." I moved to step around him, my heart achy and sore, when he put a hand out.

"Wait," he said. "I didn't mean that. I just . . . I don't want you to leave. You have six months here until you would need to make a decision about us. Can't we just see where this goes?"

I didn't want to leave either, and his dark, sad eyes were calling to my wrung-out heart. At the same time, I was too frightened to stay. It was on the tip of my tongue to promise I would look into a return ticket after Christmas, but I couldn't make that promise right now. Not when it was so messy—my feelings had just been thrown into a blender and set to pulse. "Six months, and then what? I go live in Geyserville for six months, then come back for another half a year?" I shook my head. "I need to go home. It just makes the most sense, okay? I'm sorry I didn't get to meet your Nan or try your Christmas cake. I was really looking forward to both of those things."

"Luna," he said, brushing my fingers gently as I walked away.

The touch zapped me with longing and sorrow. I turned back to him, rested my hands on his stubble-roughened cheeks, and reached up on tiptoe to kiss him softly on the lips. My heart slammed into my ribcage, and my body was slowly turning to mush. His lips were so soft, his kiss so giving. I tasted the salt of my tears, jarring me back to the present. I stepped back, wiped my eyes with the back of my wrist, and went for the pub.

He didn't stop me.

THIRTY

THE WILD HARE WAS TEEMING WITH PEOPLE. IT LOOKED like everyone had left the Christmas Fair and come here, much as Rhys and Ruby had predicted. I weaved through the crowd; some faces I recognized and many I didn't. Hamish stood at the bar, leaning between two people on stools, watching Ruby flit around the kitchen. I did a quick sweep of the room, but so far no one looked green from undercooked meat or like they were forcing down burned or salty pie crust.

Instead, Frank was sitting on a leather armchair near the fire, a cast on his broken arm and Ned dozing at his feet. Maggie was gesturing wildly to Katherine, who wore the same 90s windbreaker she'd sported at book club and listened intently, sipping her drink. Arthur, the bald knitter, was digging into a plate of some sort of chocolate dessert. Flo sat at a table with a nicelooking man who nervously pulled at his cuffs, Finn kneeling at their feet and feeding pieces of pie crust to a little black terrier.

Warmth from the fire and the bodies—and probably the building's heating system—cocooned me. The general sense of merriment and joy permeating the room made my heart hiccup and threatened the tears again. It was home. This pub had actually begun to feel like a place where I could see myself still happy five years from now. For the first time in a long time, the future was vivid ahead of me, and I wanted it.

I swallowed against a tight throat. The dream dangling in front of me wasn't meant to be *mine.*

The front door opened, and Rhys brought a gust of cold air in with him, throwing water over the glowing coals heating my daydream. I shook myself and walked through the crowd without stopping and up the stairs.

I needed to pack. I needed to sleep a little before my alarm would go off at four-thirty in the morning. And I needed to be gone from this magical place. Which meant I needed to stay away from the people who could change my mind.

A knock sounded on my door about an hour later. I'd showered, folded my elf costume and piled it on the chair, and started packing. My suitcase was open on the foot of my bed and everything was spread out, organized and ready to go inside.

I inhaled and opened the door, sagging slightly upon finding Ruby standing there with a plate and a glass of dark, bubbly soda.

"How's it going down there?" I asked, trying for a bright smile.

She frowned. "What's going on?"

"Nothing."

She looked pointedly at the open suitcase on my bed.

I grimaced. "I planned to say goodbye to you later, once the party died down a little."

"So, you're leaving. That explains Rhys's sulking. Here, I brought you something." She held out a plate with a small slice of cake edged in crisp white frosting. It looked familiar.

I took it and sipped the soda. Dr Pepper—exactly what I needed right now. "I take it your cooking was a success?"

She shrugged. "People still prefer Rhys's pie to mine, but so do I, so I can't really blame them for that."

I set the cake and drink on the dresser and pulled her in for a hug, my throat growing tight. "I'm proud of you."

"Thanks, Lu. I'm just glad all those health and safety and cooking classes were worth it. Rhys said if he passes the night without food poisoning, I'm welcome in the kitchen with him."

I leaned back, my eyebrows up.

"He didn't mean that bit about the food poisoning—at least, I don't think he did. My food safety certificate means I'm allowed back in the kitchen again. And now the people of Snowshill won't boycott us either, because they've tasted my improved skills."

"And Hamish?" I raised my eyebrows. "He's tasted your skills too."

Ruby guffawed. "I was going to kill you for that, you know. I told you to throw the mistletoe in the bin."

"But then he kissed you."

She grinned. "Yeah. More than once, actually, so your life is safe again."

"I knew it."

"He won't leave me alone down there. And he won't stop watching me. I'd say I hate it, but it's actually lovely."

"He's been watching you like that since I got here, Ruby. I would have been worried it was some sort of weird stalker situation if it wasn't clear how close you two are. He loves you."

"He's always loved me. But now I might wonder if he *love* loves me."

"You'll keep me posted, right?" I asked, my heart doing the weird achy thing again. I pressed my fingers to my chest to make it stop, but it did nothing. "I want to hear about your life when I'm gone. I want to stay friends, if we can manage it."

"We can manage it," Ruby said with confidence. She pulled me in for another hug and kissed my cheek. "Have a safe flight, and call me when you land. I want to know when you're home."

"Of course."

She left to return to her people and her kitchen, practically floating away from me, her long, red ponytail swinging behind her. It took me another fifteen minutes to finish packing and to make sure I hadn't left anything in the drawers or underneath the bed. When I sat on the soft chair in front of the unlit fireplace and took a bite of the cake, my senses were immediately consumed by it. The cake was moist, the icing sweet, and bursts of orange and spice hit my tongue. It was Christmas in a cake.

I nearly dropped my fork when the realization hit me squarely in the heart. The iced cake had looked familiar because I'd seen Rhys frost it in his kitchen earlier. It wasn't meant to be cut until Christmas Day, but he must have done so because I told him I'd wanted to try it.

I cut another bite and savored the flavors, enjoying every last morsel on the plate while my insides crumbled.

Rhys had given me Christmas.

I WAS a zombie by the time my plane landed at SFO. Callie was waiting in her blue Highlander when I came outside, and I threw my bags in the trunk and climbed into my seat before she could get a good look at my face. I hadn't really smiled since last night, and I wasn't sure my facial muscles were capable of it right now.

She wore a soft yellow UCLA sweatshirt and leggings, her highlighted hair up in a messy bun. Eying me from the side, Callie kept her tone neutral when she spoke. "You realize you are the most depressed looking version of yourself I've ever seen, right? You're like George Michael coming home and crumpling face first on the floor."

Her *Arrested Development* comparison was on point, because

that was exactly how I felt. "Just play the Charlie Brown theme music for me all week then, because it's how I feel."

Callie pulled onto the 101 and headed toward the Golden Gate Bridge. It was the middle of the day in California, and the sun shone against the rust-colored bridge and sparkled off the water in the bay.

"If you're that sad, why didn't you just stay?" she asked.

"I couldn't stop thinking about Aubrey's baby or her wedding. As much as part of me wants to punish them forever, I don't really want to be the reason she has a bittersweet wedding day."

"That's big of you."

"Yeah, well, I guess I'm finally growing up."

"Growing up sounds awful," Callie said.

"What are you talking about? You've been a grown up since you were like five."

She laughed. "Somehow, Mom missed that memo."

"Where is she? I thought she'd come with you."

"She wanted to, but I didn't let her. I wanted to come for you by myself."

And here came the inquisition.

"I won't ask you anything," she said. "But I'm here if you need to talk about it."

It was too fresh. The Band-Aid was still covering open wounds I'd incurred by leaving Rhys behind. I hadn't seen him since that last night in the pub, and my heart was sore. Being home again was oddly discomfiting, though. It didn't feel *right*. I couldn't help but feel like maybe I'd been too hasty in my decision to leave—but no. I couldn't question what was obviously a necessary step in moving on from what had happened to me with Jake and Aubrey over the last year.

The silence stretched between us as we left the city behind and entered the golden, rolling hills of northern California.

"How do you know when you've made the right call?" I asked.

"Were you never listening when Mom and Dad would tell us to be quiet and listen to our hearts?"

"Yeah, but . . . I mean, how do you *know*?"

She shrugged. "You just know. You have to have faith in your decision-making abilities and your gut. You have to have faith that your heart would never steer you wrong and the wisdom to know the difference between what you're actually feeling and what you want to be feeling."

"Right now I don't know anything except that I miss Rhys."

Callie shot me a sympathetic look. "Things didn't work out between you two?"

"Work out? We live in different countries, Cal."

"And?"

"And I realized I'm crazy. Like *certifiable*. Because Rhys asked me to extend my trip, basically, to see where things go between us, and I was actually going to do it. I had six months of legally living in England before I'd have to decide, you know? Like move home or apply for a visa or something."

"That actually sounds kind of reasonable to me," Callie said carefully. "It's not like he proposed to you. He just asked to date you. And you can work from anywhere."

I closed my eyes and slid lower on the seat. "Well, it hardly matters now. I left him, and we never talked about the possibility of me returning after Christmas."

She didn't say what we were both thinking, what Rhys had said: that I got scared and did a runner.

"There was no winning in this situation," I complained. "I swore I wasn't going to run from my problems anymore, but no matter what I chose, I was running from something. Either Rhys or Aubrey and Jake."

"I think coming back to fix things with Aubrey was really big of you, and you'll probably be glad you did. It'll give you the closure you need to move on with your life."

"Glad I sacrificed a relationship with a man who could probably make me happy and fulfilled to fix my relationship with the couple who slashed my future to bits?"

"Yeah. Like I said, the bigger person. I mean, Jake and Aubrey did a crappy thing, but they might have given you the opportunity for a better future than you could have had if you'd stayed with Flake."

She was right, but that didn't make this any easier. "Being the bigger person sucks." The sun glared at me, and I slid my sunglasses on and reclined my chair. "I know it's not midnight, but my body feels like it is because I've been awake for so long. I'm going to be antisocial and sleep."

Callie reached across the console and squeezed my hand. "Love you, sis."

THIRTY-ONE

MOM AND DAD BOTH RECEIVED ME IN THE WAYS THEY had my entire life: warm, squeezing hugs that lingered. Dad was silent, as always. Mom was practicing self-control by not bombarding me with a thousand questions when I walked through the door of our restored Victorian home.

"I'm going to crash," I said, my Jell-O body pretending to be human. "I can't stay awake."

"But we're going to the wedding?" Mom confirmed. "Do you need to tell Jake?"

"I have it under control." I went toward the stairs, but stopped. "What do you mean *we*?"

They were silent. My family all looked at me with varying degrees of guilt.

My hand tightened on the banister. "You were all going to the wedding anyway?"

"It's Aubrey," Mom said as if that explanation should cover it. "We were undecided, but now that you're going, we will come and support you."

I nodded. I couldn't erase our history, and I knew my parents both loved Aubrey like a third daughter. I hadn't really considered how fixing the rift would be good for my entire family.

"Maybe tomorrow we can go shopping," Mom suggested while I made my way slowly up the creaky stairs. "If you're going to your ex's wedding, babe, you might as well look good doing it."

I'd been considering calling Aubrey and meeting up with her tomorrow. I didn't have anything formal in my closet Jake hadn't already seen, but I didn't feel the need to try to impress my ex-boyfriend. I'd never say no to a new dress, though, or a little more time to get my head on straight. "Maybe we can find a long, white dress," I hollered from the top of the stairs.

Light laughter followed me, and I could hear the concern lacing their mirth.

"Kidding," I called.

If it wasn't clear before, it was obvious now. I was becoming unhinged. Besides, if I was going to wear a symbolic color to the wedding, it would obviously be black.

GEYSERVILLE DIDN'T HAVE MUCH in the way of shopping, so we drove down to Healdsburg and wandered the overpriced boutiques until I landed on the perfect dress. A stone blue midi-length wrap dress that made me look and feel good but didn't send any messages like *I'm trying too hard* or *Please take me back, Jake!* We got cupcakes at a boutique bakery and found ourselves walking through the park in the middle of the plaza. My bag hung from my bent elbow and hit my hip with every step.

"Want to sit?" Mom asked, gesturing to an empty iron bench.

Callie shook her head. "Too cold for sitting."

"Moving keeps our blood flowing," I said.

"Oh right. I forgot your blood ceases to pump once you sit," Mom said thoughtfully.

I grinned. "It slows, doesn't it? Besides, we didn't all wear five layers."

Mom laughed. She looked like she would fit in with the locals in Snowshill with her sweater, coat, and scarf. "I was cold this morning."

"And preparing for a trip to the arctic," Callie said.

"Which works to my benefit, since I'm the only one warm enough to entertain the idea of sitting on a bench."

"You can question Luna just as well if we're walking."

I nudged my sister in the arm. "I thought we'd gone over everything." We'd talked early this morning when my body woke up before the sun and Mom had come in from milking the cow. She'd listened but held her advice back. It was weird for her—the woman who could fix anything.

"We have," Mom said. "But you're still unhappy."

"I'm probably going to stay this way for a while. I need to get over Rhys."

Mom stopped on the path and stepped in front of us. She clutched each of us by the arm and looked from my face to Callie's seriously. "I love you both. I will always love you both. But you need to know I support your life choices, and I support you deciding where and how you want to live. I always will, no matter what." She swallowed. "Your father, too," she added. "He just struggles with these conversations. You both know he agrees with me."

We nodded obediently, but it was true. I'd never doubted my parents' love for me.

Her hand squeezed tighter on my arm. "That said, if you changed your mind and wanted to go back to Rhys, you have our support, babe."

"You don't even know him," I said.

"I know he made you happy, and I trust your judgment. Lu, loving and being loved are the most important things in this life. If that's happening for you in good old England, then so be it."

"He runs a pub," I reiterated. "It's been in his family for generations, and it's a job that stays right where it is. He can't just up and move here. If I tried to get him back, I'd be committing myself to potentially having a life over there." I gestured wildly to the side, as if England was located south of the plaza.

"That's why I'm saying this," Mom said gently. "I didn't know if you needed to hear it or not because you're an adult and don't need permission, but Dad and I will be fine. We love you, we'd visit you, you'd visit us, and we have FaceTime."

My heart swelled with appreciation for my mom, and I pulled her into a hug.

"No one asked me," Callie said, "but I'm *not* okay with you living an eleven-hour plane ride away."

"Says the girl who lives a seven-hour drive away."

"Definitely not the same thing."

"I know." I gave her a hug. "We're all operating under the assumption that he'd even want me back."

Mom and Callie shared a look.

"What?" I asked. "I know my life isn't actually a Hallmark movie and you guys haven't flown him over here or something, so explain that look right now."

Callie shrugged. "You just sounded like you'd already decided, that's all."

"If you've decided he's worth trying for," Mom added, "then I can't see any reason he wouldn't agree." She teared up. "Oh, this is going to be hard."

I tried to shove down the hope and possibility running through me. They were wrong, though—I hadn't decided. The fact was that Rhys hadn't stopped me from leaving, and he hadn't approached me once after parting ways in front of the pub that night. Their confidence in us was a lot stronger than my own.

Opening the cupcake bag, I pulled out another one while we walked to the car. The carrot cake was good, but it only reminded me of the Christmas cake and the man who'd thoughtfully sent a slice up to me on my final night in the UK.

I slid into the backseat of Mom's car and pulled out my phone. I hadn't texted Ruby again since letting her know I'd landed, and I was anxious for a connection to Snowshill.

Luna Winter: I need my Snowshill update, please and thank you.

Ruby Norland: We talked yesterday. I can tell this is going to become my full-time job.
Ruby Norland: Pretty much nothing has changed in the last two days except the fact that you left a giant, gaping hole in the pub, and I'm a regular in the kitchen now.
Ruby Norland: Also, Hamish says hi. He has a pink front door since Linscombe figured out who messed with their sign. They painted his door hot pink and left a note that said "we know how to paint, too." HOT PINK, Luna. *crying-laughing emojis*

Luna Winter: Poor Hamish! If I was there I'd paint it black for him.

Ruby Norland: I think he plans to keep it pink for a while. Show them they don't bother him or something.

Luna Winter: That'll show them. I want a picture of this door next time you're at his house.

Ruby Norland: Consider it done. Evidence will be along shortly.

Ruby Norland: Or you could come back and see it for yourself. We miss you!

I could picture them now: Hamish on his regular stool while Ned lazed about at his feet, Ruby leaning against the counter while texting. My chest squeezed, yearning to be there with all of them. Especially with the man in the kitchen working on dinner. *No. Do not let your mind go there*, I commanded.

Luna Winter: What about Ned? I'm sure he misses me the most.

Ruby Norland: You and I both know that's not true. Hamish misses you the most. x

I laughed out loud, and Mom stopped mid-sentence.

"Sorry," I said, sliding my phone into my purse. "I missed that."

Mom looked at me through the rearview mirror. "I just asked if you plan to call Aubrey today."

With the wedding tomorrow, it was probably better to take care of the reconciliation before that. But I worried that if I did so, she would rope me into being a last-minute bridesmaid and I would accidentally commit myself to a trip to Ireland or something just to get away.

"Would it be awful to just show up at the wedding early and talk to her then?"

"And make a pregnant woman sob when her makeup is already done?" Mom asked.

I was a little disturbed by her confidence in this fact. "Who says she's going to cry?"

Callie turned around on the seat and lifted her eyebrows at me. "Her hormones do."

"Fair enough."

"I'd call her today," Mom said. "If it was me."

"I'll think about it."

By the time we returned home the sun was already fading, and the Christmas lights on the tree were visible through the window. The old Victorian wraparound porch was sprinkled with lights that hadn't been plugged in yet, and I walked around the side of the house to turn them on. Callie took my shopping bags inside for me, and I nestled on the porch swing.

My contacts list was long, and the H-names weren't anywhere near the A-names, but I found my finger hovering over Hot British Guy's number. I missed Rhys, and I just wanted to hear his voice.

But what would I say to him? *I made a mistake. I want you back. Please let me return to The Wild Hare and do my yoga in the dining room and eat your delicious savory pies.*

Or, maybe what I needed to say was *I know the kiss between you and Jenna meant nothing, but your history scares me.*

Yeah, the truth was better. I *didn't* make a mistake in coming home. My mistake was in not talking to Rhys more and forming a plan to go back. But I couldn't think about being that raw over the phone while I had Aubrey's baby looming over me. I scrolled down to **Aubrey Schenk** and dialed before I could talk myself out of it.

To my equal parts of surprise and dismay, she didn't answer. I left a voicemail. "Hey, it's me. I know it's the night before the big day, but I just wanted to—oh, look, you're calling me back." I hung up the voicemail and accepted her call. "Hello?"

"If you tell me that was a butt dial, I'm going to be extremely embarrassed."

A smile curved my lips. I couldn't help it. This was the sassy best friend I'd had for most of my life. Our encounters over the previous nine months had been so awkward and void of her wit that it had been easy to not miss her as much. But *this*? I missed this girl.

"It was intentional. I, uh . . . I spoke to Jake." Better to just rip off the Band-Aid.

"He told you, didn't he? Dimwit."

"Should you be calling your fiancé a dimwit the night before you marry him?"

"I can if he goes behind my back to tell you I'm pregnant when I specifically told him not to."

"Should I be offended that you didn't want me to know?" Mom and Callie were so off-base here, it wasn't even funny. There were no tears. Aubrey was drier than the Sahara. Was rage another pregnancy symptom?

"It's not about wanting you to know or not," she said. "I didn't want you to reach out to me just because of the baby, and I knew the second you learned about him, you would."

I didn't know whether to be relieved that she still knew me as well as I thought I knew her, or annoyed that she'd pegged me.

"Which," she said, "you've obviously done exactly that."

"I didn't call you because of the baby. I called because I don't want to be the reason your wedding has a rain cloud over it."

"Which you decided *after* you learned about the baby, right? I know I'm right."

"You know, you could have just told me yourself and then none of this would have even happened."

She scoffed. "Yeah, like I could do that to you. Like I hadn't broken you enough as it was. I wasn't going to dangle my baby in your face and guilt you into forgiveness."

"I mean, you could have, and it would have worked, but I would have been faking it then."

Aubrey was silent for a minute. "*Then*? You aren't faking it now?"

"I flew home from England early for you, Aubrey."

"You're *here*?" Her voice lifted an octave, flying up on the wings of hope. "Does that mean you're coming tomorrow?"

It had always been my plan to attend the wedding after I returned to California early. It was why I had come back. I took stock of my feelings and was pleasantly surprised to note the pain was ebbing. The dull ache that usually accompanied my interaction with Aubrey or Jake was absent, and a void sat in its place.

I toed the floor and set the bench swinging softly. "If it's not too late, yes. My whole family wanted to be there."

"We have them down already, in case they showed up," she said. "It was you I didn't know about. You know, it's not too late to find you a matching gown—"

"I can't," I said, firmly but kindly. It was time for me to offer rejection without running away. My hands clenched and my body tensed, but I'd done it.

"Okay, I understand. Listen, Lu," she said, softening her tone. Preggo Rage Aubrey was gone, replaced by Contrite Aubrey. "I never *meant* for any of it to happen. We never cheated on you, and I didn't set out to fall in love with my best friend's boyfriend. I know it will never make up for anything we've done to you, but we both love you and want you to be happy. I can't say this part for Jake, obviously, but I am sorry." Her voice was laced with tears. "I can't regret the way it turned out, but I am sorry you had to be collateral damage. After my mom and Jake, I don't love anyone else in the world more than I love you. That hasn't changed."

"Well, it will soon."

"Yeah, this baby boy is shooting up to number one on the list pretty quickly." She drew in a ragged breath. "Do you think you can ever forgive me?"

"I forgive you, Aubrey. I don't want this hanging over us for the rest of our lives. I'm happy for you, and I will be there tomorrow to support you."

I felt like one of those broken Japanese vases, put back together with gold and fitted until I was whole again. Maybe I would never look the same, like my relationship with Aubrey would never be the same as it once was, but I was no longer fractured into jagged pieces and missing parts. I was whole. I just had a few new, golden-hued scars.

She blew out a heavy sigh that made it obvious how fast her tears were falling. I wiped my own wet cheeks and leaned back on the bench. "Well, I better let you get your beauty rest."

"Ha! No such thing once you hit the second trimester. But thanks." She drew in a ragged breath. "You know how much I've looked forward to my wedding day, and I can't express how inordinately happy you've made me just knowing you'll be there. Love you, Lu."

"Love you."

I hung up the phone, closed my eyes, and rocked myself gently on the porch swing. It wasn't lost on me that I had come all the way back to California to make things right and then had the conversation with her over the phone, but I didn't regret my choices. I would be there for her at the wedding tomorrow, and that's really why I was here, after all.

When it came down to it, facing Aubrey and hearing her real, unfiltered apology had been freeing in a way my frustration and anger could never have been. She'd been honest, and I didn't like everything she said, but I could recognize the truth, and it resonated with me.

After meeting Rhys, I couldn't exactly regret the way things had turned out between me and Jake, either.

The bench was comfortable, even if it was numbing my butt, and the cool breeze washed over me in a way that felt cleansing. I marveled over the changes in my heart since going to Snowshill. I really was the Grinch now, post-heart change. The Luna of one month ago who had seen Jake and Aubrey in the taco shop never would have been able to attend their wedding with a healed heart. Rhys had done this for me. He was my Cindy Lou Who. He had freed me from the bonds of anger and helped me release my hurt and find my way back to contentment, to love.

Footsteps treaded up the shallow porch steps, and I drew in a deep breath, ready to scoot over and make room for my dad.

"Care if I join you?"

My eyes shot open. "Rhys?"

THIRTY-TWO

RHYS STOOD ON MY PORCH. YES, *THE* RHYS FROM Snowshill, England. He was currently five feet away from me, hesitating, his clothes a little rumpled and his hair perfectly disheveled. His face glowed in the Christmas lights hanging on the porch, but it was otherwise dark outside, and I was in such a state of shock I didn't move.

"I am starting to wonder if I've made a grave error."

"How did you find me?" I asked.

He ran a hand over his jaw. "Ruby helped me. She found your sister on Instagram through a tagged photo on your feed and DM'd her to get your address. They've been talking since then, and I got a rundown of your schedule." He stilled. "That makes me sound like an utter creep, doesn't it?"

"I guess that depends on if you're just here to steal locks of my hair and toenail clippings, or if you came for another reason."

"Well, you certainly know how to give me a solid, romantic headstart, don't you?"

I shook my head, unable to reconcile his accent with the surrounding California wine country. Two different parts of my life were intersecting, and it took a moment for my brain to catch up. "What are you doing here?"

Rhys sat beside me on the bench. "I came for you."

"For me? Like to throw me over your shoulder and carry me away?"

"No. For you like to be here *for you*. I didn't want you to have to go to the wedding alone."

My heart melted into a puddle, but somehow also made my pulse race at the same time.

He reached for my hand, and I let him hold it. The gold adhesive healing my cracked, broken bits was thickening, my chest filling with warmth.

"When you told me your reasons for leaving, I understood, but I was angry," he said. "I thought it unfair that I finally found a woman who made me happy and she had to live on the other side of the world. I thought if you were willing to stay for a few more months, we could be together and worry about the future later. But then you left, and it scared me. I didn't . . . I didn't know how to fight for you."

His fingers started playing with mine, running up and down each one lightly and then over my palm. A thousand little butterfly wings tapped against my insides, and I calmed my breathing to give him the quiet attention he deserved. "Jenna leaving did a number on me, as you are well aware. I tried to fight for her, to fix our problems, and she still chose to leave. When you presented me with your plans to leave the wedding right after discussing Jenna and the kiss, I froze. I should have fought harder for you then. Or offered to accompany you. Or at least done something to prove I was serious about us, but I was scared. Last time I fought for someone, she still didn't want me."

Those words were like a knife to my heart, and I hurt for him. "I wouldn't have accepted your offer to come," I said gently.

"You have the pub to think about, and your Nan, and Christmas with her and Ruby."

"Ruby has Hamish now," he said, a grin widening his lips. "They're so in love it's revolting, and I only had to be around them for a few hours. They'll keep the pub going while I'm gone and spend Christmas with Nan, and all will be well."

I grinned. "I was right about them."

"You were, and that's part of why I'm here. After Ruby got your address, she gave it to me and left me to make a choice. The idea of you going to that wedding without me was a large part of my motivation, but I also needed to be here, in person, to tell you something."

"Because video chat doesn't always cut it?" I asked.

He smiled. "Not for this." Rhys stood, pulling me up to stand in front of him. "I started falling for you when you accepted my grandad's old costume beard as collateral for your car keys, and every minute with you since was another nail in the coffin."

"I don't know how I feel about you likening your feelings to death."

"I'm *dead* serious, if that helps."

"A little."

Rhys cupped my cheeks, much like I'd done to him in front of the pub when I was saying goodbye. "I love you, Luna. I'm utterly besotted with you. I don't know how we're going to figure it out yet, but I want to be together. I want you in my life, and I want to be in yours."

Heat from his touch permeated my entire body, making me warm and weightless as I basked in his gaze. His shimmering dark eyes were honest and good, and I saw myself reflected in them, in the way he saw and loved me. It was vindicating to hear the same words from his lips that had been bouncing around in my head for days. He loved me. I knew it with certainty, because I felt the same way.

I circled his wrists, holding onto them while his hands still cupped my cheeks, cradling me with care. "I love you too, Rhys."

The smile that broke out on his face could have lit the entirety of San Francisco with its glow. Rhys lowered his lips to mine and kissed me deeply, shoving away all the questions and fears and unknowns of the future, replacing them with his confidence, love, and devotion.

A whoop let out from inside the house, and we broke apart. Callie stood in the window beside the tree with her arms up in the air, doing a happy dance.

I pointed right at her. "Sneaky!"

Callie did an elaborate curtsy, likely owning her part in all this by talking to Ruby.

I shook my head. "I'd be more embarrassed about my sister if I wasn't so happy right now."

"That makes two of us." He kissed me again to prove his point.

When I leaned back, my hand found his easily. "You ready for a California Christmas?"

"It's odd not having snow, but I think I can survive it."

"Good, because I don't plan on letting you leave anytime soon."

MY BLUE DRESS WAS PERFECT, and Rhys looked even better in a suit than any man had a right to look. It was a good thing men didn't have to worry about upstaging the groom or we'd have a little trouble on our hands. Rhys hadn't earned the Hot British Guy nickname for nothing.

We drove out to the little winery up in Cloverdale where the wedding was being held and found seats in the small, white church.

Rhys held my hand and leaned in to whisper in my ear. "You look beautiful."

"Thank you." I would have made some quip about spending hours at the mirror perfecting this revenge look, but it wasn't true. I'd expected to need a shield of makeup and perfectly curled hair in order to face this day, but I was doing it on my own, and having Rhys with me was an added benefit. His hand leant me strength, and I was no longer hoarding the grief I'd expected to carry anymore.

I'd texted Aubrey last night to let her know I was bringing a plus-one, and she was excited to meet him.

People filled in the seats, and the groom came out to take his place at the front of the room beside his best man and grooms-men. It was strange seeing Franky here, since the last time I had seen Jake's best friend was last year, when we were still together. The entire thing looked so similar to the wedding me and Aubrey had designed in high school—the most recent scrap-book. It was oddly comforting that some things hadn't changed.

Jake looked up and caught my eye, and his entire body seemed to freeze. I had to believe he'd known I was going to be here, and when his mouth did the little half-smile I was so familiar with, it was confirmed. He mouthed *thank you*, and for some inexplicable reason, tears sprang to my eyes.

I nodded softly, but his attention was stolen by the preacher.

"You good?" Rhys asked, probably having just witnessed that whole interaction.

I faced him. "Actually, yeah. I'm glad we made it here, and honestly, I wouldn't have it any other way."

He squeezed my hand. "Good. I'm glad you have some closure. I'm just here to judge their caterer."

I laughed quietly. "You'll be disappointed if you plan to hate it. Aubrey's aunt is probably catering, and she's incredible."

The music began and the bridesmaids started down the aisle. I scooted closer to Rhys, breathing in his soft cinnamon and warmth smell, and felt content. The rest of the wedding passed without additional tears. Aubrey looked amazing in her empire waist gown —*not* the dress she'd picked out a few years ago, but I assumed the baby made this one a better option—her blonde hair curled and loosely piled at the nape of her neck. Dinner was delicious, as expected, and when it was time for dancing, Rhys proved he had hidden skills. He took Callie out when I danced with Dad, then he spun Mom around when Dad wanted a break, so it was safe to say that all the Winter women were fully on board the Rhys train.

I was carrying a glass of lemon water back to my table when Aubrey stepped into my path, and I slowed my steps. I'd been able to get by without speaking to her yet, instead sending her wide smiles across the room. But I couldn't leave now without being obvious. Not that I wanted to, but I was nervous to speak to her face to face. I didn't even have my shield by my side.

"You look lovely," I said.

She lifted her hand to gesture to me. "So do you. I almost regretted going with the sage green bridesmaid dresses when I saw that color. It's so pretty."

"Your friends looked good in the green. It was the right choice." She'd once told me she wanted the bridesmaids to blend in with the greenery so she would stand out more, and she wasn't off base at all, because that's exactly what had happened. I cleared my throat and looked at her rounded belly. "Are you telling people?"

"Not on social media or anything, but everyone in this room knows. I'm twenty-nine weeks along, so over halfway now."

"You'll have to send me pictures when you have him."

Aubrey hesitated. "You won't be around here?"

I looked to the dance floor, where Rhys was dipping Mom to the slow crooning of Whitney Houston. "I'm moving to England, actually."

When I tore my gaze away from Rhys and set it back on

Aubrey, Jake had joined us. He stood at her side, and he couldn't have looked more surprised than if I'd taken a glass of champagne from the nearby table and chucked it in his face.

"England?" Aubrey asked.

"So that's why you went," Jake said.

"It's why I'm going back," I corrected. The song ended and Rhys was making his way back to our table with Mom. He spotted me and lifted his eyebrows. I nodded. "Do you want to meet him?"

"Yes," Aubrey said, and I could practically feel her excitement.

Rhys stepped up beside me, sliding his arm around my waist in the way as old as time that said *this girl is mine.* "Lovely wedding."

"Thank you."

"Aubrey, Jake,"—I leaned in a little to his side—"this is Rhys. He's just out here for Christmas, and then we're going back to Snowshill."

"Oh, that's in the Cotswolds, isn't it?" Aubrey said. "I think I drove through once when I went with my mom in high school. That whole area of the country was so dreamy."

"Your area of California has so far looked beautiful, as well," Rhys said.

"Just wait until you see the redwoods and the ocean. Lu might convince you it's worth staying here."

I looked at Rhys and we shared a smile. We both knew that wasn't in the plan for us, but I hoped we had many California vacations in our future. "I guess we'll see."

"It's good to meet you," Jake said, his gaze sliding from Rhys to me. "I'm really happy for you, Lu."

I nodded. "Me too."

We walked away from the bride and groom, and I knew with certainty that facing them and this wedding wouldn't have been as easy without Rhys by my side, but I was glad I had done it. And I was glad he was there with me.

"Now can we get out of here?" he whispered in my ear. "I thought kissing you at your ex-boyfriend's wedding might be a little tacky, but I've been dying to do it all night."

I grinned up at him. "Let's go."

THIRTY-THREE

UGH. I COULD NOT MAKE A DECISION. I'D PULLED OUT AN old notebook and lined one side of the page with pros for why accepting the collaboration with Stella Fit was the right thing for my business and the other side with cons, but neither list ended up being very long. The short of it was I didn't like Stella's stipulations, but being connected with her name would do wonders for me on Instagram.

But it wasn't good business sense to make decisions based on what I liked or didn't like, was it? This was where Jake always had come in and advised me. As a lawyer with a good logical brain, he had a knack for these things. I knew I could credit him for part of why my channel took off the way it had. If he hadn't pushed me, my growth would have been substantially slower.

I sucked in a breath and blew it out with puffed cheeks. It was Christmas Day and everyone was somewhere else, so I had the living room to myself. I lounged on the overstuffed rocking recliner Dad kept in front of the TV, staring at my list. Rhys was in the kitchen learning how to make Dad's famous chocolate fudge, and Callie was outside with Mom tending to the animals.

She'd started to help train Dusty, the new horse, but the poor guy wasn't really having it.

I stared at my list, chewing on the end of my pen.

Pros: free clothes, more followers/subscribers, it would look really good for my brand if I was one of the exclusive ambassadors, have I said free clothes?

Cons: overposting, annoying my followers, working with Stella and Jenna, being an obvious ad.

I dropped my head back and closed my eyes.

"Who wants fudge?" Dad asked from the kitchen.

Um, me. "Always." I tossed the notebook aside and went into the kitchen, where Dad and Rhys were licking spoons like a couple of children. The pan of fudge still needed to set, situated on the counter behind them. I scraped out a spoonful of warm fudge from the pot before it could get filled with soapy water and washed out.

"Not bad, Mr. Winter," Rhys said.

Dad pointed his wooden spoon at Rhys. "Think you can do better? I'd like to see you try." There weren't many things my dad was competitive about, but his chocolate fudge was one of them.

Rhys put his hands up in surrender. "I'm afraid you've found my weakness in the kitchen. Sweets have never been my forte."

He must have been trying to downplay his skills in front of my dad, because I recalled a certain cake he'd happily nurtured for days.

"Luna has you covered," Dad said. "She makes a mean batch of caramels."

Rhys's eyebrows shot up.

I licked my spoon clean. "It's the only thing I can do, and only because Mom taught me. She's the real master."

"I think I'll need to try those."

I booped him on the nose. "Maybe if you're good, we can ask Mom if she's willing—"

"Ask me what?" Mom stomped her feet outside and came into the kitchen, letting the screen door shut behind her.

"Caramels," Dad said.

"Oh, I saved you some." She went into the pantry and came out with a bag of homemade caramels cut into bite-sized squares and wrapped in wax paper.

"What? Why? You didn't know I'd be coming home."

"I was saving them for when you got home. I knew you would eventually."

I opened the bag and gave one to Rhys. He popped it in his mouth and moaned appreciatively—much to my mom's delight —and asked for another one.

"Did you make a decision?" he asked me.

This, of course, made Mom's eagle eyes shoot to me. "About what?"

We moved to sit around the kitchen table while Mom started on dinner, and I filled them in on the meeting I'd had with Stella and Jenna.

"I guess you have to ask yourself if the benefits outweigh your reservations," Dad said.

Rhys nodded.

Mom paused at the stove, where she was stirring the boiling potatoes. "If you're worried that accepting the deal makes you beholden to her, then don't do it."

"I would literally be beholden, Mom. I have to sign a contract. I've always had a consistent number of videos per week, but I've never followed a strict schedule, and I've never pushed products at my people. There's such a big difference between sharing a new protein bar with an honest review and basically becoming a Stella Fit ad."

Mom stopped stirring. Dad leaned back in his chair. Rhys's brow furrowed.

"Why are you all looking at me like that?"

"You went to the meeting knowing you were there to talk about a collaboration, right?" Dad asked.

"Yes."

"You've done them before, often enough to understand the basics?" Mom added.

"Yes."

Rhys leaned back in his chair and crossed his arms over his chest, his knee resting against my thigh. "So, to sum up, you went to a meeting about becoming a Stella Fit ad, and you walked away concerned they were asking you to become a Stella Fit ad."

I looked at each of them. "Yes."

"Then what is it about Stella Fit you don't want to promote?"

"Her," I said simply. The answer flew from my mouth, and I knew at once what I would have to do. "I don't want to promote someone who makes clothes so expensive they're impossible for the average person to afford. The bulk of my audience is probably moms and low-income men and women who don't have the time or money to go to a yoga studio—let alone afford Stella's clothes. They're at home, doing yoga in their sweats or whatever, and they don't have loads of cash to spend on designer yoga apparel. I'm afraid if they watch me promoting the clothes that hard, they'll think they need them—or that I think they need them—and that isn't my brand."

"There you go," Mom said, returning her attention to her potatoes. "You had the answer yourself all along."

She was right. "I did, didn't I?"

Dad pushed up from the table. "I'm going to help Cal with the horse."

"She's getting the hang of it," Mom said.

But still, he went.

Mom drained the water from the potatoes and started mashing them with plenty of butter and salt, just like Granny had taught us. We were giving Rhys an American Christmas dinner, and Mom wasn't holding back.

Rhys found my fingers and threaded his between them. "I can see why you're such a helper, Lu. You get it from your parents."

He was right. They were always doing something for someone else, and I supposed that was just how I had been raised. I smiled at him, noticing how seamlessly he'd fit in with my family. It was a shame Snowshill and Geyserville weren't closer to each other, but that didn't have to mean he couldn't have a relationship with Mom, Dad, or Callie. Who knew? Maybe we could even convince Callie to come stay with us sometime.

"They're pretty great," I agreed.

"So are you. You know, you've been worrying over this Stella Fit thing for a few days, but your mum was right. You had the answer all along. We just helped you see it."

All these years I'd thought I needed Jake's wisdom, but Rhys was right. I'd had it in me the whole time. This was the kind of support system I wanted and needed: people who helped me see the right way to go, not just told me what to do. I hadn't identified before going to Snowshill how much I enjoyed helping others, but Rhys, Ruby, and Hamish had helped me see how naturally it came to me.

That was the way I wanted my channel to be, moving forward—a free option for those who couldn't afford classes otherwise. I still got paid through ads and whatnot, so it was still a legitimate job for me, but when I took the focus away from growing my brand and my name and instead shone the spotlight on the real reason for keeping up my channel—the *people*—my heart warmed with the confirmation that it was the right thing for me and my future.

I looked intently at Rhys's chocolate eyes. "You know, it's actually something your cousin said that had me thinking."

"Ruby?" he asked. As if he had another cousin who was friends with me.

"Yeah, she mentioned something about the channel being great for people who couldn't afford to attend classes or didn't have childcare. It made me look at my subscribers differently. I'd been thinking about letting the channel go and teaching in-person classes again, but I think if I pull back a little I can still manage to do both. One for me, and one for the people on YouTube who need it to be virtual for whatever reason."

"That sounds like a good plan." He laughed. "I'm not surprised, though, that the root of your reasoning is how you can help other people while still doing the career you want. We can find you a place to hold classes. Maybe empty out a room in the cottage next door. Frank doesn't need all that space, and he's at the pub half the time anyway."

"You have such a strange relationship with your tenant."

"He was my grandfather of sorts for a while," Rhys said. "I don't think he ever stopped treating me like a grandson. Besides, I think he'll love the idea if we set boundaries and give him a discount on rent."

"Is it weird for you, though, having me do the yoga thing with all your history?" Jenna was, after all, still very much a part of the yoga world.

"No. You aren't Jenna, and I've never thought that way. I love that you are so passionate about it."

"Good. I can't wait to get home and set up a studio. Maybe we can even become peacemakers and get some Linscombe people—"

"I'll draw the line there."

I grinned, leaning across the table, and Rhys wiped it from my face with a kiss.

When I leaned back, I caught Mom watching us with a goofy smile. "I have a feeling I'll need to chat with Aubrey's parents soon."

"Why?"

"Oh, you know," she said, swinging around the potato masher like a fairy wand. "Just catering and venue info."

My cheeks bloomed red at her insinuation. I'd known Rhys for a month. It was definitely too soon to talk weddings. I hazarded a glance at him, worried that she might have said something to hurt him. He'd been married and divorced, and I didn't know if marriage was something he was even looking for again in his life.

But he startled me with the directness of his gaze. "Maybe hold off on that conversation just yet," he said, unfazed. "Maybe next Christmas, we can have a snowy, winter wonderland wedd—"

"Okay, let's not get ahead of ourselves here," I said, but I leaned forward and sealed his promise with a kiss. The confirmation that it was a possibility was a relief, and I didn't want to push things yet.

Rhys stood. "Can I help you with anything?"

Mom pulled out a floral apron and handed it to him, complete with tiny purple flowers and a pleated lilac edging. "Sure thing. Let's get you going on the green bean casserole. Next year, you're making pies. I hear your crust is incredible."

"You've got it."

Next year. Mmmm. I liked the sound of that.

EPILOGUE
ONE YEAR LATER

THE UNEXPECTED CALIFORNIA CHRISTMAS I'D GOTTEN TO share with Rhys last year had been a magical experience, but now my whole family had flown to Snowshill for the holidays, and Rhys was determined to prove his hometown could offer up an equally lovely Christmas experience. He didn't realize, I think, that he wouldn't need to try very hard. Snowshill performed well for the holidays with very little prodding. It was a Christmas haven. Though I did think taking my parents and Callie up on Hamish's property to cut down a Christmas tree and then decorating it in the pub with hot chocolate and Bing Crosby was a nice touch. Mom seemed about ready to move out here and join us in the Cotswolds permanently.

It was the night of the Snowshill Christmas fair. So far this year there had been no tent trouble from Linscombe, though Hamish had yet to paint his door again and it still shone bright pink, clearly visible from the road. I had a feeling the lack of trouble between the villages was because we hadn't rented tents this time around. Hamish's barn had worked so well last year that the council voted unanimously on using it as the location for the fair again.

And guess what Rhys and I were doing? You guessed it. Santa and his little elf. Though I did order myself an elf costume that fit my personality better than Jenna's had.

I was sitting in Santa's big chair now, bent to fix the jingling slippers over my shoes. The barn loft was a little musky, but I'd come to notice a lot of the old buildings here carried that scent, and it didn't bother me. It was familiar now, homey.

"You alone in here?" Rhys asked, coming up the last few steps fully decked out in his Santa costume and fake beard.

"My bells were giving me trouble." I tugged them into place again and stood, walking across the floor to meet him in the center of the room. Each step jingled, and I was pleased with this addition to my costume—so long as they quit drooping to the side.

Rhys slid his arms around my waist. "Think we could get Callie to bring us up some hot chocolate halfway through the night? I might need a little boost. There's a long line of kids out there."

"Already? We don't open for another ten minutes."

"Hmm. Ten whole minutes. How should we pass the time?"

"You aren't ruining my makeup, Rhys. Do you know how long it took me to perfect this red lipstick? Besides, I don't want to scar the kids with a red-lipped Santa."

"Okay. I had a better idea anyway." He stepped back, disengaging from me, and fished around in his pockets for something, his overstuffed belly shaking while he rummaged. When he finally pulled his white-gloved hands free from his pockets, his brown eyes locked on me, and he went down to one knee.

"What?" I said, much too loudly. "Now?"

He grinned. "I told you last year I started to fall for you when you agreed to take my costume beard as collateral. You didn't realize then you were giving me your heart. What's more fitting than a proposal while I'm fully dressed as Father Christmas?"

A laugh bubbled up from my chest and spilled out. It was so

absurd, but he was right. It was so perfectly us. "Yes, of course. Please, continue."

Rhys grinned up at me, his teeth visible beneath the scratchy, white beard, and popped the ring box open to show me an oval bezel-set ring that made my breath catch. "I cannot imagine any other elf by my side, and I want you, Luna, to be there always. I love you more than anyone in the North Pole. Please, make me the happiest Santa Claus in the world, and agree to be my Mrs. Claus."

"You absolute goober," I said, wiping tears from my previously perfectly mascara'd eyes. "I would love to."

He slid the ring on my finger, pulled the beard down under his chin, and stood to kiss me. I didn't really care about messing up my lipstick anymore. I had expected this proposal for about a month, ever since he asked me in not-so-subtle ways which kind of ring I'd prefer. But *this*? This was so utterly perfect for us.

"You've made me really happy, soulmate."

I stilled, my fingers digging into the velvet covering his arms. "I thought you didn't believe in those."

Rhys's dark eyes roamed my face, and he shook his head lightly. "I was afraid to. But I've thought a lot about this, and I think soulmates have to be equal. Each of us committed and loving to the same degree. Our previous relationships weren't that because they were lopsided, right? They don't count. I can't imagine a life without you—or my life with anyone else. You're it for me, Luna. Just you."

I reached up on tiptoe and pulled him down for another kiss. I'd long since believed I was meant to find him and we were meant to make a life together. Maybe I would have ended up just as happy with someone else if I'd never come to Snowshill and we'd never met, but I like to think that wasn't the case. It was just Rhys for me. Rhys and no one else.

"Can we have tacos for the reception?" I asked, leaning back.

He'd been working on his carnitas, and they only seemed to get better and better.

"I assumed so. Right next to the Dr Pepper bar."

I threw my head back and laughed. "Sounds perfect to me. But what do you get out of that?"

"Oh, come on," he murmured, laying a kiss on my lips and then leaning back to hold my gaze. "You know I'm only marrying you for your Granny's mashed potato recipe."

"That dies with me."

"Swap for Nan's Christmas cake recipe?"

"I'll ask Nan when we see her tomorrow."

He growled. "Shoot. Foiled."

"I guess you'll just have to marry me for me."

"Jolly good, that. It was my master plan all along."

A throat cleared from the doorway. I looked up to find Ruby standing there, her arms crossed over her pregnant belly, Callie just behind her. "You two planning to look presentable? Kids are coming up soon."

I lifted my hand, turning it so they could see the ring, and they both squealed, running toward us and pushing Rhys gently away.

"It's bloody gorgeous," Ruby said.

"Dreamy," Callie agreed.

I noticed Rhys looking in his phone camera to check how badly my lipstick had smeared over his lips, then using a tissue to wipe it away.

Callie sighed. "I want to help plan the wedding."

"You will. You know you can have six months out here without a visa," I reminded her.

Ruby grinned. "Maybe we'll have to find you a Brit of your own so we can get you to stay longer."

Callie rolled her eyes. "Fat chance getting my mom on board with that. Oh, speaking of. I should go get Mom and Dad."

"They were going to come up when they finished shopping

the stalls downstairs," I said. "I'll tell them then. Or maybe I'll just dangle my hand and wait for them to notice."

"Ten bucks it will take Mom less than ten seconds to notice. She's been dying for this engagement for months."

Her and me both.

I was just glad there would be no more back and forth between America and England while Rhys and I worked the visas out and made it possible and legal to be together. A wedding was exactly what we needed to ensure we could always stay together.

He caught my gaze over Ruby and Callie and smiled, and my heart fluttered. *I love you*, he mouthed.

I love you back.

CHRISTMAS ESCAPE SERIES

*All sweet & clean romances that can be read in any order

Christmas Baggage
by Deborah M Hathaway

Host for the Holidays
by Martha Keyes

Faking Christmas
by Cindy Steel

A Newport Christmas
by Jess Heileman

A Not-So Holiday Paradise
by Gracie Ruth Mitchell

Later on We'll Conspire
by Kortney Keisel

Cotswolds Holiday
by Kasey Stockton

AUTHOR'S NOTE

When I had the fortune to visit Snowshill, England in 2021 I knew immediately that I needed to set a book there. It was such a gorgeous, quaint village, and the church was such a beautiful centerpiece to the village. I loved the turquoise-painted doors set against the yellow stone and rolling green hills. The churchyard was especially touching, and the headstones that had tilted with age, which inspired the scene in Linscombe.

While Snowshill is a real town in the Cotswolds, The Wild Hare is not a real pub. In order to keep my artistic freedom, I invented the pub, all of the characters, and Brumsworth Manor. I also invented Linscombe and the rivalry between the towns. If Snowshill has a rival, I am not aware of it—though I would not be surprised. What high school doesn't have one?

While in England, I also had the opportunity to visit a church where my ancestors were married in the 1600's, which inspired Luna's desire to go to Linscombe. My mom also texted me many details about those ancestors while I was there, and I inherited my interest in genealogy from her. She's the real family history MVP.

Another interesting thing I noticed while visiting the UK was how many restaurants and pubs had a dog menu available and how many canines were allowed in the dining rooms. It's not something we see a lot in the States, and I found England & Scotland's attention to dogs really sweet, so I absolutely had to make that a part of Luna's experience too. That, and their complicated showers. If I hadn't been traveling with author friends who could help figure out the shower situation, I'm certain I would have been destined for many cold showers as well.

Luna's hometown, Geyserville, is a real town in Northern California. It's just north of where I grew up. El Azteca, though also real and delicious, is located elsewhere. So if you stop in town for tacos, you will not find that particular restaurant there. I'm certain Geyserville has amazing tacos, too, though.

I hope you enjoyed this little trip between two places that have my heart: Sonoma County, where I was raised, and the beautiful English Cotswolds.

ACKNOWLEDGMENTS

Thanks, first, to Jon for being the inspiration for Rhys's thoughtfulness. Like Rhys, Jon also wears a lot of plaid and sports a dish towel over his shoulder anytime he's working in the kitchen, and I love it. I'm blessed to be so wholly loved by my own American lumberjack husband. (Okay, so he's not really a lumberjack either, but a girl can pretend.)

Next to my kids for supporting me, putting up with my plot discussions, and helping me come up with goofy scene ideas. I love you goobers *the most/to infinity.*

This series was such a blast, all because of the Christmas Escape authors and their willingness to be silly on Instagram reels. I've enjoyed getting to know each of you and look forward to working together in the future! Deborah, Martha, Cindy, Jess, Gracie Ruth, & Kortney. You are all talented women, and I love learning from you.

To my beta readers, who helped me fix the awful ending and tighten up the story. Your feedback is forever and always important and helpful: Nancy, Karen, Brooke, Melynne, Nicole, Melanie, Martha, Jacque, Cindy, and Jess. Thanks ladies!

And a special thank you to Ashley Weston for being willing to read at the drop of a hat and cheerleading the story for me. I am so grateful for your friendship and help with this book.

Thank you to my critique group, who supports me in every way along this author journey. Martha, Deborah, & Jess—you all mean the world to me!

Thank you Melody Jeffries Design for the most perfect cover, and thank you Karie Crawford for your editing and polishing.

I would not be able to do any of this without the small miracles I see daily, and I know God is watching out for me and my writing journey.

And finally, thank you Maisie Peters, Olivia Rodrigo, Gracie Abrams, and all the many romcoms who collectively inspired this story. This one goes out to all the fictional women who lose their boyfriends to Hallmark's leading lady.

ABOUT THE AUTHOR

Kasey Stockton is a staunch lover of all things romantic. She doesn't discriminate between genres and enjoys a wide variety of happily ever afters. Drawn to the Regency period at a young age when gifted a copy of *Sense and Sensibility* by her grandmother, Kasey initially began writing Regency romances. She has since written in a variety of genres, but all of her titles fall under clean romance. A native of northern California, she now resides in Texas with her own prince charming and their three children. When not reading, writing, or binge-watching chick flicks, she enjoys running, cutting hair, and anything chocolate.

Printed in Great Britain
by Amazon